She waited for the inevitable like a trapped and frightened hare, but still cried out when a long, muscled arm snaked around and held her stiffly against the tree. She risked a look downward and in the twilight could see his cloak swinging forward, nearly encompassing her lower half in its folds. She was just about to cry out her abject fear again when a strong, gloved hand clamped hard and ruthlessly over her mouth and nose. She had difficulty breathing and though she felt frozen with horror, she protested in a little whimper.

"You are more beautiful than you are valiant, but I've little faith in a frightened woman, so keep still and I'll relax my hold on you. But stay, I warn you," a silky smooth voice breathed in her ear.

Then Aurora's breath escaped her body and she seemed to be floating on air. What was happening to her? she wondered in a wild moment of abandonment. Like a tumult the light contact of his lips shivered through her as he kissed her eyes and the softness at the nape of her neck next; then pressing her back against a cedar, he bent to kiss at the quivering corner of her sweet lip—and the nectar of their lips mingled for the first time.

# PHANTOM LOVE

## SONYA PELTON

**ZEBRA BOOKS**
**KENSINGTON PUBLISHING CORP.**

ZEBRA BOOKS

are published by

KENSINGTON PUBLISHING CORP.
475 Park Avenue South
New York, N.Y. 10016

Printed in the United States of America

Calm and dark he descends,
Winging his way through the misty darkness
That dismally shrouds the dawn.
His presence transforms
The shy daybreak into splendid morn.
The knitting of his raven's brow
Makes men tremble with fear.
What value a talon of finest steel,
In dirt, in murk, in corrupt slime—?
Yet the dawn sings, and her song
Makes her fierce listener shiver,
Giving him a taste of the sacred bliss,
That once Aelf-wig experienced in a dream,
In a dream, Aelf-wig—
Somewhere in tomorrow's mists.

*Prologue One*

*The Fairy Hollow*

*Virginia 1670*

By leaps and bounds, the young doe broke from the dew-sparkled edge of the forest, then suddenly stopped tall with ears pricked. For several moments the beast became still as carved stone. A slight stirring to her right set her back into motion, to the dense sanctuary from whence she came.

A small, willowy girl with delicate heart-shaped face and skin like a windblown rose, sat on a stile out back of the summer house, where from the grassy hillock she could gaze out over the enchanting shores of both the James and the Chickahominy rivers.

This fine, golden April morning, Aurora Gregory had slipped outdoors at dawn to enjoy the return of spring to the colony. She breathed deeply of the sweet-smelling aroma that rode on a balmy breeze from the forest. The smell of pines and of fresh buds was in the air, along with the bird-song of geese and wood pigeons.

Then Aurora had spotted the doe, lovely in her graceful, long-limbed flight. Little Ro had frozen so as not to frighten the wild creature and gaze upon it awhile longer. But a blowing strand of raven hair had tickled her petal pink cheek and so she lifted a tapered finger to flick it back.

"Ohhh," Aurora breathed her disappointment,

watching the white flag of the doe vanish into the wood.

"Missy Ro, are ye out there?" the Scotswoman's burr called from the back door creaking open.

"Be right in, Hetty!"

Lithe Aurora skipped down from the stile and hastened toward the house, having sniffed hot porridge wafting out. A small jug of sweet cream and a pot of honey would be there waiting to be poured over the cereal, Aurora knew, and she licked her softly curving lips.

Aurora wiped her clogs on the flimsy doormat before entering the warm glow of the cheerful kitchen. The huge brick hearth spread light and welcome. This was her very favorite room in the summer house. At night she would sit in here and watch the sparks fly upward through the great chimney throat to join the stars above. So far, this was the only home Aurora had known since she was two years old. Her birthing place was England, and her eyes, the color of the heather that grew wild on the moors, had been too young to see what she left behind.

The girl sat, spreading the skirt of her brown wool dress with golden-rod-dyed collar, and picked up her pewter spoon. Hetty, the girl's charge, stopped what she was doing and waited for something to happen. Aurora smiled and bowed her dark head.

"I crave to thank God who gives me food to eat every day of my life. Amen."

The housekeeper nodded, busying herself once again. Hetty, who did all the cooking and baking, was also personal maid to Aurora and Deana, the girl's mother. A lad of eighteen did all the hunting for the table's meat.

Rufo was a half-caste, part Indian and part French, and had been homeless when his father died of the swamp fever. Some three years back, Captain Strang, Aurora's stepfather, had dragged the lad home from the woods on a length of hempen rope. Strang had given Rufo a last name—appropriately, *Savage*. He had indeed been wild, but was now tamed. Hence Rufo never wandered, but to hunt, and always returned with a fresh kill. After a time, Strang had allowed Rufo to labor in the fields of Raven Keep, in exchange for part of the rent he owed the landlord each month.

Rufo and the little girl had become fast friends. He had taught her all he knew about medicine—the magic of herbs for dosing the sick. When not hunting or skinning hides, Rufo looked after his little friend whose hair was as black as his own.

"You are white. Why you have hair like mine?" Rufo had asked Aurora one day.

"Black? Mayhap because my grandfather was full-blooded Irish. Mama said in that country, Ireland, there are many dark-haired colleens."

"Co-leen?"

Aurora had giggled. "Girls—like me." She had pointed at her still undeveloped chest.

Rufo had grinned. "Yea. Girl."

When Rufo had turned back to his work, Aurora had peered down at her chest and pinched the front of her smock out with two fingers of each hand. Then she had shrugged and dashed off to play, unconcerned whether she ever developed or not. There was

11

much fun in just playing and being a girl for the time being.

Scooping up a spoonful of cereal, Aurora canted her head at the housekeeper. "Are we ever going back to England, Hetty? Are we always going to live in the summer house? Oh, there are fine houses here, too, like Uncle Edwards's big plantation house. They even got bayberry candles and real snuffers, made of silver. How come we don't live in a big fine house near Jamestown like Cousin Melly and Aunt Margaret?"

Aurora looked wistful as Hetty set a dish of apple butter down in front of the girl she'd known and loved and cared for since she was a wee bairn.

"Ye've got a busy little mind, ye hae. Finish up yer breakfast now," Hetty said, turning back to the hearth, a stern air about her.

Hetty Moireen, birthed in the snowy highlands of Scotland, had been with her lady Deana for nigh onto thirteen years now. Hetty had found herself without position or penny when arriving in Lincolnshire in 1658. She had no kith or kin since the age of twenty-and-eight and had worked as a scullery maid for ten more years. So it had been on a cold, bleak night that she had knocked on Lady Gregory's door, begging a morsel and a pallet for the night. Deana had hired the poor woman on sight, and ever since, Hetty had been excessively fond of her lady and doted on Little Ro still more.

Aurora continued with her probing. "How come I've a stepfather and Cousin Melly has only a father? And how come I have but one last name, while Mum Deana has . . . let me see—one, two"—she held up a

12

third finger—"What's this one, Hetty?"

"Ye hae three up." Hetty halted here, beginning to worry that Aurora was badly in need of a tutor. She went on. "Yer mother's doings are her own. Dinna ask me what I canna answer, luv. Now. 'Tis getting late in the morn. You canna play in the house, because yer mother's got a fit of wheezing again and needs her rest."

Hetty knew some of the answers, but not all. She believed that Deana had never loved anyone as she had Colin Gregory, an English lord in whose veins had flowed half-Irish blood. Deana possessed the countenance of a courtesan and many men had said this. It was sad, but Colin Gregory had died in a duel defending his wife's name.

If Deana had hoped to retain some of the aristocratic status she had known while in London, she was sorely disheartened to find that this portion of the colony called Virginia, in the New World, was a unique community very unlike the English ones she'd known.

Aurora would someday reflect back and be saddened that her mother had never known, as she herself would in years to come, the gay plantation life, and the expansion of the population that would fill out the Virginia skeleton, with Jamestown as the seat of eastern splendor.

"Who am I, really?" Aurora tried again.

"Whew! Ye're Aurora Gregory, a well-born lass. Lord, mon! You be full of wondering for such a young lassie. T'ain't proper."

Even though bombarded by these troubling questions, Hetty padded happily across the puncheon floor. A good fire was going in the kitchen fireplace under a vast kettle and she went there to stir the turkey giblet stew she was brewing for her ailing mistress. Over her shoulder, Hetty glanced at the girl's puckered face, bespeaking the intensity of her thought.

"I'll hae some puff apple pies for ye, so never ye mind the giblets."

"From those pretty red apples we put up last fall? Mmm," Aurora murmured eagerly.

Aurora studied her breakfast intently for a moment with her luminous, elfin eyes, and then continued chattily on a different subject this time.

"Oh, I saw the *pretty* deer this morn again!"

"Doe."

"Dough like for bread?"

With a wag of her head, Hetty answered, "Nae, they be spelt different."

Aurora went on impishly. "Yea, but they *are* the same color. Course *dough* has to be baked before 'tis brownish and all white inside, like the chest and throat of a deer outside, and some of the smaller ones have spots."

"Fawns."

"Yea, fawns." She smiled a knowing pixie smile. "You can hardly see them in the greens and browns of the forest glades—they kind of melt together. Oh! I saw a big one with bony things growing toward the front of her head. I snuck up behind a tree, silent as a mouse, close enough to see that they looked like they were covered with soft velvet, those bony branches. And her tail was like a white flag when she put it up and—she looked a little angry with me for being

14

there. I mean, her eyes looked all dark and stormy, like a thunderhead was resting on her brow."

"Whew! What ye saw was a buck—"

"Yea, but before she was frightened away, she was riding the back of the other one—the one with no bony things on her forehead. Oh! They looked to be having such a frolic! There was many of the smaller ones and the one with—with—"

"Antlers. *He* be the buck, lass. The others are the females—like you and me and Deana. Ye should be cautious of the bucks during rutting season. Ye could have been harmed. The buck attacks when he's wi' his harem. He could've ripped ye apart wi' his hooves, just as he does when battling another male for the does. Sometimes two bucks will fight a long time over the harem—"

"Oh! Really!" she said, luminous heather eyes lit up.

"—and canna be separated by neither thunder nor the need to nourish themselves. They even perish of starvation battling for love of the females."

"Do *men* do that too?" Aurora breathed excitedly, but then her urchin grin faded to seriousness. "Fight over ladies until they both drop dead of hunger?"

Hetty suppressed a hearty laugh. "I told ye the buck has a harem—many females. Man is called a roué or a rogue if he takes more than one woman— like one after the other—to pleasure himself with. God help ye, luv, that ye never meet up wi' one of their kind! They be men with horns just like the bucks!"

"Does man ride woman like the buck did the doe that I saw? And why don't the little fawns play too?"

15

Aurora nodded her pixielike head at the end of her questioning.

Hetty cleared her throat, her wooden spoon suspended in the air. In suspense, Aurora awaited an answer.

"Later your mother, God help her, will hae to give ye a good talking to on the birds and the bees." She showed the inquisitive one her broad back as she turned to stir her stew.

"Oh. Do birds and bees play games too?"

With a hot splash Hetty dropped her spoon in the stew and had to fish it out before she turned to answer in a sterner voice.

"Whew! I got work to do, so dinna tarry and make me head spin, else I canna put my mind to it."

"Mmmm, I love the smell of that strong black coffee you are brewing."

Hetty bit back a retort. "Ye can have a wee bit later on, luv. Ye've had too much coffee to be growing proper, 'tis said it stunts a lass's growth."

"Poo! Old wives' tales!"

"Look at ye, why yer but a willow switch!" Hetty couldn't help but smile at the little sylph though.

Hetty went back to her stirring, pondering over the fact that the lass lived in a fairy world with little people running around in her head. The poor lass would no doubt settle for nothing less than a knight in shining armor on a white charger. It was due to the many sugary fairy tales the Lady Deana had filled her child's head with. But who could set Aurora on the path to reality at this late date? It would take a very strong, intelligent person to come along and accomplish the feat. Otherwise—Hetty shrugged sadly—the girl would continue to walk through her little fairy world the rest of her life. Maybe even *by* herself.

"Hetty—"

The older woman halted Aurora. "Maidens should be mild and meek, quiet to hear and slow to speak."

"Well . . . all right. For now," Aurora quickly added.

Dismissing from mind all the questions she'd had, Aurora devoured the remains of her delicious breakfast, then skipped back prettily outside to play. Hetty shook a fat spoon out the door at the youth, warning her not to wander off into the deep of the woods.

"There be Injuns out yonder, Missy Ro. Dinna wander far and gie me yer promise you won't go near Raven Keep, the landlord's house. I canna be looking after ye, and Rufo's out hunting, so ye've got to be good."

"Oh, yes, Hetty!" Aurora called back. "Promise, Ro will be good," she added to herself softly as she made her way toward the pink and yellow buds blooming wild on the knoll.

Aurora halted long enough to peer back over her shoulder, saw the vacant doorway, and giggled impishly, disturbing the fog in the hollows as she headed next toward the forest, humming as she went, skipping fairily.

The dark band of clouds that had crept upon the horizon, now rolled ever closer, but slowly, as Aurora slipped out from the forest. She stood very still, just like the doe she had seen earlier in the day. She had

17

wandered, despite the housekeeper's warnings, deep into the wood and was now on the other side of the forest, a good two miles west of the summer house. The river flowed somewhere to her left. She could hear it and smell the moister air.

*Dinna wander far,* echoed in her mind uneasily.

She had not meant to be bad, but there was something of the adventurer in her that desired to search far and wide, discover for herself what lay beyond the summer house. Besides, she had gone in search of the precious mint leaf which she could brew to ease her mother's congestion. Her own various bags of dried herbs were dwindling low, but soon she would be able to plant her seeds outside in the kitchen garden after the ground was well warmed.

It was much too early in the spring to discover the lance-shaped leaf, she decided now, feeling foolish in her searching for it, and made to head back home.

Suddenly Aurora was startled by the three-note whistling of a bobwhite; at the same time two men became visible against the gray outline of woods across from where she stood in the fairy hollow. Not wishing to be sighted by the strangers, she backed up apprehensively until she was hidden behind a tangle of myrtle.

The wood grew darker, even as she stood there, and a misty rain had begun to fall, bringing with it cooler air and a deepened silence. The birds had even ceased to sing. Aurora reached behind her shoulder, slipped her camlet hood up over her dark curls, and secured it beneath her chin. She shivered in the deepening gloom of late afternoon.

The men had begun to converse with each other,

but from this distance Aurora could not distinguish the words. Nor did she want to. Suddenly she blinked her eyes, shutting them tight for an instant. In the lowest part of the hollow she had seen a vision of a lovely Indian maid, had imagined hearing a plaintive weeping that lifted in melancholy song.

Aurora reopened her eyes wide, expecting to see the vision. All she could see was the lowering sky. It looked angry, threatening. She just wanted to be gone from this place, and home in the cheerful kitchen with Hetty or in the parlor with Deana!

Aurora stuck out a heavy clog to head back from whence she came, but a twig snapped noisily in the hush of the hollow. She snatched her foot back and stood still, shaking, waiting for the men to go. Curiosity overcame her fright. She leaned closer to peep through the tangle. The men were coming toward her, and they were dragging something between them. A man . . . it looked like a man!

"'Tis a man," Aurora caught her breath, thinking that he looked awfully ill. Shakily she wondered what the two were going to do with the poor man.

Aurora continued to stare at the strange scene. Curiosity turned to disbelief—mostly because she knew one of them. As if in a dream, she stepped out from her hiding place, tilting her head, not realizing that her hood was slipping off.

"*Dios mio!* What in hell are you doing here?" the angry voice hissed across to her, ending in thunder.

Captain Strang came briskly to her and stared down into the little, upturned face. He could barely restrain the fury that raged within. Aurora gulped, realizing that she had been more than bad, wandering so far from home.

"Do you know where you are?" Captain Strang questioned the girl, who was now studying the ground.

"Nae, not really," Aurora answered truthfully. "I went for a walk in the woods, Stepfather, looking for herbs to cure Mama's cough."

"You are on the grounds of Raven Keep." Javier Strang frowned darkly. "You see there on the bluff?" He waited impatiently for her to look up toward the house. "You did not see it before? You should not be here, you know. There are nasty watchdogs here. They could eat up a little one like you. You have been very disobedient this day," Strang chided in his deep voice with its trace of Latin accent.

Aurora dared not look up at him, but kept staring at his bright green silk coat. It was the work of a master tailor who could have found employment with the king himself. His silver-brocaded vest was crossed by a velvet baldric that an earl might have envied. His naked rapier hung from a lean hip down to a rakish leg. To one as young as Aurora, he looked very impressive in his finery. Little did she know that Captain Strang could never be a gentleman. He was naught but a seafaring adventurer, an imitation gentleman.

"Stepfather, what is that red stain on your coat? Have you been eating berries?" Aurora blurted in her curious innocence.

"*Berries?*" Javier repeated, his black velvet gaze slipping down to his coat. He lifted a hand, brushing, as if shielding the stain from her sight. "Ah—yes, Ro, I lunched on a berry tart this—"

"Captain!" the younger man shouted a warning, dropping his human armful to the wet ground.

At the same moment Aurora said, "Stepfather, is that man sick?" She pointed to the lifeless, dark-haired figure that had slumped forward like a rag doll.

"*Jesu*," Strang swore softly. "Come, I will take you back to your mother. Now!" His step hastened as he ushered her into the wood.

Aurora held her silence until breaking from the forest and coming upon a smaller hollow behind the summer house. The roof of the dwelling was misty with a light drizzle falling around it, and the chimney steamed while the smoke from the hearth fought vainly to spiral evenly upward. The wind had freshened, coming briskly off the river. The sun had long ago bowed below the horizon.

"Stepfather," Aurora began again, "was that man sick? You know, the handsome one with the black hair, like mine? He was slumped over horribly, and you and the fair-haired man had to half carry him. How come that other man you were with ran away and left the poor man there? And who was the man with the big gun, coming from the way of the house?"

A deep breath expired from her stepfather. "The man with the gun will no doubt care for the—ah—sick man, my dear." He then said something beneath his breath the girl could not hear, before he went on. "You will remember nothing of what you have seen, you hear? Nothing! This is business of men, not of little girls."

"Ay, 'tis done, my stepfather. You have my word.

You will not punish me?" she said, trying to strike a bargain. He had only whipped her once before for disobeying, and she had not liked it.

"You may call me Javier. We are friends, yes?"

"Aye . . . Javier," Aurora answered tiredly, blinking heather-hued eyes against the rain and the new, keening wind.

Suddenly Aurora stopped dead in her tracks. Something was terribly wrong. Now she was running as fast as her thin legs could carry her, hearing Hetty's mournful evensong.

"Mama! Mama!" she cried in great gulps, breaking into the house.

Aurora had seen the vision of death: the skeleton carrying the scythe.

Prologue Two

The Letter

England 1670

*In another place in the world, where sovereigns, lords and their ladies, gentlemen of the bedchamber, maids of honor, guards and servants were housed in the pomp and splendor of Whitehall. . . .*

Bran Fayette Ravenleigh, known from birth as bastard of the highest rank, discarded his small sword and began to sport the long military blade that his grandfather had worn in the days of Charles I. There was a fierce silver glimmer in his piercing gray eyes above his long aquiline nose. And when he smiled, which was not often, it was usually a jaded half-smile that mocked rather than pleased.

Elegant, arrogant, the English cavalier was not in good humor now as he entered the sprawling palace that stretched from the Thames to Westminster. Slapping his thigh with his gauntlets, his cape sweeping out behind him like black wings, Bran strode through winding corridors until he reached his private quarters which faced Bowling Green. He paused for a split second, then moved like a brisk wind into the chamber.

"And what are you doing here?" he said in a clipped tone, whipping a cream-colored hat with drooping pink plume from his head.

"I should ask what became of you last night, mi-lord Bran," Elspeth Woodville said with a pretty pout.

"Don't," Bran warned, tossing his hat carelessly onto the huge bed. Eagles and cupids gazed down with silver orbs from the lavishly decorated headboard.

Elspeth had been staring longingly at the bed before the cavalier entered the room, but now her heart fluttered madly at the sight of her lover. Not even the king's bastards slept in such a fine bed. She herself, before coming to court, had been born and raised in a bawdyhouse near Covent Garden. One of the queen's ladies-in-waiting, Elspeth was a sly, showily pretty woman in her early thirties. She had just completed her elaborate morning toilette; her pale copper hair gleamed in contrast with her yellow satin gown, that was looped up on one side, displaying a full underskirt of cloudberry satin. She was a beauty with white-powdered flesh, a merry and dissolute lady of the perfumed Stuart court.

"Why did you not attend court?" Elspeth went on undaunted. "La! There was much gaming and fun . . . but alas, gaiety was lacking without your presence." She swung a white arm around the bedpost, peeping around it coquettishly and cocking her head.

"Were you perchance ambitious again last night?" Bran countered with a question of his own.

Elspeth ignored his ill humor, watching the man who never failed to excite and mesmerize her as he moved about the room restlessly, catlike, his hands locked behind his back. Bran was very tall; his broad shoulders tapered down to a narrow waist, and further down to lean flanks encased in well-cut breeches. His shoulder-length black hair with the sheen of a raven wing was not curled in the fashion but brushed back carelessly from his high brow as though windswept.

Starting at an early age, Bran Ravenleigh's education had been in the hands of the queen's monks. Being a bastard, with only his grandfather to answer to, he had grown into a man without ever having experienced youth and innocence; the only kind of love he had known had come from the ladies of the court, about whom he had become overly curious when he was just a gangly lad.

Elspeth studied those long fingers now, with a tingle growing inside her as she recalled how cool and tender, as well as hot, his touch could be. There was always about his very presence a crackling, electric vitality. To both men and women, there could be no denying that the tall cavalier was the epitome of male virility.

A wave of despair washed over Elspeth. Finally it was beginning to dawn on her that their relationship had been suffering a slow and painful death. She had not wanted to recognize the signs. One was that Bran no longer sought her out to share his bed. She should not be surprised, of course; she had known long ago that Bran's reputation was that of a ladies' man. She herself had gone through much chambering and wantonness. But how could she forget this man, whose kisses were almost savage, who excited her so greatly, driving her almost insane with physical desire?

At this very moment she would feel no shame in throwing herself at his feet and begging him to take her. But he would just be repelled by her actions— again. Oh! she had almost done just that several nights ago when her overwhelming desire for him had become uncontrollable.

"Take your pleasure, Bran, damn you, hurt me!" she had cried at him. So, he had very unceremoniously pushed her from him, none too gently, as if he couldn't stand the very sight of her!

"Why do you torment me like this, Bran? You know what you do to me. Do you even care?"

"Hurt you?" he had said coldly. "Elspeth, you hurt only yourself. Remember, we had a mutual agreement right off. There would be a beginning and an end to our act together. The curtain has come down, sweeting."

"Oh! How can you push me aside after—" she groped for words—"after all you've taken from me. Now I shall be no good for other men—"

"By God, you act as if I'd taken your cherry!"

Elspeth fell silent.

"No hard feelings, hmm? Now—go away like a good girl before you become utterly tiresome. It's my bedtime—alone!"

He had shut the door firmly in her shocked face.

"Darling?" Elspeth tried softly now, wiping the meditative gaze from her face.

But Bran Ravenleigh wasn't listening. He was staring out the window, as if no one else was in the room. Elspeth tipped her head. What was he thinking? About the past? Perhaps his parents again?

Though Bran would never discuss it nor give it

much thought, rumors circulated even now that his Saxon-born mother had been a much-besotted creature, blind in her adoration of a rogue who had made coarse sport of her love, left her heavy with child, and abandoned her to go on his merry, lecherous way.

As a lady of the court who could in her heyday have become a duchess by marriage, Lady Juliet loved deeply and foolishly, and had been laid to rest shortly after the birth of her bastard son. She had withered and expired of a broken heart, many had said. Consequently her son had become a romantic figure in and around court, from London house to country manor. The story was whispered and sighed over even now, twenty-four years later.

The tough old Cavalier, Sir Eric Ravenleigh, had given his only grandson the family name. Sir Eric had fathered the rapscallion who had abandoned the Lady Juliet, and then had banished him when he had been arrested as a highwayman. Sir Eric sent his natural son from his breast, banning him from ever setting foot in England again. Sir Eric himself had ridden off with the horsemen, set his son to ship on the early morning tide. That had been when Bran was still a babe. Sir Eric hadn't laid eyes on his son since, and had banished him not only from land but from memory.

"Bran—I . . ."

He turned partly around. The afternoon sun was filtering in through the ivy so that everything was bathed in a soft green light. It would have been romantic, but Elspeth's words faded as she saw the cold indifference in his opaque eyes. His lips sneered a little. The silence grew thicker between them and she shuddered. Her eyes strayed to the walnut writing desk. His sudden change in mood had something to do with that letter he had received from the New World. She had read it, without his knowing. But he saw where her gaze lay.

"So"—he moved menacingly toward her—"you have been snooping perhaps?" He lifted one rakish eyebrow.

Elspeth heaved a deep sigh, exhibiting the deep décolletage of her yellow gown's bodice. She knew she was beautiful, one of the most gorgeous at court.

Bran looked down into the vacuous blue eyes and cheeks stained artificially red, noticing the slight puffiness of long nights under her eyes. Men would ever boast of their conquests, and Bran knew she had bedded down with several others of late. Aye, he could take her right now, and the pleasure to be found in those white-powdered, secret valleys and curves would be great indeed. But he shook his dark head, his deep voice loud in the room:

"Well—?" he ground out.

Elspeth drew back from him, blue eyes wide and staring from under their artificially long lashes. But she was glad he was finally noticing her, even if it was a chilly acknowledgment.

"Why, milord, I thought you'd forgotten I was in the room," Elspeth said with the excited little break in her voice that Bran knew so well by now. She knew he awaited her answer, but she went on nevertheless. "You do not look exactly pleased though—"

He cut her off. "Pleased! *Pleased.*"

For a second he just stood glaring; then he grabbed hold of her arm. He looked so furious that she thought he was going to hit her.

"I'd advise you very strongly *not* to enter my rooms while I'm out. You were snooping in my desk, Elspeth, and you know I know it!"

"I was not," she said, mock-indignantly.

"That is a bare-faced lie." He released her arm and she pretended to rub a pain out of it.

"How dare you say a thing like that?" Elspeth ended with a pout.

"Lord, you can actually stand there and honestly say that you were not? I as much as caught you in the act—that desk over there appears as if a thief had rifled through it, you damned little liar!"

Her face went scarlet. "Yes, yes, I *did*," she cried. "And I'm glad I did!"

He snorted disdainfully through his long aquiline nose. "Sir Eric informed me that you would interfere if you could—"

This time she cut him off. "You are going to the New World!" She appeared wounded now.

"*That* is none of your business, and you'd better mind your own. Now get the hell out of here—go get laid or—or something!" He felt very much like throttling her.

"I oughtn't to have confessed—" She broke off. "What's *wrong* with us?"

"Us—*Us!*" Bran moaned next. "Sir Eric warned me it would be like this." He paced the floor, holding a conversation mostly with himself.

Now that slate-haired gentleman was just entering his grandson's apartment, very unceremoniously

31

and indifferent to Lady Woodville standing there, posturing; she was waiting on her lover, as if she had nothing better to do than toady at his feet, begging Bran's favors.

Loosing his large falling collar, Sir Eric snorted disdainfully as he chose a brightly patterned chair near a low table, where he could leisurely pour himself a tot of his grandson's favorite brandy.

"I'faith!" Bran growled. "A man can never seem to find time to himself these days."

"Hrumph! Send that empty-headed chit, that royal doxy, out then! I would talk with my grandson alone now. Hie from my sight, slut, begone!" With a waft of his hand, Sir Eric cruelly dismissed his grandson's latest mistress. Their affair, this old man perceived, had been long cut-and-dried, anyway.

"A pox on you!" hissed Elspeth at the viperous elder Ravenleigh.

"Look you—" Sir Eric began, but Elspeth showed her back to him.

"By your leave, milord Bran!" She then curtsied to Bran before rustling to the door.

"By your leave, milord," Sir Eric mocked in a high voice; and she left the chamber posthaste.

Though he was feeling quite the opposite this morn, Bran could not help but loose a thin smile, and this time it was genuine. It was one of those rare gestures of affection, reserved for the only person in the world special to him. As for women, he could take them or leave them—literally. They had begun to cloy him, making him wonder what was wrong with him.

Bran felt as if he'd been wallowing half-drunk in a

stagnant pool. The white-powdered flesh, the clacking tongues, the late nights of gambling and making love to beautiful, bad, gamesome, and stupid vacuous women like Elspeth Woodville—all this gaiety and empty wit had at first excited him. However, the games people played here at court now palled on him.

Even now Bran felt jaded as he looked over the breathtaking Elspeth. Something was missing from his life! He turned from the window where outside Elspeth strolled, her eyes lifting now and then.

And now the letter that had arrived from the New World, dated five months back, would finally give Bran an excuse to depart the perfumed atmosphere of the Stuart court. A long voyage across the western ocean was just what he needed. He loved the sea, delighted in the salt spray and the wide expanse of blue fading into gray, as far as the eye could see.

Bran doffed his sword and leather jerkin, then lounged on a plush seat across from Sir Eric. He eyed his grandfather narrowly as he spoke, but the twinkle remained.

"Did you have to be so hard on Elspeth, Sir? You give her a bad case of the nerves, you know. She has a rough time of it sleeping afterwards."

"Silly vacuous twit!" Sir Eric grumbled, then squared his shoulders, which were still strong and straight, as he leaned forward. "Yet, I'll warrant you knew she was wearing a yellow petticoat last night, eh, lad? Must have spent a wicked night yourself, impaling her to that oft-rumpled bed of yours!"

"That—umm—was exactly what bothered Elspeth, sir," Bran began. "We didn't."

Sir Eric punched his thigh. "That's really rich, lad. Kept her panting at your door while entertaining another, eh?" He waited, then said, "No? Where in hell were you last night, then?"

"Pondering," Bran answered tersely.

"Pondering? Whither?"

"As I rode along the Thames, pondering the fact that I've no future here. But now, as you, I've a mission in life. Murder will out," he declared, and only Sir Eric knew of which he spoke.

"Think you that is true?"

"Indeed! You too have changed the past few days. I've noticed your fresh swagger, the tough old Cavalier surfacing once again. You were not blathering—to Virgnia we shall go and seek the man responsible for the murder of our kinsman!"

Sir Eric lifted a thick eyebrow imperiously. "Man? How do you know it was not a woman who put your uncle in his grave?"

Bran shrugged. "Man, woman. Whoever it was, they will pay. Perhaps even more than one." He turned more serious. "Damn, but I do wish I'd been old enough to have met my uncle before he sailed for the New World. But I had been a babe back then, you said. Was—was Jason much like my father?"

Sir Eric squinted one gray eye at his grandson and waved a hand negligently in the air, saying, "Don't rightly know. Don't recall. Yet . . . a mite perhaps, lad." He suddenly appeared very old and very sad.

At first Bran had objected somewhat to the old cavalier's decision to remove themselves suddenly from England to the New World. For the rest of his life, Bran would remember that morning when the letter had come from Virginia, written in the neat hand of one Colonel Thomas Ludwell. It explained that Jason Ravenleigh had been murdered in mysterious circumstances. His body, lying in a misty hollow out back of Raven Keep, had been discovered by a man named Harris, the steward of the old house. Jason Ravenleigh had been thrust clean through with a rapier.

Jason's diary had been discovered by an investigating member of Governor William Berkeley's council, with only two names giving clue to the whereabout of any kith or kin. Scrawled in it was merely "Ravenleigh" and right next to it "Whitehall." The council member advised Sir Eric's presence without delay.

Bran had lifted his cool gray eyes from the closely written pages he had been scanning. His expression had greatly altered that morning, being first one of disinterest and boredom, but soon he had whistled softly between neat rows of white teeth. He had come swiftly to a decision then. Justice, no less than fortune, demanded their presence at Raven Keep in faraway Virginia. Indeed without further delay.

"Zounds! The day is wasting. We've not a moment more to lose, must attend to matters at hand," Sir Eric said hastily, rising on the carved walnut cane with silver knob. He merely sported it, for he was by no means a cripple. "I've sought and received audience with the king. We go there now, lad."

"After you, sir," Bran said lavishly, sweeping his hand out the open door.

Sir Eric bustled from the chambers, his handsome grandson on the heel of his bucket-top boots.

After King Charles had given the Ravenleighs their leave and his blessings, arrangements for the voyage began and within a fortnight had been completed, with special provisions for their comfort aboard ship.

So Bran bade farewell to his queen and, with that intense light in his eyes, gave a meaningful look to her ladies. To the stern-faced tutors, the monks of his younger days, he gave his most generous and mocking regard as he received their blessings and then cheerfully followed his straight-backed grandfather. As he passed through the portal, one of the ladies-in-waiting's whispers could be heard, "Lud! Hate losing that one. He had indeed been a stud ready to mount, from on early age. Poor, poor Elspeth . . . But, la! We had vied with one another for his favors, and with the lad gone away, ladies, this court shall indeed be impoverished!"

"Faugh!" snorted Elspeth Woodville full in the other woman's face, and stomped off down the corridor.

The morning of their departure, Bran stood watching the river as wispy veils of mist rose from the ruffled surface and gray clouds hunched low over the city. Sir Eric thoughtfully watched his grandson lift his dark head, seeming to see beyond the city to the far off moors.

"I shall miss but one thing," Bran softly told his

grandfather. "All else here in England has grown sour and stale."

"What's that, my son Bran, what will you miss so very much?"

Bran breathed in deeply. "The color of the heather growing wild on the moors," he said poignantly.

# Part One

# The Map

# One

"What manner of young woman have you become, Aurora Gregory!" Jeremias Edwards lectured his niece. "Tutor Aylmer tells me you have become as spirited as a gypsy wench, riding wild through the forest, letting the wind tear your hair loose from its binding."

Aurora said nothing, just sat with her hands folded prettily in her lap.

"Answer me, Ro! Why these complaints? You are behind in your studies. I thought you liked calculating and history, but still you are far behind and have been tutored over half a year now."

Aurora swallowed hard, glancing to the left and right like a startled fawn, her sweeping, velvet-black lashes fluttering downward and hiding heather-hued eyes.

"Ro, you do not fool this old man one bit. Now, what of your lessons? Egad, you are now a young lady of thirteen!" He sighed impatiently. "Well then. Aren't you happy?"

"I . . ." she stammered, then stopped. She spied a silver snuffer, and all the other things she had used to dream about having around her. Since coming here to live, all these nice things and fine furniture seemed

41

less important to her. She had learned something about herself, as young as she was. Love. That was all that mattered to her. She wanted to love and be loved. That, and Cupid, and the forest.

"Do you want to go back to living with Hetty, only the two of you in the summer house? It has been long boarded up, you know." Jeremias would not tell her that he could never send her back there, nor why. The landlord, Jason Ravenleigh, had been murdered the same day that Deana had died of a lung inflammation. It was now rumored that the place was haunted by spirits—whether good or evil, no one knew.

"N—No," Aurora finally said. "I like it here with you and Cousin Melly and Aunt Margaret, Uncle. I am in—indebted to you, sir, and—and I've nobody else in the world, no other kin. Only Hetty," she ended pathetically.

Jeremias continued to frown at her demureness, but in spite of himself, he looked with inward pride at his sister's daughter, who so much reminded him of Deana. When alive, Deana had come weeping to North Creek at least once a month, with little Ro along. His niece, he realized, had enjoyed these short visits, and the spinning wheel never ceased to fascinate Aurora. Often she would beg his wife to teach her how to work it. Margaret thought the child was charming.

Captain Strang had called Aurora's mother a witch, a female demon, an Ishtar brought back to earth to snatch away a man's senses and drive him mindless with the sound of her husky-sweet voice, her coy smile. Strang had even said that the child was born with the taint of sin on her, Deana had cried to her brother.

Even the way Deana had walked at a slow pace, not striding, her carriage moving with a feminine grace, had driven the captain into an unreasonable jealous rage when in the presence of other men. Jeremias himself would have skewered the man through had Deana just said the word! But she always dried up her tears and returned meekly to the summer house, and Captain Strang.

It may prove detrimental later on, but to be sure, Jeremias thought to himself now, Aurora had inherited her mother's perfection of beauty. It should not be too many years before Aurora found herself a husband.

The merchantman, rumored by some to be a pirate, had left his stepdaughter alone with the housekeeper a whole month after Deana had passed on, until finally, Jeremias had whisked the girl away to his plantation situated in the region just north of Jamestown.

"I want no more complaints from your tutor, Ro. I am doing only what's best for you. Do you understand?" His voice became less stern. "You are no wild illiterate gypsy. I would very much dislike punishing you. So, do you want to keep the pony I gave you?"

"Of course, Uncle! I love Cupid! And do you know she is almost as big as a Berber stallion, Ivory said," Aurora animatedly informed him of what the butler had told her just that morning.

Jeremias softened, finding it difficult to conceal a smile. "All right, Ro, go and study your Shakespeare now."

43

So Aurora had knuckled down to her lessons, and Jeremias had less cause for vexation. In the afternoons, though, she still continued to ride as free as the searching wind on her pony. The forest to her was like a great cathedral, with its vast arches and its glorious, ever-changing colors, jewel-dipped in the early morning dew. She loved the music stirred by the wind among the autumnal leaves and through the tall pillars of timber.

Aurora looked forward with anticipation to riding in the winter with the snow crunching beneath Cupid's hooves. For now, she rode the glebe near the old log church. Most of all, the rides in the Virginia forest cleansed her mind of memories of death in the summer house. Aurora allowed everything that had happened that day to slip from memory.

To Bran Ravenleigh, as he stood by the rail on the lower deck, Virginia at first glance was nothing but forest—green savagery of primeval land. As they drew closer, he was unable to believe his senses. Enormous pines rising skyward, larger than the greatest oaks and yews of England, stood like sentinels guarding the wide river. The air, fragrant with the clean scent of pine and fir, was stimulating against his newly bearded face.

One of the sailors stepped to the rail as the fat-bellied ship nosed closer to shore.

"There be man-eating birds in the forests. And savages—they're hiding under every tree!" He shuddered visibly.

"Surely, you jest!" Sir Eric exclaimed, but not completely set at rest.

"Hah!" Bran scoffed at the sailor's fears. "Man-eating birds?"

The quartermaster pulled his curled black pipe from his mouth and pointed with it toward the forest, which faithfully clung to the land's edge.

"Aye, 'tis a strange land of beauty, and sometimes of terrors unknown. There's food and shelter, though, for those who know the woods and come to respect the dangers there, like creatures of the wild and, of course, Indians. But ain't never heard of feathered beasts eating a man alive," he ended with a chuckle, sticking his pipe back into his mouth and sucking deeply.

Bran slid his regard over to a man he had become acquainted with by the name of Tom Bone. He was a wiry, middle-aged man, a bonded servant and colonial of many years' experience. He wore leather clothing of a strange cut, the likes of which Bran had never seen before. In truth, Bran was seeing many things alien to him, and he expected to see much more.

"You will have to learn to handle new weapons. Bet you don't have anything like this where you come from," Tom Bone boasted as he handled a small French hatchet. "Take that sword there. Won't do you much good in warfare against the Indians."

Bran shrugged broad shoulders. "Who said I had any argument with the red barbarians, anyway." He showed the man the length of his back then as he turned away from him.

"Want to try it?" Tom Bone said tauntingly.

Bran peered over a shoulder, then turned back to face the man wielding the hatchet. "Why not," he answered smoothly.

As Tom Bone handed over the hatchet, Bran gave him a penetrating stare. Bran handled the thing with a flexible wrist, then, he flung the hatchet; it went spinning along the deck and stuck, blade deep, in the mizzen mast.

"Hmmm, maybe you don't need much learning," drawled Tom and looked, even as the sailors did, upon the lean young man from England with a new respect—and perhaps a little awe.

"A great asset in your forests, I'll wager," Bran sniffed arrogantly as he offered the weapon back to Tom Bone.

"Yea, and I'll bet we could drop your whole England into the forest here and lose it like a pebble in a stock pond," Tom returned coolly as he swaggered over to ready his master's luggage for going ashore.

"Nice chap. He's got pecker," Bran said of Tom Bone to his grandfather. "He sort of grows on a person. Think I'll have a chat with his bondmaster later."

"Buying up bonded servants already," Sir Eric laughed. "And we ain't even got to Raven Keep yet!"

If Bran had expected Jamestown to be a city like London, he would have truly been disappointed. But, as it was, he expected and found it to be nothing more than a village among the tall pines of a peninsula. Small boats moved lazily away from shore, some under sail, some rowed, as their own ship was warped into a berth alongside the jutting wharf.

Bran saw in the town situated on low land none of

46

the neatness of England. Large brick houses were terraced beside dirty, unpainted huts where smoke from cooking fires drifted lazily upward. The triangular fort was a great brown scar, and part of its log foundations had already been washed away by the restless tides. Beyond the little town the forest loomed dark and formidable.

"Zounds!" Sir Eric exclaimed. "Methinks we have traveled back in time to an ancient civilization, no less!" He craned his neck then. "Look there, to the befeathered fellows. Wrapped in fur mantles they are, and it's only autumn."

Tom Bone chuckled. "Indians, that's what they are. Yep. Indians," he said, swinging a bulging sack onto strong shoulders.

"Damn me all to perdition, 'tis a strange place, this Virginia!" Sir Eric said sharply.

Strange and beautiful, Bran thought, with something wild in the air—a certain romantic enchantment. He felt a shiver of premonition go through him.

Several jolly-faced wenches shouted to the sailors, posturing and waiting until the seamen could be released from their tasks. As the ship was made fast, the captain called to the wenches to stand back, and they laughed gaily, tossing kisses up to him.

"Anything there, my fine cock, that takes your fancy, you'd like to do it with?" Sir Eric asked as he peered sideways at Bran.

"I believe so, sir," Bran returned, mock-seriously.

"Bah!" Sir Eric grunted. "Say, you look immensely bored, son. What say you to a few flasks of

47

brandy and a good bench beside the hearth to strip our backsides of mold and mildew?"

*"All ashore!"* the mate bellowed.

Bone's bondmaster spoke briefly with Bran and then went his own way, leaving the servant with the Englishmen. Bone wondered what was up but did not question as he was ordered to follow with baggage, as the Ravenleighs were escorted ashore and directed to Lawrence's Inn.

A small group of farmers garbed in leathern breeches and blue linen smocks guffawed in passing. The reason was quite clear, thought Tom as, with a low chuckle, he shook his bearded chin.

Bran Ravenleigh, indifferent to the insults, attracted more attention than a flashy whore in red. He wore a suit that the queen had given him as a parting gift. It was an outfit of pearl-gray, topped off with a white-plumed hat; he sported red Moroccan top boots. Sir Eric attracted slightly less attention, clad in his finest silken coat and largest beaver hat. His colors were blackish purple.

Snatches of song drifted to the tavern from the wharves where half-naked Negroes were busy loading and unloading cargo. At the tables were elegantly dressed planters from the upper James, those who had come to examine indentured men and women. They paid less attention to the Englishmen than the farmers had.

As the evening waxed and waned, Bran could not take his smouldering gaze from the young wench waiting busily on tables. Her face was comely and she appeared to be in her early twenties. She wore a pert white modesty cap which shrouded all her hair. As she weaved her way in and out of tables, Bran could detect graceful lines and a goodly shape beneath the formless smock. Her dark eyes glanced his way more than twice during the evening.

The serving wench came later to his room, with charcoal pan in hand, to turn down the sheets and warm them. Bran chuckled softly to himself as she displayed some surprise and embarrassment at finding him already abed.

"No need for that. It's quite warm here in bed," Bran said, and his mouth, large and sensual, twitched in a mocking, all-knowing smile.

The charcoal warmer clattered on the hearth and she started to flee.

"Wench!"

His sharp command made her freeze at the threshold like a startled hare. Then, under his commanding stare, which bore deeply, mercilessly, as if penetrating her very soul, Rachel glided slowly, like a linnet charmed, toward the feather bed.

Bran reached up and, taking her hand, kissed it, back and palm.

"You came to warm my bed, Rachel," he said in a low voice, using her given name for the first time that night. He blew out the candle.

The morning dawned chilly at the inn as Rachel quietly removed herself from the crook of the sleeping man's arm and rose from the bed. Her full breasts, bruised slightly, swayed as she added a big log to the fire and stoked up the last few remaining live embers. She stretched at length, rolled her hips in sensuous remembering, then gathered up her work-smock and skirts, which had been tossed carelessly and hurriedly onto the floor the night before. She took one last glimpse of her lusty lover, blew him a kiss, and then slipped quietly downstairs to busy herself. She tugged on her clothes, haltingly, as she went.

Lawrence, the proprietor and owner, shot Rachel an elevated eyebrow as she rushed into the long dining room with her pert cap askew and wearing a most prettily flushed countenance. He shrugged concedingly then. The handsome newcomers from England occupied his best rooms and the youngest dandy was no doubt responsible for Rachel's tardi-ness. What could he say with such well-paying customers? he shrugged again.

The ship that had carried the Ravenleighs from England's shores also brought many needed house-hold items, besides fancy furbelows and warmer materials for the winter months. Therefore, the early morning shoppers, several of whom were ladies, already breakfasted here. The hot meals had been laid out, and Rachel was just in the process of scooping up a heavily laden tray, her step turning in the direction of a young couple seated at the center board. Another serving maid had just smilingly served a few gentlemen in a booth against the wall and now halted at the table nearest the fireplace where two young women had just sat down upon the straw-cushioned chairs.

"Oatmeal and coddled eggs for ye both?" the

50

serving wench inquired, resting her generous weight on one leg, which to her delight attracted attention to her thrust-out hip from the gentlemen in the booth.

"Aye," the eldest of the two young women answered. "And milk for my little cousin here," she added, tossing her head and boasting her newly purchased bonnet with its froufrous.

Unconcerned with the blond woman's showiness, the serving wench ogled the two gentlemen as she sashayed away from the table. Whispering together, the men chuckled as they shared a private joke, then gave their full attention to their hot meal.

"Melly," Aurora began softly, "I do not crave milk this morn. I would have ordered apple cider. You know how very much I love apples."

"Hush up, Ro," Melanie chided her young cousin. "You'll do as I say when Mama and Papa aren't about to supervise. Anyway, you need the milk, your breasts need some filling out. Don't you know you're still as skinny as a newborn horse? Now"—she pursed her naturally pink lips—"cast your eyes downward, for those men in the booth are looking this way."

"Melly"—Aurora glimpsed up once—"you do not lower your eyes. Why me?" The midnight curtain of lashes lowered at once.

"Hush now, Ro, you are embarrassing me! Here comes our meal. Be good and just keep staring at the table, or else I will have to tell Papa that you have misbehaved. You wouldn't like not being able to ride your beloved Cupid for a whole week, would you?"

Aurora shook her head furiously, causing her long

braids to brush her small shoulders and then bounce back to trail over her bodice front. A pewter tankard of foaming milk was placed beneath a nose that wrinkled unhappily. A set of coddled eggs followed along with an earthenware bowl of oatmeal. Molasses and honey. Thick cream. Aurora finally licked her rosebud lips. She shook out the serviette, laying it upon her lap in a most ladylike fashion, then attacked her breakfast like a burly woodsman.

Aurora heard the tapping of Melanie's shoe beneath the table and so proceeded to eat less heartily. She sighed drearily. How she did struggle to be obedient! It was so very boring to be a tea-and-doily little lady. Ugh! She did truly and dearly love her aunt and uncle; they had taken her in shortly after her thirteenth birthday. She had been wild and unruly, and lonely. She had labored hard to maintain proper progress in her academic studies, but the fascinating wilderness that surrounded her uncle's home remained her dominant interest over the long months since she had come to live at North Creek.

"Now, stay here, Ro," Melanie ordered as she stood after completing her meal. "Finish your oatmeal, but be sure to drink all of your milk! I am going outside to see if Papa is back from his business to pick us up."

With her eyes still cast downward but slitted askance, Aurora saw her chance as one of the wenches swept by with a tray of dirty plates and brass goblets. The milk was poured swiftly into one of the empty goblets, and no one in the room, not even the serving wench, had caught the young woman's furtively executed gesture. Aurora smiled to herself as she placed the now empty tankard back down beside her plate of half-eaten eggs. Glimpsing the serving wench just going into the kitchen, Aurora caught the frown and then the disinterested shrug as the wench spied the milk sloshing in the goblet.

Aurora now shrugged her frail shoulders in boredom. She sighed as she twiddled with the serviette in her lap. She could feel those two gentlemen still staring her way. She blushed a little, wondering if they had caught her sneaky little act. Oh, well, what do I care, she thought to herself. As long as Melanie hadn't seen, she was safe.

Toying with the spoon as she pushed the oatmeal about in the bowl, Aurora let her gaze lift above the mantel of the fireplace. Cocking her bonneted head, her eyes roamed over the oil-painting which hung there. The tall figure was so darkly clothed that she had to strain her violet eyes to make out the sweeping lines of a cape and the wide circle of a Cavalier hat. The face was so dark, though, that it seemed like the artist had forgotten to paint the countenance into the canvas. She was so mesmerized by the standing portrait clothed in mystery that the suddenness of Melanie's return startled her half out of the straw-cushioned chair.

"What's the matter with you, Ro, 'tis only me. Ah! Have you finished your milk as I told you to?"

"Melly, really! I am not a child anymore. Alas, I shall be four-and-ten very soon!"

"Well, you sound just like a pouting child, and keep your voice lowered!" Melanie snapped. *"Have you?"*

"Of course—see!"

Aurora tipped the tankard upside-town and Melanie reddened profusely as the two well-dressed gentlemen chuckled in passing by their table. A single teardrop of milk fell to the table as Melanie shot Aurora a murderous look, but the sooty lashes were already fluttering down as Aurora scooped up a healthy blob of oatmeal into her mouth most ceremoniously. One side of Aurora's cheek bulged out hugely, and just when Melanie would have kicked the younger cousin beneath the table, a tall man in splendid finery entered the dining chamber.

"Aurora . . . you are an imp!" Melanie hissed, sweeping a bold glance over the young dandy making a leg as he passed by and halted at the next table.

Melanie blushed demurely, but when she looked up again she noticed that the gesture of gallantry hadn't been meant for her and her cousin. The young couple at the board were just rising and the man wasn't looking at all pleased with his companion's ogling the clean-shaven dandy cavalier.

Aurora's nose twitched curiously as the fresh odor of milled soap wafted their way. Melanie's look warned Aurora to hold her tongue and keep her eyes cast downward, especially now that this dashing rogue had entered. Melanie had only caught a glimpse of him, yet already she sensed the sheer magnetism of male virility that he emitted.

The dining chamber was quite emptied now as the tall man scraped up a chair and set his long length down. He spoke to the busy serving wench with the generous hips. She was not so busy now, though, as she stopped to stare at him as she'd slowly done the night before, with her large mouth agape.

"Where is my bedmate, that lusty wench Rachel?" Then, brusquely he waved the stunned wench on her way. "Never mind, I see her now."

Rachel had just stepped from the kitchen, casually sipping a hot rum, unaware of her lover until now when he beckoned her to his side with a bejeweled hand.

Aurora leaned across the table to Melanie. "Bedmate? Does that mean they are married?"

"How would I know! I care naught, and hush up, Ro, 'tis none of our business," Melanie whispered harshly, but kept half an eye trained upon the comely wench weaving her way between the tables, until she stood directly behind them.

"Good morningtide, sir, did you sleep well?"

Aurora heard the breathless question followed by a throaty laugh that bubbled up from Rachel's high-bosomed chest. Melanie was unable to resist perking up her already burning ears. Aurora tried not to eavesdrop, but she too could not help but listen as the wench Rachel murmured.

"M-m-m, you smell good, sir. Oh!"—Aurora could almost feel this Rachel being fondled or pinched—"You are too bold, lover. Now stop that, Lawrence might see."

Lover. Now that Aurora understood. Still, what she knew about lovemaking between a man and a woman she could put into a thimble in her rail, the loose fitting garment with several pockets for sewing items.

Suddenly Melanie, who could not restrain herself any longer, glanced over at the amorous pair, and her eyes widened at what she saw. It was then that curiosity overcame caution in young Aurora, and she twisted about to see what had shocked her cousin. With a sharp intake of breath, Aurora snapped her head back to its former stiff position. Now Melanie looked to Aurora with that smug I-told-you-so expression.

Aurora quivered from head to foot. How dare they! She wanted to get out of here fast, but somehow her shoes were glued to the wood floor. Splotches of bright red stained her youthful cheeks.

"The customers, love," Rachel chided as she rearranged the bodice of her smock and Bran lifted his head from its bent position.

"Ahem, sorry ladies," he tossed over his broad shoulder as he rose, then followed Rachel into the kitchen as if he owned the place.

"No doubt that one will get more than a hot meal in the kitchen," Melanie remarked, almost to herself.

But young Aurora wasn't listening. Her eyes were fastened to the swaggering male figure with the short black queue hanging down in back. She had never seen such familiarity pass between a man and a woman and had experienced her first taste of sexual stimulation. She hadn't liked it one bit. The scene had caused funny little tremblings in her belly. Melanie must not have liked it either, Aurora decided, for her face was flushed almost magenta and her lily-white hands fluttered about her now untied bonnet.

Just then the door opened wide, and Melanie made a sound which resembled a sigh of relief. Uncle Jeremias had paused there, holding the door open for his niece and daughter while he beckoned them with a quirk of his graying head. Melanie rose, her bright smiling mouth belying the turbulent emotions raging within her. Aurora made to follow suit, but again her gaze was riveted to the portrait.

Now the canvas breathed life as it was bathed in autumnal rays of sunlight. An eerie halo of light played about it, then rested momentarily upon the dark countenance before flickering back outside the frame. Her spine tingling up and down, Aurora gasped and fled from the room.

The horses were brought around from the shed, and Aurora mounted expertly, hauling Cupid's reins up with her. Melanie was given a hand up into her perch, and soon the three of them were heading in the direction of North Creek.

The ride back home afforded Aurora an interlude of dwelling upon her thoughts; some were troubling to her young mind while from somewhere out of the darkest recesses of her mind she discovered a brand-new kind of excitement that caused her frail limbs to tremble.

She had trained herself to push the most unpleasant things far back into her brain. Like the dark-haired devil with the English sneer in his voice. Arrogant! Conceited! She would forget that crude dandy in no time at all. After all, when you forget, it always lessens the pain. She had taught herself well along those lines. She hoped that in the future she would never have to meet *that* man. One thing, though—she would not soon forget the portrait of the dark-caped figure.

The man in the vizard, the masked man, would always remain etched in her mind, for ever and ever.

# Two

"A small spark makes a great fire, milord. With you it does not take much," Rachel purred provocatively, running warm hands across the naked chest matted thick with crisp, curling hairs.

Bran cleared his throat. "Speaking of fires: Why is the one in your fireplace merely glowing embers? And another thing: Why are your curtains always drawn? Do you have some deep dark secret, like a disfiguring scar you'd rather I not see?"

"Mmmm . . ." she stammered secretively, "I like it dark and mysterious when we make love. Do you mind, if for me it makes it all the more exciting? If I am pleased, love, then you are too, huh?"

Bran pulled her closer, coming in contact with her full breasts. She allowed them to dangle over his chest, tempting him with the fruitlike ripeness of them. He caught one roughly in his large hands, smiling roguishly as she thrust a pink tongue at the tip of his aquiline nose.

"Wicked wench, it does not seem to matter much of indeed you conceal something from me—just as long as you continue to pleasure me!"

"You beast! What about pleasuring *me?*"

"You have already said you are pleased. So, tell me, were you not so a short time ago?" He put his hands beneath her buttocks and squeezed the plump moons.

Never before had Rachel's ardor been so completely quenched. The night before had brought her many pleasures of the flesh; it had been she who had collapsed in near-exhaustion. He was like a stallion, and oh! how he gave it to her as no man had done before. She had taken it all, too! He had made her deliciously sore with his rocklike member. This hadn't happened to her since her very first time with a man. She had felt the *virgin* all over again. He remained in action for longer than she had ever known or even dreamed in all her vast experience.

"Say, sweeting, are there more biscuits and ham?" he murmured, tossing an arm carelessly across her still moist belly.

"Your appetite is really something, you know that? Should watch yourself, lover, else you'll end up with a fat belly."

"Zounds! Am I hearing right? Methinks that 'twas I supposed to be warning *you* of that." His fingers began a methodical exploration at the top of a swelling breast.

"Bran," Rachel was suddenly thoughtful, "did you happen to notice the two women downstairs breaking the fast?"

"There were lots of women here today. But two together? Not really." He nibbled at a bare shoulder, himself becoming wonderfully hard and erect all over again.

"You *should* have seen the younger, less finely dressed one. The shock on her sweet maiden face when she caught you at it, nibbling my breast. Oh! but she was a china doll, did you see?" Rachel felt herself beginning to breathe harder.

"Nay. I was busy, as you yourself just stated."

Bran's fingers, aristocratically long and hard, made a hot trail up her inner thigh, then teased and tugged the dark curls there. The need for deeper stimulation was foremost in Rachel's mind, and all conversation now ceased. They concentrated their efforts on lusty love play now. It didn't last, though, for Bran was soon mounting Rachel and at once entering her, plunging his hugeness into her deep, wide canal. She received all of him easily, without any pain. He penetrated her to the hilt, and she grasped his enflamed organ tighter with herself.

Rachel began to shudder before him, rocking her hips in frenzied movements until one final thrust brought her to explosive heights, bringing the sweetest release she had ever known.

"Lord!"

Bran rolled over onto his side, releasing a long-winded breath. He watched Rachel's generous form, white and moisture-glowing, rise from the mussed bed.

"You will need to wash again, lover. Should I fetch hot water from the kitchen?"

"What will Lawrence say?" Bran said deeply.

"You *know* you've lined his pockets with extra coin to lend me the free time in your arms, lover. Oh—you!"

Reaching out, he had slapped her bare derriere, snapping out an order at the same time for her to get going.

"The day's wasting, wench! Fetch me my bath water, and be quick about it!"

After breaking the fast—with Bran having had his "dessert" upstairs in Rachel's room—the Ravenleighs received word that Governor William Berkeley would be pleased to receive them at the Statehouse directly before noon. Tom Bone would stay behind to direct the unloading of the heavier baggage and arrange for their departure upriver to Raven Keep on the morrow.

On their way to the Statehouse, Bran reflected back to several hours before when he had stood beneath the portrait of the dark masked man. It had intrigued him. A sense of awe had swept over him—and something else he couldn't put a name to. On questioning Rachel, he had merely received a noncommittal shrug. And Lawrence, who had bought the inn and all its furnishings, leaving everything in its place, could only offer that the artist had chosen to remain anonymous.

"Well, how do you know that?" Bran had wondered out loud.

"I have studied it thoroughly. There's not a mark on it indicating any type of signature—that's how."

Bran shrugged as they neared the Statehouse, dismissing the painting as unimportant. His mind was busied with more important things today.

The handsome Statehouse faced the river and both visitors were impressed by the large and well-appointed rooms, as well as by the courtly manners of Sir William Berkeley. He was richly garbed in velvet, the color of which matched his clear blue eyes. He had a high forehead, a straight nose, and sported a large coal-black campaign wig.

On the second floor of the tall house, Berkeley welcomed his guests in his antique-cluttered salon, and waved them to be seated. Bran chose to remain standing while Sir Eric took a seat across from the ruler of the Dominion of Virginia.

"Are you comfortable at the inn?" Governor Berkeley inquired, a tiny bit uncomfortable as the younger Ravenleigh leaned his tall frame on one of his most prized possessions, brought downriver from Green Springs. It was an inlaid walnut Sillón de Caderas chair and he had just polished it most lovingly.

"Most comfortable, sir. We leave on the morrow for Raven Keep," Sir Eric returned politely.

"You will find the Ravenleigh house in good order," the governor continued, eyeing Bran askance, his nervousness growing. "Harris, your steward, is quite invaluable and I have already sent a barge upriver to notify him of your arrival. Harris would have been here to greet you himself, but your captain brought you in a week ahead of schedule."

"The captain took the northern route, I understand," Sir Eric remarked. "'Twas a good voyage, but in truth I am happy to be relieved of the rocking and rolling motion of the vessel."

They spoke briefly then of mutual acquaintances

at court, and shortly took their leave of the governor who at once flipped out his handkerchief and wiped the precious chair free of any possible fingermarks.

Bran swore as they made their way down the street to the tavern. "He didn't mention Jason's death. There is something strange about that cool old buck," he said with a frown.

"Hell's bells! You barely said two kind words to him," Sir Eric recalled with some surprise.

"Didn't have to. He knows what I think of him."

"You do not give a man a fighting chance, do you?" Sir Eric squinted.

"I know immediately if I like someone or not, that's all."

Early the next morning Tom Bone procured horses and, after having dispatched the baggage upriver by boat, guided them along a trail that would wind for a score of miles through the mighty forest.

They rode unceasingly through vine-hung pines, oaks and cypresses, the crimsoned trees arching above them like the beams of a giant's abbey. As they journeyed past a marsh, they flushed a flock of turkeys which took wing like clumsy vultures and perched high on the branches of a long-dead pine with their necks thrust out like parsons reading prayers.

"Stupid-looking birds," Bran observed out loud, taking a last peek over his shoulder. A low-hanging branch snatched painfully at his hair, and he tugged it free. He swore.

Laughingly Bone began to think there was not

another in all Virginia who could equal this Englishman in profanity. Tom's dark eyes, gold-flecked, flashed. The younger man sure sat a horse good for a London dandy; proud and ramrod-straight, it was as if he had been born on the back of a horse. With a thrill of premonition Tom looked on ahead.

As if he shared the man's thoughts, Bran tossed back, "Glad I bought your bond papers, Boney."

His new manservant laughed and Bran fell back to ride beside him.

"So, friend, tell me about the Indians, you being a frontiersman and all," Bran asked.

At first reticent to speak of them, Bone began slowly. Then, as Bran's eyebrows, full and prominent—the sort a man should be wary of—moved like question marks, humorously and indicative of the parade of thoughts crossing his brilliant mind, Bone soon launched into his speech.

After a time, Bran was wishing he hadn't plied the manservant with so damn many questions. Now there would be no stopping the well of words that bubbled forth. Still, he found Bone interesting, and he soon relaxed to the rhythm of his mount.

"The fierce fighters become war chiefs," Tom went on. "Also there are wizards who we call medicine men, and they've more influence than the chiefs even. They wear masks and make magic. A tribe lives together in peace, and the barbarians treat one another kindly and generously. They—"

"Heard some conversation back on the ship," Bran interrupted. "Is it true that the Indians will rob and murder strangers any day of the week, including Sunday, and are as cruel to their enemies as the notorious Roundheads or Spaniards?"

"Aye, you heard right," Bone said simply and strangely fell silent.

At the river, a horn hung on a post beside a small boat wharf, and Bone, putting it to his lips, sounded a blast across the broad stream. Soon Bran saw a ferry coming into view around the bend—a barge rowed by four wild-faced men and commanded by a squat, bearded man who appeared to be a farmer. He greeted Tom like a brother.

The small group boarded the craft and proceeded with the tide to a landing where stood a log tavern and stable shed. For some odd reason, Bran was suddenly reminded of hot-blooded Rachel. Melding with him, she had looked like tawny fire in the moonlight stealing through the curtains, more passionately sensual in her appeal than any woman he had ever known. Her moist lips, without the phony red coloring he had become accustomed to, had branded his body with forbidden fire, in places he thought only the ladies of the court could have dreamed of. His own lips still burned.

On passing a summer house, Bran asked Tom Bone about it, why no one lived there. It was plain to see that no one did, for it was boarded up, and weeds grew up around it as if they had for several months. Tom answered that he had never seen the former occupants, and that was that. But Bran gave it a long study over his shoulder, feeling that same shiver of premonition that he'd felt earlier go through him. As with the mysterious portrait, too.

Raven Keep appeared small in the distance, but Bran could tell as they rode up the slope that it was a place of roomy proportions with good attics for servants. Indeed it was larger than any fine house in Jamestown. Double-storied, with the upper floor jutting out beyond the lower, and with the main-floor windows like narrow, midget-sized slits, it was a castle in fact as well as name.

As they passed the heavy gate that marked the entrance to the immediate grounds, yelling house-boys ran out to help them dismount. Harris, the steward of Raven Keep, joined them. He was a lean, nervous, sallow man, but his squinty eyes brightened at the arrival of the Ravenleighs. Also he was much pleased upon learning that Tom Bone, the noted forester, would now be a member of the house-hold.

"Lo and behold!" Harris exclaimed as he pounded Tom on the back in a friendly greeting. Tom hardly knew the man, but he pumped his extended hand just the same.

Harris turned then, as the other servants had gathered at the entrance, and proudly presented them to the new masters. One of them was hatched-faced Mr. Minter, who would be personal manservant to the Ravenleighs.

Inside, the hall boasted a timbered roof. With all its play of light and shade, there was a suggestion of mystery and gloom. Bran thought at first the entire setting seemed somewhat ancient, but soon found it furnished as luxuriously as the governor's Statehouse. But here, masculinity was the order of the day, for prize specimens of black walnut and massive oak could be seen here and there. The house displayed no touch of femininity. There was even a suit of armor guarding the main hall, silver shining and formidable-looking.

"Yes, sirs," Harris began in a halting, stumbling way, "Jason Ravenleigh—God rest his soul—maintained the old manor against pillage from land and river. He *sure* did."

Bran decided there was no arguing that point.

The hallway which they traversed was softened by Turkey carpets, colored in bold reds and blacks. The windows boasted hangings of native doeskin, and on the walls were painted leather shields. The western room was the plantation's armory, and through the door Bran saw racks of muskets, and two brightly polished breastplates graced the wall.

Housekeeper Ida Minter, in her rustling black silk, showed them to their private chambers, her thin frame leading the way up the wide staircase to the upper hall. The windows here were wider, and the leaded glass casements permitted the sun to play on cleanly scrubbed paneling and floors. The bedchambers were furnished with massive pieces in the Tudor style that had been brought over from England, and in each there were huge feather beds. Tables of black walnut, chests, and bedstead were all covered in a riot of carving, which hardly left an inch of wood unfretted.

Bran, in his own bedchamber, was mildly surprised when he saw the scarlet red bedspread, matching heavy drapes and valance, all very old and embroidered by hand. The Ionic bedposts shone with polish.

"I am surprised . . . and pleased to find things so well arranged. Thought Jason lived like a barbarian. Bran—?" Sir Eric asked askance as he tested the bed with his hand, which sank deep into the softness. "A fortune in feathers—we'll sleep well."

"You'll sleep well," Bran called from the adjoining chamber. He was pondering the female servants, not a one of them having given him the urge to grab her by the hair and drag her off to his bedchamber. Nothing lost, he deduced. There was always Rachel.

With Eric Ravenleigh roaming the house, accustoming himself to his new voice of authority. Bran spent two days at work on accounts with Harris. As most of the figures were in the steward's head, they balanced by every style of reckoning.

Jason, Bran discovered, had not neglected his lands. While taxes were sky-high and the navigation laws had impaired the tobacco trade, their receipts were ample, with reserves to the credit of the estate on deposit with several London merchants. Equipment, boats, outhouses, all were in excellent condition. Too, there were men enough to cultivate new plantings.

Harris's amiable face grew cloudy when Bran questioned carefully about his late master's death. Harris, sensing trouble, had gone out to the hollow with gun in hand and had found Jason's crumpled form, blood trickling from a wound clear through to his back. He had seen someone fleeing, but when he had lifted the gun to his shoulder to fire, the figure had already vanished into the rain-soaked wood.

Bran turned back to the desk, filing this much information into his brain for now. It was not long before Harris spoke up again, this time hesitatingly.

"A young female used to come here. You . . . know of her?" Harris bit his tongue then. Of course, how could he?

But Bran spun around from some papers he had been going over. "What female?" he asked harshly.

"Well . . . she had raven-black hair, you know. Like yours. She was pretty and . . . you know—"

"No, I don't know," Bran snapped, then recalled that Harris was by nature a very nervous man. "Any more?" Bran said more gently.

"Didn't pay too much attention to what her and Jason's business was," Harris said sheepishly. "Excepting she come by here a lot more than other visitors did. Jason didn't go off galavanting much himself, you know. Women had—ummm—always come to him."

"Well, where is she now, my good man?" Bran pressed.

"I know not, young sir. About a week after Jason's death a black brigantine anchored offshore . . . and I saw *her* board it."

With that Harris went back to his calculating, the telling of the details pertaining to Jason's death

70

causing him to be more nervous than ever, as he fumbled about ineptly at the papers on the desk.

For a time Bran stood motionless, a dark vengeful figure, and vowed he would find the young woman, this black-haired wraith, if it took him the rest of his life.

# Three

Five years made sweeping changes in Aurora Gregory. Having been taught carefully by her English-bred tutors, she now possessed the gilt of her native heath.

Aurora had the carriage, grace, and charm of a woman much older than eighteen. Gone was the moon-faced little imp, and in her place was a gorgeous creature—remarkable to the point where young and old men's hearts fell down into their shoes at the mere sight of her. Aurora was even a little amused when she could flutter her long sooty lashes and thereby wordlessly flatter a helpless male when the heather-hued lights, alertly brilliant like a wild thing's, danced in her eyes.

With luminous, light-complexioned skin, which contrasted startlingly with her lustrous midnight hair, Aurora Gregory was the envy of all her friends. The happiest moments of her life happened when Aurora strolled the cedar lane in front of the manor, dreaming, delighting in the smell of the earth and soft breezes after a spring rain. She was sometimes called the moonstruck maid by her neighbors and friends.

With the aid of tutor Aylmer Tobie's London-born

wife, Aurora was now so graceful in carriage that her posture was that of a Diana. Her voice possessed no colonial sharpness, even though she had retained most of her Virginia accent. With her well-turned speech, she could discuss the latest books, court affairs, and French fashions. She had studied her uncle's classics—Caesar, Virgil, Homer, and some of Euclid. *The Canterbury Tales* and Shakespeare's historical plays were her favorites, among English poetry. Also, Aurora knew the Bible and her prayer book; and she could heal the sick with her magical herbs.

"That one has no trouble making conquests," Jamestown spinsters had cruelly gossiped of Aurora. "She forgets men quicker than you can say Jack Sprat! She be a heartless *Ashtoreth,* her with her witch-bag of herbs and her long, gypsy-dark hair. . . ."

Hair, Melanie Wellbeloved née Edwards thought now as she sat in the drawing room, that possessed unnatural lights. Blue lights like the sheen of a raven-wing played along the thick strands. Melanie measured her cousin's face, so like her own. They could have been twins, but for their coloring. Melanie's own hair was as bright as ripe maize silk, and her own violet eyes were large and merry, not the haunting and mysterious violet depths that now gazed dreamily at the woodland scenes in the wallpaper above the dark oak paneling.

"For heaven's sake, what are you mooning about now—perchance a lover? You are incurably romantic, but do nothing about it." Melanie chided the cousin who sat on a low-cushioned stool. "You barely touched your dinner and you've had that faraway look again all afternoon!"

Aurora wrinkled her slightly freckled nose as she toyed with some woolen yarn she had made on her Aunt Margaret's great spinning wheel. Then she rubbed her pert nose in deep thought, ignoring her cousin's taunts.

"Lord, don't keep me waiting, Ro. I'm dying of curiosity! You aren't homesick, are you?" Melanie questioned chattily while at the same time she thought of a rakishly handsome sea merchant.

"Home? This is the only home Hetty and I know now, Melly." She sighed then. "I was merely dreaming about making a pretty quilt from this yarn. The nights can be very cold in the winter, and we need some extra coverlets anyway."

"Dreaming about a quilt. Alas! a man's body is warmer than any old quilt. Foolish one, what you need is a husband to keep you warm," Melanie said importantly. She had five years on her cousin and thought this made her more sophisticated.

"Does Mr. Wellbeloved keep you warm, Melly?" Aurora asked playfully, but hitting a sore spot, thinking of the emaciated man upstairs who wheezed and coughed most of the night despite her herbal remedies. He was a sad old man, but Aurora loved him just the same. Elvy had told her many tales of his past adventures as a pirate. Secretly she realized that Melly rued the day she had become his wife.

"You're a clever one, Ro. You should have been Elvy's wife, not I. You two have more in common than bees and blossoms do, I swear. But a man needs to be stimulated, old as he is, right? That's all the old goat wants, anyway, to see if someone can top him in an intellectual argument."

"In truth, he still has a mind as fast as a whip, Melly."

"That is all that's fast about the persnickety old man. I know just what you're thinking, too. I can see that freakish little imp in your eyes again. Our marriage is a human comedy, a mistake from the first, you know it, and like to rub it in. Even though you keep your lips sealed on the matter!"

"Nay, and I do not think Mr. Wellbeloved stuffy at all. Perhaps if you spent more time with him and created a more loving, friendly atmosphere, he would be happier. He truly has a soft heart, Melly, has it ever occurred to you?"

"Alas, he doesn't have a soft head, Ro. And his leathery body is as tough as a crab shell. You ask me if he keeps me warm? By the time he blows out the candle, I've made my way to the edge of the feather bed. Ugh! I can't stand it when all he can manage to do is pet my breasts. He can't get it tense, you know, he's too old."

Aurora giggled. "Did you perchance happen to fall out of bed the other night? Oh, and such a crash as I have never before heard!"

"Hush up, or you'll have the looney bird pattering down here in his tasseled nightcap and knee-length bedgown, wondering where all the merriment is coming from. As decrepit as he is, you know he can't pass the chance by for a little gaiety. So . . . now you're dying of curiosity, instead of me. Why did I marry the crotchety grandpa?"

Aurora unclamped her hand from over her smiling

mouth. "I have always been a little curious, Cousin, but not overly much. I shall not bombard you with questions . . ." Impishly she let it hang.

"I married him"—Melanie sniffed with chin held high—"because there was wind of a jingle in his pocket. Alas! Little did I know at the time the old bean was as poor as a churchmouse. He could have fooled anyone—by the way he strutted around Jamestown in his Venice lace stock, silken hose, and buckled boots, and burgundy-lined cape—and he did!"

"He *didn't!*" Aurora squealed mock-scandalously, extracting a blinking frown from her cousin.

"Blood of Beelzebub! Not so loud, Ro."

Aurora leaned forward with her chin in both hands, squashing her pink cheeks. "Now you have me impatient to hear the rest," she mumbled between her hands, her eyes bright as sun on heather.

"Well, you know! That was all he owned, what was on his scrawny back and bandy legs! Otherwise, why do you think he'd be living here—nay, croaking here—at North Creek!" She had sunk farther down into her small armchair. "He even had Mama and Papa fooled, you see, saying his ship would soon be coming in. Verily, he didn't even own a barrel of hardtack on one of them!"

Aurora canted her dark head, saying, "Well, it was not nice of Elvy to fool you so. But, who knows, perhaps he has a fortune hid somewhere, like a treasure. One can never tell with old folks, Melly."

"Oh, stop it, Ro! You are making me ill. You don't believe that hogwash any more than I do. See, you are grinning already." Melanie turned a pert profile to her younger cousin, this ending the conversation.

Melanie Wellbeloved sighed deeply, pensively. The nights were dark and full of longing, and her dreams of being the mistress of a wealthy plantation had come crashing down before being fully erected. She desired everything that smooth London bitch, Catherine Tobie possessed—and more. She wanted, too, to feel the thrust of young loins again. And not just some witless farm boy or less than properous tobacco planter who already had snot-nosed brats twined about his threadbare legs. She'd seen it too often, and it was not for her. When the right man came along she would play the waiting game. How otherwise would she be able to snare a young planter whose mama would settle for nothing less in a daughter than Snow White? Well, it would not be long before she would be free of her shabby-genteel husband and able to tie the knot again and rise from the smoldering ashes of her defeated dreams.

A feverish wanting shook Melanie and her white hands clenched so tightly her fingernails dug into her palm. She had thought that when all Elvy's wealth was hers she would rid herself of *him* and cast about for a better mate. Perhaps even David. *David Wiley*. She still remembered the pain when he had deflowered her. She had been thirteen at the time, David several years older and experienced. . . .

"No, no," she had sobbed, beating like a trapped butterfly against his chest. "Don't—not any more. . . ."

"Shhh, Melanie. Just let me . . ."

She had tried to fight him off out in the loft of the barn. She had made claws of her fingers and

77

scratched but little, trying to rip at the handsome, lust-twisted face above her. He had thrown her down first, one leg pinning down her own legs. One of his cruel hands had torn her woolen gown, ripping it clear down to her belly. She had tried bouncing away from him on her buttocks, but his other hand had imprisoned her by clasping her thighs, fingertips dipping into her flesh. One full, young breast thrust at him impudently as she had heaved and strained on the dirt and chaff to get him off of her; he had pinched the peak of a brown nipple before his pink lips had closed over it, teeth nipping the little tips.

"David," she had panted. "Oh, David, quit, please, oh please! That hurts me so!"

He had lifted her very gently to meet him then, nibbling now softly at a corner of her mouth, soothing her into a false sense of security. He had fumbled low to draw his human blade from its scabbard. She had tossed a glimpse downward at the hideous thing just before it drove deep, tearing tender tissue while her scream was muffled by his pinching hand clasped about her mouth. Her blue eyes, eyes as blue as his, had gone wide and fixed unbelievingly on his face. His organ had thrusted, withdrew, plunged ever deeper . . .

David had finished with a grunt and a low moan, his lips drawn back from his teeth in a savage grimace of ecstasy. She had looked first at him in stunned shock while he had been buttoning his breeches, then at her own virgin's blood.

"David, you almost killed me!" she had cried in her innocence.

"Don't tell your parents about this, Melly. We'll do it again and again, to be sure, and it'll keep getting better—you shall see!"

The memory now flooded her being of the next time and all those following the ravishment; it had indeed become better and better. The third time in the loft she had emboldened herself to kneel over him, hands clutching the blade that had first impaled her, before she tossed back her blond head and lowered, opening herself up. With a hoarse cry he had thrown himself upward, bucking like a wild horse, while Melanie screeched and cried out, sharing with him the culmination of their lusty lovemaking. She had been seventeen one night when David pressed his lips to her throbbing throat, after they had finished. . . .

"Marry me! Tomorrow!"

Melanie had shaken his arms from her waist and stood to step into her wrinkled dress of soft lawn and cotton lace edging.

"No, I'll not marry you, David Wiley. You are not the man I thought you were. You said you had a home—a plantation. You do not. You said you had wealth—you do not"—she whirled to face him—"You always lie!"

His pink lips had widened in astonishment. "You—you bitch, you refuse *me?*"

He received a curt nod, Melanie's love-curls bouncing over her shoulders.

"Tah! You slut! Harlot! Dirty bitch!"

Her face had convulsed. "*You* dare call me that—you who came here and stole my maidenhood when

79

I was but a child? You bastard, filthy lecher in penniless pants, get out and never come this way again!"

His hand had closed into a ball, he had strode forward two steps to catch her by the wrist, almost snapping it as he spun her viciously about.

"Do *you* think you can win yourself a better choice as husband?"

"No! When I come to think on it now, men are all such stupid creatures—you the *most* of all!" She had wrenched free of him and flounced from the barn.

That had been the last time with her and David Wiley. Not long afterward she had met and married the old and crotchety Wellbeloved—indeed the most stupid of all male creatures.

She sighed now; there would be no wealth should Elvy die. An arrow was suddenly planted in her heart.

"David, David. What a fool I've been." And oh, how she ached to have him hot inside her just now! Melanie shivered despite the warmth of her wool shawl and glanced up from her ruminating. But Aurora had already retired for the night. So Melanie thought.

Aurora stood just inside the bedchamber, which was illuminated by two large, greasy candles, which were smoking. A row of books—prayer and hymn books and various editions of the Bible—stood on a shelf nailed to the wall. She ran her hands lovingly over the cracked leather bindings. This was where Elvy Wellbeloved was spending his last days on this earth, for everyone for miles around knew that he would soon sputter out like a dying candle.

"Mr. Wellbeloved? May I come in, sir?" Aurora

tentatively asked when no movement came from the huge armchair pulled up in front of the fire. She could see him, though, the top of his head, silver-gray unkempt hairs standing upright, his thin and blue-veined arms and hands resting, one dangling over and one on the worn velvet upholstery.

He sputtered awake. "Who's there, damn it!"

"Oh, sir, I'm sorry. I did not know you had been asleep. I've bothered you and shall come back later—"

"Sounds like a spunky English girl. Catherine Tobie had done a good job on you. Damn it, come in, Aurora Gregory, and visit with me. Tarnation, but I've been lonely. Come on, come on, don't dawdle, girl. I haven't a whole hell of a lot of life left to be sitting by the consarned fire alone. Come around, Ro, come around!"

"By your initial imprecation, sir, it sounded like company was the last thing you desired," Aurora said as she skirted an unpainted pine desk and came around into the circle of hearth-light. "Are you cold, sir? Shall I tuck your robe about you and tend your fire, M'Lord Aelf-wig?"

Faded black eyes lifted to Aurora. "Ahhh, you are enchanting, little Ro. Aurora, the ancient Roman goddess of the dawn . . . No! I don't need no silly-sally fussing and prancing about me. I just want good conversation and a glowing"—he coughed—"crackling fire on a chilly damn night. Sheesh, it's so damned cold the ink is freezing in the inkwell! Where's Hubble, my cat, where is he? I've missed the big puss."

"I fed him some pease pudding and let him out, sir.

81

I shall let him back in before I retire."

"Heh, see that you do, else his whiskers'll freeze right off his nose. Well enough. Now! Sit on the stool here and wrap your shawl tighter about you. It's damn cold in this room."

Aurora reached into the pocket of her rail. "I have brought you some more syrup for your cough, sir. I brewed it just this morning, so it is fresh and potent."

"Good, good. I'll have some upon retiring. Your brew does wonders, Ro. I would expire of a coughing fit had I not my little physician around to make me medicine. Doc's medicine makes me cough even more, so I hid it under my pillow."

Aurora frowned at his strange words. He was failing fast, and he had no kin to love him. No one knew Mr. Wellbeloved's roots, or where he originally had come from. Elvy himself had forgotten most of his younger days, but not the rollicking adventures he'd had at sea.

"How about your young gentleman, that—ah— what's his name, the towering lad that come courting last week? What about him? Where's he been hiding his face?"

"Rodney Quick? Oh! He is not my gentleman. At least I should hope he did not take me seriously. I mean I've never given the lad reason to. He is forever stumbling on a leaf or a blade of grass, and he has the most abominable way of always sniffing. Like this—" She showed him with a fist sliding up her nose to form a pig's snout.

"Ha! That's rich, Ro, that's rich." Then he sobered abruptly. "We can forget him. Damn, don't any of the other young jackanapes come round anymore?

82

No? Don't have a beau, eh?"

"No one, sir."

Elvy Wellbeloved thumbed a leathery, unshaven chin. Aurora had turned a pale shade, and then the color had spread rampantly across her face in a red flush.

"Don't need a man yet anyway, child. You got lots of time . . . whene'er you wish . . ." He snored suddenly, dozing.

*No one.* Aurora breathed the words again, this time to herself. For she was thinking of a certain portrait of a masked man that she had gazed dreamily upon . . . five years ago?

Why did the vision of that man clothed in mystery come to haunt her just now, after all these years?

Aurora had made it a habit to forget—especially Deana . . . and Captain Strang. Most of all she must forget the awful last day that she knew caused her nightmares sometimes.

Now she must contend with a different matter. She had never felt again that strange sensation since glimpsing those lovers at the inn. Just eighteen and mature of body, she had already attracted many a hopeful beau. None had stirred her to anything except neighborly interest. Neither Alan Hackett nor Rodney Quick fitted any of her young dreams. They always wanted but one thing—to steal a kiss or pet. Even Silas Randolph, the widower supposedly skilled in methods of attracting women, was just another visitor.

Outside a light snow had begun to come down. As Aurora stared out the window, tears came readily to her eyes. Just what was wrong with her? She wanted to be in love—totally. Then why could she not feel? Was there never to be a love for her?

"Missy Ro? Can ye not see the old man's asleep?" Hetty's soft voice invaded her troubling thoughts.

Hetty again recognized that strong, tearful emotion that played across Aurora's face, something that altered the whole aspect of her lovely face, illuminating it, and yet causing a strange distress.

"Thought ye'd be hungry, lass. Come to yer room now, there's sassafras tea and hot scones waiting for ye. Yer cousin will be coming soon to put her old man down for the night."

After Aurora had made one last tuck of the lap robe around Mr. Wellbeloved's ankles, she followed the Scotswoman down the hall to her own room where a bright hickory-log fire was burning on the hearth. Hetty placed the tray on the nightstand. All the furniture in her room was made of simple, unpainted maple and although most would consider it plain and drab, it was as she liked it.

"Thank you, Hetty, it was kind of you to think of me," Aurora said, sipping the hot tea she had poured herself.

Despite Hetty's contented little humming tune as she bustled about opening and closing bureau drawers, Aurora felt a certain aloneness. She sighed pensively as she stood and began to undress, unfastening the center hook-and-eye closings of her corseted bodice, then removed the yellow homespun skirt that was divided in front and caught back in a loop to form a simple drape. After her petticoat was removed she put on her nightgown, gathered at the neck, its fullness reaching all the way down to her now bare toes. All her clothes were hand-me-downs from Melanie, but for a few her mother had left her that were still in good condition. The purple-patterned silk was her favorite.

"Ye should'na have any trouble sleeping now, with that warm tea inside ye."

She glanced at Hetty in surprise. "Trouble sleeping?" Aurora said, wondering if her loneliness showed all that much.

"Aye," Hetty returned, bending down to bear-hug Aurora. "Just in case. Sometimes, luv, we've all trouble getting to sleep." Warm understanding was aglow in her kind eyes.

She bid Aurora good night as she left the room, taking the empty tray with her. Aurora leaned from the bed to blow out the candle, then stopped halfway to it. Hubble. She had forgotten to let in the cat. Elvy would miss the cat that usually curled up at the foot of his bed after having been outside.

Rising, she went to slip on her shawl and stepped into her slippers beside the bed. Downstairs all was still, but for the murmuring of voices in the living room. Aunt Margaret and Jeremias. Aurora slipped by the door silently.

At the back door, Aurora called for Hubble; as she stuck her head out she felt the wet flakes of snow tickle her face. She called and called, but no Hubble. Hugging her shawl tighter, she stepped out, making the mistake of closing the door softly, thus blotting out the beacon flooding from the kitchen hearth.

"Hubble," Aurora called. "Hubble, Hubble, come

sweetheart, come!'' She walked on, continuing to call, until she reckoned she was several yards from the back door.

The snowflakes floated down white and rampant, a blinding curtain before her. Blinking her wet lashes, Aurora whirled but with the knowledge beforehand that the bulk of the house would not be visible to her anymore. She wavered, having forgotten the poor cat as tentacles of fear began tugging at her heart.

Aurora had heard often of people freezing to death in a snowstorm, having been almost at their doorstep, or perhaps a hundred yards or so from the house, their tracks going in blind circles and meandering trails about their stiffly frozen bodies. It had even happened to Indians, Jeremias had once warned her with loving care.

Aurora hurried faster toward what she hoped and prayed was the direction of the house. Poor Hubble, she thought. Poor Aurora, too, she added; for though she kept trudging, the snow was harder to plow through now that it was piling up and her feet were fast becoming icicles. The shawl draped over her head and shoulders was shrouded with a wet mantle of white now, she knew.

''Hubble—'' she cried weakly. Then—why was she calling for the cat when she herself was lost? Well, perhaps a meow would lead her to shelter. If only the snow would ease up a little.

There was still no sign of the house. Nothing but white. White speeding down in front of her eyes until she was made dizzy. Cold. She was so cold. Lord, her

86

limbs were numb.

"Oh, God, if I cry now my tears shall surely freeze. Mama . . . Oh, someone, please God, help me. Help . . . Help . . ." she cried weakly and tripped on the hem of her nightgown, her frozen hands splayed out to break the fall to her face.

Lying helpless, she thought never in her entire lifetime had she felt so utterly alone. This must be death, or near to it. Panic consumed her. Numbness was stealing all through her as she snuggled in her snowy bed, trying vainly to find warmth. Where was her courage now? Had she ever had any to speak of? This was the end. She was going to die! She closed her eyes, waiting for the inevitable.

Seconds later she opened her eyes and saw something black amid the snow. Was it night she was looking at? As she watched, the thing moved and began to fly in the oddest way. It was a bird—a huge bird! She lifted her head, feeling renewed strength as she watched the bird that darted to the left, disappeared for a second, and then reappeared to beat its wings frantically above her. Its harsh cry seemed almost human. Over and over it repeated the same motions, darting away, disappearing and then reappearing. Aurora suddenly realized what the bird was doing. The harsh cry was saying *Follow me!*

"Missy, what you been doing out there in the freezing cold!" Ivory's voice surrounded her like a soothing, warm balm when Aurora stumbled in the back door. "Lord, babe, you look just like a snowman. Come over here by the fire where you can sit and be warm, while I get you a blanket and something hot to drink."

Aurora was already thawing out beneath the woolen blanket Ivory had tucked around her from neck to toes, when he set down a cup of hot tea with stimulating lovage herbs in it. Aurora poked an arm out of her warm cocoon to reach for the steaming cup.

"Better wait, babe, I made it too hot to drink just yet," Ivory warned, rubbing her slightly blue feet between the folds of the rough blanket. "I learnt that from you. It's a good rememdy for what ails you, that lovage cordial. Now tell Ivory, what were you doing out there strolling about in the snowstorm for? You trying to turn into a big old icicle at your young age, babe?"

Aurora managed a light laugh. "I was looking for Hubble when I found myself foiled and wading through a snowstorm. Alack! a huge bird saved my life and led me back safely."

Ivory tucked his chin into the black folds of his neck, his face registering that he was not buying this tale. "Strange things happen, babe, when one's afeared. You shore looked spooked when you come in all white and red-nosed. Lord! Lord! You says you was looking for the cat?"

"Aye. I promised Mr. Wellbeloved that I would let Hubble in before retiring."

"Babe, I let the cat in over an hour ago. I'm shore sorry, I wish I'd known you was looking for him. You ask me from now on before you go galavanting out there in a snowstorm, you hear?" Ivory turned to pour Aurora some more tea with herbs, adding, "You just snuggle up there and don't you worry none about nothing. When you falls asleep I'll carry you up and tuck you in bed jest like I did when you first come here, babe.''

Trusting the old butler, Aurora did just that after she had finished her second cup of lovage tea. Her eyelids grew heavy. Before she fell asleep, Aurora thanked God for her miracle with black wings.

*Four*

Astride his barrel-chested hunter, Bran rode through the wintry fog toward the York River after having spent the night at an inn situated on the outskirts of Jamestown. The low, cold wind breathed hard through his woolen cloak, but the sun showed promise of sending its lambent light glancing over the thinly iced face of the river. The sensation of cold was beginning to leave him by the time he entered the primeval silence of the forest.

During his five years residing in Virginia, Bran had learned from Tom Bone and Harris much of the geography of the colony and its great distances, endless forests, and bewildering water courses. Thereafter, he had begun a methodical search for the young female who, he was certain, held the key to the slaying of his uncle.

During the summers, Bran had practiced almost daily with his weapons until he became quite adept at various sword tricks that he had learned as one of the prince's captains of the horse, but had not mastered until now. Tom Bone, meanwhile, taught Bran wrestling and some of the arts of forest warfare which had been a mystery to the young Cavalier. Sir Eric's grandson learned to wield the short blade and

90

razor-keen French hatchet and to load a fusil so it would throw an accurate ball.

The forest remained a mystery to most planters, and not one soul traveling alone dared venture two miles inland from a river. But Bran, as a challenge to his strength and nerve, ventured daily into the deep forest, and sometimes Tom Bone went along. To his amazement, Bran soon discovered that land trails to the west were in many cases much shorter than the water routes and, with knowledge of the forest, mounted on horseback or not, he could outspeed the swiftest barge between points on the winding streams.

"I have become a woodsman," Bran bragged to Tom one day. "Me, a dandy Cavalier of darling old England. Our dovelike neighbors would be indeed horrified to learn that I've become a savage!" He laughed aloud and Tom joined in.

Tom Bone never seemed to relax in the woods. He slept with one ear open, and even when he ate he paused between chews to listen, or when smoking a pipe of fragrant leaf. When they hunkered down to a supper of venison and pones, the man's nose as well as his eyes and ears always remained alert to danger. Bran marveled that Tom could smell a thunderstorm and even estimate its intensity. He could track a deer with stealthful expertise, and in every respect the manservant was a better woodsman than any Indian Bran had so far met.

Bran dismounted now at the new plantation on the York River. He had traveled here to visit Colonel Ludwell who he had learned had been a close friend of Jason's.

The colonel now graciously received Bran, even though Ludwell had come down with strep and was beneath a pile of quilts on the daybed in his library. A blazing fire crackled in the grate as they conversed lightly for several minutes, and then Bran came right to the point.

"You knew my uncle well?" Bran waited for the weak nod. "Jason was murdered six years ago and damn! if I haven't searched Virginia from head to tail for five of those years."

"Yes, I, too, have heard from sources of my own that you still search for the murderer. Would that I could help you find the coward who thrust him through!" His voice rose as he lifted himself on an elbow to meet Bran's intense gray gaze.

"I shall never give up, Colonel," Bran returned in a dangerously soft voice. He could trust no one anymore—too many people knew of his quest. For now, he would withhold any mention of the raven-haired wench.

His eyes sulfurous, fever beading his high forehead with sweat, the colonel leaned closer. "Look for Javier Strang. Captain Strang. I think he knows how your uncle died."

"Captain Javier Strang?"

"A merchantman . . . actually a pirate in sailor's garb, most believe. And go to seek him carefully, Ravenleigh, for the captain is well-liked in Jamestown," the colonel advised.

Dizzy and weak, Ludwell slumped back to his bed and Bran graciously made his exit. He retraced his tracks to Jamestown, and was discreet in his inquiries about the sailor.

In the subtle shadows of evening, he first went to the local tavern where Rachel worked. Resting his mount in the stable shed, he sought out Richard Lawrence, the innkeeper who was later to become his friend.

"There was some argument between Jason Raven-leigh and the trader Strang. Was right before Jason died, too, but I couldn't tell you what the cause of it was"—the innkeeper shrugged—"That's all I know, sir."

So—Bran concluded as he stepped outside into the cold, starry night—his uncle and this Captain Strang had been mild acquaintances for years, then suddenly seemed to become unfriendly. The reason? This was obscure, but he would be damned if he did not find out pretty soon. What made him even more incensed was the fact that the wraithlike young female Harris had mentioned several years back seemed to be virtually unknown by the gossips of the taverns. They had been exceedingly reticent to speak about Strang. Whatever else he might be, this Strang had high connections at Jamestown, and it was plain to see that it was unwise to question overly much—especially not about so close a friend of Sir William Berkeley!

There seemed to be some connection between Strang and the raven-haired wench, though. Damn! Not one soul knew where Strang could be found. Bran left without even seeing Rachel Smythe. He had not looked for her, nor was he in the mood for wenching, satisfying as she had been to his lusty appetite on many a long night.

\*      \*      \*

Outside, the dark green of the pine and juniper were decorated with snow-crystals, while inside Raven Keep the halls were as cold as Christmas by morning when Bran rose and made his way downstairs to breakfast with Sir Eric. Bran entered the hall, masculinely garbed in doeskin breeches and buff waistcoat. His high boots had been well varnished.

Bran expected his grandfather to question his whereabouts the past several days, but he saw only Harris seated at the long table.

"Has my grandfather come down yet?" Bran questioned the steward.

"Sir Eric is still abed, Master Bran. He awaited your coming late into the night, you know. The hound woke me when you slipped in at four of the hour, but Sir Eric did not budge. He is well, though, but grumbles often that the weather is as cold as that of Scotland here."

Bran nodded, then reached beneath the napkin for several hot cakes, which he forked onto his platter and poured maple syrup over. Harris passed the ham, and then proceeded to rise from the table, having had his share of the breakfast.

"What's your hurry? Sit back down, Harris. I would have a word with you."

Halfway out of his chair, Harris eased himself back down. He wondered nervously if he had made a mistake in calculating. He had come up short in the books, but then, naturally the drought had been calamitous and had completely ruined the harvest.

"It is not the books, Harris. No fault of yours, as your reckoning proved exactly true to the letter." Bran paused a minute to chew a bite of ham. He washed it down with a swallow of rum-spiked tea, then went on. "What do you know of Captain Javier Strang?"

Harris thumbed his bewhiskered chin in thought before he spoke, slowly. "I can't be certain . . . but it seems to me that's the name of the fellow who rented out the summer house. It was quite some years back, sir," he ended hurriedly.

"The summer house," Bran said reflectively, almost to himself. "Ah, of course, the little house on the eastern tip of Raven Keep. Hmmm, could it have been about the same time that my uncle was slain?"

"Sir? You mean did the captain rent the house that same year?"

"Certainly."

"Why . . . why, yes, I guess he did," Harris recollected. "Seems to me he had a family, too. Sorry, sir, that is all I know. Jason took it upon himself to deal with his renters personally."

Bran slapped his napkin down and rose from the table. A muscle worked in his lean cheek as he strode brusquely to the door and called for Minter to fetch his woolen cloak. Harris padded up behind him, helping his young master into the puce coat.

"I should remind you, sir, we are having guests for dinner. Will I tell Sir Eric to expect you?"

"Aye," Bran said absently. "And tell one of the houseboys to fetch me a turving spade and a handful of pegs. I shall be ready and mounted out front by the time he returns."

The boards crisscrossing the door groaned free of the doorframe as Bran worked with the tool. With the weathered boards lying at his feet, Bran gave the door a push and the wood-and-leather hinges creaked forbiddingly, as if protesting and deeply resenting this stranger's presence. Brushing snow that had fallen onto his broad shoulders, he stepped into the bleak kitchen cast in semidarkness, and noticed at once a bittersweet presence that seemed to reach out to him.

There was sadness here, and strangely enough, joy had been shared between these walls. A child's joy. He could almost hear the silvery, tinkling laughter as he moved through the two lower rooms and climbed the narrow stairs to the tiny bedrooms in the loft. Up here, pale twinklings of wintry sun struggled through the wavy-glass window, and dust motes rose to play in the frail beams. Bran spun about on his heel as he tilted his dark head, staring hard at the rickety rocking horse he could have sworn moved just a minute ago. Tinkling again. It was a little girl's laugh he heard. Sweet.

Absurd! Bran turned and ducked his head as he made his descent back to the kitchen. He halted and stood still, listening, glancing up sharply as a frail and mournful sound lifted and hung in the musty air—like death itself. Then he espied the little pouch. Hunkering down, he gently lifted the pouch from the corner where it had, no doubt, lain all these years. He held it up to his nose.

"A medicine pouch," he decided, and the herbs crumbled between his hard fingers. "I know this was yours, little girl. Who are you? Where are you? And why are you haunting this place—and me. . . ."

"Ouch!" Aurora said as she accidentally pricked

her finger with her embroidery needle. Her head lifted, her wide eyes registering surprise, and she automatically sucked the tiny speck of blood from her finger.

"Someone is thinking about you," Melanie jested in a singsong voice.

"Do you really think—" Aurora began, her eyes misty—"I did have the strangest feeling that someone was thinking about me, as if a whispering arrived on golden wings."

"Or black wings," Melanie began cryptically. "There was a raven outside the window a moment ago. Didn't you see it?"

Aurora sniffed and lifted her hanky. "No," she answered distantly and then sneezed loud, wiping her nose daintily.

"What's a raven doing—? Well, anyway, I say fiddlesticks! I was merely mocking Aunt Bertie and her old wives' tales. Well, Ro, it's too bad you caught the sniffles. I could have told you that chasing pussycats in a raging snowstorm wasn't good for a soul. Now you can't go with us to the Ravenleighs' for Thanksgiving dinner."

Melanie sighed and set aside the tea cosy she had been embroidering. She frowned down at the ill-made stitches. She could never be as good with the needle as her cousin. Aurora's own stitching was considered comparable to that of the best seamstress in France. The younger woman knew how to judge tapestries and her needlework was to be envied. Melanie was indeed extremely jealous of her cousin's various talents. If that wasn't enough, the gossips said the Edwards's niece sat a horse better than most lads in the colony.

"In a quarter of an hour the Tobies will come to take us—I mean Catherine, Aylmer, and myself—in their sleigh to Richard Holder's and from there we will go to the Ravenleighs. How do I look?" Melanie spun around for her cousin to inspect her new clothes.

The skirt of Melanie's purple gown was turned under and looped back, displaying the quilted petticoat beneath. An ornamental, gold stomacher covered her chest and abdomen in a triangular shape. The woolen cloak she would wear during the journey was trimmed in fur. Her pale hair was turned under in side-locks and tied with purple velvet ribands, while the back hair was fastened in a coil into which more ribands had been twisted.

"I'm glad Mama could do my hair before she and Papa left to go to the Randolph's for Thanksgiving."

"The style is most becoming, Melly, and your new dress is gorgeous. You are the image of a lovely princess," Aurora sighed, looking down at her own gray rail which hung loose and shapeless. A brass chain suspended from her waist held her scissors and pincushion. Her dark hair was covered with a pert little cap of quilted calico that fitted exactly to her head.

Sleigh bells jingled gaily outside as the snorting, blowing horses came to a halt below the delicately frosted window. The snow was falling in earnest again.

"Have a good time, Melly, and do not worry about Mr. Wellbeloved as I shall check on him often and make sure he gets turkey dinner and pumpkin pudding."

"Oh, I will have a grand time," Melanie announced, forgetting that she even had a husband. "Just think, finally I'm to meet Bran Ravenleigh. I hear he is quite splendid to look upon. Like a prince! Keep yourself warm, Ro, and don't stuff with too much turkey"—she giggled as she whirled from the room, calling back—"I know I will!"

Alone now, Aurora sniffled into her handkerchief again as she rose and went to stand before the window. Huffing on the window, she wiped a spot clear with the end of her shawl. She gazed from her wintry porthole, listening to the faint tinkling of sleigh bells—and then pin-drop silence. It was as if the world had suddenly gone away, leaving her all alone.

Aurora stirred after a time and glanced about the room. If she didn't know better—that there were others in the house besides herself—she would now believe that she, Aurora Gregory, was the only human being that existed in this whole wide world.

Yet sometimes, as had happened while sitting with Melanie, and before she had known this startled sense of vacancy, she had felt surrounded by a warm force—a presence? As if something—more like *someone*—had tried rifling her thoughts from afar.

What had come over her? Gazing upward now, a starry snowflake suddenly dipped out of a multitude of others, as if to mock her foolish ruminations, then dashed away.

"Do you feel what I feel?"

Aurora pressed a palm against the cold window. Her own voice had startled her.

*Who are you? What do you look like? I wonder*

*what you are doing now. You are out there somewhere. I feel your fire heating my body.*

*Are you real, or just a figment of my imagination? I believe and yet—it's like a whisper riding on the wind. Feeling; reaching; searching. Why?*

Aurora's blood raced through her veins. This was a little scary; nothing like this had ever happened to her before. Would this feeling go away?

*Where are you, and what do you want from me?*

Again, it seemed to her that she was not alone. Or was she only imagining this mysterious stirring, in her loneliness?

What if this someone—this man—yes, he was *man*, having no physical reality, was suddenly given substance and came to her? What then?

With the twin fireplaces roaring, a grateful warmth with the odor of blazing hickory wood filled the room. Dinner was being served in the great hall of Raven Keep, where the guests had assembled at a long oaken table. Mr. Minter and Henry carried in the roast venison, boiled bacon, wild turkey, quail, and hot meal cakes, pease porridge and dried grapes. Ida Minter followed, bearing on a tray pewter tankards of beer and tall bottles of Madeira. As the huge room had fireplaces at each end that glowed with beds of wood, the chill was soon extracted from the place. Fat candles in sconces on the walls flickered and lighted the board.

Tom Bone was bent at the fireplace helping the black cook, Cuffee, roast the oysters and chestnuts. Richard Holder, the Edwards's closest neighbor, stood close by, sniffing the succulent aroma wafting from the hearth.

Sir Eric's brows rose, and pleasure lighted his eyes, when Cuffee placed the shellfish platter at his elbow. Richard Holder chose the seat nearest his host, his eyes never leaving the platter of deliciously roasted oysters, except maybe once or twice to look in Melanie's direction. Within several minutes all were enjoying the repast in fine humor. They talked of home affairs, and of the threatening weather that had come early to the colony.

"Oh, and the ice that floats in the river," Catherine Tobie said. "I'm afraid we shall have icebergs as big as horse-sheds before long."

"Not all that bad, my love," Aylmer Tobie cheered his wife. "At least they won't come floating to our doorstep," he chuckled, and Richard Holder joined in.

"You men are funning me," Catherine said as she blushed very becomingly, in a courtly fashion.

Richard Holder came to Catherine's rescue by changing the subject at once. He spoke of the topic of the day—Nathaniel Bacon—saying that he was a young man of wealth and the best English training, but a bit on the melancholy side.

"Though his name is linked with it, he seems to care little for political life," he ended.

"Nathaniel Bacon," Bran pondered out loud. "Seems to me we've been hearing of him a lot recently."

"Ah, but he is a nephew of our present Nathaniel Bacon and, they say, the older one's heir," Holder explained.

Melanie could not take her eyes off Bran Ravenleigh. He had changed into his dark-gray waistcoat, and breeches which fit snugly on his lean flanks. His white collar was beyond reproach in its lacy perfection. Melanie sat just opposite him and more than once had become nervous and ill at ease under his steady gaze and had to look away. He outstared her every time, but her sparkling violet eyes, as if possessed of a will all their own, could not help but wander back to him. She felt scalded by his silvered scrutiny.

Bran wondered what Mr. Wellbeloved would think of his young wife's undisguised interest in a stranger—a man she had only just met. She had made excuses for her family, said they had gone to neighbors for the "big dinner."

But Melanie did not explain why her husband hadn't been able to come, and never once did she mention her cousin who stayed at home with the sniffles.

With dinner finished, Catherine struck up what was to be a long conversation with Bran Ravenleigh. They sat at a proper distance apart on an upholstered walnut bench with a hinged back. The men, smoking fragrant pipes, took their places before the fire, seated on a massive piece of Gothic furniture—a crimson-velvet cushioned settle which had been designed to seat several persons.

Sir Eric eased down into his favorite chair, made of oak, with a high panelled back, sides, and arms. Tom Bone chose to sit, as was proper for a servant, on an oak stool, trestle form, with medallions facing each other. His rough bearded face reflected full contentment at being included in such fine company.

With Catherine monopolizing the young host's time, Melanie became quite bored and stood to excuse herself from the hall. She pled a sick headache and held up her lily-white hand when Richard rose in mild alarm.

"Don't fuss with me, Richard. You just go ahead and have a good time. Do sit," she almost snapped when he just stood there gaping at her. "I will find the housekeeper and go upstairs to lie down, please." Her regard, though, snagged hotly on Bran Ravenleigh before she swept out into the main hall, her steps muffled by the Turkey carpets there.

Bran watched her go, his gaze hooded by thick black lashes. If circumstances would have been different—but no, she was a married woman. And besides, Richard Holder kept vigilance over her like a Tom with a mouse.

Catherine put round eyes upon Bran Ravenleigh. "You—?"

"Nay, mistress," Bran answered her barely formed question. "At least I've my doubts she's in the family way."

"Oh?" Catherine blinked, followed by a sudden blush. It came to her that in all her life she had not met a more outspoken young man. It had been evident all throughout dinner.

"You read people very well, Bran Ravenleigh," she went on. "You never flinch with embarrassment either, do you?" She smiled genuinely though, having already decided before this conversation that she liked him very much.

"I must warn you, madame, that compliments move me not one inch. As for your question, I'd say—no."

"Well, I must confess that I have been spying. Is—do you think she is waiting for you upstairs? I mean, Melanie means well, but she is a trifle lonely being married to a man four times her twenty and three years."

Bran almost laughed aloud at that. "So, madame, you were not about to say that the good Mrs. Wellbeloved was in the family way, I presume? Unless—"

"Ah, do not be cruel," Catherine chided. Then, "I am sorry, but have you not heard there is smallpox in that Nottoway town upriver? The infection was said to have been caught from a Scottish peddler."

"Aye, madame, but they were savages. The pox has not, much to our relief, reached Middle Plantation." Bran took a deep breath before he went on. "Mrs. Tobie, I believe we have been talking in circles. Why don't you tell me about yourself—and your family. Like Sir Eric and myself, I hear you too are from England?"

That did it, Bran thought contentedly as Mistress Tobie immediately launched into a lengthy, one-sided recitation, one that would have made Sir John Suckling envious had he heard her airy English prose, and each and every one of her elegant relatives who must be *sooo* lonesome for her merry company.

Bran sighed, relaxing his long silk-stockinged legs stretched out before him, Catherine's voice humming like bees in his ear. He nodded now and then to indicate that he was still with her.

With Bran half-listening, Catherine turned the one-sided conversation to Aurora Gregory. "She captures hearts, young and old, the lovely darling. Oh! and Melanie is fit to be tied for all her jealousy. And them cousins, too. You should have heard Melanie just a week ago when Aurora had playfully fashioned her dark hair in the French manner and had awed and scandalized their more sedate friends. La! How little Ro can speak of the latest fashions from Versailles. Of course I suppose I should take some credit for schooling Aurora in charm, fashion, and grace. The darling would so make some man a fine wife, with all her pleasing attributes." Catherine looked askance to young Ravenleigh with a sly twinkle in her blue eyes. What a handsome couple they would make, Aurora and Bran, with both of them ebon-haired and gorgeous!

Up until now, Bran had been mildly bored with the soft chatter around him. Suddenly his ears perked up as he harkened to what Holder was saying to Aylmer Tobie. Melanie chose to enter the room, sleepy-eyed, just then. But Bran barely acknowledged her presence as he sat tensely alert.

". . . Captain Strang has visited the Welcome Inn every evening the past week, I've heard from one of my servants. There's a—pardon, ladies—dark-haired wench who goes there to meet him and . . ."

Bran shot Tom a lightning fast look and together they rose, without any preamble. Catherine suddenly turned around and found her company had vanished. Oh dear! Was it something she had said to make him go off in such haste? Perhaps she had chattered too much and bored him, she decided with a deep sigh of abashment.

Sir Eric dozed in the oaken chair with a bearskin

rug wrapped around his legs, thus missing the glances exchanged by the guests—swift liftings of the brows that held more than surprise. Was it apprehension? Catherine wondered.

The Welcome Inn, built on the lee side of a huge tobacco wharf, was a forbidding sight at dusk when the two weary travelers approached. Unpainted, gray from the salt spray of a hundred squalls, its timeworn and blistered sign creaking ominously on its chains like a gibbered wood skeleton, the bleak structure overhung the icy creek, making the old building seem to float on the dark glassy waters.

Bran and Tom had ridden most of the day after having set off at dawn from Jamestown. Now, ten cold and biting leagues later, wrapped in wolfskin mantles, having drunk from skins of ale and eaten lightly of jerked beef, they had finally reached their destination. Dismounting, they fastened the horses to two pines and stole through the dusk.

Two men cautiously entered the common room where the proprietor, and his two broad-bottomed wenches were at the fire, basting a saddle of mutton. The huge greasy man frowned when he heard the door open and close, felt the blast of wintry air nip his backside. Mr. Sparrow turned and at once fluttered about his strange-appearing guests. Plainly, Mr. Sparrow's movements indicated that his mood was indeed fearful and nervous.

Tom Bone sauntered to the window, cleared a spot free of hoarfrost and looked out over the broad, icy creek. Bran doffed his beaver hat, but when he began peeling off his gauntlets, he halted as he noted the landlord's trembling. The wenches, after admiring the dove-colored doublet and black breeches which fit like a second skin—especially about the pelvis area—caught his steady, piercing gaze as they perused him, looking up his magnificent frame, and scurried out of the room like chickens fleeing the hatchet. Bran's lips quirked in a smile that did not reach his hooded gray eyes.

"So, you are expecting Captain Strang?" Bran inquired as he swung about, catching the proprietor off-guard.

Above his pelican-like throat that worked like a bellows, the proprietor started to shake his sparsely thatched head. There was a moment's silence, then Tom moved like a cat and took the man by the fleshy throat.

"You are," Tom stated rather than asked, backing the man up to the fireplace.

"Speak out, damn you!" Bran commanded, and Tom shook the man until his overgrown melon-head rolled back and forth within an inch of the oak mantel, and his rheumy eyes popped from Tom's mighty grip.

"He—he come and gone," cried the proprietor. "Ye missed 'im!"

Bran swore and then pressed, again with impatience: "Do you also know of a raven-haired wench?"

"N—No, yer worship. Been no women but the wenches in here tonight," he gulped. "I only kept the good captain victualed for a week or more, I swear."

107

Bran snorted and then turned to the window, studying the dusk-darkened water. Suddenly he pulled the one glove back on and turned back to the man.

"Say nothing of our being here this night. Understand?" he clipped.

The man bobbed his huge head. "Aye, I understand—Aye!"

"And see that the wenches keep their lips sealed," Bran warned with gloved fingers on his sword.

"Aye, aye, your worship! Me girls know no English. They be Dutch."

Bran and Tom left the inn, going out into the chilling blast of wintry night. As they strode in silence, Tom scratched his head in puzzlement. What did his master have in mind next?

"The forest, then, instead of the inn?" Tom finally inquired as to their resting place for the night.

"Yeah," Bran said. "Of the two evils it seems the lesser. I shall sleep sound this night, at least for several hours. I could not trust that greasy fellow back there, Tom, and would much rather wake to a howl of a wolf or the scream of a panther than find a kitchen knife slicing at my throat."

Still, when Bran paused in his stride to glimpse over his shoulder to the inn with some indecision, Tom nudged him ahead.

"Forget it, my friend. There will come another time for a meeting with the pirate Strang."

The way ahead lay as dark and cold and still as the air of a cave and from out of the wood came the long-drawn howl of a hungry wolf. With his countenance given to a sinister cast, Bran wondered out loud:

"Where is she, where is this raven-haired wench?"

"Hell," Tom laughed softly. "She's a phantom, master, that's what."

*"Phantom,"* Bran repeated softly. He was thinking of the black cloak and silk vizard he had discovered in Jason's trunk. Perhaps, just perhaps he could put the disguise to some good use.

# Five

Buxom Margaret Edwards stood at the window in silence, her steely blue eyes studying the darkening winter sky. Of fair hair like her daughter Melanie, Margaret bore herself as if born of royal blood. It was her husband who had come down from an English stock of lords and ladies. But still Margaret possessed a certain delightful timidity which made her attractive to Jeremias at first meeting. Her temper could flare, though, and she was not without her womanly emotional outbursts.

She now awaited her husband's return. Jeremias was over at Middle Plantation,* the village halfway between the James and the York rivers, where he had gone to meet a visiting shipmaster. He could improve his purse in the springtime by selling to the merchant captain several head of cattle he had bred himself. Since there were many planters selling tobacco, the buyers could just about set their own prices. He was lucky to have a substantial income in a time when taxes were heavy and unfairly distributed. Virginia had been ripe for insurrection and it had begun with the Indian uprising in the summer past.

---

* Middle Plantation, now known as Williamsburg.

110

Margaret shuddered now. Her husband was one of the few planters who realized that peril was forever hovering near them. Tribes of Indians flowed back and forth through the forest like haunting mists, and no one planter could guess their intentions. Margaret thanked God that they did not live in the northern neck of Virginia. Since autumn, at least fifty plantations had been abandoned and over two-hundred men, women, and children slaughtered. All this continued to worsen because the governor refused to take a firm hand against the Indians for fear of losing his profits in the fur trade, Jeremias had decided.

"I refuse to believe," Margaret had told her husband just that morning, "that the good governor deliberately draws Indian profit on the blood of his own people."

When angered, Margaret could become quite tyrannical and unreasonable, so Jeremias had backed off, speaking no more of politics and Indians.

*On no account will I rest until my good husband is come home*, Margaret fretted as she twisted her handkerchief. She had stood now at the snow-scened window for over an hour, watching the gray sky change to a deepening winter purple and finally to midnight blue. Ivory had come in several minutes before to light candles behind her, she never realizing that he had come and gone out quietly. She stared reflectively at the flakes of snow winking up at her in the square of floodlight below the window.

Margaret recollected that her daughter's sudden and most scandalous marriage to Mr. Wellbeloved four years ago had thrown Jeremias into a long-term fit in which he had stormed and sputtered. He was the type who had desired his daughter to marry more to his own advantage. Where he had failed miserably with his own closest flesh and blood, Edwards now pondered a suitable match for his beautiful young niece.

So who was there to pair with Aurora Gregory?

In her mind's eye Margaret saw again the sight of Aurora returning from a long ride, as she had often done before the snow became too heavy and Jeremias would not allow her to ride out. Strands of that mysterious midnight-black hair, which the biting wind had torn loose from the hood of her cloak, had blown wildly about the creamy, heart-shaped face. Her cheeks and lips always had roses in them when she took her airing, which reminded Margaret that those same lips were fashioned in such a way that Ro always appeared to be throwing a kiss one's way.

But for the dissimilarity in hair coloring and height, Melanie and Aurora could have been cast in the same mold. In a bonnet or lacy modesty cap which concealed most of the hair, or in semidark, a person would find it most difficult to tell them apart. And Melanie was *but a half foot taller* of the two cousins.

*Who?* she again wondered. There was always Rodney Quick. Heavens, that clumsy lad would never do! Jeremias had not been introduced to the Ravenleigh scion yet. Still, Bran Ravenleigh's reputation with the tavern wenches had already caused much gossip; so had his long journeys through the western counties. It was even rumored that he

112

dressed—indeed!—half-naked like a wild Indian. To the quiet planters of the parish, the young man seemed old beyond his years. What age? Twenty and eight? Nine? No one knew for certain. The planters treated him with great politeness and a bit of awe, but gossiped behind his back as though he were a blood cousin to the devil. Law-abiding elder citizens spoke also of him as a dangerous and mysterious person to reckon with.

Forsooth! Bran Ravenleigh wedded to Jeremias Edwards's niece? A man possessed of a reputation for adventurous violence seemed to no hell-born brawler in the colony and the most gentle and exquisite girl—mated? Now, that would fan the flames in the scandalmongers' kitchens!

"Mistress Edwards?" Ivory came up behind Margaret. "Sorry to bother you at this time, but it's Mister Wellbeloved. He's done taken a worse turn."

Margaret fluttered her hanky all the way upstairs as she followed the black, middle-aged butler. Aurora was already there, sitting pale-faced at the bedside of the fever-tormented old man. The emaciated figure was rasping something to the young woman when Aunt Margaret quietly entered the bedchamber, which also seemed bathed in sweat.

". . . and I left my beloved England for the New World. Why, child?" He wheezed and Aurora drew a cool cloth over his sweat-curded forehead as he went on. "Most the land was owned by nobles. Hard for a poor man to save enough to buy some . . . land. I dasn't tell you what happened at sea—"

"You needn't explain yourself to me. Rest now,

113

Elvy. You can tell me later. . . ." Aurora's thin voice trailed as she pushed the straining man back gently to his damp pillow. She had given him strong infusions of Peruvian bark, but the frail body could not retain the medicine.

It was probably useless to plead with him to save his strength, Aurora thought sadly as he continued to ramble, for now that dark clasp of death held on to him tightly. She knew this as well as everyone else here, including Melanie who just stood at the foot of the bed, not daring to come closer in her fear of death, her lace handkerchief wept into with much noise; otherwise Melanie was very dry-eyed. Old Bertilde Lacey sniffed, but it was for real.

"I shall make bold for this once, Ro, and speak my piece," Elvy said with much pause between words. He went on in the same manner. "Even had I saved the money . . . in England there weren't much land for sale. I'd hoped to better meself by sailing to the New World, this deuced, savage co—colony. 'Tis so big and lonely and empty. Even the rivers are dark and silent. You should look upon the Thames, alive with boats 'n' barges 'n' noise." He waved a bony arm toward his young wife. "I done your cousin wrong, eh, Ro, my heart? Needed somewheres to die, I did not want to . . . ."

"Aye, Aelf-Wig, milord. But you must not speak such things just now. Save your dear breath. Here— drink this medicine I prepared for you."

"Save my breath—for what!" he croaked, waving the herbed brew that she proffered him aside. He crooked a finger at her then. "Lean closer and listen

114

well, little goddess of the dawn.''

"Aurora Gregory! I forbid you to play nursemaid any longer," Jeremias demanded from the doorway. "You'll soon be ill yourself. You have been in here all day, since I left early this morning. Begone from this room now, niece." He shed his coat, tossing it into a chair.

"My good husband," Margaret exclaimed, rushing to his side. "I worried that you be detained by the heavy snows." She then indicated the sickbed with a waft of her hand. "Couldst thou call a boy to fetch the good parson here by morning?" she beseeched in a rush.

"God's nightgown!" Elvy rasped from the depths of the bed. "I be hearing the angels—or devils—call me now. Don't need no parson. He be seeing naught but a corpse by morningtide," Elvy finished in one long whispery breath.

Jeremias lowered his voice. "The old man is delirious in his final hour."

"I beg of you my husband"—Margaret all but wept—"let Ro stay. In truth, there is so little time left."

Aurora had paled snow-white after the old man's words. She looked so frail and helpless in her total sorrow. Elvy clutched the small hand to his scarecrow breast, drawing her closer, but even at that she had to strain to hear him.

"I have seen it in a dream. Great love and riches await you—" he muttered in his supposed delirium, but his mind was not gone yet.

"Please lie back, sir," Jeremias begged as he

slipped to the foot of the bed. He too would go no closer.

"—prithee listen, Ro," Wellbeloved continued but in a failing voice. "Awaiting the dawn is the raven's kiss. Find the other half, Ro, and you shall find love . . . too. . . ." He sighed his last words on earth.

"What was that he said?" Melanie wondered out loud. "Oh, look! Papa, is—is he gone?" she said almost excitedly.

"Find the other half . . ." Aurora breathed and unwound death's last grip on her hurting hand. In her palm there lay a piece of yellowed parchment.

Unconsciously Aurora tucked the paper safely in the pocket of her rail. She bowed her head in her hands, praying for Aelf-Wig's departed soul, the dusk of her hair veiling her tear-stained cheeks. After a short time had elapsed, Aurora kissed the dead man on the brow and crossed the thin hands upon his breast. She then slipped quietly and reverently out of the room.

"Ye are tired, luv," Hetty said to Aurora as she sat near the cold hearth. "Come now, eat something and seek yer bed. Dinna grieve no more. My heart aches watching ye. I hae brought ye up a pasty, my wee bairn."

Hetty placed logs in the grate and put fire to them, making the chilled bedchamber soon bright again. There was a keen wind outside that battered at the house and windows, and the night sky was wild with ghostlike clouds. When Aurora at last was ready to sup, her lashes were still wet but a newborn peace had stolen over her.

"Ye have lost two loved ones, but ye've grown prouder and braver each time, ye hae. Ye've a heart of gold, my bairn, and a loving one. You gie your all to love. Dinna gie it to one who canna return yer precious love," Hetty ended with a little catch in her voice.

Crossing the room, Aurora pulled the bit of parchment from her pocket, and pressing it to her breast lovingly, she then placed it in a little box with the rest of her meager treasures. Tomorrow she would read it, but for now she wanted to commit to memory everything Elvy Wellbeloved had imparted to her on his deathbed. The last words from his lips had for now escaped her mind. But she had heard them. Someday, somewhere in time, they would flash across her memory.


Aurora had fallen into a deep winter sleep. . . .

The scene opened with blue-violet fog tumbling across the floor. She entered the dining chamber at the Inn, like the shadow of a somnambulist. The fireplace at the far end of the common room flickered with magenta tongues shedding blue light. Half-hidden in the murk and gloom was a darksome man seated with long legs stretched out before him at a table, a table that had no legs. He too was bathed in opaque shades of evening, with penumbra surrounding him.

Moving in slow-motion, Aurora looked down to her fuzzy toes, bare and blue; extending an arm that was also haloed by a penumbra. She felt like a spectator taking in her own lethargic movements.

Her dream-filled vision slipped by slow degrees across the room to where the serving wench had suddenly appeared. Stepping from the misted doorway that had momentarily frozen her movements, the wench walked as if she dragged behind her a heavy burden as the dark dashing rogue at the floating table beckoned her with the bejeweled fingers. Mesmerized by the blue flashes at the man's hands, Aurora tried to move toward him also, as if competing with the wench as to who would reach the rogue first.

The penumbra seemed to be weighing her barely moving limbs down, but the wench had put on speed, and would reach him first if Aurora did not move faster. As if peering through smoked glass, Aurora strained her eyes seeing the wench and the rogue already embracing. She had lost the race.

With silvered eyes the rogue looked up and noticed Aurora for the first time. She came to a standstill not far from the amorous pair. A slow smile spread his sensual lips while Aurora took in the bare, heaving breasts of the wench; the pendulous rounds of flesh were tinted blue, the nipples peaked like purple strawberries.

Shocked, whirling in slow-motion, Aurora tried to fly but her wings were clipped suddenly by a pair of strong, ruthless hands. Looking over her shoulder Aurora saw that as the rogue gripped her with one hand, the other was releasing the wench who was slipping away fast. Then the wench's body was gone into the blue fog, her fingertips stretched in supplication before they too were swallowed up. The dark rogue ignored the disappearance of the wench, his attention solely on Aurora now.

She was totally alone with him now; the Inn that had surrounded them before had vanished as had the fireplace and the floating chairs and the tables. The only spark of color other than that of blues was in his eyes. Gray—*silver*-gray—eyes that seemed to be looking into her soul. They stood—were *floating* on a piece of blue earth outside now. It was sultry. Alone with the swaggering rogue, a scoundrel. His words she could not understand but he was scoffing at her apprehension.

The rogue drew her closer, and closer still, his lean hardness melting into her, his blue kisses showering her face and neck, hard blue hands exploring and then lifting her filmy skirts, claiming her body as well as her spirit. A maelstrom of pleasurable excitement, of sensation, of color, and drama surrounded her. Her dream-world burst into a fantastic display of color, and plaintively wailing music entered her head, while the rogue whispered love words into her ear. He was melting hotly, further into her; they were becoming as one.

Then something began to dart deep within her. She woke with a start, trembling, terrified of discovering someone in the bed beside her. But she *was* alone. The room was dark and chilly with orange-gold embers dying behind the hearth stones. Her thighs still quivered and when she explored between them with tentative fingers she cried out of exquisite pain. Her own moisture frightened her, for this was not her time of month.

Aurora rolled to her side, knowing a curious mystery of longing stir deep inside of her, leaving her wondering as a twinkling of the dream, becoming elusive as a firefly flitting about at night, remained . . . wondering . . . curiously wondering . . .

## *Six*

At North Creek the verdant stems of flowers were already poking through the warming earth, and the essence of the forest wafted on a lazy breeze. Beyond the sprawling manor, the turquoise waters of the lagoon lat quiet for the ducks and the geese had escaped north. The screeching gulls were at sea, trailing and circling the pirate ships that roamed outside the capes.

Aurora Gregory, also in her golden season of life, stretched out on her front and belly in dewy freshness beneath the cedars west of the manor, flitted out of a daydream for a moment as she remembered her Aunt Margaret's advice.

"'Tis not proper to rest your cheek against your fist, Ro. This causes wrinkles and makes the structure of one's face misshapen."

Stuff and nonsense!

Again Aurora impudently leaned her rose-petal cheek on her fist and gazed through the hazy cedars toward the west. Perhaps it was not proper to lie here on the ground, either. She might become flat as a fluke from making a habit of this position. Nothing could make her as underripened again as she was at age twelve! She giggled.

"Keep the elbows back, chin forward and up. It is very fashionable, Aurora Gregory," Catherine Tobie had instructed her often during social manners lessons.

Aurora laughed again and flipped onto her back, her senses pierced suddenly by the sharp tang of the woods come to life in the spring. She thought of how nice and warm it would be to roam through the forest now after the spring thaw and breathe with pure joy the smells of newborn nature. As it was at one time, it was now again unsafe to roam the forest or even be near it because of the Indians. The governor, she heard often from Uncle Jeremias, seemed unable to unwilling to accord the colonists adequate protection from ever-widening Indian massacres and raids.

Aunt Margaret's spinsterish sister could remember when the first Indians came in 1644. Bertilde Lacey was almost as old as the colony itself. She could recall when Opechancanough was killed and when Governor Berkeley was the handsomest cavalier in all the world. Now Sir William had become tyrannical and inefficient, Bertilde sniffed disdainfully.

Aurora turned her thoughts to love, as young maids were wont to do in springtime. Quaint Bertie had never known love, the passionate kind between a man and a woman. No matter how old they might be, Mistress Tobie said, women who had been loved showed it in their faces. And she, Aurora Gregory? No man had loved her except Mr. Wellbeloved. Well, at least not in the way she hoped someday to be loved and cherished by a man. *Love.* What a charming four-letter word, she sighed dreamily.

Aye, the house had been filled with suitors, all

those that had visited her here at North Creek during the long winter. Now with spring there might come others, too. Wealthy girls with dowries were not plentiful, and pretty ones were rarer even. Melanie was both wealthy and pretty. Melanie would have many suitors once she packed away her widow's weeds, any day now.

Am I pretty? she wondered. Her suitors had thought so, said she had ceased to be a child four summers ago and had become an alluring young woman. She now noticed the difference every time she saw herself in Melanie's wavy mirror, or when drawing a pail of water from the shallow garden well.

As Uncle had often said, it was high time she chose a husband. Pressure thus, she would have to examine all men closer now. After all, she was just not the type to be dependent the rest of her life like Aunt Bertilde on the Edwardses. It was a woman's duty to wed and raise a family. All women married if they could. But who was there to turn her head?

The other day Melanie had again spoken of Bran Ravenleigh. Now that she would soon be free to wed again, Melanie was of a mind to give that young man a more careful inspection, she'd said.

"Always," Melanie had told Aurora, "he wears a murderous-looking weapon upon his hip or carries a fusil. He is known as a brawling favorite of tavern wenches—and a lover. Some believe he is as cold and pitiless as a mountain Scot, and that he sometimes runs with Chiskiak Indians. They are the friendly treaty Indians, but still barbarians to my thinking. Could you believe, Ro, he's rumored to sleep with squaws! Bran no doubt has bastards strewn about the countryside. He loves a woman like a lord one day, 'tis gossiped, then longs for another the next. Even a comely wife, should he ever take one, could not keep him long at her side.''

"Ugh!" Aurora had exclaimed. "I hope that I should never have to meet *him*. I would loathe such a man."

"Cousin, don't bet your milly petticoat on it! Even you, known to be as elusive as a bird in flight around men, would be tempted to meet this man who is as ruttish as a devil buck!"

"Melly!" Aurora had pursed her lips primly. "A meeting between two bodies—male and female— that is all love means to his kind! Not even hands held in tenderness for a time before—well, before— you know!" She had shrugged in perturbation.

"You'll see, Ro," Melanie had said to the frozen mask of bewildered beauty. "There's no resisting his virile charms. He's known, you see, to be able to hypnotize a woman right out of all her good intentions."

Aurora had looked her cousin directly in the eye. "You mean *you'll see*. I, for one, shall not be waiting in line to be trod upon by this . . . this ruttish buck, as you call him. With all the fuss you make over him, Melly, you might as well get it over with and go over and throw yourself bodily upon his doorstep! Now! Today!"

She had flounced out of the room, with Melanie's shrill laughter following her all the way to her room.

Scowling in remembrance, Aurora now turned her thoughts back to Elvy Wellbeloved and the bit of parchment he had left for her keeping. She had studied it, but the thing meant nothing to her, except that it was possibly part of a map of some sort. Without the other half . . . She shrugged, dismissing it for now.

Beyond the lane the blood-red sun was dropping below the forest as Aurora stood, brushed off her skirts, and drew her shawl more tightly about her shoulders. For some odd reason she shivered as she made her way back to the house. Her shiver was not due to the suddenly cooler air, either. Her steps lagged and she stopped beside the line of cedars. Dusk was falling, bringing a pinkish cast to the grounds. A strange sensation coursed through her limbs, and she felt oddly as if someone watched her from behind the bole of a cedar or peered from some bushes. Dry cones crunched not far from her and she started.

"Prithee, who is there?" she questioned the shadows where the twilight deepened with each passing minute. She was almost afraid to glance behind her, and her feet became as leaden weights, as though in a slow-motion nightmare.

Beneath her white cambric cap, Aurora's scalp prickled hotly, and nervously she tucked the loose strands back up inside. She chanced a look around. It was very still among the cedars, but there in the shadows lurking . . .

Muffling a strangled cry with the back of her hand, Aurora fled to the deepest of shade, opposite from the direction she had been going—and away from the man. But was it a man she had seen? Or . . . she was afraid to think of what it could be.

In terror Aurora had half-glimpsed "it" walking toward her very slowly, like a panther—nay, like some beast standing on hind legs, stalking its prey. A male beast. It seemed as if he could smell her out, even as she tried concealing herself behind the stand of trees. She whirled, and with heart drumming wildly, pressed her back to a trunk. If she tried a dash toward the house he would be certain to catch her, for she had already sensed the alert mobility in him, so all she could do was pray that he would somehow go away.

Oh, why didn't Hetty call for her and scold her for staying out in the night air? Why didn't someone come searching for her, she wondered frantically as she inched her back around the bole and braced herself to flee if danger warranted it.

She waited for the inevitable like a trapped and frightened hare, but still cried out when a long, muscled arm snaked around and held her stiffly against the tree. She risked a look downward and in the twilight could see his cloak swinging forward, nearly encompassing her lower half in its folds. She was just about to cry out her abject fear again when a strong, gloved hand clamped hard and ruthlessly over her mouth and nose. She had difficulty breathing and though she felt frozen with horror, she protested in a little whimper.

"You are more beautiful than you are valiant, but I've little faith in a frightened woman, so keep still and I'll relax my hold on you. But stay, I warn you," a silky smooth voice breathed in her ear.

With desperate courage, Aurora nodded her head, so hard in fact that she bumped it against the tree. He came around then, releasing his hold as he did so, but stayed just in front of her so that escape was an impossibility.

In the course of the last quarter of an hour the pink had melted and the moon and stars had come out, bathing the bemisted grounds in a dreamy, silverish cast. Her heart jumped in her breast. Black-cloaked, this dangerous-looking stranger wore a dark-plumed hat whose wide brim dipped low over his forehead, shadowing a face which was further made secret by a jet silk vizard over his eyes and nose. There was still sufficient light, however, for her to see the cold-steel eyes that contrasted with the curled, smiling lips. Smiling! What was he smiling at? Her cowardliness? Her sensory knowledge then told her that this was no ordinary man, this masked and bearded . . . ranger.

The hooting of an owl sounded, and with it she thought she heard the blowing of a horse close by— or had he merely come on silent tread through secret winding trails that pierced the darkest green of the forest beyond the lane?

"Melanie Wellbeloved," he said simply, in a deep purr, ignoring the frightened look that swiftly was altering to one of surprised confusion.

Strange sensations now tingled mercilessly along Aurora's spine and down into her trembling limbs.

"M—Melanie," she stammered, trying to clear the fog from her befuddled brain.

He tilted a half-bearded chin. "Aye, Melanie. That is your name, is it not?" he said, almost impatiently.

Aurora blinked her confusion. "How—?" she paused and her hand slid up almost of its own accord to the ruffled cap which concealed her dark-as-night hair. "Who are . . . you?" She breathed the question tentatively.

He snorted softly. "Fay . . . a ranger. That is all you must know, for now, but don't let it get around," he said smilingly, but the gesture ended swiftly.

"I—I am not accustomed to seeing masked men, or any wild rangers around here for that matter." She gulped loud, keeping her eyes averted from the glittering eyes.

"You are indeed more lovely than I remembered, Melanie Wellbeloved," Fay said half-mocking the last name, totally ignoring her bold comment.

"How do you come to know m—me? I have never seen you or your kind before," she said, thinking of Melanie as she drew upon her imagination. Her perfectly formed lips trembled then as she realized she was baiting him but without actually intending to.

His tall frame moved closer. "Your skin is as delicate as dawn and I wonder if your body is—feels as softly rounded as it looks."

"You must indeed be a wild ranger—one of those border men from the west," Aurora began, her voice shaking for want of courage, "because you certainly are as rude as one!" She had almost choked on her last words as it came to her, recalling the awful stories of those men and their murderous cruelties, where in those filthy frontier cabins they bedded women on the bare floors like rutting pigs.

As if he hadn't heard her, he said, "Melanie," almost like a caress; then, "I am not entirely savage, but then again I am not always the fashionable blade either. Is telling half the truth a lie, milady?" He suddenly reached out to clasp her trembling hand.

"Do not touch me, I—I do not even know you," her voice shook as Aurora peered up from beneath sweeping lashes at the half-masked, half-bearded face. Her head barely reached his shoulder. But then, she did cower just a little.

Disregarding her feeble warning, he drew her nearer to him. Her warmth and soft loveliness started Fay's heart to beating a rapid tattoo, the feel of her young body setting his flesh afire. Aurora stirred weakly, her bones defying her by turning into jelly and her chin coming up automatically. She saw this wild young man up close, he who was as motionless as a hunting cat ready to devour tender flesh. Consequently and for all her unwillingness, the tips of her young breasts grew hot and erect.

"You have a perfume—like a misted dawn," Fay murmured as he caught this young woman in his arms and held her fast.

Unresisting, Aurora's breath escaped her body and she seemed to be floating on air. What was happening to her? she wondered in a wild moment of abandonment. Like a tumult the light contact of his lips shivered through her as he kissed her eyes and the softness at the nape of her neck next; then pressing her back against a cedar, he bent to kiss at the quivering corner of her sweet lip. The nectar of their lips mingled for the first time, and they flowed together with a hot whirling surge of dizzying sensation. Aurora's whole body seemed to melt into his while his lips continued to crush hers in a possessive, passionate kiss.

Aurora was being swept along, blind and helpless

in experiencing the first pulsations of desire. He was giving her delight beyond anything she had ever imagined even in her wildest dreams. She was now engulfed in a torrent of thunderous sensation, and it was useless to struggle for some measure of dignity beneath this storm of freshly awakened passion that permeated her entire being.

The shadowed head lifted. "Melanie, I never knew—" Fay began, but his voice trailed off into a hoarse murmur.

The deep male strings of his voice woke Aurora. The man seemed more than half barbarian! He wore the costume of a masked border man and yet he had the cavalier touch. He was as quietly alert as a wild animal. It suddenly dawned that truly this man had no feelings whatsoever, but was a cold-blooded animal, a hunter out to devour what it might in his path.

What a fool she was!

"Why are you trembling? Cold?" he asked near a cheek that flamed to belie his question.

"I am not trembling!" she said as she tried thrusting him from her.

"Come now, Melanie, do not quell your desires. I have a pantherskin hidden in the trees over there. You will be warm, you'll see," he ended on a low, mysterious note.

"Nay!" Aurora cried, her voice fraught with great fear as she broke the tight circle of his arms and stepped back.

Viselike hands slid down her arms until gloved fingers forced an entwinement with hers. "I know you will, Melanie. Come—"

She heard it again. The low and gentle neighing of a horse. He had come by horseback; now she was certain. This presented another puzzle to her. Why would he hide his mount so far down the lane? He certainly must have something to hide.

For all she knew of this tall man in dark mask and cloak, he could be one of those sent to Virginia for their political crimes, from the dregs of London or Liverpool to the plantations. An escaped convict from a nearby plantation? "Go away. I know not who you are and never want to!" she protested in a small, lifting voice.

"Ah, but you do, sweeting. You will remember someday, soon," he argued softly.

"Nay, never. You are a wild, ruthless stranger!" she continued, knowing that his silvered eyes bore into her with that inscrutable look. At the same time she said this, Melanie's ethereal image loomed before her. What was she saying? Melanie was in the house, and she, Aurora, was taking the place of her cousin. And just what would this quietly dangerous man do if he discovered that her concealed hair was not gold but as black as midnight?

"You are still mourning your late husband?"

His eyes, Aurora saw, which the moonglow had found between the slits, were taking her in with a strange glimmer. Most surprising of all was the fact that Aurora was finding herself being mesmerized by them.

"Of course not," she finally answered truthfully, in Melanie's behalf. She hung on desperately to a fine thread of her will, fearing that she would again be swept away and her maidenhood spent here on the grass. For naught, with a mere stranger. She went on. "But I must not, can not do what you ask me—Fay," she said the odd-sounding name for the first time, and it thrilled and scared her all at the same moment.

The first impact of his wave of desire had been spent. "Why play the role of modest maiden now?" he asked slowly, coolly.

She stiffened. "You come here dressed like an outlaw knight of the road—why? Do you always attire yourself thus? I have a feeling 'tis not your wont," she said, avoiding his bold question.

"I have already told you—not always. Let's just say I must keep my identity a secret while traveling from Jamestown to the western forests, and let it go at that? There are more important matters pressing just now. Cast fear aside, Melanie, and come lay with me. I shall unmask over there in the dark, fine lady, if you like."

"I am not—Oh! Let me go now, please, I prithee," Aurora implored. She was feeling utterly strangled and confused. "You impose upon me with your greater strength!" she added.

Now quick to temper, Fay stepped back from her as if she had suddenly grown ugly, the cloak flapping forward like a raven wing. "Devil take it! Who are you to make me shiver like a white-livered milksop! Do you think you are fashioned of pure gold, or a saint, that I cannot touch you, much less bed you?"

"Alack! You are a vile, black-hearted beast!" Aurora retorted, this time intrepidly, surprised at her own recklessly daring venom. "Why came you here—for what?" she thrust again while her courage yet reigned.

"That question is passé by now, wouldn't you say?" he snarled into her face and widened violet eyes darted to either side of him.

Aurora stood trembling as though she had caught the ague when the tall bucket-topped boots were silent on the leafy turf as he pivoted sharply from her in a swirl of black cape. Then like an owl which speeds noiselessly through the night he disappeared.

She spun about as though he might have hidden behind her, but the young ranger had indeed gone. Aurora broke into a run then, as if all the demons in Hades followed, as fast as her feet could carry her up the lane toward the house. Wraith-like she ducked through some low-hanging branches in taking a shortcut and tripped on something. Wondering, she bent to pick it up.

It was the pantherskin—a cloak that smelled fragrantly of wood smoke. In his haste to be gone from her he had forgotten it.

*Seven*

Below the rough wood-beamed ceiling, the tables glittered with brass and silver goblets, and the odors of roasted meat and wine and tobacco mingled pungently. There was a center board in the tavern with benches at which the commonalty was entertained. For gentlemen there stood booths around the walls with individual tables and straw-cushioned chairs.

Bran chose a seat that faced the door and carved himself a rich slice from a juicy leg of mutton, which he surrounded with lentils and a portion of spring vegetables. His appetite had grown during his long ride here and he attacked the fare with much relish. Then, as the rich fare began to warm him, some of the agony of his heart and mind departed. The saturnine innkeeper came over to the black-clad man to learn the latest news from the upland country.

"Good Lawrence," Bran finally asked the question, "have you heard any news of the sea captain?"

"No, Bran, there's nothing new," Lawrence replied. A failure as a planter, he lost his mortgaged holdings years before to a protégé of the governor who challenged his title before the court controlled by Berkeley. Lawrence undauntedly opened a tavern

134

which soon qualified as the favorite stopping point of visitors to Jamestown. He fared better now than as a planter, while man and beast alike discovered Lawrence's to be a place of cheery warmth and plenitude.

Bran shot a glance over his shoulder as a mighty roar of laughter sounded from the center table where two dark-skinned sailors nodded over their mugs of ale.

Bran lowered his voice. "What have *you* heard of our friend Nathaniel?" he asked.

"In defiance of the governor," Lawrence began softly, "our good Nathaniel has taken field against the Indians. Sir William has proclaimed Bacon and his followers rebels and mutineers."

"Aye," Bran nodded. "I yield that I enthusiastically support Nathaniel Bacon. I think we've had enough of Berkeley's injustice, this governor who has a warped love for power and is fast becoming rich from trade in beaver skins."

Lawrence inclined his head. "You have ridden with our friend then?" he said in conspiring tone.

A dead silence followed his words, giving Lawrence his answer.

"By the way, my friend," Bran changed the subject, "where is that pleasure-seeking wench?"

"Rachel had a hard day at work, so she is already abed," Lawrence said, poking a thumb toward the narrow stairway. He grinned next. "She will be no less than willing to wake for you, though, I'm sure."

Bran poured himself a mug of the tavern's best sack, then strode across the room to climb the steep, narrow stairs to her bedchamber. The innkeeper pursed his thin lips, shook his head at the man's lusty appetite. He had detected an ardent need in Bran Ravenleigh this night for a bit of feminine comfort. Alas, he doubted that the man would find solace in Rachel's arms this night, for he knew full well what tormented Bran. It was an exquisite madness, an affliction that occupied the heart and mind; and lust could never satisfy it. This innkeeper wondered what the name of Bran's tormenter could be.

Upstairs, Bran paused listening at the door for signs that Rachel stirred inside and was awake. No light shone beneath the door. She could be asleep. But then again, Rachel was in the habit of sitting in a darkened room. In fact, Bran smiled here, she preferred always that the room be pitch when they made love.

Bran leaned with a hand splayed against the wall, his dark head down in indecision. He clenched the hand into a tight ball. A sound of wakefulness came from within. His somber mood brightened, then just as quickly dampened. Damn women all to hell. Why couldn't a man live like a hermit, and take matters into his own hands, and be better off for his being separated from women? Bran thought his cynical thoughts over, but came up with no conclusion.

Why could he not make up his mind now? What was holding him back? The answer was more than just women. It was singular—*woman*.

"Ah, Hell"—he ran long fingers through rumpled hair—"I am just not up to this tonight." And especially not *this* night!

With a ragged man-sized sigh, Bran straightened from the wall, paused again, shrugged, then made to move toward the stairs when the door opened a crack.

"Bran Ravenleigh," Rachel said breathlessly. She moved toward him, looking him over suspiciously and taking in his surprised expression.

"Leaving already, luv, without seeing me?" she said.

The room was indeed a dark cavern behind her. Why did she always dwell in the dark, he wondered momentarily, as if she was afraid of the light.

The intimacy of Rachel's lovenest beckoned Bran with remembrance of many past nights filled with passion's fire. Lust tugged him forward while a love so sweet and fresh it made him ache inside held him back.

In tune with his need of a woman, Rachel moved against him and brought his hand up to the delicious curve of her breast. While her own fingers slid downward to play in a slow and sensual arousal. He stirred then, and as usual, Rachel sucked in an amazed breath at his size. A frown drew her full, dark eyebrows together.

Suddenly, inexplicably, his hardness started fading. A strained smile flitted across his handsomely darkened features. Their eyes met in the neardarkness of frail light escaping up the stairs from the common room below. Rachel looked aside.

"I would not do you justice this night, Rachel," he said. Then reached out in a gesture of apology. "But I need you, at least I—"

"Piffle." She stepped back out of his reach.

"What?" he said.

"You are right, lover. I noticed your problem at once. Not tonight, hmm? Another time, Bran?" She

137

nudged the door open to go back inside.

Bran nodded, and then deciding the best course was to remain silent, walked away. He would wonder later who it was that actually made the choice. But for the remainder of the evening, he was going to be immersed in the tavern's best inebriant. To forget or try reliving the day—Bran was not sure which just yet.

A half-breed Indian with a long horselike face caught up with Bran the next afternoon as he left Jamestown and struck for the woods. The Indian was garbed like a frontiersman, in canvas breeks and a white linen shirt which contrasted with his copper-toned skin. He sported mantle and wore moccasins, and his hair was as black as Bran's.

"You are Bran Ravenleigh, grandson of Sir Eric, and nephew of the man numbered with the dead?" he inquired, trotting his small spotted pony up a short incline.

"That's right," Bran said, puzzled and wary at the same time. "By what name are you known?" He then patted the big head of his startled horse to calm him down.

"There has been much talk," the Indian went on, as if he hadn't heard the question. "I have heard from many of my men who have worked in the past for an evil sea merchant. When this man drinks like a pig the firewater, he boasts of an evil deed from the past. *I* know, too, there was no duel with this man and your uncle, as many have said." The Indian slowly watched the man stiffen in the saddle; he had expected this.

"You mean Strang? Captain Strang?" asked Bran

138

with a slanting regard to his informer. His chopped hair swinging as he rocked in his seat, the Indian merely nodded. Then, slowly, he spoke.

"Aye, he is the one. He is the devil you seek. He drove his sword through your uncle's heat—a heart that was always good to me when I worked in his fields. Another held Master Ravenleigh down and the coward pig did his evil deed. The other who I know not by name is a slinking white-haired man who finds lodging and feeds himself on the charity of others."

"Where is this other now?" Bran rapped out between taut white lips.

"I have not laid eyes on him for many moons now."

"What then," Bran began silkily, "does this man look like?"

"I know him only as 'white eyes,'" the Indian answered, wheeling his pony back in the direction in which he had come.

"Wait!" Bran called to the proudly mounted figure moving off the path slowly toward the forest's entrance.

"I know no more," came the deep reply as he kept his pony's head straight ahead.

Later and on questioning Harris, Bran discovered that Rufo Savage was the name of the half-breed who, along with his forty some workers, was a traveling overseer. They went where field work could be obtained, and in the past, during the planting season, Rufo had labored in the tobacco fields of Raven Keep.

"What does 'white eyes' mean?" Bran continued to

question Harris.

"Indians call one who has pale blue eyes by this name," Harris explained.

So, he was fair-haired and had blue eyes. Bran shrugged. There were many men with this coloring in the colony. But how many were human parasites as this Savage had said "white eyes" was? Damn, that would take some looking into and tomorrow would be the first of many investigations.

The following day Bran sought audience with the governor. After waiting for a half an hour, this time at Berkeley's plantation Green Spring, one of the largest in the colony boasting a most stately brick manor, Bran and Tom were received with the warmest cordiality. But thereafter, the governor made it a point to ignore the buckskin-clad bondsman.

"You have been a stranger, Bran Ravenleigh. I have been anxious to discuss a matter of importance with you. First things first. How goes it at Raven Keep?"

"All's well, even Sir Eric, your Excellency," Bran returned as graciously as he could under the circumstances.

There was a new weariness in the governor's usually sparkling blue eyes, as he went on. "I have, as you may already know, ousted the young Nathaniel Bacon from my council, Ravenleigh. Bacon has taken serious affairs into his own hands with his three-hundred volunteers and attacked the Susquehannocks. Bacon's expedition is a dishonor to the English nation!" Berkeley ended hotly, unembarrassed by his sudden outburst of rage.

Bran allowed his gaze to roam out the leaded casement window, envisioning Bacon that day he had crossed the James to meet the soldiers at Jordan's Point. As soon as they had seen Bacon coming, a shout went up from the volunteer soldiers. "A Bacon! A Bacon! A Bacon!" He agreed to lead them, and Bran had been much moved to hear Nathaniel's friends—not the scum of the country, as some believed, but men belonging to the elite crowd—shout that they would go along with Bacon to take revenge upon the Indians and ever be true to him. Along with the volunteers, Bran had signed the round robin, in which they wrote their names in a circle, so that the group leaders might not be found out.

"I had it in mind to ask you, Ravenleigh, if you would do us the honor of joining our council," the seventy-year-old governor said.

"I am greatly flattered, your Excellency, but I—" Bran paused, catching the sudden light in Tom's almond eyes. It said: Here is your chance to further aid Bacon in his cause. You are already a rebel, why not a spy!

"Then I may count on it," Berkeley said, taking Ravenleigh's pause as agreement.

There went his plans to swear out a warrant against Strang for the murder of his uncle, Bran thought with some annoyance. Perhaps now, though, he could kill two birds with one stone. He was well aware that Strang and others of his kind were shown favoritism and had the governor's protection. And there was no one in the colony higher up on the ladder to investigate the governor himself. No one but King Charles, who was in faraway England.

"Well, what was on your mind, Ravenleigh?" Sir William wanted to know why he was afforded this special visit.

"As you said yourself, Governor, I have been a stranger to you," Bran began, quirking a corner of his large, sensuous lower lip in a half-smile. "But no more, sir."

"Ah, good. I shall see you then in June at the opening session of the House when we shall meet with the council members to resolve this Indian problem."

"Good day to you then, your Excellency," Bran said pleasantly with an incline of his dark head, for he thought it was time he and Tom absented themselves.

Sir William watched Bran Ravenleigh and his manservant exit the room. After he was certain that the butler had let them out, he turned toward the door to an adjoining room.

"Captain Strang, you may come in now, please."

The seaman was dressed immaculately in a dark blue coat brocaded with silver threads and a white linen shirt that was spotless; he stepped into the room, his eyes fathomless black pools and the planes of his long face stretching tautly.

"Dangerous fellow to cross, that Ravenleigh," Javier Strang said cryptically. "I hear he has been looking for me for a long time. I have a strong feeling he wanted to bring charges against me today. For the murder of one Jason Ravenleigh, it is known."

"Why . . . how can this rumor be true? Jason

Ravenleigh was a friend of yours—when he was alive," Berkeley said to this favorite henchman of his.

With an effort hat mottled his rakish complexion, Javier managed to control himself as he said: "Too bad, but we had a little misunderstanding before he died." He sighed affectedly. "Too bad."

"If this is true, what you say, then I am afraid we shall have a bit of trouble from him. There shall be no charges brought against you, my good captain. You must stay away from Jamestown for a while. So—ah—is it not about time you take another voyage?"

"*Si*, but I am no coward." His laugh was evil. "*Gracias*, I will go now, *Excelencia*."


"You have met a woman," Tom began. "A special woman, I think. To every man some woman is a witch in the mist. She is yours, perhaps?"

"She is almost that, Tom—almost."

"Is it Tadewi?" Tom queried as to the small-bodied Indian girl that Patamon of the friendly Chiskiacks had presented one summer to Bran as simply as a new bow with arrows or a beaded belt.

Bran stretched iron-sinewed arms, recalling that Tadewi had been a comely barbarian, a lusty little beast of the woods—nothing else. But his memories of Tadewi would be treasured. Since then he had held another's lily-white hands, had breathed the sweet fragrance of her warm young body. Those rosebud lips that he had kissed beckoned his mind even now; and his loins ached to know her.

"Nay, Tom, it is not Tadewi nor any tavern wench," Bran supplied as he spurred Nimrod on. He

143

looked down from the tall horse. "Don't pull such a serious face, Tom Bone, it is not all that bad. After all, she is just another witch. All girls become the same." But his smile did not reach his ash-colored eyes, now deep with some exciting emotion.

With the white wolfhound curled at his feet, Sir Eric was still awake in the Hall when Bran arrived at Raven Keep. His grandfather was seated in the dark by the southwest window, smoking a pigtail twist* and staring out at the starlit river which appeared like a night-mirror against the forest cast in shadows deep.

"So, night cock," cried Eric Ravenleigh, tossing back his aristocratic head, "you've been making bold with the wenches?"

Bran merely lifted a dark eyebrow as he proceeded to the board to pour himself out a cup of smallbeer.

"Beelzebub's nightgown! Clad in buckskins again, hah? You are a veritable savage," Eric sniffed disdainfully.

Bran eased his tall frame onto the scarlet, up-holstered bench and Duchess, the bitch, padded across to him to be petted then lay at his feet. Sir Eric didn't wonder. Females, be they human or beast, always fawned at his grandson's feet.

"I'd some business the latter part of this day that best was accomplished in my western garb," Bran explained to begin, "but at daybreak I shall don my cravat and silken hose again."

"You have become a rebel and followed Bacon into the wilderness, eh? Meant to teach the Indians a

---

*pigtail twist—tobacco soaked in rum.

bloody lesson, you and his other followers, didn't you all," he stated rather than asked this last.

"You yourself knew from the first that I did not favor Berkeley"—Bran snorted softly—"him and his separate laws for the favored rich and the frowned-upon poor. There he sits at Green Spring, while three-hundred whites have been murdered—men, women and children shattered to death over the winter, and now he waits to learn the will of the assembly. Devil take!" He would not add that he would sit on the council to Sir Eric, and have him add "spy" to "rebel." Eric was not proud of what he was doing already, so why add more fuel to the old man's wrath.

Still, Eric looked down his long, broad nose at his grandson, wearing that imperious look of his. "You are bursting with hatred for the redskins! So, how many of those savages have you alone murdered, then?" he all but snarled.

"I have slaughtered no children, sir," Bran allowed, but tersely. "The women and children were loaded into canoes after the battle and were free to go."

Cuffee entered just then bearing a light repast for his young master. When he had padded back to the kitchen, Eric took up again.

"Not only have you become a ruthless murderer, my son, but you are also a hypocrite, I'm sad to see. Well . . . do you not favor the savages over the governor and his council?" the older man then inquired painfully.

"Ah, but there is a marked difference between the Susquehannocks and the Chiskiacks. Where the first

145

are hostile killers, the latter are friendly, peace-loving. They are a separate nation of proud people. I am not a hypocrite, my grandfather, I only speak with candor."

"This land is rotten with rebellion!" Sir Eric snorted low as he leaned forward onto the window sill, this ending the conversation.

With brooding aspect, Bran finished his meal and his drink in silence and then respectfully left Eric. He climbed the stairs to seek his sorely needed rest.

Alone, the older man squared his chin, tucking his lower lip sourly. This deuced wilderness! Would they not have left Whitehall, his grandson could have not grown apart, and forgotten his motherland and the king. He blamed himself. He should not have urged Bran to come here to live, to avenge Jason's death. Damn Virginia! Jason had always been a fool!

Sir Eric agonized that indeed Jason reached from his mossy grave with his wild rogue's soul to blacken his own flesh and blood.

## *Eight*

Aurora had seen him from the leaded casement window upstairs. She did not know this tall man who had arrived on an equally tall horse just minutes before. He had on the finest wig, falling in rich, coal-black clusters down his straight back and over his wide shoulders. His linen shirt peeping out was Holland, his bluish-gray vest was fit for a duke, and his riding coat, befrogged with silver brocade, fitted his rakish form as though he had been born with it on his shoulders. She had seen the Negroes all come to stand at the edge of the orchard to gawk at this man whose elegance was greater than anyone else who was here today at the party.

For some odd reason, in that dead-still moment when the wickedly handsome man glanced up from beneath his wide cavalier hat, she had been more frightened than she had ever been in her life. Not even when she had encountered the masked man in the lane had she been this removed to horror— ironically a horror that had evolved into a great longing to see him again.

When Bran had dismounted, a horseboy had run up to take his mount out back to the stable. Striding the short distance from lane to house, glancing up,

147

he thought he had detected a presence at one of the upper windows. A blurred white face had indeed peeped out, then the drapery had fallen back into place.

Lifting her skirts high, Aurora sped out of her room and into the hall. Voices floated up to her now as she stood frozen at the top of the stairs, unseen, her dropped skirts swirling about her ankles.

"Bran? Bran Ravenleigh?" a breathlessly excited voice called from the doorway as he neared. "Why, yes it is you! What took you so long to visit North Creek?" A pretty pout followed.

Melanie, gowned in a fashionably looped skirt and long-waisted bodice adorned with extravagant bows, stood there with arms stretched out before her, hands invitingly reaching out to Bran's. She pouted again when he grasped her hands in greeting for but a moment, then dropped them back to hang languidly at his sides. He poked his head inside to the hall which was lighted by a myriad of candles, but he could see no further beyond the glare of them.

"A party? And I was not invited? Tsk, tsk," Bran said playfully as he entered and left his feathered hat in the hands of the Negro servant. He turned to Melanie. "I trust your parents are well?" He cocked a thick eyebrow down at her.

"Indeed," Melanie began, "but you are too late, Bran Ravenleigh."

"Late? Really? It looks to me as if the party had just begun to liven up," he returned, hearing the tinkling of glasses and the gay murmur of a sizeable crowd inside.

Melanie loosed a coquettish laugh. "I mean you

are too late to meet Mama and Papa. Jeremias has taken my mother to the Carolinas. Mama's youngest sister is on her deathbed. They left a fortnight ago," she said chattily.

"So, you stayed behind to hold up the fort?" a muscle twitched in Bran's cheek.

"Aye, and take care of Bertilde Lacey, my other aunt. She's much too old for traveling."

Bran studied the little face spotted with impudent black patches and Melanie blushed very prettily. Her lashes fluttered downward in a sweeping gesture that allowed him a striking view of her arched brows.

"Hmmm, so, while the cats are away the mice will play?" he said but there lurked a wicked gleam in the depths of his deep gray eyes.

Behind the bannister upstairs, Aurora could feel even from this distance the sheer animal magnetism of the man. Just like . . . She would not go back down and rejoin the guests! She could not. Even if she decided to, her trembling legs would have crumpled beneath her like a newborn fawn. It was only by conscious effort that she now kept her knees from shaking as she slipped back into her room. She sat down gingerly on the edge of her bed.

What a silly coward I am! Aurora chided herself. Bran Ravenleigh. She had finally seen the man, but she doubted whether she would ever desire meeting him face to face. What was it about him that frightened her so? No power in Heaven or on earth could make her go down now; she strengthened her resolve.

It was merely that—he frightened her. The whole countenance of him. The brooding brows. The large,

149

sensual lower lip. Even the tight breeches that displayed so much manhood. She blushed crimson now for having been so observant. It was indecent!

"I shall seek always to remain hidden from him who frightens me so!" She lowered her dark head then, and prayed for a moment. "Elvy, Elvy, why am I such a coward? Is this the Raven you warned me about in such a way as to make my heart burn with such fear? Aye, but he shall never, ever kiss me. . . ."

"It has already been done," Bran murmured to himself downstairs, cryptically, himself confused, and Melanie lifted a surprised brow at her newly arrived guest.

"Already have what, Bran?" she wondered, having half-heard him.

Bran frowned and then shook his buzzing head. "Are you all right?" Melanie awaited his answer, but then let it drop as with a curling smile she leaned toward him touching his tanned wrist which contrasted beneath the lace of her ivory fan.

Bran continued to brood, but Melanie missed it in her absorption to impress upon him what a delightfully charming creature she was. She even went so far as to ape Catherine Tobie's exclamations, knowing that Bran Ravenleigh was an Englishman.

"La! I hope you are not so wild as people here have gossiped that you are," she said intimately low. Then she straightened as cold signs of disapproval came their way. Her voice lifted. "But you should not stay away, Bran Ravenleigh. I have been dying to see you. You are one of the few people who make me forget the sorrows of widowhood when I am with you." She feigned the look of a woman who was lonely and

150

mourned her husband's passing.

At that Bran quirked his mouth in a lazy grin and paused before going into the room where dancing was going on. He caught his image in the great mirror and it startled him for an instant, not because of his elegant attire but after what she had said. He certainly did not look the mystery man now. Had she indeed seen through his fine clothes?

With her back to him now, Bran studied the delicate nape of Melanie's neck, pondering: Why do I desire you? Why was his head not dizzied as it had been in the dusky cedar lane? She is radiant, then why am I not thoroughly shaken again? There was now neither no aching sensation in the center of his tall body but he would wait for those exciting pangs in his loins to afflict him as before. Damn . . . why not? He was a man much enamored, foolish though the thought of being smitten by a woman had seemed to him in the past.

Here punch was plentiful and there was much feasting, drinking, and card playing. Gossip flowed about the Indian crisis, but more than a few left their circles to step forward and greet the newcomer as he entered the glittering room. A pretty young woman by the name of Belinda Culpeper was introduced to him next.

"You are quite notor—" Belinda broke off. "Uhhmm, I mean famous, Bran Ravenleigh." She had been about to say "notorious", and Bran hardly paid any attention to her, lest he become obnoxious.

Bran inclined his dark head to Belinda and then moved away. An elderly woman whose name Bran had already dismissed from his mind as unim-

151

portant, examined him thoroughly before she detached herself from a group of gossiping ladies, coming over to tap him on the arm with her painted fan. Bran remembered hearing her mention in a high nasal voice that she had just returned from a long stay in England.

"I have heard many tales of you, Bran Ravenleigh," she said in an imperious tone that belied her politeness.

Bran stared rudely into the shrewd eyes, then purposely fastened his regard to the straight nose which left much to be desired.

"You hag—" he coughed—"I mean . . . you *have* been away in England far too long to have heard so much of me, madame. Ah, excuse me, but I hadn't caught your name in the introduction?" he said, obviously cutting.

Melanie rustled her skirts nervously as she tried tugging Bran away from the rapidly growing circle of guests burning with curiosity. He finally relented, after having given the matronly old hag a stiff but formal bow. Her lackluster hair had suddenly seemed a shade grayer, and the wired curls which framed her pudgy, powered face, too, seemed to sag.

"Why, the very cheek of that young man!" she blustered as he moved away, his nod to her laconic.

After swallowing the lukewarm wine and giving a shudder, Bran set the empty goblet on a table. With Melanie on his arm he ushered her at last into the privacy of the sitting room and shut the door firmly on the scandalized faces.

Outside in the dusk, birds of spring caroled from trees and thickets as Bran pulled Melanie into his arms the moment the door was closed. If she was mildly surprised at his immediate passion, she was doubly so when he lifted her with steely arms and bore her most improperly to the sofa among the velvet and silk pillows strewn there. .

"Bran Ravenleigh!" Melanie said huffily, rising to straighten her gown's long bodice and flowing skirt. "You are like a rutting Highland bull! I am not like your tavern wenches you take liberties with, you know. Do you measure me with such women?" She did smile, though.

Bran said nothing, but put one hand on her knee as he studied her intently, his gaze sweeping round her face in a measuring gaze. A frown grew between his eyebrows, then relaxed and softened his eyes to a pearly gray. Somehow her gown had slipped again from both shoulders, leaving the pale, round upper swells bare. He bent over them to rain hot kisses lower and lower.

"Bran—I say!" Melanie gasped for air as he grew bolder. "So, do you want to take me to wife?" She lifted a naked shoulder flirtaciously against his elegantly cut coat.

"Do you know, your eyes are almost the color of heather?" Bran began in a velvety soft tone. "Almost—but not quite."

"You are avoiding my question," she said poutingly.

"Perhaps," he finally allowed.

"There have been others who would gladly wed me," she began with bated breath, "but I already had a husband, and none of them were suitable, anyway. Now I am free and want a husband." Her look was

153

appraising, liking what she saw in this thrilling young man with the sometimes stern visage and at times brooding. Too, he was very wealthy, she knew.

"I suppose I should be flattered, Melanie Well-beloved," he said with an air of hauteur as he pushed her gown back into place.

His breath came quickly for a moment, blowing hot and cold. What was he getting himself into, he who always preferred bachelorhood? Hell! He would have to wed someone someday; mostly because he wanted sons. Too, he wanted no simple, immature maiden for a wife, rather a woman like Melanie who had had experience in the bed. He had never known a virgin, neither had he even any desire in the past to deflower one. But something here bothered him. He should be hot, not cold as he was now.

"Wait, Sir Ravenleigh," Melanie was saying, "I am not finished. Don't believe that you are a last forlorn hope. There are other men I could wed in an instant's notice, some of them handsomer than you—and richer." Here she lowered her eyes at once.

Bran appeared bored all of a sudden with the conversation. "Then, my dear Melanie, why not choose one of them?" He made to rise but she held him there.

"Because . . ." she faltered beneath the burning eyes suddenly perusing her. "Mmmn, I have heard that you leave behind you a trail of brokenhearted girls—"

He broke in. *"That* excites you?"

"Let me finish, milord. Also, you are courtly, shrewd, and rich, but ironically you do have high standards, the gossips say. All that and a man who

154

can turn into a gentle and tender lover"—her big violet eyes blinked affectedly—"What more could a girl hope for?"

"And you, Melanie, how do you measure up to my—uhmm—high standards?"

"Well, I am beautiful, witty, charming, and am ravishing, so I've been told. Above all, I am not some fragile-petaled blossom but a strong and very determined woman. I know what I want, you see. All this makes me an incomparable companion, and also, to a man such as yourself—a salve to your vanity," she ended, laughing provocatively as Bran stared boldly at her quivering bosom.

Momentarily, disturbingly, a flashback of a certain moon-drenched night of early hour came to Bran. He shook himself free of the vision and the sensations.

"Have you ever been in love—Melanie?" His piercing question could be seen to have startled her.

She laughed a bit nervously. "Love? I don't know what you mean, Bran. That I be swept away on a milk-white charger by a tall handsome knight? Hah, me? A winsome bride?"

"Is that all love means to you, merely a fairy tale romance? Nay, Melanie, you have never been in love, but you did speak of a gentle and tender lover. Does the thought excite you?"

She shrugged the question off, saying, "Maybe you could persuade me to fall in love?" She fluttered her lashes. "Love as you see it, sir?"

"My heart has never been occupied with that childish sentiment," Bran said, his voice thick with sudden irritation.

Melanie mistook this as a means for evening the

score, for she had caused his male pride to suffer. With a man like Bran Ravenleigh, she would have to tread cautiously, bide her time until he did indeed fall for her. She had been too lavish with her favors before, and this time she didn't want to lose by giving in so willingly. Her swift brain worked fast planning now.

He will soon smile at me, Melanie tried to comfort herself as she pressed his brown hand.

Bran did not return the pressure, and declined her offer of a goblet of wine. "Had you no feeling for your late husband?" he suddenly asked, his eyes probing relentlessly.

Melanie's face was at once pale, as though some inner wave of terror was afflicting her. "You trouble me, Bran Ravenleigh. Why all these questions?"

"Answer me!"

My, he is jealous, Melanie thought deliciously, and licked her lips like a cat. She bent her golden head demurely.

"Mr. Wellbeloved was lonely, Bran, and I thought if I could give him a few more happy days on this earth, well then, I would have done a noble deed surely. It wouldn't have been very proper if I had seen him without being properly wed. So I brought him to North Creek, where he spent his last days—as my husband. Sure Papa was angry, but he soon got over it when he saw how happy I made the old man." She paused here for a moment. "I never failed to tell him what a really wonderful, intelligent person he was. I guess . . . aye, I did love him a little." She sighed sadly next. "But he never once made love to me, you see. There hasn't been anyone, Bran, can you believe that?'' She ended, hoping she had not made too grave a statement, one that would affect her future as the mistress of Raven Keep.

With her violet, vivacious eyes, her glowing pink skin, and her golden hair, Melanie seemed too angelically fair to be human, Bran thought to himself as he perused her. Again it came to him: Why . . . why do I want you? Where was that flame burning within?

But aloud he said: "I do have high standards, believe it or not, and you would indeed have to measure up. What I mean is—you would need to tread very, very carefully where other men are concerned. Added to all those wild descriptions of me—I am by nature a very jealous man." He stood abruptly then, his leg grazing hers thrillingly through her skirts. "Until then we shall meet as before," he said without thinking, then wondering if she had caught the meaning. Anyway, he would soon find out if her affections were genuine, and she certainly would discover his dual identity. Soon.

He left her by striding out unceremoniously. Behind the closing door, Melanie sat openmouthed for a time, feeling a little confused with his parting words. Suddenly she was racing out the door, lifting her skirt that was fashioned recklessly high and, with a flutter of scarlet petticoat, went squealing up the stairs to brag to her moody cousin. Gaping after Melanie, several of her guests went to find their wraps in a huff.

Upstairs Melanie burst into Aurora's room.

"Ro, guess what! I am going to be a bride again!"

"That is wonderful, Melly," Aurora said absently.

"Well! What has happened to the once gay little Ro, who used to forget men quicker than one can say Jack Sprat?" Melanie taunted as she swept airily across the floor. "My, my, have the tables been turned on you? You look a little lovesick, dear cousin."

Aurora ignored the jab as she combed out the long "heartbreaker" curls which Hetty had tied with a gay bow in a fashionable cluster over each ear. She placed her comb on the table now and twisted the dark hair into a neat but somewhat simple knot at the nape of her neck. Before Melanie had come upstairs, Aurora had changed back into her old dress, a modest gown with a high-collared bodice and made of violet-blue homespun. She always donned it when she was feeling blue. But her favorite gown of purple patterned satin was back in the thinning wardrobe. After Margaret had left for the Carolinas, Melanie had *borrowed* back one each day of the gowns her mother had altered to fit the slightly slimmer girl. Aurora's wardrobe now had become quite sparse.

"Belinda Culpeper was looking for you, why did you disappear all of a sudden and not return?" Not waiting for an answer, Melanie went on. "Bran Ravenleigh has asked me to become his wife! Isn't that just too wonderful?"

"He is awful! He frightens me!" Aurora blurted without thinking.

"You have met him?" Melanie said with suspicion. "I did not see you once downstairs after he had arrived."

"I happened to be looking out at the weather when he rode up the lane mounted on that beautiful horse."

Melanie shrieked. "Afraid of a man you have never even met? I do believe you've had a bad shock of some kind lately. Have you grown senile, Ro? Ha! You spent too much time with that old man I'm ashamed to say was my husband."

"How can you say such things, Melanie! Sometimes I daresay you seem a wicked woman," Aurora said softly as she bent over the pantherskin cloak in her lap. She blew into the sleek fur, the sharp tang of woods and smoke rising nostalgically to her nostrils.

Melanie sauntered closer. "Whatever is that thing in your lap, may I ask," she wondered, sniffing the wood smoke. "Whew! What is it?" she repeated, pinching her pert nose.

"You believe I love a phantom, but I know better." She bent her head wistfully.

"In love? Now I know you are senile, and you just a young innocent. Poor Ro, I thought you were jesting when the other day you asked me to keep an eye out for every stranger who comes by. Don't tell me you have met one of those murdering bordermen!"

Aurora lifted her chin proudly. "He is not what you say!"

"And he gave you that thing?" Melanie went on as if she hadn't been interrupted. "Oh, what will our friends say when they learn you are enamored of a ferocious bounder!" She bent her bright head closer. "Tell me, has he bedded you in the forest?"

Aurora stood so abruptly that the pantherskin slipped to the floor. She was herself like a wild thing as she stood her ground, her eyes flashing into narrowed slits of purple. Melanie sniffed disdainfully, then gave the pantherskin a little kick with her toe before she whirled and went unswerving to the door.

"At least, Ro, I shall marry into wealth. La!" Childlike, Melanie stuck out her pink tongue before she shut the door firmly in her cousin's rigid face.

Aurora closed her eyes for a moment as her shoulders slumped in weariness. She was indeed tired of Melanie and her constant cutting words and antagonistic attitude. It would be ever so nice if they could live together in harmony. What had she ever done to make Melanie display such ill will toward herself? She could not understand it. She had always tried to act kindly and good-humored with Melanie, even have some good times, but Melanie, in the usual run of things, managed to make her utterly miserable.

Aurora bent down to pick up the pantherskin, cuddling it against her cheek until its wild fragrance penetrated, as that first blushing night, into her heart and body. Her thoughts of Fay, the man who seemed part phantom and part flesh and blood, came more often to her now. He might be a menacing figure, a cloaked evil, and he was, perhaps, a borderman, but he had bewitched her with his kisses and had given her daydreams that were things of fire and fury, making her body burn and ache for him. His voice was as deep as the baritone echoes of a sultry, distant thunderstorm. She was becoming acutely aware of her womanhood, and she was suddenly afraid of her brand-new feelings, and yes, a little ashamed, but still she did yearn desperately for another glimpse of him. Another touch of him.

Really, would he come again? Should she continue

with her masquerade—falsely claiming to be Melanie—or tell Fay who she truly was? She just did not know what to do anymore. She was miserable in this, her dawn of love.

That night Aurora fell into an exhausted slumber, dreaming of a masked man stepping boldly from out of a dark canvas and encompassing her trembling form in a tenderly loving embrace. When she half awakened floating in her twilight sleep, Aurora found herself totally alone, wrapped in her covers. She wept then, trying fiercely to summon him back. But when she slept soundly again, she walked the cedar lane alone, crying out to her love. He never came.

# Nine

It was a fortnight later as again Aurora strolled the cedar lane. Night birds called from the dusky forest, their cries coming with the wisps of mist that stole from the river. The chickens in the coop, having been a-flutter and cackling excitedly for some reason, settled down as before. She was impervious to the ruckus they had set up, as she was heedless in her melancholy state that it had become increasingly dangerous to venture outdoors alone.

The tears stung her lids, but she fought them down. She would not let Melanie see her face all blotched again so that she could gloat that she, Melanie, was happy in her love life while Aurora was reduced to lonely tears.

There was hope no more. She would never see the dark ranger again. Even if she did, she agonized, he thought her Melanie, but, oh, she would be fain to change places with Melanie just to be with Fay. She laughed a tiny, ironic laugh that dried her eyes. It was as if she were possessed and left haunted by the mystery man. She, Aurora Gregory, was betrayed by a maiden's dreams into believing that Fay could have cared for her a little. *Her,* not Melanie.

"I knew you wanted me to meet you here this night."

A deep thrilling voice came from behind Aurora and she whirled about, uttering frightened little gasps. But she had felt when first he spoke, the strong magnetic force drawing her. Her blushing could hardly be recognized for what it was in the dusky light as she cast a brief look up at him, then lowered her chin shyly.

Fay moved one step closer, no more. She stayed. The music of the night swelled as if on a silver note, and the pale moon seemed to rush to its zenith in the purple sky when he gave utterance again.

"There is a certain magic in the air when we meet like this . . . wouldn't you say, my precious?"

There was a note of joy mingled with surprise in her fluttering heart as she regarded the tall ranger. He had arrived so soundlessly, as if on a gentle breeze, but he looked even fiercer than he had the first time. He was dressed in leg-length buff doeskins. His cloak and mask were almost invisible in the quickly gathering darkness. She could not utter one word of greeting. He seemed to her unreal, phantomlike.

One brown hand reached out to touch her frilled white cap and Aurora realized with horror that he wanted her to remove it.

"Nay!" she gasped. "You—You frightened me." She beheld with some apprehension the startling gleam of white teeth as he lowered his hand at the same time that he smiled. As if he were amused!

There was a long unearthly silence before he said, "You didn't answer me." He paused, then sighed deeply, his virility touching her to the quick. "Are you still afraid?"

"I—I am not—afraid!" she exclaimed in short breaths, the last word rushing out.

He reached out for her again but she stepped back nimble and quick.

"Ho, but you *are* afraid of me."

"Nay! I am not," she ended with a soft whisper.

"Then why do you draw back and shiver? I can scarcely see you and yet sense your fear. Why? Come forward here, and let me hold you to feel how your heart trembles. I will gentle your fears, little dove," he said huskily, cajoling.

"Prithee, do not come any closer," she murmured in a suffering, barely heard voice. Her foot turned as if to flee, but she could not.

"Will you answer me then? Why are you, the air around us, and this sweet lane all filled with magic? There seems to be a veritable witch's incense surrounding us beneath these branches and—" He snatched her to his chest as he stepped forward like lightning. "Ah! How I have hungered for your lips, to be alone with you, my precious," he murmured, his breath harsh-sounding and hot against her burning cheek.

Aurora wrenched her face aside, but only worsened her position. Now his warm lips nuzzled her ear, and she swayed as his steely arms banded tighter about her small waist, then one swiftly reached up against her back to keep her from swooning. Whimpering and digging her nails into his flesh, Aurora felt a wave of intense desire sweep over her, washing away all the loneliness she had felt for several weeks.

Danger signals, though, registered in her brain as she felt the tension build and tighten in him. He seemed to be drawing her into his very male self. But she was heedless to the danger, for she was already dying a sweet death called ecstasy.

"Love, precious love, can you give yourself to me?" he moaned in his throat, giving her a butterfly kiss on her cheek.

"I cannot, F—Fay. Oh, please, I prithee do not ask me. My heart is breaking!"

Aurora brooded momentarily in the midst of her passion on how it was that Fay knew her cousin. Now, in his arms, it hurt so to think of them together—Fay and Melanie.

"Why? There is someone else who claims your heart? You are perhaps—betrothed?" Fay asked, his voice suddenly chilling. "Never mind," he altered quickly. "Someday you shall know all that is mystery now. For tonight, for now, there is naught but this magic between us that must not be spoiled."

Aurora tried breathlessly to converse, for she was becoming faint and limp against him. "Where do you sleep, where do you lodge?" she asked him. She was alarmingly aware, too, that all will to resist his lovemaking was shrinking fast. "Please—do not—" she began, but he was already capturing the sweetness of her lips.

It was a long, demanding yet gentle kiss, and Aurora was on fire for this wild young man who had entered her heart but a fortnight ago. He was smothering her whimpering, half-protests with his lips and she was returning his kiss with an ardor so fierce that it belied her maidenhood. She could feel his impassioned shiver mingle with hers.

In their nearness, she felt his manhood pressing against her even as the kiss deepened. This frightened her. This excitement and desire were so very new. Just when she thought she would surely swoon from the tumultuous sensations flowing within her, he lifted his head and spoke.

"How much do you know of the art of making love—tell me, precious, I would know."

"M—Making love?" she stammered.

"Aye."

"I—I cannot!"

"I did not ask you to. I merely asked what you knew of the pleasures. Perhaps—"

With deliberation he began to kiss her again, more demanding than before, crushing her lips and extracting little moans from her throat. With his arms tightening like bands of steel, he pressed her closer, making her very much aware of the difference between man and woman. He was so crushingly hard against her that she began to whimper.

"I don't mean to hurt you, but I can't seem to hold you close enough. I shall try to be gentler."

A darkly tanned hand had just reached up to cup a breast when all at once there came a worried call from the house. It was Hetty's voice Aurora heard through the befuddled fog in her brain:

"Hoo-hoo! If ye be out there, lass, ye've best be getting yerself in now. 'Tis late!"

Hetty broke the spell that had been woven like an inescapable, loving web all about the cedar lane, the spot where the lovers stood with arms entwined. Now

Fay stood frozen in frustration, his hand just a fraction from her breast as he peered down at the face he could barely make out, but knew was lovelier than the fairest rose that bloomed in England. Yet somehow Melanie's blurred face appeared smaller than ever to him. He relaxed his fierce hold on her.

"Ah, Melanie, flame of my life, my own heart, you tempt me mindless, that I know not what I ask of you. Why aren't you—" he began, and groaned deeply. "But you must go—for now." His lips merely brushed hers, then lingered, then crushed deeply again. His frown went unseen before he lifted his dark head. "Precious Melanie, my fair-haired vixen, God above only knows how I love you."

Suddenly the night air shivered with a long-suffering cry. In the twinkling of an eye, his arms were let cold, and he was left staring ahead as far as the darkness would permit; in a moment all he could see was the pert white cap moving through the dark like a vaporous wraith. Then he could see no more of her; only the sweet essence of bayberry lingered.

The moon was shrouded by a dark cloud, the lane pitch now, and Fay stood alone with heavy heart beneath the faintly stirring cedars. A bird of omen, of lustrous black color, gave a harsh, loud cry once, then passed silently overhead.

Aurora hastened up to the garret where she knelt down on a hooked rug and dragged out her large, beloved bundle from an old chest. A huge tear glistened as it rolled down her flushed cheek and onto the soft black thing in her lap. The glossy hairs sprang up beneath her hand, like a living beast flexed and crouching to bar an unwanted presence from entering this private sanctuary. Aurora felt as though her young heart had fallen onto the fur and was slowly shrinking, dying there.

"Fay . . . Fay!" she sobbed as though her chest would swell and burst.

Hetty searched within and without for her wee bairn. But Aurora did not budge from the garret for hours, so great was her grief.

That night Aurora burned many candles as she sat up in her room. Sleep evaded her like a wraith continuously floating out the door. Fay's parting words professing his love for Melanie made her feel as if he had stabbed her and turned the blade back and forth inside her heart.

An hour earlier up in the garret, as the latch clicked behind her and Hetty had stepped into the little room with slanted roof, Aurora had hastily stuffed the pantherskin back into the chest. Hetty had moved into the light of the one stubby candle that squatted in its dish on the floor.

"Why hae you been hiding yerself in here, luv?"

All of a sudden Aurora stood, ceremoniously dusting off her hands. She sparkled with animation—for Hetty. She would not forever share her distress with this woman who had always been a loyal servant and true-blue friend.

"I have been rummaging through these old trunks," Aurora began in a forcibly chatty manner. "I like to come up here and look at all the old things Uncle Jeremias purchased at the Stourbridge Fair in

England. 'Tis strange all the bric-a-brac one collects in a lifetime, only to be stashed away at the top of the house, lovely things that do naught but collect dust and—"

"Whew!" Hetty had interrupted. "Please, luv, I been having quite a go around with that pawky Bertilde Lacey, and her quaffing the fume agin. I canna stand a man smoking tobacco twists, much less a woman. 'Tis dangerous to the lungs and brain," she ended, rolling her "r's."

After dining on a small portion of vegetables and fowl, Aurora bathed by the little fire, sunk to her shoulders in the huge wooden tub brought in and filled by the houseboys. She kept up her gay pretense under Hetty's watchful regard, but now alone and brushing her hair dry, she continued to let her thoughts dwell on that romantic woodland knight.

For the hundredth time Aurora wondered who this Fay could really be. While with him she had sensed that he was born of gentle blood, but she knew most of the better families of the colony, and he fitted none. She cared naught if Fay were rich or poor. She herself valued neither wealth nor social position, as her cousin did.

Aurora was bewildered by her attitude; she was not the same girl who had not long ago been carefree. Yet in spite of her gloomy mood, her young body had begun somehow to feel relief. At least she had seen the one who had been haunting her dreams for weeks. She had been with him, held him close to her breast. Her nipples hardened and of a sudden she crimsoned. Oh! she had returned his kisses shamelessly, but something in the contact had made her feel a womanly glow and a strengthening beneath a man's desire.

Now the owls and whippoorwills outside her window made cruel sport of her, seeming to mock her thoughts that she would probably wed a stumbling, bumbling, sniffing oaf like Rodney Quick. A likely prospect, for Fay loved Melanie, as did Bran Ravenleigh! But the English-born gentleman meant nothing to her; in fact, she felt something close to loathing for the man.

She was unable to endure the thought of matrimony with another. Fay would then vanish forever beyond her reach. A disturbing thought occurred to her suddenly. Even though it seemed a near impossibility that Fay change his mind about Melanie should he learn the truth, how could she go with him? Where would they live? In the wilds? She called to mind some lines from the Book of Ruth then:

Intreat me not to leave thee,
    Or to return from following after thee:
For whither thou goest, I will go,
    And where thou lodgest, I will lodge.
Thy people shall be my people,
    And thy God my God.
Where thou diest, will I die,
    And there will I be buried. . . .

"Fay, Fay, my heart doth fly to you, even would we be oceans apart," Aurora murmured, pressing her face in her curled arm, still smelling the sweetness of

170

bayberry soap that clung to her clean, rosy skin. "Do not leave me so sad, so lonely, my darling wild Fay." Oh, Lord, why did he have to be the one she had lost her heart to!

With the sudden lifting of her head, Aurora heard the murmur of voices outside her room: Melanie's voice, loud, harsh, and Hetty's slow explanation, as if she had tried to complete the lines several times over. Aurora sniffed and dried her eyes as she came to her feet.

"I tell ye, I did'na know him. I've told ye the Gospel truth, 'tis all I know of him. He said—" Again Hetty was interrupted rudely by Melanie.

Her hair flowing, her feet bare, Aurora appeared outside her door. Hetty looked to Aurora entreatingly.

"Hetty," Aurora said as she glanced at her cousin's sneering face, "what is this all about?"

"I been trying to tell yer cousin what the man said, he who come to gie her a message."

"What man, Hetty?"

"Whew! I did'na know him. He was a complete stranger, lass. He come to the kitchen door and"—Hetty looked askance at Melanie, almost expecting to be interrupted again—"said 'Dinna be afraid, I only came to gie you a message for the Mistress Melanie.' Now . . . he said for her and all her folk to come to"—Hetty scratched her frilly-capped head, then went on—"to Raven Keep on the morrow. There was no one wi' him and I could'na hardly see him standing wi'out the door in the dark."

"*Well*, why didn't you tell me, old woman!"

Melanie snapped, her eyes flashing blue-violet sparks in the dimly lighted hall.

"I tried to tell ye that part, but ye kept cutting me off, asking *who* the stranger might be. Ye dinna ask what words he—"

"Ignorant Scot! You just didn't want to tell me all, afraid that Mama and Papa would object to our visiting Raven Keep in their absence, without their approval."

"To be sure, ye should'na go without their say," Hetty instructed, pursing her thin lips. She turned to the younger cousin. "Luv, I am weary to the bone, so I'll be going to me bed now."

After Hetty had gone, Aurora perused Melanie with something close to exasperation. "'Twas very cruel of you to speak so harshly with Hetty. After a full day's work, how can you expect her to be wide awake when some stranger comes bearing a message at such an ungodly hour. Melly, could you not have exercised a bit more patience with her?" Aurora realized that Melanie's prejudices were many, her reasons few. But why the Scotswoman?

Melanie tossed her unbound, bright hair over her shoulder. "Ha! Speaking of wide awake, what was she doing in the kitchen at such an *ungodly hour*— filching a midnight snack again? Let me tell you, cousin, I run this manor with my parents away, never forget. If I wish I can even have both you and your haughty Scot servant tossed out on your backsides, where you can fend for yourselves. Your mama left you nothing, save for a few ragged garments. Out in the cold, cruel world, see how far you and she can get,

172

penniless and adrift!"

What could Aurora say?—for this was the cold hard fact that she had been afraid to face ever since their coming to North Creek. But she never thought Melanie would put it to her so cruelly and baldly. Really, where would she and Hetty go if Melanie carried out her threat? There were murdering savages out there. Aurora sent up a prayer that Aunt Margaret and Uncle Jeremias would return from the Carolinas safely; circumtances would return to normal again then. At least the Edwardses kept some peace in the house.

"I too am weary. So I shall bid you a good night, Melly," Aurora said with a defeated droop of her shoulders, as she turned to retire.

Melanie glared imperiously at the slim back moving away from her. "We will go to Raven Keep on the morrow!" she ordered with a parting shot, delighting in being masterful and having the upper hand.

"I shall be one not to go," Aurora tossed over her shoulder softly, her hand gripping the knob tightly.

"You will do as I say! Or else Hetty is the first one to be out of this household! Understand, dear cousin?"

"Aye," Aurora breathed, but the next words came hard. "It shall be as you say, Melly."

"And stop calling me *Melly*, it's sickening! I am Melanie, soon to be Mistress Ravenleigh. Bran's wife! And tomorrow we three—that includes your doting servant—will depart for Raven Keep, escorted by the stablehands. They'll not be needed here, anyway. We'll need all six horses, including your precious Cupid, to carry my favorite gowns and personal belongings. We might as well stay there awhile."

Aurora said no more, but went quietly and submissively to her room, hoping and praying that soon the Edwardses would return and put an end to their daughter's unfairness and cruel demands. Aurora slept hardly a wink that night, for in the back of her mind lurked the frightful premonition that something horrible was about to take place.

Indeed, ill fortune was in the wind and it broke the very next morning. For the Edwardses were never to return to North Creek. But their escorts did, bearing the tragic news.

The dawn was shrouded wtih dark clouds before the riders approached the manor and dismounted. Melanie, for some reason having awakened with the birds, was the first to greet the sad and bedraggled travelers. Her face was a deathly hue of white as she invited them shakily in for hot coffee, and there in the kitchen the grisly tale unfolded.

There had been a drenching rain the morning before. After stopping at an inn ten miles this side of the Caroline border, the riders said they had gone on ahead to check out the trail and see if a detour had to be taken. On returning they had found "Indian sign," and the Edwardses had vanished from the trail. That was all, but Melanie could guess the rest.

"Yea, 'tis a bad thing that's come to pass," Hetty said to Aurora an hour later. "And may God Almighty help us all now," she added, meaningfully.

174

Aurora knew exactly what Hetty was driving at. If Melanie's dictatorial manner had been bad before, it was now utterly appalling to everyone in the household; even Aunt Bertilde found no peace in her old rocker, and Melanie gave full vent to all her resentments against her cousin and the Scot house-keeper.

So mean and overbearing had Melanie become in her new status, both as the future bride of Bran Ravenleigh and now the mistress of North Creek, that she barely mourned her parents' most probable death.

"Could she be a dragon, she would send forth flames!" Hetty announced as she came in to aid Aurora in her packing.

"Aye," Aurora returned wearily. "'Tis unbe-lievably selfish that Melanie would still have us go to Raven Keep. Ah, Hetty, Melanie shall not spare us one peaceful moment, I'm afraid. Most certain am I that Bran Ravenleigh will be no kinder than she. She has spoken of him as being a rake, but she cares not if he be the devil himself. My guess is that he is completely ruthless. Alas! When she becomes his bride, he shall no doubt put us through as much misery, if not more."

Hetty sighed as if the weight of the world rested upon her thin shoulders.

"To be sure, luv, I've seen his kind before, and wi' him to lord over us, the stormy seas ahead have but begun to blow and be felt. Dinna fret over much; perhaps ye've a groom in yer future too, and a kindly one I pray."

"Alas, Hetty, I wish I were not such a coward!" Aurora half-sobbed.

Hetty rushed to the young woman and tossed her arms about the sagging shoulders. "May the good Lord gie you strength, me gentle-hearted little Ro. And may he give me some too, luv."

## Ten

The earth was already toasty warm as the small group left North Creek with midday just an hour away. They rode unceasingly along the northern trail through the forest. The branches with their springtime foilage in full bloom almost obscured the sun so that there played a ghostly yellow-green light along the needle-and-leaf cushioned floor. The escorts were armed, ever watchful of savages, and their going was slower than if there had been just the two men.

The colors of the forest in springtime were impressive, with the white blossoms of the dogwood and the purple-pink blossoms of the redbud seen everywhere. The scent! The pink blossoms of the azalea filled the air for miles around with a delicate perfume all their own. The variety of trees marching through the forest was endless: towering pines, hemlocks, cedars, locusts, hickories, sycamores, beeches, birches, willows, maples, and oaks of nearly every kind.

Aurora was remembering a certain night . . . she remembered it well. A moon of silver with a nimbus of yellow-gray surrounding it. A kiss, deeply and feelingly given. Deep purple clouds drifting lazily

177

by, with a paler hue of violet lacing where the moonlight caressed them. She remembered the night well.

"Into my life you stole . . . in spring . . . like a phantom," Aurora murmured to herself as an arrow planted itself in her heart.

Aurora sighed and continued to study the life around her—the squirrels, both red and gray who grew fat on the huge supply of acorns and hickory nuts; red-headed woodpeckers, almost the size of black crows; quail, whose sharp whistle could be heard coming from the meadow when the forest opened now and then. In some places the forest floor was covered with a thick growth of underbrush and again the trail would curve and the forest would open onto a floor dotted with little patches of sunlight, where it was possible to ride or walk easily over the soft carpet of fallen leaves or pine tags and needles.

"I love him . . . with all my heart," Aurora breathed the words softly, fiercely brushing away tears with the back of a hand.

She felt an aura all around her again, like a living thing, growing stronger even as she rode, something beckoning and drawing her and filling the emptiness of her heart. She couldn't understand it; she did not try to. It was much too frightening.

The trail cut sharply westward leading them to a broad savanna where they would traverse head-high marsh grass and then on to the Chickahominy River. Once there they would board the ferry, horses and all, and proceed to the landing.

Aurora had donned the black of mourning, her cap laced with long black riband streamers. The dress was old; she looked like a dowdy serving-maid, and just as well for she had been reduced to servitude anyway. She would remain unnoticed, too, without having to mingle with the guests at Raven Keep. There were surely others, she decided, that had been invited there this weekend, but they would never believe she had been gentle born, for she was dressed no better than the meanest servant.

Hetty, saddened to see her fine little mistress so lowered, thought that it seemed to please Melanie to such a degree that she had beamed when Aurora appeared outside with her meager baggage, garbed in somber black and gray. Melanie herself had donned her best, for she detested black after having worn the widow's weeds for so long (Margaret had insisted), and had ripped the black thing asunder from collar to hem, so she had no other mourning clothes to wear.

Hetty had sniffed disdainfully at Melanie's russet gown with ornamental stomacher and silk camlet cloak. Shockingly, Melanie also wore a frilled cap with long streamers of gay ribands and high-heeled leathern shoes with splendid buckles. Contrasting bleakly with her cousin, Aurora had on her serviceable clogs and a loose gray cloak made of strong durable stuff. To be sure, Hetty thought sorrily, little Ro would be one not to draw attention to herself at Raven Keep. But the secret was that Hetty had packed the purple patterned silk and white varnished shoes—just in case.

Upon leaving the manor, Hetty had lavished some pity on poor doddering Bertilde Lacey. She had been like a tearful child, losing the last two of her kin, first the one in Carolina on her deathbed and now Margaret. Thank the Almighty for senility, Hetty sniffed wtih one hand on her reins, the other shaking out her hanky—for Bertie quickly forgot the circumstances surrounding her. Hetty had been lenient, and the old woman had returned to her rocker, chuckling to herself and quaffing the fume.

Once on land again the small party approached a small weather-beaten house. Aurora recognized it at once, having known early in the day she would look upon it again after five whole summers away from this place that was now boarded up and bleak. Ah, memories came flooding back, some gay, some heartbreakingly poignant. Did the Ravenleighs have knowledge of who had once resided here? she wondered. What did it matter anyway? Nothing seemed to matter.

They passed the gate after riding up the slope and the houseboys and stable hands were there to help them dismount and take the weary mounts along with the Edwardses' servants out back.

In his bedchamber upstairs, Bran had just removed with a well-honed blade a two week's growth of coarse beard. It was close to the hour five and he had just wiped his chin with a moistened linen when he heard the ringbits jingling musically outside. As he was tossing his towel to his servitor, his heart beat a little faster. Melanie had arrived safely. But damn, he should have been more thoughtful earlier and sent his sloop to pick up Melanie and whoever had accompanied her. Sometimes, of late, he wondered where his finer feelings were. It was no wonder, though, that he was confused when it came to his feelings for Melanie. She was indeed a mystery. But then, he was no less, he supposed.

Seating himself to pull on his tall cavalier boots, Bran negligently waved aside the coal-black periwig that Mr. Minter brought perched atop his upraised hand. Mr. Minter was a reserved and dignified man, as most of the Ravenleigh servants were, as had been their parents that had served before them.

"Anything but that, Mr. Minter," Bran said, indicating the wig.

The white wolfhound, Duchess, padded in and sniffed the black curling wig, then backed away snarling. Mr. Minter held the wig higher, as if the big dog were going to spring forward and attack it.

"Ha! There, you see, Minter, even the bitch abhors the thing," Bran said laughingly as he tucked his gathered breeches into his tall boots.

"Well! You do look very handsome in the wig, young sir," Minter reminded as he placed the periwig back on its stand. The manservant turned to aid his young master in tying the long neckcloth of white linen.

"Never mind, Minter, I'll have a go at it myself," Bran said as he passed the neckcloth twice about his neck and lapped it in front after the French manner.

"You sometimes remind me of the first master of Raven Keep, sir, although of course you are a head taller than Derek Ravenscar was. Still—"

"Raven*scar*?" Bran inquired lifting a black brow.

"Oh, yes, sir, he named his place himself. He had been a fierce sea-wolf in his day. My own hair stood on end when my own father first sought employment with the rumored buccaneer Ravenscar. We had come over on the good ship *Elizabeth*, me being a Dutch lad of only nine years."

Bran frowned in puzzlement. "Why have I not learned of this Ravenscar before this, my good man? I thought my uncle named this ancient hall."

Minter shrugged his bewilderment. "Don't rightly know, Master Bran. I thought you knew that was the very reason your uncle purchased Raven Keep—because of the name befitting his own. He never said if he was relation to Ravenscar, though."

"Well, this *is* very interesting, Minter. Do tell me more."

"Shouldn't you be greeting your guests, sir? They've only just arrived."

Bran waved a hand. "Your wife will show them to their rooms and get them situated before the evening banquet. Now, damn, unfold this mystery," Bran urged, settling himself into a massive black chair with a red cushion and crossed his long legs.

Minter sighed and began: "Derek Ravenscar had looked to be in the prime of life when I first laid eyes on him. His frame was sturdy and vigorous, his skin unwrinkled—then. His dark eyes were bright but full of the devil." Here Minter loosed a chuckle, then went on. "He had made a great deal of hellish noise about the halls that he shared with—ahem—a willowy Paspahegh squaw. He laughed, he sang ribald songs, and swore like the pirate he was—or had been—until Raven Keep rang with his merriment. To the Indian maid he gave the English gypsy name of *Rawnie*. How they played like wanton youths," he sighed, reminiscing.

"Hmmm, so this tale has a sorrowful ending?"

"Oh, yes, a pity, but when she died of the swamp fever, his soul seemed to depart with Rawnie. Small wonder that his mind failed him for quite a time afterward. He grew old of a sudden. The Indian love song in his heart was deathless, though. He never took another mistress to this house, and he raved quite madly about the halls, crying out to some dark Indian spirit that he was a fool for never having given her his name while Rawnie was alive and healthy."

Bran glanced around his bedchamber in a new light, almost seeing in his mind's eye an almond-eyed squaw with skin of a light-tan color. Too, he imagined he could hear her lovely, plaintive song. Suddenly Bran sat upright in his seat.

"Tell me, Minter, where is this Ravenscar now? Has he passed on?"

"Well, Master Bran, last I heard he changed his name, then disappeared. Never seen him around these parts after he sold Raven Keep to your uncle Jason. When Ravenscar left here he was a thin, gray shadow of his former self."

"Did he leave a diary or journal of any sort that you know of?" Bran continued to probe, now that his curiosity was piqued.

"Mmm"— Minter scratched his chin thoughtfully—"can't say that I know of any. Jason had all Ravenscar's personal effects packed in boxes down in the cellars under the house beyond the wine cellar."

Bran rose as if shot. He tossed on his cape and strode brusquely to the door, moving so quickly that the sleeping wolfhound woke with a low growl, swung her long nose around and, sensing no danger, padded to her master and traipsed behind into the hall.

"Young sir, what will I tell the guests? Can we expect you for the banquet?" Minter called worriedly.

"Tell them nothing," Bran tossed over his flowing cape.

After Bran had gone, Minter again scratched his head, shrugged, then went to see if he could be of help in the kitchen. Next to being the young master's servitor, he delighted in aiding Cuffee with the preparing of the meals. Minter's flesh crawled as he made his way down the steep back stairs in Bran's wake, but upon reaching the ground floor he headed for the kitchen. He was relieved that the young sir hadn't asked him to accompany him down into the rat-infested cellars. Minter would go no further than the wine cellar; beyond that was the dank dripping unknown that was rumored by a few of the servants who had dared venture there to be haunted and filled with frightful spirits.

On the ground floor, Melanie had entered sweepingly into the hall as if she were already mistress here. Aurora and Hetty exchanged quiet looks as Melanie introduced both of them as her personal servants. Mrs. Minter was quietly pretty woman of thin frame and middle age, but she ran the house with one leg in each room and refused to put up with insolence from her underlings. Melanie's saucy remarks about the massive furniture raised Ida Minter's graying brows in suspicion. Having felt immediate dislike once before when waiting upon the surly blond woman, Ida now wondered what prompted Melanie Wellbeloved to act so high-and-mighty in this household.

The affairs of Raven Keep and its furnishings were none of her business!

"If you would care to rest up, the bedchambers are on the first floor up the staircase here," Mrs. Minter said meaningfully as she indicated with a wave of her hand the principal staircase, which was beautifully rife with Renaissance detail.

"I know where the bedrooms are," Melanie returned petulantly. She whirled and sauntered directly into the great hall of the east wing.

The two of them feeling silly just standing there facing the staircase, Aurora and Hetty picked up their bags and followed Melanie into the banquet hall. But Ida Minter halted them with an imperious chin in the air.

"You two can just wait there and the footman will be along to take up your bags. At the top of the stairs to your right, you both can share a bedchamber. Master Bran"—her voice rose a pitch for Melanie's benefit—"has left orders to put Mistress Melanie in the west wing, next to the—umm—nursery." Ida frowned to herself, wondering why that word "nursery" should disturb her just now.

"I do not want to be put next to the nursery," Melanie argued, despite Bran's orders. "I would much rather have a room close to Master Bran's."

Ida concealed her scandalized shock well. "That is quite impossible, mistress. The room next to Bran's is occupied by Sir Eric himself," she said flatly, clasping her long fingers over the crisp white apron that protected the black silk dress she wore.

"Humph," Melanie muttered under her breath as she continued to give the hall a measuring scour, as if she planned to make changes in the decor.

Aurora stood below the lintel, also viewing thoughtfully the banquet hall. Its heavy dark shelves shining with copper tankards and cups of glass and silver, its twin fireplaces of massive stone, one at either end, hung with gleaming pots and kettles, she could almost imagine the masculine timber-beamed room come cheerfully to life, with the two fires roaring on a night when the winter wind wailed and blew against the toasty warm walls. She sighed, fantasizing that she could be the mistress of this house that reminded her of a castle with its dark mysterious corners.

Ida Minter swung her head toward the younger servant. She had caught the soft release of breath and now peered measuringly into the heathery eyes, eyes exactly Master Bran's favorite color. The mistress with blond hair had pale purple eyes too; strange, but there was darkness and light both in the servant's eyes. Like heather in both sun and shade.

"A lordly feast will be provided," Ida announced, turning back to Melanie. "But I can't say as it will be this day. Many guests from the parish have been invited, but alas, most of them fear traveling because of the Indian raids up north. More often than not folks have turned back, even ones escorted, after entering the forest trails. Safest travel is by boat, I always say."

"Pshaw," Melanie exclaimed. "The Susquehannocks and the Doegs never venture this far south . . ."

A low cry from behind Melanie was quickly muffled, but she whirled just in time to see Hetty gently unclamping her hand from around the small chin. Ida frowned as she noticed that the young servant appeared totally crushed with grief at what she had just heard.

And rightly so. Melanie crimsoned recalling to mind the horrible tale of her parents' capture—and on the southernmost tip of the colony at that!

As if she had been slumbering all the day, Melanie suddenly received a belated shock. Her parents were dead. Dead! She just knew it! Her posture began to wilt, taking on an aged appearance, and her face went from red to deathly white.

"Dear, dear, how tired and ill you are looking, Mistress Melanie," Ida clucked as she gave an arm to the drooping woman. "Here, I'll help you up to your room where you can take off that tight-looking stomacher and rest." She gave a sly wink to the visiting servants. She then indicated with a nod for them to procede her and Melanie up the main staircase.

With the footman arriving on the scene just then, the small procession moved slowly up the grand staircase. As Aurora was mounting the wide stairs, glancing back down with a little thrill at the standing suit of armor, there grew within her the feeling that someone walked stealthily beside her. Was it more like an aura that surrounded her, had ever since entering these ancient halls? A flickering orange light flashed briefly before her eyes, and rubbing them, at the same time it came to her that she had been predestined to be here at this time. . . .

. . . and the torch continued to flicker in the crevice of the stone wall where it had been wedged above an old chest. Bran was intoxicated with the reverie of buried pirate chests overflowing with pieces of eight and glittering jewels. The thrill and adventure of discovering the cache was in his blood, intensifying with every passing moment as he stood in the underground chamber, trying to decipher the mildewed pages of the journal. Derek Ravenscar's journal. He had discovered, too, a map stuffed in between the pages.

Damn, but only half a map!

The latter part of the journal itself seemed to have been scribbled with the last of Ravenscar's strength, drained by some painful emotion. Bran put in himself that it had been because of the Indian girl's death. He strained his eyes now in the orange glow of the torch, putting in letters where they were missing from splotches of black ink:

A [n]ew Century has turned. My beloved Rawni[e] is gone. Perhaps someone else can find [u]se for the trea[sure].

Bran flicked back to the front of the journal and read:

The crew bureed it somewhere betwixt the Trees—to Keep out of Hands of attacking Indians. They Fleed in such Haste & were unable to Recover the Tresure before leaving. The vessel *Mysterye* leaking badlee—crew sunk Lower Norfolke before they could return for Cache. Their part of Tresure is now mine. Shall leave it bureed—for now.

Further on:

—large amount of Golde and Silver and contained in Kegs and Chests—bureed in—

The last word had been destroyed with ink splotches! Bran cursed. And the map:

At a pointe just to E. of—

Of what? Where? Trees were his only clue. And Virginia was nothing but trees!

"Ho! I have it now," Bran breathed out in the dank chamber. "This all is linked with Jason's murder! He was murdered because of a pirate treasure—ill-begotten booty Jason himself had known nothing about!"

But then, perhaps another pirate had knowledge of the treasure. Ah-ha! Strang! The bloody murderer had been after treasure!

Now, he knew that Jason had also kept a journal, for mention of it had been made in the letter Sir Eric had received at Whitehall concerning Jason's death.

Stuffing the journal and map into his waistcoat and snatching up the torch, with a scowl drawing his black eyebrows downward, Bran left the cellar with rapid strides.

Mr. Minter knocked and knocked. Finally the call that bade entry came, but gruffly. Minter saw the younger master studiously bent over, absorbed in what looked to be a ledger at his huge black desk.

"Ah—Master Bran?"

"Aye, Minter, what is it?" Bran asked dourly.

"Sorry to bother you, young sir, but Mistress Melanie and her servants are the only ones that have arrived so far."

Just as well, Bran thought as he glanced up for a moment. He had no desire for festivity this eve. He was busy studying Jason's journal and wished for nothing more than to be left alone. Minter took note of this and set forth to put the young master at ease concerning the fact that Bran should have been available to greet his first and most important guest. Bah! Important! The blond twit was not very well liked by the servants, and they gossiped about her downstairs even now.

"The mistress Wellbeloved is abed, Master Bran. I fear something has befallen her parents, the reason for her being indisposed. Her youngest servant had spoken in her behalf, saying that the Edwardses have been captured by Indians. She knows not whether they are ever to return, but presumes them dead. . . ." Minter let it hang, trying to put the situation across in as delicate a manner as the lovely girl had done.

Bran half-rose, clutching the desk. "Alas! Not the Edwardses. I was yet to meet them. I say—I shall go to Melanie at once." But he lowered himself back down heavily then.

"You wish to see her when she wakes," Minter began, reading Bran's tired movements, "after she has taken nourishment, of course."

"Of course," Bran repeated dazedly. Then, "Have a houseboy run out to the stable in an hour's time and bring Nimrod around to the front for me, will you?"

"You are . . . going for a ride?" Minter finally summarized, almost to himself. He looked to the window that was all a yellow glaze in the falling sun. "It will almost be dark by then."

"Aye, there is a bit of daylight left yet," Bran answered. "I—perhaps I shall go sooner." In quiet meditation he stared up from the journal. "Tell me, Minter, where did the family go that used to live in the summer house?"

Minter shrugged dumbly. "In faith, I have no idea, sir. You could ask Harris."

"Aye, I shall ask Harris later."

Minter slipped out quietly then to go and find a houseboy. Bran lifted his dark head. His eyes as gray as the deepest forest mists, he stood suddenly while at the same time he snapped the journal shut.

# Part Two

## Flame Burning Within

## Eleven

The forest closed in on every side, its gloom menacing as never before. The trees shut out all but a few beams of feeble light in the thickest part of the dense mass where Aurora had wandered. She could hear small animals scurrying through the undergrowth. She had always loved the forest and its mysterious sounds and scents, the tall trees that looked to God all day, but now her heart was beating wildly. After what had befallen the Edwardses, she must surely have been insane to have ventured into the wood.

Who would miss her? she had thought upon leaving Raven Keep. After putting their few belongings in the small wardrobe, Hetty had gone immediately to sleep, exhausted, on the pallet in the smallest bedchamber in the house, the one they had been appointed to share at the top of the stairs.

Now she stood at the edge of the forest, the summer house squatting dismally, boarded-up, neglected, before her eyes, as if the place had become a part of the yellow-green flora that snuggled up against the weathered gray boards. Her girlhood had flowered here and she had been saddened to think of it while, during a golden sunset, she had walked out that door and not returned since. Not until today.

Aurora experienced a shockingly sudden thrill. It was as if she had never left here at all, had only been dreaming these past years. Because a gilded sunset of like kind was in the making, stroking the scene with orange-and-gold dipped brush. She laughed at herself then. It was merely a certain kind of déjà vu, that was all.

The remembrance of joyful hours beyond recovery stole back to her poignantly as she made toward the house.

"You are enjoying the sunset, *senorita?*"

Aurora received a second shock then as she spun about in search of the voice that had enveloped her like an evil embrace. Her head turned in the opposite direction of her body, as if she were doing a difficult exercise. There was no one here, nor there. Just where had the voice come from that had seemed to be so near? She hunched forward to peer into the trees and, as she was doing so, a hand touched her shoulder from behind. Automatically, as she whirled about, her hand went to her heart in a shock that nearly bowled her over.

"Captain Strang—" Aurora stammered, staring directly into fox-like black eyes. "Is—is it really you?" The black orbs darted toward the river, over to the forest, and then back to her—in one second's time.

"So, it is you—my little stepdaughter," Javier Strang said slowly, seeing Deana all over again. "Certainly, you are not a little girl any more. Can you forgive me for leaving you to grow up so lovely all alone?" He reached out to lift her hand and kiss it, but she shyly pressed it into the folds of her skirt.

"I—Stepfather, it is beyond my ken how you appeared of a sudden. Have—you been here long?" She reddened. "I mean, you do not live here anymore, do you?"

He swept his black cloak back. "Here? Ha-ha, I do not think so. Like you, I have just come here for a visit. Well, tell me, can you forgive me, or no?"

"I—I do not live alone," Aurora halted, becoming uneasy with him here alone, wondering too, why he appeared so nervous . . . and strange.

"Well, it does not matter who you live with now, only that you are here." He cleared his throat. "And so am I. Cozy, eh?"

"I—I think I should be starting back now. They will miss me at Raven Keep—"

"Ah!" he interrupted. "You live there—"

It was her turn to interrupt him. "I—we are just visiting. So, if you will excuse me, I shall go now."

He stepped closer. "Not so fast, my lovely stepdaughter. We have not had time to visit. Would you like to come for a ride on my ship? It is not far from here. Come with me, eh? You will like my sailor friends. Come, no one will bite you. We will just have some fun like we used to, no?"

Aurora felt a surge of fear send shivers down her spine. Danger signals were sounding in her brain. Something was all wrong about this. He was not the same man upon whose knee she used to perch while Deana looked on smilingly and Hetty hovered in the background. She sensed what the change was then: Here was a man; she was a woman fully grown now. His feelings had suddenly altered toward her. His intentions, she realized, were not purely of a fatherly nature any more. He wanted something more from her. But then, come to think of it now, had she ever really known him, his personality?

Before he reached out for her, Aurora caught sight of two men, sailors by the look of them, and one had slung over his shoulder a tool for digging. What they were doing here meant nothing to her. Foremost in her mind was that she was a woman alone with three men. They had to be the sailors Captain Strang had mentioned. Were there others too? On the ship?

"Let me see your hair," Javier said as he snatched the ruffled cap from her head, causing the black hair to tumble free, gloriously auburn-black in the sun that dipped low.

"Captain Strang! Alas, what are you doing?"

"Come here, little *belleza*, I want to give you a fatherly embrace. Ah, do not fight me like that, I will not harm you—not you, my little stepdaughter."

"Nay! You must not do this, you are frightening me!"

"*Dios*, but you are a hot little virgin, no?" Javier murmured as he caught her to him, struggling, but fast in his strong embrace. He rained hot kisses upon her flushed cheek, seeking to capture her sweet lips.

Aurora felt him try to lift her and carry her off, she realized with horror, to his waiting ship. Struggling was useless, for Javier Strang was a man stronger than his lean and long frame suggested. Out of the corner of her fright-wide eyes, she could see the two sailors pause in what they had been doing to watch the struggle, that no doubt appeared half-intimate to their lecherous eyes. Indeed, she was almost swooning in her weakening state, and Javier continued to try and make love to her and carry her off.

Unknown to Aurora and her ravisher, two men emerged from the dusk of the forest and reined their mounts to a sudden halt. One of the mounts sensed the fear that surrounded the place, and he reared up; the younger man clamped a hand over the muzzle of the beast and then soothed him with quieting fingers. The slightly older man of the two spoke then, low, so the sound would not carry.

"Look there, Master, her gypsy-dark hair. And that man . . . he looks to be your enemy."

"Exactly. I agree. Come on, Tom!"

Alerted by the watchful sailors, the captain shoved his armful from him so abruptly that she stumbled and fell, rolling in a tumble of skirts to the ground. Captain Strang was off and running, following in all due haste the fleeing sailors. Their destination was the shore ahead where the black ship sat at their ready disposal. Bran spurred Nimrod faster and Tom Bone followed in his wake, both of their mounts churning up clods of damp turf.

"Damn! I've no weapon," Bran called to Tom. "How about you?"

"None, Master!"

"Hold the wench, Tom. I'll get the bloody bastard!"

"Aye!"

The weather-stained craft sat rakishly low in the water. Bran swore, as he came to a skidding halt, seeing the two-master with her four guns showing and a dozen men, perhaps more, on her cluttered deck. Captain Strang was nowhere to be seen. He had vanished like a wraith into thin air. But now, there he was, the captain wading strongly into the water, shaking his fist after the two sailors who had already gained the schooner. Bran had no choice but to turn back, otherwise be blown apart, for one of the sailors on the poop had a fusil out, covering his captain. The sailor fired, but the bullet fell just short of Bran's dark head.

"Good try," Bran called back over his shoulder, gritting his white teeth in frustration that he had not caught the captain. Ah, but now he had the raven-haired wench in his clutches!

Bran halted to throw a glance over his shoulder. There she was, the black schooner, out in the shallows and already slipping stealthily downriver. But his immediate interest was the woman that he knew Tom was holding captive. He had her. Damn, he had her!

Prancing and blowing, Nimrod brought his master to a halt beside Tom Bone and his struggling armful that ceased up her squirming and shrieking when the tall horse and rider loomed over her. From his high perch, Bran took in the wild visage of the young woman, thinking she could have been an Indian squaw but for her fair skin and civilized raiment. The sun was half gone now, making her eyes looking up at him dusky in her fright, the color of them unrecognizable, and her hair a fringe of black that shrouded her countenance from his thorough perusal. Still, she was dressed like the lowliest servant, as a tavern wench.

Aurora knew him as Bran Ravenleigh. He appeared in foul mood, with his black brows drawn together in a scowl, eyes like an angry gray sea, as he dismounted and hunkered down to study her like she was a creature they had just caught. She had never seen him up this close, and too, had never witnessed a more wrathful countenance. She shivered and her heart plummeted down to her toes as he glanced meaningfully in the direction the captain had gone, and then back to her.

Alas, he did not think that she and Captain Strang—that lecherous beast—had been having a clandestine meeting, did he? His perusal completely pierced her thoughts, it seemed. He looks inside of me, Aurora thought, as she fixed him with a wild-eyed glance, then dropped her sooty lashes. What was worse? she wondered. Almost having been spirited away by her own stepfather—or this? The timbre of his voice shot clear through her when next he spoke.

"Pity, Tom, that the good captain has neglected his demure little mistress," he said laconically, and Aurora decided that indeed, without Bran Ravenleigh even touching her, this fear right now was far worse than that she had experienced with Javier Strang.

Spying the digging tool that had been cast aside forcefully during the sailors' haste to be away, Bran rose to his feet.

"Were you and your friends peradventure searching for something with that?"

At first this didn't register in Aurora's whirling brain, but then she found her wits and spoke tentatively. "Not I. Those men—were not with me. We—I mean Javier—nay, Captain Strang, you see . . ." She could not go on, not with them both regarding her as if she were some dangerous criminal.

"Bad scene," Tom put in with a drawl, and Bran followed with a snort of settled doubt.

"What do you know of my Uncle Jason having been murdered here?"

"Murdered? I . . . I . . ." she stammered but hadn't a moment to hash this over in her mind, for he was speaking again, harsher this time.

"Never mind!"

"I—I must speak—now!" Aurora muttered with voice quivering.

Bran bowed mockingly. "Be my guest, wench," he said smoothly, and then to his servant, "Let her go, Tom, she is powerless to flee."

"My cousin . . ." Her voice cracked. Why did her throat dry up just now to betray her? She wanted to rise, but her legs too betrayed her.

"What say you?" Bran sarcastically barked, his teeth gritted all impatiently as he pulled her to her feet.

Fingers of twilight were groping across the earth as Aurora felt herself being lifted roughly. Suddenly the words blurted from her stiff lips. "Captain Strang is my stepfather and Melanie Wellbeloved née Edwards is my cousin!" She crimsoned horribly now.

With hands on lean hips, Bran leaned far back and his deep laughter rumbled in the hollow near the summer house. He inclined his head forward then, peering cynically into the shocked little face. He was about to speak, but something had come over him.

"Who are you . . . really?" he ground out, frowning inwardly.

"I—I am as I say," the frightened young woman answered, "none other than Aurora Gregory." She felt strange tingles go through her limbs, watching his unsmiling mouth.

"Shall I kiss the hem of your garment now, or later?" Bran questioned lazily, trying to see her face through the curtain of disheveled midnight-hair.

"Sir, you asked and I but answered truthfully," Aurora said softly, bending over to pick the trampled cap up from the ground.

Above her, Bran snickered. "Aurora Gregory, Melanie's cousin, you say. Well, we shall just see about that." He turned to Tom. "Escort Miss Gregory to your horse, Tom. I shall ride ahead and make certain that Mistress Wellbeloved—I mean Melanie—has awakened."

"Melanie has been indisposed since we arrived at your manor," Aurora shot at his back.

Bran stiffened and whirled to face her. He stared for a long searing moment. What she spoke just now was Gospel truth. He was totally confused now. Never had he seen this "cousin" of Melanie, nor had he known she even had one.

"Tell me," Bran began, his gaze riveted to the black strands of hair, "are you also servant to your own flesh and blood? None other had accompanied Melanie but her servants."

Aurora balked. She would not, could not let this arrogant man learn that she, Aurora Gregory, born of gentle blood, had been reduced to servility. But what could she say to make him believe Melanie was truly her kin?

"I am—Melanie's cousin, as you shall soon

discover for yourself," Aurora returned, her chin held high.

With an indifferent shrug, Bran showed Aurora the length of his broad back as he strode over the turf to snatch up Nimrod's trailing reins.

When Bran entered the bedchamber, trailed by Aurora Gregory, Melanie was sitting up in bed against the plumped-up pillow. She was faring better now after a generous repast and several goblets of wine.

In his courtliest fashion, Bran went to lift a pale hand which he touched gently, briefly, to his lips, espying at the same time on the bedside table an empty bottle of Madeira standing next to a freshly lighted candle. His swarthy face was so near to Melanie's that she could recognize the smallpox scars on the planes of his cheeks for what they were.

Melanie cringed inwardly. Although the marks did not detract from his good looks, Melanie disliked, in fact was disgusted by scars, or any such disfiguring mark, even though smallpox scars were a familiar sight of the times on many a handsome face in England, she'd heard. For some reason this brought David Wiley, her childhood sweetheart, to mind. David. He had skin, flawless and rosy-cheeked as a green schoolboy.

Bran had read the revulsion that had flickered in the pale eyes, knew what had caught Melanie's attention. He could have said, "What is it, Melanie, do you find disgust in a little mark here and there?" but he was self-conscious enough as it was about them, so why strike up a conversation on an epidemic of smallpox, that which had taken place so long ago, when he had been but a small boy.

Behind Bran Melanie caught sight of Aurora, looking wan and weary. Melanie shrugged against the pillow. She had warmed to Bran's affection and was feeling her old flippant self once again, especially since she had begun to imbibe.

"I am sorry to hear the bad news of your parents' capture," Bran began, then waited graciously while Melanie shut her eyes as if pained by his words. But when she reopened them, appearing lighthearted again, Bran took up. "Our other guests have not yet arrived . . . perhaps tomorrow. My steward wrote the invitations to extend the welcome over the weekend."

"Just as well, Bran, I am feeling quite weary," she said with affected languor, before she concealed a belch beneath her hand.

Hanging back, Aurora wistfully watched the lovers. She was beginning to look at Bran Ravenleigh in a different light. It would be so wonderful to be with somebody who really and truly loved you, for yourself, forsaking all other loves; a man who held one special woman in his heart forever and ever. Perhaps, Aurora thought poignantly as she gazed upon these two, she could find such a love someday. Then she realized there was but one man for her, he whom she had pledged in her own heart to love until death. Aye, she had already found him, and Lord, how she wished fervently he were here.

Bran frowned askance just then, acknowledging the presence behind him. "Ah, I've forgotten. Sweeting, your servant is here to perform her duties. What would you have her do?" His sea-gray eyes narrowed, unseen as Melanie looked beyond him.

"What? Oh, of course, Ro. Fetch me some more Madeira, with a bit of muscovado in it," she ordered and sat back with a languishing sigh.

"*Ro?*" Bran echoed, elevating an eyebrow.

"Of course, Bran darling—my servant. Her full name is Aurora Gregory. She—umm—dresses my hair among other things, and Hetty who is also here, is my housekeeper, who will keep my room tidied up while I am here. Hetty is a Scotswoman," Melanie ended loftily, while Aurora stood stunned by the proud announcement.

Bran lifted his chin that had been resting on the back of his wrist and placed his forearm along a lengthy thigh as he regarded Aurora Gregory. "Well, servant, why do you linger?" he asked, his deep voice filling the room in a rich timbre.

Aurora paled visibly but took herself immediately to the downstairs. She had been thoroughly humiliated, by not only Melanie but Bran Ravenleigh as well, and had very shamefacedly backed out the door. Aurora halted her steps as her hand slipped to her head. What a mess she was. Indeed she felt utterly disheveled. She sorely needed a bath, a good scrubbing after being manhandled. And along with all her other problems, she had misplaced her ruffled cap. It was just as well that Fay was not here to see how dirty and drab she looked!

Upstairs, Melanie longingly awaited the Madeira. She tried stifling a hiccough now and then, but was only embarrassed further by a deep rumbling that began in her stomach and ended in her throat. And try as she might Melanie couldn't keep her eyes focused on Bran Ravenleigh. She had already imbibed too much, but really had no care, for she felt so nice and warm for the time being. She knew also that she afforded Bran a very fetching sight, with her silk wrapper draped loosely about her, the mounds of her milk-white breasts peeping provocatively out. It mattered neither that Sir Eric would be thrown into a fit should he discover his son lingering overly long in her chamber. Too, Bran would go if she but said the word, but she was feeling especially naughty after all the liquor she had tossed down, brought up by one of the more tractable housemaids. If imperious Ida Minter had but known this she would have added another year for the new bondservant Lucy to serve.

"I noticed you eyeing my servant Ro, Bran. Does she interest you in some way?" Melanie managed somehow to keep the words from slurring too much. There was a jealous little devil in her that she held in check, as usual, when she was vying with Ro over some gentleman's attention.

Bran looked up finally from some deep reverie, his countenance immobile. "She appears troubled and anxious about something, that's all, sweeting," Bran returned, making emphasis on the uttered endearment.

Melanie desired to learn just to what extent his seeming interest stretched concerning the mousey girl who was her cousin. He appeared to be waiting for her to go on, so she baited the hook. "Being a man you wouldn't know what troubles Ro . . ."

Bran did nothing more than appear utterly bored with the conversation as he blew upon immaculate fingernails, holding them up to the candlelight.

Melanie herself could not stand the hovering air of suspense, wondering of a sudden who it was that had first created it.

"Well, Bran, don't you want to know?"

Bran yawned. "Please, don't keep me waiting," he said.

Melanie squirmed and tittered. "She fancies herself in love." She snatched his attention from his long-fingered hand by drawing it toward her waist.

"In love—?" he began, feigning surprise. "Her?"

"Well! Why then do you think she's so mopish and craving?"

"Her? Craving what?" he asked dumbly.

"You know, for a man to lie between her thighs. Alas, for Ro, that love is denied her."

"Why," Bran began, boredom yet reigning, "does she pine for a secret lover, perhaps of disreputable character?"

Melanie, after pondering a thought deeply, blurted, "Why, Bran, you sly fox, you have guessed exactly!" She squirmed suddenly, trying to settle herself more comfortably against the pillow. "Now, where is Ro. I would have some more wine."

"Have done, Melanie. Enough is enough," Bran said.

He caught her completely by surprise next, bending over her fair head, then kissing her and slipping his tongue through moist parted lips. Melanie offered no resistance as the kiss became more insistent, and she did not shrink from him as his hand slid down to cup a silken breast, teasing a pink, hardened nipple. Melanie moaned. When his caresses became more urgent, however, with long fingers sliding down below her waist to explore the moist cradle, then penetrating forcefully, she knew even in her befuddlement that the moment had to be halted, and pushed him away. She told herself she must play her maiden game a little longer; at least until they were safely wed she would not give him what she knew he craved most.

"La! but you are rough. Were you trying to hurt me, Bran?" she whined, drawing the coverlet between her thighs to halt the throbbing there.

"You taste just like a tavern wench," Bran said coolly as he rose from the edge of the bed. He pulled from his breech pocket a handkerchief and dabbed at his lips.

"It's written all over your face that the kiss displeasured you," Melanie pouted. "You have had a lot of experience with whores, haven't you, darling. Never mind, I like a man who knows how to pleasure a woman. Oh! I mean what bride would want a green schoolboy for a husband." Melanie frowned here, first at him, then at herself.

"Indeed," Bran returned with a smile he didn't feel. He was at the door the same moment the knock sounded, having heard the steps in the hall. "Come in—ah—Ro, is it not?"

"Aurora to you, sir," she said just as coolly as he just did. But her insides boiled in a turmoil she could not still.

With the green wine bottle and silver tray, Aurora made to sweep past him but he caught her wrist, almost sending the bottle crashing to the stone hearth. Melanie sat up straighter in bed, her eyes wildly flying from one to the other.

Aurora tried hard not to tremble but the attempt was useless. "Sir?" she questioned his motives.

"Ro, get that bottle over here, I die with thirst!" Melanie demanded in an unnaturally high voice as her fingers picked at the coverlet in frustrated boredom.

Bran disregarded Melanie's command, still holding onto the frail wrist while Aurora continued to peer up at him quizzically.

"My bath is being filled in my bedchamber just now. It is an old English custom of ours that the youngest servant scrub the master's back. I believe you to be the youngest in the house just now, Aurora Gregory," he murmured, his breath caressing her crimsoning cheek.

"But, sir, this is not England, and besides, I am not a servant of yours," she finally found her voice to brave the words.

"Nevertheless, 'tis the custom here, too, so I shall await you to do my bidding at the bath," he ended as if he hadn't heard her, finally releasing his painful grip.

Aurora did not tarry but hurried over to set down the tray with a loud clatter. She stood abjectly rubbing the painful bruise in her wrist as she inwardly took back the nice thoughts she'd had of Bran Ravenleigh. He had demeaned her, and just when she had thought there could be some gentleness in him.

While Melanie was uncorking the bottle, Aurora, unstrung, cast a quick glance over her shoulder just in time to see the door closing. Aurora released a shuddering sigh. She would not think of later and what she must do, or else try to get out of.

Melanie poured herself a generous goblet and downed the fiery white stuff noisily in one hasty gulp. Aurora wrinkled her nose, praying that she would never find herself in Melanie's circumstances, drinking like a lush to ease her grief. Poor Melanie.

"Hah! You should see your face, Ro. Every time Bran looks at you, it turns ripe red. Handsome, is he not? Kind of makes your forget your wild ranger and crave him, hmm?" She tossed her fair head toward the door that had just closed. "Well, cousin, hands off—he's mine!"

Aurora looked on with sickening disgust as Melanie belched out loud, then, toppling backwards she quickly passed out. Aurora put a finger to her puckered lips in thought, but then discarded the idea as quickly as it had formed. Still, if need be . . .

## Twelve

The moon, a huge lopsided orange slice, rose above the darkened forest. Inside the Keep, beeswax tapers had been lighted and positioned in sconces, aiding the single log nestled between the large brass andirons in warming and lighting the deeply colored bedchamber. Even at that, there remained an air of forbidding mystery. Just like the rest of the house, here was light and shade, cheerfulness and gloom— day or night.

In the brass-banded wooden tub, with darkly bronzed arms dangling over the sides, Bran lounged in the now lukewarm water, helping himself to the earthenware pitcher of wine that sat on a low table beside the tub.

"Damn, where is the wench," Bran ground out, grim-visaged and scowling. "Ned!" he shouted, to which a young houseboy stationed outside the door immediately responded by rushing in with two more vessels of water that had just been lugged up to him from the kitchen. "Not so fast! Slow*wwwly*, Ned," Bran gritted out between his teeth and the strapping lad applied more caution to his labor. "Ahh, that's better. Now, Ned, go and fetch me that little servant of Melanie's. She was to scrub my back. Do you know what is keeping her?" Tipping his goblet to sensuous lips, his brows rose in interrogation above the rim.

Oddly, Ned blushed. "Don't know, Master Bran."

"Well then, go and fetch her to me, anyway!"

"Be she with the Scotswoman in the upper west-wing?"

"How would I know!—Aye," Bran growled. Then, "Have done with your questions, or I'll tan your hide till it glows in the dark. Just fetch her, hear, fetch her!"

The houseboy had caught the dangerous warning tick in the lean cheek, and so he scurried off to do Master Bran's bidding. Ned's fawn-colored eyes brightened as he went along the hall that stretched from east to west wing, then took a sharp right, passed the stairs, now stood before the door. He gulped. His young heart beat like a drum as he hesitated. Sure, he had seen the pretty little Ro in mouse-colored clothes, but it was her eyes that had dazzled and struck him to his heartstrings.

Ned knocked once, waited, gulped, drew a hand across his high forehead and said "Whew!" just before the door slowly opened, a dark head appearing in the crack, the pale face peeping out. She was without her pert cap now, her midnight hair satiny clean and unbound. Ned knew for a certainty he had never in his life beheld a fairer maid.

"Stay there," Aurora whispered, so as not to awaken Hetty, who had dragged back to her pallet after supper chores. Aurora rushed to her bed, tied her hair back neatly with a long riband and then returned to the lad waiting there.

"Whew!" the lad had been exclaiming to himself again.

"Pardon me?"

Ned stared unblinkingly. "Ah—umm . . ." he stuttered, almost forgetting the errand he had been sent on. "Master Bran's waiting for you to come scrub his—*his back.*"

"Never!" Aurora snapped, making to shut the door in the lad's flushing face, but he stuck a foot between, which became pinched in the process.

"Ouch!" Ned painfully exclaimed.

"Oh! I am sorry," Aurora said, reopening the heavy door.

Now Ned Minter was afeared for his own sake. He was no dunce, but quite the opposite when it came to obeying the Ravenleighs' orders. Both Sir Eric and Bran had wicked tempers, and besides, his father would flog him himself for disobeying the Ravenleighs. But would he ever be able to forget this little face that wore such a miserable and doomed expression?

"I understand," Aurora said, reading his agony. She came out with him into the hall. "I shall do it for you—" She hesitated.

"Ned. Ned Minter!" he almost shouted, his distress vanishing.

"Ned," she repeated, liking him from the first. "You may call me Aurora. Will you accompany me back to the master's bedchamber and await me while I do his bidding?" she asked in a mocking tone meant for the taskmaster.

"Aye, 'twill be a pleasure . . . Aurora," Ned

breathed as already they hurried along the south hall.

Aurora sighed in inward resignation. Why had her life become so complicated? Was she forever to dwell beneath Melanie's shadow, her days on this earth one long masquerade? Why was she allowing Melanie to do this to her? She found her answer next. It was solely for Hetty, her beloved servant who Melanie would feel no mercy for if her own impudence surfaced. Sometimes she just wanted to slap Melanie so hard! And now she was doing Ned Minter a favor by not disobeying the *master's* lecherous command. Aye, if Ned was afraid of Bran Ravenleigh, how was she to find the courage to face the scoundrel in his nakedness? Oh, unholy thought!

"Damn, it's about time. What took you two so deucedly long?" Bran barked and scowled, cooling his backsides in the bath. "Ned! Go down and fetch me some more hot water. What are you waiting for, hell to freeze over? In my tub? Now!" His eyes defrosted then as he took in the female.

Aurora stood in fear and trembling, trying hard not to show it, but her glance widened at the broad shoulders jutting out at the top of the deep tub. She watched instead as Ned Minter rushed out the door, closing it behind him so as not to lend draught to the chamber, and she dared not even peek back at the tub.

"Well? What is it, Aurora Gregory, haven't you ever looked upon a man in the buff before at bathtime?" came the question, followed by a little splash as the bar of soap was shot from his squeezing hand.

Aurora chose not to answer, it seeming improper to respond to such a boldly put question. Instead she filled her roaming gaze with the huge black-oak bedstead, draped with scarlet red hangings, then quickly on to the foot of the bed where an enormous leather-bound chest squatted with its brass fittings gleaming dully in the chamber's half-gloom. The Turkey carpet beneath her was woven rampantly in reds and golds on a solid black background. With its dark massive furnishings, the room bespoke masculinity just as she had expected it would.

"Come here," he said suddenly, startling Aurora.

She obeyed, walking slowly onto the footcloth protecting the carpet from being splashed upon, and looking at him so reproachfully it was as if he'd just wounded a small creature of the woods.

"Have done with your maidenly act, Aurora Gregory. You came to scrub my back . . ."

"When'er you wish, s—sir," she said lamely, sidling up to the tub shyly as at the same time trying to avoid looking into those disturbing gray eyes.

"I am not a satyr, you know. Nay, I guess you would not know. We are barely more than strangers to each other."

She appeared so chaste, Bran was thinking, that he could hardly believe he had seen her locked in a loving embrace with Strang. In fact, her actions were like that of a fledgling where men were concerned. His regard savored her form as she bent down after he had handed her the soap and the cloth. Dipping her hand into the water, Aurora noted with a blush the heavy growth of dark hair on his arms and legs.

"Brrr," Aurora shivered, averting her gaze from seeing any more of him. "How can you stand it, sir. 'Tis terribly cold!"

"Don't you think I know that! It won't be for long, though, I hear Ned coming. Wait," Bran halted her as she was about to soap his back.

Ned hauled in another two buckets and began to pour, slowly this time. Bran watched the lad who seemed at loose ends and indeed red-faced in the presence of the dainty servant girl. Aha! There is something afoot here, Bran decided.

"That is enough, Ned. You may go now," Bran instructed the lad who was trying hard not to gawk at Aurora.

"B—But . . ." Ned stammered.

"Go now, Ned, your parents await you downstairs to partake the servants' evening meal."

Ned cast one more yearning look in Aurora's direction and then dipped to take a bucket in each hand. He walked with slow progress, as if the door would never be reached.

"Ned!" Bran growled, growing impatient with the enamored lad.

"Going, going, Master Bran!"

Even at that, the door shut slowly. Once again Aurora and Bran were alone. He swung around to face her so sharply that she jumped, uttering a little shriek. He shocked her even further by snatching the riband from her head, causing the black mass of hair to tumble in slow-motion about her shoulders. Black strands uncoiled and bounced across her clad bosom to rest in soft disarray.

"This hair," he murmured, "midnight dark as my own. How can you profess to be Melanie's cousin with locks such as these? In very truth your countenance resembles hers much now that you have cleaned yourself up. But think you that I believe you when you say that Strang is your stepfather?"

"Yea, sir, all I have said is truth, so help me God. But you must believe whate'er you wish. I swear by all that is holy, sir, and may the Almighty strike me down here and now if I have deceived you one little bit," she ended, seriously grave.

Bran lifted his gaze to the ceiling as if expecting a bolt of lightning to come down and strike the servant. Aurora could not help it, but she giggled behind her hand. Her eyes sparkled mischievously then. Though not carried away with joy, she was actually relaxing in the presence of this man who possessed that same animal magnetism and roguish appearance that she had so feared from afar. But now, now his silvery gaze bore into her and he appeared dark and frowning all of a sudden.

"Scrub my back—now!" he commanded as he presented his long muscular back to her.

What Aurora had not realized was that her old self had surfaced, if but only for a few minutes. It was that same Aurora Gregory who not long ago had captured the hearts of many men. She had been tutored well by Catherine Tobie in the art of charming coquetry. What Catherine had failed to teach her student of several years was that if used incorrectly, especially by virtuous maidens, the effect could be quite damaging, downright dangerous in the presence of a lusty gentleman.

Bemused now, with a rapid rise in her pulse, Aurora bent to her task. Her long hair tickled Bran's wide shoulders as first she scrubbed, then sponged clear water onto him, washing away the soap suds.

Aurora was about to straighten from her bent position when a long arm snaked back and caught her about her tiny waist. Curious tremors shot through her at the sudden contact, and she tried to draw back. He was fast to snatch her against the tub, her hips in dangerous proximity to his face.

"Now that my bath is over, I would like a bit of recreation, Aurora Gregory," he uttered huskily, a suffering tightness felt in his groin.

"R—recreation, sir? I—I do not understand," she faltered, desperately tense.

"Your prudery fools me not one bit, Aurora. This is not debauchery, on my part. And you know full well what I am driving at. Sensual pleasure, the very same you give to the captain, most generously no doubt."

Finally his words rankled, forcing her to speak her mind. "My—Javier *is* my stepfather, not my lover! 'Tis sinful what you presume, sir!"

"Aha! Javier again, hmm? You play the innocent as well as I do the eunuch. And if I am an eunuch then this *thing* that has found its way into my bath must belong to another. Yea, you are as artful as a demimondaine. Come, Ro, forget your captain for the night. I would fain taste new meat and am certain that soon, once we get going, you shall have the same craving." He made to rise but first released her. "Fetch me the linen over there, Aurora, but let me warn you that I am swifter of leg than you should you try for the door."

Aurora seethed inwardly. "Swaggering cock! Too big for your boots!" She wanted to toss at his dark head.

Her thoughts whirling rapidly, Aurora displayed a slim back while going to snatch up the towel that had been warming on a low bench near the hearth and turning, she handed him the towel at arm's length.

"Snuff out the tapers now, Aurora."

Doing as he ordered, watching the room bedarken, she paused all at once as a devilish plan struck her, and she lost no time in executing her stratagem. May the Almighty forgive me this fool's errand, she prayed, but she couldn't devise another to safeguard herself from being violated and deflowered by that rakehell.


With countenance darker than a summer thunderstorm, Bran carried a thoroughly sodden, listless Melanie back to her bedchamber. She was babbling incoherently when he deposited her in a silly heap on the bed. But it was when he was striding to the door that she surfaced for a minute, her languid words coming across to him. He paused, listening as her words made more sense.

"Bran, my handsome groom will be waiting for me in bed, Ro? I must go to him?" She giggled, then went on. "Wake up, Melanie . . . Help me, Ro, I can't walk. Shhh!" Melanie waggled a finger drunkenly before her ruddy nose. "Awright, if you're sure thish is my wedding night. But just one more drinky, Ro. Ish all gone? How . . . Walk straight now, Melly, you mush be sober for your groom. Aye, right into hish arms. Sober up, Melly, but not too much!" Melanie fell to giggling again, was then swallowed up into a stupor, the pillow claiming her head, with its nightcap askew, for a long time to come.

Bran left the bedchamber and went along the hall to the east wing, his feelings for Melanie quite dampened and unromantic at this time. And to think he had almost made love to her, thinking her none other than Aurora Gregory. Damn, it was most ironic! It had been the sweet odor of mint leaves on her breath and the savage warmth, the luscious body pressing close to him as she had climbed into his bed, that had blinded him. He could have had her, for she had been quite willing—up to a point. Then Melanie, not Aurora Gregory, had collapsed against him like a rag doll, clingign listlessly to his neck.

Mint leaves! Who would carry herbs around with them, ready to be used if need be at a moment's notice? Surely not Melanie. Something tugged at his memory. The summer house; the herb pouch; a child's sweet voice. Haunting him.

Abruptly Bran slowed his steps. He shook his dark head, causing a wave to fall over his forehead. Just what the devil was he doing? This was getting him nowhere, except into more damn confusion. He spun around at the sound of the back stairs creaking.

"Master Bran."

"Ah, just the person I wanted to see. Tom, have Jonsey get the *Enchantress* ready. We shall take the sloop first light of dawn."

"You must have read my mind, Bran. I was just thinking we should take a jaunt downriver. Do you think your guests will miss you?" He grinned, the gesture lifting his chiseled countenance.

"Fat chance of that!" Bran snorted cynically. "At least not until tomorrow night, Tom. The other guests should have arrived by the time we return."

"*If* we return," Tom muttered to himself as Bran went forthwith to his bedchamber and closed the door.

# Thirteen

At the other side of the house, Aurora nodded in a chair, but remained alert to every creak and groan of the old house. She fully roused herself then, swung her legs from their curled position to place her feet on the bare floor. Had there been footsteps just now out in the hall, or had she only imagined them? It must be that she was just apprehensive.

Aurora had been terrified after giving Melanie a little push into Bran's room and then closing the door on her. She had stood there in the hall, waiting for the house to come down around her ears, but all she had heard was the snapping of a log in the grate and an occasional creaking of that huge scarlet-and-black bed. She had blushed then, expecting that her naughty deed had been accomplished. The master was bedding Melanie, his bride-to-be. She had hurtled herself back to her own sanctuary then, shutting the door and leaning back against it, her heart beating rapidly. That had been an hour ago.

Come morning Melanie would not remember the past night's strange events. But Bran Ravenleigh was certain to! How perfectly she had deceived him, saying she would change into something more "comfortable" and be back promptly after that. Even

223

as she had stood there in his room, the little violet demons dancing in her eyes, she was certain she had impressed him with her charms. He had actually believed she would skip back merrily to his waiting arms!

Alack! If he hadn't found pleasure in Melanie's limp arms, he would most likely lie awake the night, figuring how to get even with her.

She shivered now as she drew her linen nightgown over her head and tugged it down over her body, wondering what destruction Bran Ravenleigh had in mind for her. Well, one thing was certain, if nothing else had come of it—she had thrown cold water on Bran's craving for her!

Aurora lay down on the cool bed, her mind all awhirl as she tried to envision the tall phantom Fay so that she could dream sweet comforting dreams of him. Her lashes fluttered shut. Tall . . . handsome . . . just like . . .

Such a lovely place to escape to with sundrops all around and buttercups swaying in a gentle breeze. The woodsy air smelled pungent. Or was she only imagining it? No matter, for now there wasn't a care in the world and all she wanted was to have nature touch her while she strolled in sunshine and in tree shadow.

Who is that, standing there against the verdant woodland scene? Or is it just a tree, spreading its arms—in a haunted forest? *Come closer and see*, it seemed to say with leafy branches beckoning her. Or were they arms of a man?

Aurora walked—or was she floating? Her turquoise skirts and pink satin petticoats stirred the grayish-white veils of swirling fog at her slippered feet. She did not own such a dress, nor had she ever seen these fine golden slippers she wore.

Her head lifted and she remarked the smoky-gray eyes of the tree. Eyes? A tree that has eyes? Was it going to speak to her too? But how could this be?

*"Do not be afraid, Aurora Gregory."*

*"Oh!"*

*"Sit here, beneath my shade."*

*"Remember the summer house?"* Another voice, softer.

*"I remember."*

*"I appreciate your coming to visit me, little Ro."*

*"Mama!"*

*"I have been so, oh so lonely, my sweet child."*

Aurora noticed that Deana wore a white dress as fine as cobweb, and her hair seemed to be made of the same. It was white and frail, just like her face.

*"Why are you here, Mama?"*

*"I am here to tell you a story, about a lovely young woman. A love story. I may not have time to tell it all, but I shall come again to finish it. Would you like that?"*

*"Oh yes, Mama, I'd adore that. Is it the same one you told me when I was smaller?"*

*"Just lie back and close your eyes. You shall see, my pet."*

As Deana ordered, Aurora made herself comfortable. Colors soon swirled in her head and Deana's voice, so soft and angelic, faded until becoming mere whispers. Aurora spun round and round, like a frail leaf in a whirlwind.

*"Once upon a time . . . live your dreams, Aurora . . .*

*"Yer Aurora Gregory, a well-born lass."*

Hetty was shaking a fat spoon at her.

*"Dinna wander far. Promise you won't go near Raven Keep, the landlord's house."*

*"Promise, Ro will be good."*

Man is called a roué or a rogue if he takes more than one woman. Hetty had said that?

The wood grew darker.

*"Do you know where you are? You are on the grounds of Raven Keep . . . You may call me Javier . . ."*

*"Mama!"*

*"You will remember nothing of what you have seen."*

*"Mama. Do not die!"*

*"Hush child, I am still here. Watch the rest of the story, sweet . . ."*

*"I like it here with you and Cousin Melly and Aunt Margaret, Uncle . . . I love Cupid!"*

*"Cast your eyes downward, for those men in the booth are looking this way . . . Finish your oatmeal, but be sure to drink all of your milk!"*

Aurora's eyes roamed over the tall figure so darkly clothed . . . sweeping lines of a cape and wide circle of a cavalier hat . . . in mystery.

She saw the rakishly handsome man tilt his head and kiss the serving wench—on the breast! How dare they!

*"Ahem, sorry ladies . . ."*

*"Mama, 'tis Bran Ravenleigh!"*

*"Yes, I know, sweetheart."*

*"Take him away, Mama! He is the one who had been fondling the serving wench! I hate him! I hate him!"*

*"You must wake now, child. You are becoming much too excited. I shall return to you, my dearest darling."*

Aurora woke with a start. Sweat bathed her upper lip in tiny beads. Was it morning? But she felt as if she had been asleep for hours, as there persisted an ache in the small of her back. Perhaps her time of month had come, for it was due. She slithered to the edge of the bed and, upon checking herself further she found that this was not the case.

"Ro, are ye awake?" Hetty's tentative voice came from out of the dark.

"Oh! Hetty! You indeed frightened me half to death."

"Sure and I be scared to death meself. Did ye not hear it?"

"Hear what, Hetty?" Aurora's own voice trembled.

"Why did ye wake, lass? Did ye not hear voices? Was nae a human's voice wi'out the door. Oooh! I canna hardly say it, luv, but 'twas the spirit of a dead person!" Hetty groaned, hiding beneath her coverlet.

"Couldst thou be imagining things, Hetty, being in a strange house?" Aurora inquired, already feeling at the foot of the little bed for her shawl.

"Nay, 'tis my thinking there be strong spirits in this old keep. Near the haunted loch in Scotland where I lived 'twas such spirits wandering the hollows."

"I shall go see to put your mind at rest, Hetty. It

could very well be that someone in the house is ill—the reason for the disturbing sounds you hear—and I could be of some assistance," the healing spirit in Aurora said as she fastened her herb-pouch to her rail. "Anyway, Hetty, my belief is that spirits of the dead cannot harm you, 'tis only the living can do that!"

And with that Bran Ravenleigh entered Aurora's mind unbidden as she slipped quietly and tentatively from the room. She checked the southest great chamber first, the room reserved for man and wife. Melanie would share it with her groom in the near future. Though one could call Melanie a mean-spirited person, Aurora felt that her cousin was getting more gay seducer than she had bargained for, as Bran Ravenleigh was no man to be faithful and true, and Aurora couldn't help but feeling sorry for Melanie.

Aurora knew a moment's sore regret at her deception of the night before—but only for Melanie. Bran Ravenleigh could go to the nether regions!

Indeed it was early morning, for she could see the daystar shining big and bright in the east through the window. There was no one in here, as she had expected there wouldn't be. But she gave one last glimpse to the Elizabethan bed which was a riot of deep carving, and closed the door softly, thinking *poor, poor Melanie*.

Her steps led her to the back stairs, for some reason, where she could hear snatches of conversation drifting up to her. My, she thought, servants gossiping so early in the morning and a mighty ruckus at that. She sighed with relief. Now she could go back and tell Hetty that what she had heard was merely gossiping tittle-tattle of the servants. Nothing in that would prevent the Scotswoman, who loved a chat, from rising swiftly and going down to a pot of tea and hot buttered scones.

About to walk back to the east wing, Aurora paused when the voice of a young female servant floated up to her.

"Young Master Bran's done up in a black mood. Snatched a cup of coffee and a scone and 'way he went . . ." She trailed into whispering and the next thing Aurora heard was "That Mistress Wellbeloved's got a swollen head this morning. Should just hear her rantin' and ravin' at this early hour about not having something already up in her belly from the kitchen. Heh! She be needing something to tidy her brain!"

"Mrs. Minter'll tidy your brain should she hear you," a deep male voice put in.

Now Aurura heard the rattling of a tray coming up the stairs. She searched frantically to the left and the right, seeking a place to conceal herself. She didn't want to be caught eavesdropping, nay, she already had the wrath of the young master on her head. She was poised for breaking into flight when another voice, gruff and all male, came from the back of the west wing. Sir Eric? It must be none other, judging by the rule-the-roost tone.

What could be her excuse for being at this end of the house, so early in the morn? Oh, sir, I was looking for spirits? Or—I am sorry to be such a nuisance, but do you thinks perhaps my breakfast is ready? Aurora stifled what would have been a tense chuckle. So, where in God's name could she hide now? There was only one answer to that, one place in the house she truly wished to avoid.

Like a vaporous wraith Aurora slipped unnoticed into Bran's bedchamber and eased the door shut, ever so carefully, so as not to make a single creak. She listened at the wood now, hearing the smart two-note tapping of tall boots and cane pass by the chamber in which she was concealed. The servant and the senior master of the house could be heard to converse.

"Has my grandson broke the fast yet?"

"Nay, sir," Lucy paused timorously as she watched Sir Eric straighten the ruff about his neck. "I mean him and the manservant Tom Bone left about an hour ago. Said to tell ya they'd be back in time to sup this evening, sir. I was ah—just taking this tray to the Mistress Wellblood. She—"

"Gone again!" Sir Eric snorted of his grandson, rudely interrupting the servant. "Ah-hah, Melanie—*Wellbeloved*, Lucy—she is still abed, poor girl." He coughed. "Losing first her husband and now her parents. Hoped she'd be up and around to greet our other guests tonight."

"Me and the other servants hope so too, sir. She's the young master's especial guest and—"

"That will be enough, Lucy! Be about your business then," Sir Eric ordered, striding in his cavalier fashion along the hall and to the principal staircase. Poor girl indeed! he thought darkly. He had heard from Mrs. Minter that she (Wellblood. Hah! That's a good one, Lucy) had been intoxicated ever since entering his household. Ida had also hinted that there may have been some goings-on in

230

Master Bran's chamber between him and the blond tart. If his grandson was of a mind to start bringing his hell-hags here, Sir Eric would put a stop to that before going too far! To boot, he didn't like Melanie's attitude. The tart was up to no good.

"No good whores. Devil-women. Wenches. Hell-hags," Sir Eric grumbled along with his heartburn to the stairs. "Thigh-bent sluts. Fallen women. . . ."

Bending an ear, Aurora had been pressed alongside the door, afraid all the while that Sir Eric might step into the room. Alas! How would she have explained her being here, if that cranky bear of a man had peeped behind the door?

She was just about to crack the door and listen if all was safe for her to beat a hasty retreat, when her eyes fell on the elegant leather-bound chest. The sight of it had intrigued her the evening before and now . . . now she was powerless to leave the room! It seemed to be beckoning her. Pushing from the wall, her feet moving as if possessed of a will all their own, Aurora found herself gazing down upon it in overwhelming wonder.

"What am I doing?" she questioned herself. "Why does something tell me I must search inside?" Her flesh-and-bones shivered. "Hetty was right." She gulped. "There *is* some strong spirit, or two, that moves me now against my will."

And so, Aurora undid the olive-green straps, and the brass lock clicked open easily beneath her hand. She lifted the leather-bound top, swinging it high and wide to rest at the bedstead. There was nothing here but some old books, journals, and at the bottom there rested a round raven-marked shield. Why was this latter not hanging in the gallery with the other coats of arms which must surely be hanging there? She shrugged, deeming it none of her business, which brought her again to wondering why she was snooping into another's personal property.

Such morbid curiosity. Shame, for shame on you, Aurora Gregory! her conscience chided.

When she would have closed the lid, her mesmerized glance fell on the journal a second time. She could not look away now, though she tried to tear her gaze from it. Her hand moved toward it irresistibly.

The journal was in her burning, trembling grip now. Running her eye over the cover she read *Journal of Derek Ravenscar*. Why, he must have been an ancestor of the Ravenleighs! Such a strong, romantic-sounding name. It almost touched on the infamous, like a pirate or a rakehell. He must have been a replica of Bran Ravenleigh, who wrote the book on rakehells. With this in mind she was just about to replace it when voices out in the corridor startled her into dropping the journal.

"Alas, now I shall be found out!" Aurora cried softly to herself, wishing too late that she had gone back to her room.

The voices of the servant Lucy and Ida Minter retreated and Aurora thankfully heard the back stairs creak beneath the weight of the two women. Aurora had heard the imperious housekeeper scolding her underling for an infraction. Now all was hushed once more.

Sweeping up the journal that had fallen onto the carpet, Aurora's fingers came in contact with a bit of yellowed parchment. It must have fallen from the journal, she determined. In the process of tucking it back into the pages, Aurora suddenly gasped, a rapt look coming over her face.

"Oh, Lord, what have I come across?" she groaned and then asked herself, "Can this truly be the other half of the parchment that is in my possession?"

It must be, she concluded next, for the wide scrawling was the same and this upper half would fit hers exactly!

Great riches. Love. Find the other half, Ro, and you shall find love too. These had been Elvy Well-beloved's dying words.

Oh! What shall I do now? Aurora agonized in this her new dilemma. Her half of the map actually did not belong to her—but to the Ravenleighs!

She must make doubly sure. She examined the map closely, poring over each and every detail. Aye, she was certain. She would have to return to Raven Keep somehow, someday. If the bit of parchment was discovered in her possession she would be accused of theft, for dead men did not speak, and no one else at his deathbed had seen him slip it to her. Theft. The word rang in her ears. Accused, especially now that she had been a visitor here. Bran Ravenleigh would wreak his revenge then. Oh, indeed, he was a cruel man.

Hurriedly and unthinkingly, Aurora tucked the parchment inside her rail, closed the lid of the chest, secured the straps, and fled the room as if those spirits nipped at her heels. Excitement overrode caution, but she was lucky as no one was to be seen in the corridor. As she sped to the east wing, her mind flew hither and yon, finally snagging on two disturbing suspicions:

Elvy Wellbeloved. Derek Ravenscar. Had they been enemies, or—now she felt a mystifying tremor pass through her being—something more than that? Like blood relatives!

## Fourteen

Candlelight winked in the small, upper room. The day's work had been utterly tiring and Rachel Smythe, having drunk too much with a lonely young sailor who had followed her up to her room, settled down for some sorely needed sleep.

Rachel smiled, satiated. The lad had done her justice, indeed, just when she had most needed it. He had tossed sidelong glances at her all evening and the stage had been set for a lusty tumble. The handsome young man had been floundering in the same lonely sea as she. He had had hair the color of ripe wheat. His arms had been strong, as had other parts of him. The smell of their lovemaking still clung to the sheets.

Why had she asked him to leave so soon, she wondered now? She was excited all over again, but there was only one man who made her a complete woman. He was the satisfier; no man equaled him in lovemaking: Bran Ravenleigh. And she'd had many. She hiccoughed. Too many.

She did not love Bran. She did not actually know the meaning of love. She knew that she would end up with a man like Jake Randolph, a man whose motto was "home sweet home." He had made love to her

235

quietly, asking no questions but fascinated with her daring seductress type. They could be happy, Jake and her. She had only to forsake her past and all other loves, even . . . Javier Strang.

Rachel started suddenly at a noise outside her door. All the wenches but one were abed, and the one that remained up, sweeping the floors and putting down fresh rushes, was a mousey girl that never took lovers to her room.

Her door opened unceremoniously and she knew at once by instinct who was there. In a daze she listened to his bold entrance into the room, the bottle and cups he carried banging against the door. On rounded hips she rolled to sit up in bed. She faced him squarely as he kicked the door shut with his heel. Even in the dim light the black coals of his eyes burned into hers. His black hair waved rakishly over his eyes, brushing the eyebrows that lifted the corners at a satanic angle. The white lace peeping from his rust velvet coat stood out from the glistening darkness of his skin. He took in the room with one glance, prying into the darkened corners as if expecting someone to step out from hiding. All of a sudden he was not so certain.

"You *are* alone?" he asked cautiously, his voice slurred thickly.

"I am."

Rachel bounced from the bed to shakily light another taper. She would rather there be more light, for she sensed something in the pirate, a cruelty that he had been unleashing little by little, as he saw her, that now he would shake out fully. The pirate personified evil, but never more than she saw in him

236

at this visit.

Pirate Strang's nose twitched curiously while he took in the carelessly rumpled bed covers. He swung his gaze back to Rachel, raking her woman's outline in the cotton nightdress accusingly.

"You would sleep with anyone." He snorted with a disgust that was ironic for him. "Scarlet woman, who was he this time, eh? Who did you spread your white whore's legs for? Ah! Do not tell me. Was it Bran Ravenleigh, master of the whores, huh, *Senorita* Slut?"

With a cry of utter fury, Rachel met his lascivious gaze. Her own eyes were steady and unafraid as he stepped closer, setting the bottle and cups down with a dull thud.

"Get out!" Rachel snarled, backing up.

Casually and unaffected by her order, he poured himself a fiery cup of liquid and downed it as if he had known a great thirst. He wiped his thin lips on the arm of his coat and Rachel stared at the dark smudge on the velvet cloth. She lifted her eyes, hating him. Suddenly Javier slapped her angry, upturned face. Blood flowed from a cut lip; an instant later it was swollen and purple. Without emotion she picked up a corner of her bedsheet and dabbed carefully to clean the blood from her mouth and chin.

"So, you are like a crazy woman when I speak ill of the Ravenleigh scion, your lover, eh?" He swiped up another drink and killed it. "Answer me, trollop! You should know something then, if you will not speak."

"How could I ever have loved your touch? I know

you and *he* did not duel." A sad bitterness was welling up in her bosom along with a memory.

"You *know* how Jason Ravenleigh died?" He hoisted a dark eyebrow higher, a dark arrow of evilness.

"Aye. You are *boasting*, I know you murdered him. Now I see why you took me from Raven Keep and—my lover."

His lips curled up over small, yellowed teeth. "You mean your dead lover, *si?*"

Javier laughed and snarled and laughed some more, his swarthy countenance glowing red and black in the deep candle glow, making him look like Satan himself.

Rachel made to move past him hurriedly, but he was quick to grab her around to face him with one vise-like hand and swatted her with the open hand of the other. Midnight hair flew out with the impact and then came tumbling back down about her half-naked shoulders. His eyes narrowed in on the shivering black strands resting on the white flesh. He snarled the hair in his hands, fingers tugging her closer while he lowered his lips.

"Nay, you'll not have me! Pig, do not kiss me with your foul lips. I hate your evil soul—"

"I shall do with you as I want, slut. And there is more to come! When I am finished here, you will be sorry you have ever met Javier Strang!"

Rachel tried furiously to squirm free of his ruthless banding arms but could not; neither could she reject his crushing and painful kisses that ravaged her soft, full woman's lips. He shoved her back with swift force, causing her to tumble in a sprawl on the mussed bed.

"Open your legs, tavern slut!"

He fell full weight on the bed, but missed his fleshy mark. Seeing her chance, Rachel bounded from the bed while he was struggling to grab hold of her ankle, at the same time trying to rise. Rachel was swifter, for Javier was by far the more intoxicated. His legs quickened then and he pursued her across the short space. He caught her at the door, snatching her by the arm and slamming her hard against the wall. He panted as he spoke.

"So, you would rather not share a bed with Javier, eh? That is much too bad." His eyes glowed with a dark threat.

Baring her breasts with a swipe of his hand, his lips fell to kiss and nibble. When he bit hard she cried out. He lifted his head, still smiling that snarling smile, pinning her shoulders and back to the wall, stretching her now weakened arms high above her head. He undid his breeches, letting them fall to the floor.

Rachel knew what was coming next and hatred blazed out at him from her dusky eyes. All emotion seemed to have drained from her by the time he thrust deeply, once, but she couldn't help crying out from the swordlike pain. His thin hips worked in vigorous, pounding action, all but lifting her as he rammed and tore. Rachel had never been taken so brutally; Bran had been rough at times, but never put her through this particular kind of hell.

The pirate grunted and wallowed in the one-sided lust, like the pig that he was. To further humiliate and degrade her, Javier, just beginning to twitch, withdrew to spurt all over her, mingling it with the blood on her thighs.

Shakily he stepped back, lifted his breeches nonchalantly and withdrew a dagger from his belt. In the other hand he grabbed a handful of silken hair, twisting it about his fingers, drawing her miserable face closer, closer.

Like a rakish pirate craft stealing through fog, the *Enchantress* had slipped away from the Ravenleigh wharf at dawn. On a southwest breeze they moved into the broad channel of the James. Bran grew restless when they were far out into the river and took the tiller from Jonsey. The new mate was a good seaman but was as yet unfamiliar with these waters.

The sloop flew like a gull at sea beneath Bran's skillful steering. Though his lean body relaxed and his lungs filled with the sweet, moister air off the river, there was no ease for the ache in his loins.

"Women!" he snorted to himself. "Are they worth all the strife which they put a man through? Nay," he replied to his own question, feeling at the moment that his displeasure and irritation touched them all. Even . . .

He turned his thoughts to a lesser evil. Hah! He wasn't sure now if indeed Captain Strang was the lesser of the two evils. Women. Revenge. The first he had had aplenty, but the latter kept evading him. With each passing day his desire for revenge plunged deeper. His hatred of the sea merchant, nay, *the pirate*, had grown to its fullest measure since he had seen from afar the bastard fondling Aurora Gregory. Her stepfather? That was a laugh, to be sure!

And Melanie. What had happened to his craving for the blond widow? Damn, he knew the answer, or thought he did. Could it merely be that he had tired of Melanie already, as he had with others before her? That was not the answer either, he snorted through his aquiline nose, for he had not even bedded the woman one time. With Melanie he had not experienced the churning in his loins as he had with the wraithful servant Aurora the evening before.

She could be shy, this Aurora Gregory, but beneath her timidity he had sensed a rather sensual nature and a desperate longing for love. Her countenance was delicately wrought and she walked more lightly than any sweet fresh wind stealing over the ground. Her eyes were like English heather and he confessed them to be set somewhat like Melanie's, but instead of a merry brilliance they possessed a deep, mysterious glow, in a face an artist would find beautiful to paint. True, there was something about her that haunted him all the hours since he had first met her yesterday. She set his body and soul strangely on fire. What was this strange desire for her that had grown until now it possessed him wholly, leaving room for no other thought, no other desire? This last enlightenment gave him a little jar. He could not rest until he knew for certain.

Damn, but he would find all his answers soon enough, or call himself a fool if he didn't. In the past he had always demonstrated a stubborn determination to get what he wanted, material or otherwise, regardless of the odds against him or the dangers involved. And now he was more determined than ever to find the bastard Strang, plus solve this new and perplexing mystery of Aurora Gregory. Was she his sought-after raven-haired wench?

If that was not enough, added to everything else, Ravenscar's journal—and Jason's—were proving to be puzzlers he must still piece together. On one page Jason had seemingly written of a "he" who was a constant "plague on his soule" and would "he" never stop harassing him and give him peace? The "two men" kept at him each and every day while he was out riding his horse "Jewel" until he thought he would surely go insane.

Now, Bran thought with a diabolical grin, that could very well mean that Strang and another had been after the buried treasure and Jason's helplessness could have indicated his trying to explain, quite in exasperation, that he knew of no treasure. Bran's smile grew more sinister. That other "he" was none other than Rufo Savage's "white eyes." He would find this blond, blue-eyed man if he must rake the entire colony by searching into every nook and corner for the rest of his life.

When Bran and Tom moored at Jamestown and disembarked, the gossip in the crowded streets centered around Nathaniel Bacon. The people were cast into bewilderment. The governor had pardoned the young Nathaniel and decided to permit him take his seat in the Assembly. Sir William promised Nathaniel a commission to go against the Indians and word was sent upriver to this effect. The elder councillors thought privately that Berkeley returned Bacon to the council to appease the people of the colony, and soon Berkeley admitted as much, for this would keep the hero of the unruly ones out of the House of Burgesses.

"In the House, Nathaniel may just provoke more trouble," Sir William was heard to have said.

Bran and Tom, having had their fill of gossip for now, made their way to the inn where they would rest up a bit and nourish themselves. Frowning, Bran could not forget what he'd heard and vented his own anger in the air of the cooler spring morning.

"The crabbed, autocratic old goat of a governor, he shall soon change his mind again. No doubt our Nathaniel Bacon and his men will be made prisoners. Sir William cares not to resolve the Indian problem in our king's colony, to my way of thinking. And all the while the savages daily spill blood, murdering inhumanely!"

"Nathaniel's men?" Tom cocked a bushy, sun-streaked eyebrow.

"Oho! Think you he will find me out and put me under arrest? Remember, my friend, soon the elections will be held, and I've a good impression from the gossip here that I shall be chosen by the electorate to represent Elizabeth County in the new Assembly." Bran removed and slapped his gauntlets against his thigh.

"Hell," Tom began, "the governor is a sly old man. He knows everything. Don't you know, Master Bran, you could be arrested along with the others?"

Bran touched his belt and weapon in almost a caressing gesture. "Think you that I would cower from the governor and his lynchmen? I never forget, Tom, that justice too has a sword."

"Aye, you are in love, my friend."

"What's that you say!" Bran almost snapped Tom's head off.

"You are not an Englishman anymore, Bran Ravenleigh, you are a wild Virginian. You love Virginia as I do, she is in your rebel's blood, this savage, wooded place, which your English king rules."

Bran grimaced. "Hell's fire, I hardly know who or what I love anymore, Tom. But you may be right about one thing—we seditionists share the same thing."

"Master?" Tom's expressive brows rose in question.

"Rebel's blood, Tom," Bran chuckled for the first time in several days.

Upon reaching the inn, Bran told Tom to go ahead and begin without him. He would join him in half an hour's time at the table.

"But be sure to have some spirits for me, Tom."

"Sure you don't need more time than that, Master Bran?" Tom chuckled, winking slyly.

"Positive, Tom. Lawrence tells me Rachel is ailing. I just thought she was in need of a bit of cheering up, that is all." But his eyes sparkled.

"Mmmm-hmmm," Tom murmured as he was already biting into a joint of turkey.

Upstairs in the small room, Rachel's face was grim when Bran entered after several knocks on the door. She had been slow to call out entry.

"I'm so happy to see you, Bran," she declared tearfully.

"You could have fooled me," the tall man said as

he moved into the mustiness of the heavily curtained room. The air reeked of bad liquor and stale tobacco, causing Bran's nose to wrinkle automatically, as it had many times before.

Rachel, reclining among the mussed covers and strewn pillows on the bed, drew from concealment somewhere beneath the yellowed sheets a lean French dagger.

"Ho!" Bran furrowed his brow in surprise. "What's this?"

"I am saving it—for a certain sailor. You alone will ever know I've got it." She shrugged beneath his deepening frown and stashed the blade while Bran watched warily.

Bran waited, tense as a black panther about to spring as her story unfolded.

"I was happy, Bran. Happy being . . . Jason Ravenleigh's mistress. No, wait and hear me out. Sit back down." Rachel gestured weakly and then went on, somewhat confused herself. "Hell . . . Jason was happy too. I had even quit my job as chambermaid for the Randolphs. Then after your uncle died mysteriously, Javier appeared one night as I lay half asleep weeping on Jason's bed. Javier, like a phantom of the night, stole into the bedchamber. I think he was searching for something—and then he saw me. Sick in body and soul, there was no place for me to go, so I went with Javier. Away from Raven Keep and its memories, on the sailor's black brigantine. I don't know why I went with him. I guess it was because that Minter woman wanted me out, and I, yes, I was afraid when Jason died. One day he was alive, the next—he was no more. Javier said we had to get away. *We*. Or be accused of murdering Jason. I had not dreamed those days that Strang had slain Jason."

"Rachel—" Bran faltered. "Rachel, remove your cap for me now, will you?"

A strangled gasp came from the bed. "No! Bran, do not ask this of me. I—I can't . . ."

Bran flew from his chair by the hearth and, seeming intent on attacking the serving wench, fell on her and snatched the pert cap from her head. Raven hair, hacked boyishly short, sprang free in all directions.

"What the devil . . ." Bran breathed in disbelief, lifting a hand to touch a broom-like strand. He could not believe this poor soul, this wretched-looking woman, was the same lusty wench he had shared a bed with so often during the several years past.

"Aye, a rat's nest!" she snorted, shoving the comforting hand aside as she snatched up the cap and fitted it around her once lovely hair.

Silence reigned as Bran took himself back to the chair, dragging his feet as he lowered himself down, continuing to stare as if Rachel Smythe were some hideous apparition. The fires of hatred churned in his belly, but he bided his time to hear the rest of the sordid story.

"Don't look at me that way, Bran. I can't stand it. I know what you think and yes, I did try to keep you from seeing my hair many times . . . before this . . . when it was long and pretty. It was always dark in this room, remember? and I wouldn't let you see my hair? I knew all along you searched for your uncle's murderer and—"

"And you did not want me to learn that you, you with the raven hair, had been Jason's mistress." Bran sighed tiredly, saw a vision at the same time of a little face framed with the same midnight hair. Alas! Why hadn't he realized it before? Aurora Gregory would have to have been a much younger woman than Rachel. Nay, Aurora had been merely a girl— perhaps only twelve or thirteen, counting back. Aye, the pieces of the puzzle were beginning to fall into place. But there were yet many remaining.

Rachel's voice broke now and then as she continued. "Not long ago, Javier came here to taunt me, boasting of the evil deed. It was no duel like some of the gossipmongers thought. When I would see that ravager no more . . . he forced me to lay as if I was a tavern slut . . . and laughed. I'm no slut, Bran!" She sobbed for a moment, then dried her eyes. "Then he did this, as if to warn me to keep my lips sealed." Her hand that had slipped up to the cap, now fell limply to the bed. "It pleased his slimy evil soul, but he did not kill me. He enjoyed my spite too much. He loved tearing me, ramming into me and making me bleed. I . . . I loved that animal for a time, and if you should ask me why I could not tell you!"

"Rachel," Bran's voice was hoarse as he began, "there is someone else, a man I must ask you about. Strang is of dark countenance, but this other I seek is fair—the total opposite of Strang. Do you know of whom I speak?" he ended with as gentle a voice as he could manage under the circumstances.

"I know of no other man. Javier was always alone when he came to Raven Keep—as far as I know," she replied, her head hung low.

Rachel stared sightlessly upon the bed, and when finally she looked up, Bran's chair was empty and the door to her room was open wide.

Bran and Tom spent the remainder of the sunny afternoon scouring the taverns and streets for word of the sea merchant. They learned that Captain Strang now had four vessels, all of them marauders. A Cornishman who had sailed with Strang but had had several bitter imbroglios with the man, said that they were in the habit of preying on Spanish slave ships at great profit. Though Captain Strang longed for Jamestown, he rarely ventured north. While in his cups, the Cornishman blabbed carelessly, his hatred for the captain unmistakable to Bran and Tom.

So, discovering Strang's home seat in Lower Norfolk, Bran and Tom hastened to the sloop. They sailed on a freshened wind downriver, and unrecognized among others who went there to trade in smuggled goods, the two stealthy men made a thorough reconnaissance of the place. They discovered that several planters, upriver and down, found business association with the pirate a great profit. Bran and Tom swaggered casually into the warehouse, as if they had done so many times before.

"So, friends, what'll it be today?" a huge man in a begrimed broadcloth coat stepped up to them. A huge, cherry-red nose attested to his liking for strong spirits. "Could you be in the market for some Turkey carpets? In good condition, you know, they come in just last week."

"Nay, my friend," Bran started out. "'Tis the good captain I am craving to speak with."

"How now, guv'nor?" Strang's agent said, his

spittle riding in a wide arc out the door.

"Business—umm—private," Bran returned.

"Waaall now," the agent drawled, looking Bran over from dark head to immaculate boot. "Most like in a week the captain should slip in with a new load. He'll have some choice household slaves, if that's yer business. Some of them even got nice big bubs. You kin buy a li'l nigger for your lady cheap enough."

"That is exactly what I had in mind," Bran took up. "Good day, mate. I shall try and return at that time."

"Eyyy," the agent called out the door as they were leaving, "better not make it any longer than that. The good slaves go fast. And if you be wantin' to catch the captain, the same goes. He ain't around long afore he ships out again."

"No lie," Bran said under his breath. "Thanks, mate, I'll remember that. Good day, again," Bran called back, then walked unhurriedly with Tom back to the sloop.

Bran's brain ticked fast with plans once on board the *Enchantress* again. He had taken note that Strang's agents were well prepared to defend the busy hive from attack by sea, being armed against other marauding pirates. But not from a surprise movement, an attack by land. Aye, he and Tom, and a few of his own well-knit Welsh servants, could pull it off and withdraw unscathed. Indeed, he would sting the pirate once, then plan the second attack, and then at last, the final sting. They would choose a moonless night, stealthily set fire to the warehouse, and burn it down with all its contents.

Revenge reared its ugly head as it was Bran's plan

to totally destroy this enemy of his and Sir Eric's.

"'Pon my soul!" Sir Eric snarled as he came bounding from the house. "Why do you pluck my prize flowers?"

"I am so very sorry, sir," Aurora said, totally embarrassed. She had concealed the sweet bouquet behind her drab, dun skirts when first he bellowed. But now she held the pink meadowsweet out for him to see.

"Hrumph! So 'tis not my prize flowers, just some wildflowers," he said gruffly, waving off the proffered bouquet. "Well, who are they for?" he asked sulkily.

"I thought mayhap they would cheer my . . ." She thought a moment, then decided truth the best course with this wise, elderly man—"my cousin, Melanie, sir."

"Melanie? Ahh, of course. How come I thought you was a servant? What is your name, girl?" He rapped out the questions.

"My cousins wishes that I serve her, sir," Aurora said truthfully, "in this her mourning time. My name is Aurora Gregory, sir, and forgive me for not asking your permission to pick the flowers."

"Never mind that now, 'tis done!"

When Aurora bobbed a curtsy, Sir Eric smiled in genuine pleasure. Aurora decided suddenly that she liked this older man who at first had seemed to her a grump. He reminded her somewhat of Mr. Well-beloved, but where Elvy had been sickly, Sir Eric was very much alive and well.

"Come inside then . . . ah . . . Aurora Gregory.

We'll put those pink posies of Melanie's into a vase. You and I shall sit and converse awhile, as the whole bloody house seems to be otherwise occupied. My grandson ain't here. The guests must've got drunk on the way. God's nightgown! 'tis almost time for the evening sup. Do you crave wine?"

"Tea will be fine, sir."

"Sit then, and call me Eric. I'd like that very much, Aurora Gregory."

And so began the first of many long visits Aurora was to have with Eric Ravenleigh during her stay. They hit it off grandly from the first sitting and Sir Eric was very pleased at her well-turned manner of speaking. He discovered, too, that she was learned in books, besides having a way with herbs for medicinal use. Aurora in turn listened intently as he spoke of the moors of Kent in England, the Stuart court, and his beloved grandson, Bran.

Even when David Wiley—a friend of the Edwardses and Melanie's childhood playmate—arrived with a man by the name of Jim Crews, they kept up their conversation. David Wiley trailed along when they moved out onto the terrace, and Sir Eric entertained them with tales from his Cavalier days when he was Master of the Horse for Charles I.

By the time the banquet was being laid out in the hall, three more guests arrived. It was the Pruetts and their pretty, though vacuous, young daughter Penelope who was fanning herself vigorously, making her blond curls blow about her pinkened cheeks very prettily.

"Alas," Penelope exclaimed in her snobbishly conceited manner, "I feared whene'er we came upon a turn in the wood that mayhap those red barbarians would attack. Oooh! I crave some wine before I swoon."

Mama, Amy Pruett, rushed to her daughter with a half-filled goblet of Madeira she had fetched herself from the sideboard. Penelope held her hand out in a limp fashion and received the libation, downing half of it, then without blinking a lash, the rest. Aurora, too, did not blink, but it was only because she was thinking that Penelope and Melanie should have been cousins, so much alike were they in coloring and mannerisms. But that was where the likenesses stopped, for Aurora concluded that Melanie was by far the prettier, and to be sure it was not because she was prejudiced.

"Pooh-pooh, baby," Amy Pruett fussed over her daughter. "'Tain't no Injuns south of the fall line. Papa says so, and you know Papa's always right, baby." Mrs. Pruett tossed a quick look into the house from the terrace. "Now, where did Papa go, honey?" She bent solicitously to adjust Penelope's shawl.

Sir Eric tapped his walnut cane on the flags to get her attention. "Most likely went up with Mr. Minter with your bags. Up in the bridal chamber, if you'd like to go check it out and rest up a spell, mistress."

"Ooh-ooh," she fluttered and giggled. "Hear that, baby, we get the bridal chamber. You are too too generous, Sir Eric."

"Think nothing of it, mistress," Sir Eric replied with a wave of his hand.

Her mind preoccupied with Mrs. Pruett's words concerning Indians, Aurora graciously excused herself from the newly arrived company and Sir Eric.

252

Her spirits had dropped low as she remembered that Margaret and Jeremias would not be joining them at the banquet.

"I shall never enjoy their loving presence again," Aurora said softly to herself as she mounted the stairs to the east wing.

Back at the terrace, David Wiley watched Aurora Gregory's dejected frame move slowly into the house. He spoke mostly in monosyllables, lending an attentive air to the company, while at the same time his mind flew to his childhood sweetheart upstairs. He had not seen her for several years, and they had quarreled just before her ill-suited marriage to Mr. Wellbeloved. David had always wanted Melanie for his own, but he had not been moneyed enough or propertied as she would have liked him to be.

"Let's go inside now, folks," Sir Eric began, "the air in this deuced colony grows chilled as soon as the sun hides its face. I shall have Minter light a fire and fetch us a fresh bottle of Madeira from the cellar." He glanced back toward the river bathed in twilight, as he wondered just what in hell was keeping Bran and Tom Bone. It would not do for Bran to stand up his guests. Again he pondered the reason for this lordly feast, snorting to himself as he thought indignantly of the blond woman upstairs who had risen early in the afternoon and had been sitting at her grande toilette since. And who was this David Wiley? All he had gotten out of it was that this David was a family friend to the Edwardses.

David Wiley swaggered to the hearth and snickered at his reflection mirrored in the gleaming surface of a kettle that hung above the mantel. He surveyed his ruffs of fine linen and girdle of gold with satisfaction, deciding that fancy new clothes did indeed make the man. He had almost had to sell his soul to obtain these new threads. He had discovered only yesterday upon visiting North Creek that Melanie had gone off with her cousin and servant to Raven Keep. And so, uninvited, he had followed his long-awaited love here. He had never been inside the walls of this big house, but now fortune smiled on him and just maybe in more ways than one. He was inside and that was all that counted.

David Wiley had met on the road a man by the name of Jim Crews who was also on his way to Raven Keep and they had ridden the last remaining miles together, with Crews none the wiser that David was not among those invited here this weekend.

With a keen eye Sir Eric had been observing David Wiley. He was a slick man in manners and speech. With a nasal-sounding voice, Wiley had displayed a sinisterly debonair manner as he bowed and kissed Penelope's hand. Sir Eric now walked over to where David Wiley stood.

"You have heard of Mistress Melanie's loss?" the older man asked simply.

"I'd almost forgotten about that, sir. Ivory, the butler at North Creek was nearly in tears, and all I could get from him was that the Edwardses had met with an unfortunate accident. Was it Indians then?" Wiley inquired, turning questioning blue eyes on the master of Raven Keep.

"Aye. Poor girl. She's been abed most of the time since she arrived. I take it you are an old friend of hers?"

"Since we were very small. My parents used to visit with hers . . . that is before mine passed on from the swamp fever. Both of them, they went just like that." He snapped together long white fingers.

"Ah, then you must know how very bad she is feeling. Why . . . why don't you go up and give her your condolences, young man?" Sir Eric offered as he kept his eyes averted from Wiley.

"Oh, sir, I was thinking of doing that, but didn't want to take the liberty of roaming about your house. After all I have come uninvited and have imposed upon your banquet."

"Bah! Think nothing of it, young man. And you have my permission to stay on and comfort Mistress Wellbeloved for as long as she is here," Sir Eric said with malice aforethought as he noticed suddenly how inscrutable the blue eyes were.

As Sir Eric went to join the ladies in the parlor he walked a bit livelier. He had a pretty good hunch that Bran wasn't going to like this David Wiley. Nay, not one bit.

*Fifteen*

"Wiley!" Melanie screeched excitedly after she had answered the sprightly rapping on her door. "David Wiley! Where have you been keeping yourself?" She was breathless as she tossed slim white arms about his neck and bussed him on the cheek. She stepped back, mussing his wavy blond hair.

David reddened with intense pleasure. "Perhaps I should have come sooner," David returned, his hands never leaving her small waist.

"Like about two years," she pouted. "Ah, but you are here now, lover. *Here!*" She paused on that note. "David, do tell me, how did you know?"

"Ivory," David replied simply. "Shame, you didn't even send me a note, dearest."

"Oh, but, David, how can one reach you when you fly from one friend's house to another?" A touch of her surliness was surfacing. It didn't last though, not when she put her eyes on his fancy new attire. Melanie sparkled anew, putting on her most flirtatious façade.

"The bottle is quite empty on the table there," he grinned. "Can we get another?"

"Ugh! I had a spree that lasted all yesterday. But I can get the maid to fetch you one if you like. I've still a nasty headache—"

"Melanie," Wiley breathed, pulling her closer. "Melanie, come away with me. I don't mean now, but soon. It shan't be long before I'll be coming into some big riches and then we'll be well off and propertied."

"Oh!" Melanie exclaimed and then snickered. "David, you have not changed one bit. You always used to promise me that." She pushed him from her then, saying, "You don't know, do you, of the new position offered me. He's—ummm—very handsome, David," she taunted, leaving the bait dangling.

"Who now, Melanie? Another old croak with empty bags?" David too taunted.

"Have you not heard I am to be the new Mistress Ravenleigh?" Melanie tilted her chin up at him.

"Not Bran Ravenleigh! So . . . that's why you have come here, eh?" Wiley asked, breathing raggedly when she leaned against him with the full weight of her luscious round breasts. "You're still a bitch, you know that? Forget him, Melanie, he's dangerous, I hear, and he runs with bad company—the greatest rebel that ever was in Virginia!"

"Pshaw, not Nathaniel Bacon. I don't believe it. Bran is just a rakehell, that's all, but I shall change all that once we are wed," Melanie boasted.

"Melanie, forget him. I am mad about you, always have been, you know that. Remember how it used to be? I was the first man who ever laid with you, or do you forget when we used to sneak up to the garret and do it all night?"

"David, hush, someone might overhear! Then you'll ruin everything for me. Bran can give me what

257

I've always wanted, even my own house. The old croak gave me nothing but grief!"

"You little bitch. I bet I could pleasure you right now over there on that bed and you'd cry out for more, over and over again, wouldn't you?" He gave her a little shake.

"David, please," Melanie begged, becoming roused against her will. "Besides, Bran thinks I'm a maid untouched and if he catches us I'll have nothing . . . nothing but North Creek. The old manor is nothing compared to this grand place. Why, this is like a castle compared to that one."

David interrupted. "You forget, dearest, that Sir Eric rules here, too, and do you think he'll let you run his old hall?"

Melanie's head towered and her brows rose haughtily as she continued. "This house may be ancient, but it's just right for all the parties and balls I intend to hold. Mmmm, I could even redecorate, but Bran would build me a new house if I should crave one."

"You are a greedy little bitch, as always," David hissed as he dug into the slot of his fancy waistcoat. He handed her a patch box encrusted with sparkling gems. "I know it's old, but it's worth a small fortune, luv." This too had cost him—his father's old timepiece in exchange.

"It is so . . . unbelievably lovely, David," she breathed, looking up at him in a new light. "David, you old fox, have you come into some riches?" she wondered out loud, lifting an amber brow coquettishly.

David was desperate now, not only because he

wanted to get her into bed; but now it seemed he had a new and dangerous enemy—a very wealthy one to be sure, Bran Ravenleigh. David had never come face to face with him and had only glimpsed him from afar. But there had been talk in Jamestown, mostly by the lower class gossipers. Ravenleigh was said to attract either fiercely loyal and dedicated admirers—like Bacon's crowd—or envious and spiteful enemies. Even Captain Strang said he had to give the man grudging respect—from afar. Javier had long known that Ravenleigh was after him, dogging his shadow, but the captain had stayed clear of Bran, being careful not to challenge him openly as he would liked to have done. The few who had carried vivid and painful reminders that caution was required in either verbal or physical attack against him. But then Wiley felt he himself was made of the same stuff as Ravenleigh, and he meant to have Melanie first. Now that she was free of the old man, David would have to plan very cautiously indeed if he was to outwit Ravenleigh. And that too meant in more ways than one.

"David, where *are* you?" Melanie wondered, waving a hand in front of the pondering, scheming blue eyes. "I've asked you a question, luv. Aren't you going to answer me, or is it a deep dark secret?"

"There will be more riches just like that, Melanie. rubies, emeralds, sapphires, gold sovereigns. But don't ask me just yet how I am to come by my, ah, new wealth. Unlike my old self, I shall never again lie to you, luv," he declared cunningly.

"Oh, my. I am just so confused right now, David. You will have to give me time to think about this, my brain is too fuzzy at this moment," she said, fighting to control her emotions as, mesmerized, she watched him proceed to remove his broadcloth coat.

"Bran Ravenleigh, I hear, has not yet returned from a little journey he took downriver this morning early. My, it could be that he won't return at all," David said meaningfully while Melanie studied the patch box from every angle, her cupidity throwing caution to the wind.

"He will return sometime . . ."

When Melanie looked up at him again his arms swooped around her, drawing her close. Before she could thank him for the gift, his lips crushed hers to silence, one hand slipping up to cup a breast. Breathing heavily, hot for this long-awaited joining, David led Melanie to the mussed bed and pushed her down gently by the shoulder. She offered no resistance, but when she began to pant as he ground his hips into hers, she sat bolt upright, clutching David by the shirt sleeve.

"David, wait!" she said breathlessly. "Go first and secure the door."

Upon returning to the bed he found to his pleasure that Melanie had disrobed; he did likewise. Their fair bodies met greedily, and with David ramming into her, they soon glistened moistly with the furor of their lovemaking. They came apart and then fused again to climb the heights of ecstasy.

Having gone back downstairs to fetch the bouquet of flowers for Melanie, Aurora halted as strange sounds from the room froze her just as she was about to put her hand to the door. Had she truly heard a man's voice?

"David, oh my! You are tense again. Again, lover, again. Hurry!"

Melanie, crying out in a frenzy of passion. And David! Aurora gulped and spun about, her back to the door as if she guarded it from whoever might be about. She must be away, though; otherwise if someone happened by they would indeed read the flush in her face and wonder what was behind the closed doors. All was quiet within now, and as she smoothed her long skirt with nervous fingers, she cast a hurried glimpse about the hall before inching stealthily back to the corridor. Then Aurora froze, feeling little shocks climb her back.

"Oh, yes, Wiley! Ahhh!"

Aurora wrinkled her nose and hastened on. What Melanie and David did was none of her affair. They must surely be insane! And if Ravenleigh should catch his intended bride in the arms of another . . .

"He would skin David Wiley alive!" Aurora loosed a rare giggle.

"What are ye so tickled about, luv?" Hetty questioned as Aurora came into the little bedchamber, tossing a bouquet of flowers onto the bed.

"Oh . . . nothing, Hetty," Aurora replied breezily. Then, "What have you there, Hetty?" She came closer to the bed, glancing at the servant suspiciously. "Hetty! You have brought along my dress . . . and shoes!"

Hetty stood sheepishly, but blurted, "Dinna Sir Eric tell ye? He demands yer presence tonight at the banquet. You hae got to do as ye are bid, lass."

"Why?" Aurora demanded, suddenly feeling

261

her oats.

"Well . . . ye just have to. And I canna stand to see ye moping about!" she ended with a snap.

Her eyes trained on Hetty, Aurora picked up the purple patterned silk with its long, pointed, corseted bodice with hook-and-eye closings down the center front. The dress was very complimentary to her tiny waist and the color drew out the purple hue of her eyes excitingly.

"Whew! Dinna stand there all day gawking at the thing. Come now, wee lass, put it on? Uh?"

A half an hour later, Aurora sat on the edge of the bed while Hetty was completing the corkscrew curls she had wound around her fingers painstakingly. Aurora had just washed her hair that afternoon and the shorter strands at her forehead had dried in ringlet bangs. Now Hetty's artistry completed the picture. Aurora looked very fashionably coiffed indeed. Melanie no doubt would wear her heart-breakers, the wired locks that stood away from her head and bounced brightly when she walked.

Aurora's full-sleeved sark, dyed a violet shade, peeped through the open seam in the dress and beneath the elbow-length sleeves which had been tied with pure white bows. Both the divided skirt and the petticoat were so long that they gracefully swept the floor, giving a peek of her varnished white shoes when she walked.

Melanie's own cloudberry dress would display her well-turned ankle, for her gowns were all cut daringly short.

Aurora caught herself. Why was she suddenly comparing herself with her cousin? Strange, she had never done so before. There was no one here tonight whose favors she vied for. Aurora brooded on this but a moment, for Hetty was pushing her toward the door. Out in the corridor, Aurora reflected a moment on going to warn Melanie that the banquet would be commencing, but thought it wiser and more prudent not to intrude. Again, she concluded, it was none of her affair.

"Three cheers!" Sir Eric hooted with laughter, adding, "Is it really you?"

Aurora paused at the foot of the stairs as a chorus of male voices chuckled deeply, and she wondered who was the object of all this revelry. Ida Minter, coming along suddenly, startled Aurora. The older woman bore a tray of steaming baby fingers of buttered spring carrots and carved slices of quail and pheasant, and a servingmaid followed with another tray of crisp bacon crumbled atop snow peas and Indian meal bread, plus a bottle of Canary. Minter took up the rear with goodly slices of beef smothered in deliciously brown gravy and several more bottles of Canary and Madeira. Besides all this, Aurora could smell apple pie, her favorite, wafting through the hall.

Ida Minter halted beside the young woman. Her pale eyes beamed at the change in countenance and attire while at the same time wondering who had been so forward as to invite her to this sitting. Ida could not help being friendly, though, to this lovely young creature who was looking so nervous.

"Come along—ah—Ro, is it? More gentlemen have arrived in the last hour, Bran Ravenleigh being one of them. One could say, as usual, this old Keep is filled with robust males boasting hearty appetites," she informed with her usual exactness. "Well, come along, you look as if you've been invited, so don't stand there being so scared." She chuckled next as she joked, "The only one that bites is Bran, the young master."

Only a few minutes had passed since Aurora had heard the men laughing heartily over something. Now as she stepped to the hall shyly but gracefully, she could sense the reason why. The dashing Bran Ravenleigh was the center of attention. His well-shaped face was framed by a coal-black periwig that would have been a credit to a duke. He was posturing in a courtly manner, himself finding this sport a diversion from the feverish pace of his life.

"Oho!" Sir Eric exclaimed and whistled. "Now that's my grandson, the foppish spark garbed in his regalia. I still don't believe you got it on, lad!" He indicated the black wig with a wave of his walnut cane and sent the table into yet another roar.

When Bran had returned an hour before, he had decided to please his grandfather and dress to the hilt for this occasion. His coat of dark gray broadcloth had brocaded cuffs, his Holland shirt and collar were lacily immaculate. A silken waistcoat was cut with a flare above his gathered breeches with their gilded cords; and his baldric, on which was hung a dress sword with jeweled hilt, was embroidered in red arabesques. On his black shoes were Italian silver buckles in which were mounted a multitude of varicolored jewels. He sauntered now to Sir Eric's chair in a rakish manner.

Sir Eric smiled like a Cheshire cat as he lifted up his eyes while Bran spoke. "You've an inclination to laughter this good eve, my grandfather. You have cocked your eye upon me ever since my entrance into this kingly hall."

"Heh-heh, I do like your campaign wig a mite more than this one. Why, the way you look tonight, Bran, one could almost call you—hmmm—beautiful." His face twinkled in fun.

"Don't laugh! Minter has once again persuaded me to wear this deuced thing. Indeed, he was almost teary-eyed, poor fellow, so I had to concede. One could almost believe he has a fetish about wigs. Ah, finally," said Bran as he turned about to see the meal being brought in, making his mouth water in hunger.

The very moment Bran put his eyes on Aurora Gregory, he walked over offering her his arm, on a reflex action he was to ponder shortly. First he had allowed the pleasant shock to clear from his mind, now a tight smile compressed his full lips as he guided her slowly toward the long banquet table where the guests gaped on the tip-toe of expectation. Especially two women, both blond.

"Mama, who is *she*? She is most dainty and fair. Do you suppose she be of royal blood?" Penelope whispered.

"Hush, baby, we shall see."

Bran scrutinized Aurora thoroughly askance as he spoke low. "I see that you have finally decided to improve your appearance, and please my guests." His gaze had touched upon the kissable lips before

265

looking away.

"Guests?" Aurora glanced at Bran uncomprehendingly.

"I am sorry, you are a guest, too, aren't you," he said tersely, slanting his eyes toward Sir Eric who was smiling at the timber-beamed ceiling, twirling his goblet.

Aurora was suddenly so dizzy with what she thought was anger that she felt faint.

"I dressed this way," she began with a snap, then ended softly, "to please myself, sir." She could not add that Sir Eric had demanded her presence here, for her lips seemed to be sewn together with a tight stitch, as she had trouble getting them to open.

Bran had been savoring her appearance, but now as she lowered her head his silvery gaze narrowed in on the shiny dark locks. His regard slid slowly from there across to Melanie who was lifting an eyebrow, her face otherwise pale and expressionless. Melanie missed seeing the twitching muscle in Bran's cheek before he left Aurora's side to come around the table to the reserved seat beside Melanie's. Bran took up her hand and gallantly bussed it before he too sat.

"Oh, Bran, I'd almost forgotten," Melanie began nervously. "I would like to introduce an old . . . friend of mine to you—David Wiley."

As Melanie completed the introductions, the men nodded to each other, briefly but pleasantly enough. Bran barely paid Wiley any mind, his thoughts seemingly elsewhere, much to Melanie's relief.

David Wiley sported a long, curling, dark-brown wig. A wig in his own shade of hair was hard to come by, and he detested the white powdered wigs such as

266

Sir Eric sported tonight. To ease himself of his own disquietude, David took up studying Aurora Gregory. So, she had blossomed quite nicely, though her small breasts did not measure up to his ideal, whereas Melanie's cleavage plunged deeper and rose to quivering, full white mounds. There was no love lost between David and the Gregory girl. For, as in the past, she barely acknowledged his presence. He prided himself on the thought that if he should ever have a craving for the dark-haired beauty, he could have her in a snap.

Indeed, Aurora hardly glanced his way. David had not changed much to her way of thinking, but seemingly he was now a more moneyed man. All the gold of the world could not tempt her into liking the man. He was still sinister of demeanor, and his shifty-eyed glances had always given her the creeps.

"A toast"—Sir Eric rose as the wine was being poured—"to our guests and especially to my most honored one." He lifted his goblet and the others followed suit, wondering. "To Aurora Gregory, lately discovered to be none other than Mistress Wellbeloved's charming cousin!"

"To Aurora Gregory!" the guests chimed, hoisting up their goblets and their eyebrows at the same time.

Melanie crimsoned profusely, at once apologizing for not having introduced Aurora as her cousin the day before. "I'd been out of my mind with grief over my parents' capture. Aurora understood my heedlessness, though, didn't you, dear cousin?" Her paler eyes begged for mercy.

"Of course, Melly, I have always understood—" She broke off, hoping that she hadn't said too much in her brief sentence.

Bran soon forgot his hunger and tilted his goblet to his lips, downing the contents to the last drop.

Aurora's head whirled, and she had no idea what was being said in the next few minutes. As the feast began, her eyes met Bran's for an instant and she felt the color rise swiftly to her face. She then gave her full attention to her plate, picking daintily at the beef and carrots. Too, she was finding it difficult to look in her cousin's direction as she recalled what had taken place with her and David shortly before. With that on her mind, her hand trembled slightly, the same hand that had rested on Bran's arm not long ago. Reluctantly she felt a remembered wave of pleasure at their contact. His lips had appeared so sensitive and yet hard and cruel at the same time when he had spoken so softly in her ear. Fay! Why did Bran Ravenleigh make her think of her love for the ranger? They were as different as night and day!

In her watered-silk gown, Melanie bristled upon hearing Jim Crews compliment Aurora on the color of her dress—so like her eyes, which reminded him of the heather he had seen on a visit to England's moors. Bran curled his long fingers over the carved-oak arm of his chair, having noted this fact when first he saw her tonight.

"Yea . . ." Bran drawled deeply, agreeing with Crews.

"You are too kind, sir," Aurora said, but pointedly to Crews.

Aurora, as in bygone days, laughed gaily and the men, including Sir Eric, were drawn to her like bees to a honey pot. All but for one across from her, whose immobile face remained a frozen mask, his silver eyes lazily hooded as he downed yet another goblet of wine.

As well as the other men, David Wiley couldn't help but coming under Aurora's charming witchery. Why was she so enchanting tonight? And why was it that he always desired what he couldn't have? Women and wealth. It irked him now that she paid no mind to him. First things first, old man, he told himself. Wherever Melanie went Aurora followed, he concluded, curling up one side of his mouth.

Devoured with jealousy, Melanie regarded her cousin with a sneer. Aurora had almost instantaneously become a sparkling, vivacious woman, amusing men with her clever, nimble-witted remarks. Jim Crews, smiling at something she was saying, no doubt felt a pang of pure pleasure. Turning green inside and out with envy, Melanie set forth to capture the attention of one and all.

"Ro can converse intelligently about almost any subject under the sun. But who in the world wants to discuss great philosophers or poetry brilliantly? Almost nineteen, can you imagine what a serious intellectual she will become in just a few more years with her nose in all those uppity books? Shakespeare. How boring!" Melanie ended in breathy affectation.

"Womenfolk aren't supposed to have a mind for such things 'tis said by many," Mistress Pruett put in, then went on, "'Tain't natural, I guess. Ohh, but I sure wish that I could read," she dared to add.

"Women can be merry and wise in several other

ways, true, Bran?" Melanie said, her meaning made clearer to David Wiley than any other man in the hall.

"That remains to be seen, sweeting," Bran challenged with a glance at her over the rim of his goblet.

A flush crept up from Melanie's neck as she began to sip her wine faster. Aurora knew a moment of panic when David openly rested his pale fingers on Melanie's wrist, then returned his hand to his utensil to fork up some dripping beef to his mouth. Aurora chanced to put her eyes on Bran and was shocked to find him staring directly at her, as if rummaging her thoughts. She felt an inrush of blood to her head as her eyes dilated. With a gaze void of any feeling, Bran next peered down into Melanie's vacuous, bloodshot eyes that matched her gown perfectly. She had again drunk more than her share, he determined. Now he ever so slowly and coldly regarded David Wiley's actions, his eyes narrowing, his mouth curling. Aurora would not for her life even glance up for she knew that Bran's lip had begun to twitch in the beginning of a smirk.

"What's your business, Wiley?"

With a reflex action, Aurora had jumped an inch off her chair, but no one seemed to notice her when Bran put the question to David Wiley.

"Business?" David leaned forward to try and see Bran, but Melanie had reached again for her goblet, putting herself between the men.

"Mmm-hmmm, you know," Bran returned. "Are you a planter? A tinker?"

Egad! Sir Eric thought to himself. Bran was acting his old self tonight! The old knight leaned back, mentally rubbing his hands together for the sport to come.

"Peddler."

Melanie almost spat out a good swallow of Canary. This time she leaned back, smiling sweetly in affectation as Bran patted her gently on the back, permitting David a view of his conversing partner. Silver eyes locked together with blue, only momentarily, then disengaged.

"Peddler. Ah!" Bran said. "Of course, you travel from place to place with your wares. What do you sell?"

Again David lowered his goblet that seemed to be having difficulty finding his lips. He pursed them thoughtfully as Melanie tittered between the two, trying unsuccessfully to strike up conversation on a different subject.

"Hats."

Melanie was by now so flustered that she began to squirm and she spilled droplets of wine on her bare bosom more than once. Her chin almost resting on her chest, Aurora peeped up between her lashes, her cheeks gone from pink to a dusky rose as she recognized the danger in this verbal exchange.

Bran remained impassive to Melanie's growing discomfort as he continued.

"I would like to purchase a hat with multihued feathers and perhaps a cocked hat for riding. Do you have either of these?"

David coughed. "Ah—I would have to take your measurements, sir," he said lamely.

"*My* measurements," Bran chuckled out loud. "My good peddler, I am speaking of ladies' hats. You don't know your hats very well, do you."

"I—I am new at the business," David managed as a round of deep chuckles swept the long table. Inside his mouth he gritted his teeth with malice. No one made David Wiley look the fool and walk away unscathed. Bran Ravenleigh's time was coming, to be sure.

"Oh, Bran," Melanie piped up. "Let's talk about the wedding!" She kicked David's foot aside as he had stomped on her instep.

Bran looked at her slantingly. "Why, Melanie, is someone getting married?" he inquired with an elevated eyebrow.

"Oh! Ummm—" Melanie clamped a hand over her mouth. She looked hastily to her cousin. "Ro, didn't you say you were going to wed Rodney Quick?" She covered herself as a new thought struck her: Bran had never actually asked for her hand in marriage! Indeed, he had not! Her vanity suffered momentarily, but she recovered shortly as she remembered David's promise to make her affluent and propertied.

"Well, little Ro, is that the truth?" Sir Eric questioned Aurora as the corners of his mouth drooped in disappointment, immediately noticed by his grandson.

"I—I have not been asked by Rodney Quick . . . but mayhap I mentioned to Melanie that my wish is to take a husband soon . . ." She shrugged as her voice trailed off and her eyes misted over with something undeniably sad.

"Well then," Bran took up, "if it is Rodney Quick you crave, perhaps I can visit the lad—ah—he is a lad, is he not?"

"Aye," Aurora softly answered, drawing thoughtful and solicitous looks from around the table.

"Lad it is then. I can drop the hint to Quick and quickly Quick shall come to beg your hand," Bran rapped out quickly.

Sir Eric pounded the table in tearful mirth, causing the utensils to quiver. "That's rich, aha, that's rich!" he cried, swiping the tears from his usually stern eyes.

"Ohhhhh!"

First came the tearful sob and then the purple patterned silk flew like a colorful tropical bird out of the hall. One and all stared agog after the girl, then collectively watched the spilled wine spreading across the table and leak through the roughhewn boards onto Bran's elegant breeches. He rose swiftly as one of the young maidservants standing by mopped up the mess with several linens and then handed the young master a wadded one, blushing from ear to ear because she dared not help in dabbing his stained breeches and one and all knew this. Melanie was very pleased now and sat like a cat licking its whiskers.

"My! but she is ill-mannered," Mistress Pruett said smugly, patting Melanie's bright head.

"Nay, luv, she's just a puritanical lass methinks. Couldst be she is merely skittish about the marriage bed."

"Papa! There are other women here, and Penny too!" the older woman chided her husband.

Weary of all the tomfoolery, Jim Crews rose to go and stand next to Bran. "Are you going to Jamestown first of June?" he inquired.

273

"I'd thought on it some," Bran returned, his hooded eyes flicking from Wiley to Crews.

"I want you to take a message to Berkeley. You are our man," Crews was saying, unconsciously leading Bran to take a seat next to his own.

"What's wrong, Jim?" Bran took up a fresh goblet.

"Hellish rumors are flying," Crews said, pushing aside a half-eaten fowl. "There is talk in Jamestown that the governor awaits the opportune moment to murder our friend. It could be just that—rumors. But you are familiar with the governor and his coterie. Still, mingle quietly and wear your sword. Jamestown will be crowded with members of the new Assembly and angry mobs. I'll tell you the rest if you will first journey east. So, back to the present. How are your breeches?"

"Ruined."

With that Bran nodded and they fell in, along with the others to exchange quiet pleasantries. Penelope couldn't keep her eyes off Bran Ravenleigh, but he was seemingly oblivious to her open stares. Actually, his thoughts and cares were elsewhere. Had he been too cruel to Aurora? Why? Well then, Bran, he said to himself, I believe you are jealous, you fickle old fool.

Now Mistress Pruett was saying that just yesterday morning a ship had landed with long due woolens, tools and gewgaws. Mister Pruett added that much of the cargo had been purchased before it could even reach the warehouse. Here Melanie smiled secretly: She had sent a servant well in advance to fetch her laces and gay furbelows.

Now Melanie and Penelope, their fair heads

together, giggled often as they soaked up the wine like dissolute ladies of the court. Bran too imbibed more than usual and ate very little. He listened to the silly gossip now with an attentive ear.

"Oh, Aurora?" Melanie was answering Penelope's question. "What's she like? Hah! Ro lives in a fantasy world. Reality is just too much a bore to her."

Penelope's papa put in: "We all must dream, Mistress Melanie, 'tis good for the soul."

"Dream, sure," Melanie went on, "but she lives in a private world of dream stuff. Alas, I wonder if she'll ever wake up." Melanie smiled as she caught Bran perusing her broodingly.

Sir Eric had risen from the table and, with big hands locked behind his back, paced slowly before the hearth. No one noticed—not even Bran who continued to ponder moodily—when he stopped to stare ruminatively at the slowly dying embers. The fire had not been fed another log, for in these last days of May-time they were experiencing a new warmth that was retained in the rooms that had been aired all day. Having arrived at a decision, Sir Eric spun on his booted heel and strode noiselessly from the hall.


"Whew! What was that?" Hetty wondered out loud as she sat in the kitchen sipping toddies with one of the older maidservants.

"Did ye hear it too?"

Bonnie, who was a Scotswoman too, had discovered in Hetty someone to share pouring out to each other their loneliness for the snowy highlands. They switched now to discussing spirits and would continue to until the wee hours of the morning. Bonnie was none surprised to learn that Hetty had felt the supernatural beings roaming the halls of Raven Keep, heard their plaintive cries of lost love, long ago. Bonnie too was conscious of the spirits, while the others in the household had no notion of the Keep's night-walking spirits of the dead.

## Sixteen

Up the back stairs Aurora fled, hot tears of humiliation and anguish blinding her as she stumbled at the landing, tugged at her skirts that had somehow become tangled about her legs, and halted her flight to her room. Falling on all fours like a crouching animal, she reached behind her to try freeing the petticoat that she realized must be caught on something. She remained imprisoned, unable to see what held her in the half-dark as she stretched the material furiously until she became tearfully frustrated and, scratching her finger on a sliver of wood, one last tug rent her petticoat up to her waist.

She was free, but unmindful of the drop of blood squeezing from her finger as now she made her way to the little room that was stuffy and uncomfortably warm for this late-spring eve. A single flame wavered on the bedside table, but it went unnoticed to her that the candle was nearly spent.

A knock sounded on the door, but Aurora waited for whoever was on the other side to go away. All was quiet now. Aurora flung herself dejectedly onto the bed, rolling to her back to stare sightlessly at the flickering shadows that leapt up the wall and tried feebly to reach the ceiling. Soon the room would be cast into darkness. That was fine with her. She wanted to be in the dark anyway. She didn't even care if she fell asleep and wrinkled her pretty dress. She felt so alone. Even Sir Eric had laughed at her!

Tears sprang to her eyes, and then her face went scarlet as she again relived the scene that had taken place in the hall. Bran was again looking at her, arrogantly, and the hot color was flooding into her cheeks.

"Plague on him! I shan't cry, I shan't!"

Aurora's head rolled on the pillow. It was so quiet in the room. She would not cry. Nay. Perhaps if she just rested a bit she would feel better when she awakened. By that time Hetty should have returned and she could help her to undress. It was so very quiet. . . .

A knock sounded on the door again, softer than before. But Aurora did not hear it, nor did she know when someone entered to place a fresh candle at her bedside.

Sometime later, though she could not know how long, her eyes flew open. Had someone been shaking her awake just moments before? She breathed deeply and a strange peace began flowing into her limbs. She took no notice of the fresh candle that wavered and gave a yellow-green smoke that stung her lids. Strangely, now, her mind began to wander.

Fantasies that always seemed more vivid at night stole unbidden to her. Just what was it like to lie in a man's strong embrace? To be taken into a strength greater than her own, to be possessed? Would she ever know? Or was Bertie's loveless fate to be her own. She shivered, seeing a vision of herself as an old woman, shriveled up on a rocker, blanket tucked in at her legs, with no grandchildren to warm her heart.

She must tell Fay who she is. She loved him dearly, wanted him . . . wanted him to make love to her—now! Once back at North Creek she would wait in the dear cedar lane every day until he came to her. Her destiny rested in Fay's hands. If he would not have her, then devil take the hindmost and Bertie's fate would be her own. There was but one man for her, one love forever.

Like a zombie, Aurora rose from the bed, stood shakily to remove her gown but found that she could not manage the hook-and-eye closings. She finally gave up. She blinked her eyes and squeezed them tight, and upon opening them, she saw that all the stout furnishings in the room were now blurred, run together. She was feeling increasingly a sense of well-being, and there were funny little butterflies in her head.

Aurora knew not where she was headed, but walked as if in a trance and soon found herself standing in the gallery. Something hot dripped onto her hand and she noticed that she held the squat candle in its tiny saucer. The strange smoke reached her stinging nostrils and she again inhaled deeply, closed her eyes, and wavered on her feet.

Aurora never saw nor heard the man come up behind her, not until he came around and stood directly in front of her. She noticed him now, but she was neither surprised nor frightened. He looked directly into the dusky violet of her eyes and her fuzzy brain determined his eyes to be almond colored; or was it just the candle flame mirrored in that intense scrutiny? It didn't matter. Nothing seemed to matter.

"Who are you?" Aurora asked him slowly, dream-like. She then tried lifting the candle higher, but her arm felt like a heavy weight was dragging it down.

The man merely grunted softly beneath his breath, as if pleased with her question and her bizarre movements. She continued to stare at him, yet unafraid and blinking her eyes to better see him. But he, whoever he was, seemed to drift in a blue haze, bodiless and at moments faceless.

"Come," he seemed to mutter from afar, "come with me, Aurora Gregory. I will take you back to your room."

In the half-gloom surrounding her, Aurora let him lead her by the hand as if she was a trusting little girl. The way seemed endless, the corridor narrow and close, the candle floating before her like a faintly blurred nimbus. His long lazy strides slowed to accommodate her unsure steps. She felt peculiarly calm, barely remembering her gloomy mood. She actually floated on top of the world.

The next object Aurora could make out—a large red and black object—was a bed. Her sense of perspective distorted, the bed came toward her, instead of the other way around. Another candle much like the one the man had taken from her to carry himself, shone dully beside the bed. Oddly Aurora smiled at this new candle as the stranger placed the shorter one at the other side of the bed. He came around then to take her gently by the hand and lowered her to sit on the edge of the bed. She peered up at him like a lost puppy as he dropped the red hangings around her.

"Where is Hetty?" Aurora murmured from between the draped-back hangings on either side of her.

"She is downstairs with friends. She will come soon," he answered softly, then turned to go. "You wait here. Don't move," he added over his shoulder.

"Where is Fay?"

Jerking to a halt, he whirled and stared down at her hard, frowned, then slipped catlike from the room. Out in the hall he joined another, heavier figure; when footfalls sounded from the east wing, mingled with a drunken song, the two shadows hastened in the opposite direction, going down the curving back stairs.

"I don't like this one bit," the slighter man growled, "and neither will he—later."

"Faugh! He will love it, heh-heh, you'll see," the older man fell to chuckling deviously.

At the other end of the corridor, Bran ceased his song, halted at the door to the little room, lifted his hand as if to knock and awaken Aurora Gregory, but then, trying to clear his head as he shook it, he thought: Nay, I am in no condition to console her now. Indeed, tomorrow would be a better time to speak what was weighing heavily on his mind.

He went on to his chamber, swaggering and feeling in high spirits. He had never drunk this much and he wondered dazedly what had prompted him to do so. He hadn't the foggiest idea what had gotten into him of late. He smiled crookedly then, knowing full well just what he needed.

Bran stepped lightly into his room, shut the door and began to peel off his coat, feeling the need to strip down completely. The night was warm and the coat had grown uncomfortable, even though this was one of a lightweight fabric. His movements were brought to a standstill suddenly. He frowned and his nose twitched curiously.

Oftentimes when the maidservants knew the young master was going to his bedchamber, one would light a candle in his room and bank up the fires if it was chilly. But now as he stood there with his coat half stripped off, he wondered at the strange odor in his room. He shrugged then, thinking perhaps the servant who made up the candles had added a fragrant Indian herb, such as vetiver, as they were often wont to do on special occasions.

"Hetty?" a sleepy voice came from his bed and Bran let his coat drop off his arm and onto the floor.

The voice was husky sweet, floating through the air like the honeyed sweetness of springtime wafting from the forest. Bran's eyes widened as from the depths of his bed Aurora Gregory stood unsteadily, offering the front of her dress to be unfastened. At least this was the way it appeared to Bran. He stared at her middle, then lifted his gaze to her somnolent countenance. He stood there, thoroughly befuddled at her unspoken request.

"Are you sure you want me to . . . do this?" he asked, but already touching on the first hook as if he hadn't the will to do otherwise.

"Aye, I am very uncomfortable . . . hot," she said, pausing, wavering. Then her violet eyes tried to focus on the figure and it was by instinct rather than by sight that she knew him. "You are here," she said simply, her eyes rolling back beneath closing lids.

"*Aye*," he breathed, looking at the turned-down

282

red coverlet, then back to Aurora. He was unable to comprehend this good fortune that had come his way, but then he was in no mood to refuse it either.

With somewhat clumsy fingers, Bran, with one arm holding her upright, undid the hook-and-eyes and helped her out of the dress and petticoat, his riveted eyes missing the rent in the one. As the silk thing rustled to the floor he trained his gaze up over the sark, the only garment left on her that kept him from seeing her in complete undress. Stepping back, he took his time in removing his waistcoat, his baldric and weapon, his periwig, waiting for his brain to partially clear so that he could fully enjoy the lovemaking that would inevitably follow this interlude.

Only his breeches and Holland shirt remained when he turned to discover that Aurora had curled kittenishly upon his bed, her long lashes pressed together to form delicate spikes. He stood there looking down, a puzzled frown gathering on his brown brow. He hadn't noticed her imbibing all that much at the table, but it could be that she just wasn't used to the rich wine that had been served. Too, it was stiflingly warm in the room. Thinking this, he went to throw open a window, noticing at once how much this began to clear his own befogged brain. There was one thing more he must do. He had never suffered such a damnable headache and he blamed it on the oddly smoking candles. He extinguished them one by one, lending the flame from the last candle to one of his own stubby ones.

Only a few minutes had passed since he entered his bedchamber to discover this pleasant surprise awaiting him in his bed. In the trembling light of the one candle, his silvery gaze roamed over the delicious female snuggled in the middle of his huge bed. Bran was ready, despite the large amount of inebriants he had consumed. It had been a long while between beds and his hunger now was great. So great in fact that he felt his proud flesh throb as never before. In another minute he had disrobed completely.

Though still in a muddled state, Aurora felt the air in the room freshen. Automatically her lashes fluttered open, giving her a view of the man coming toward her as if in a drifting haze. She lifted herself on her elbows weakly, to better see him but he blurred before her as he worked at the sark to remove it. Loosely she shook her head, but still it would not clear itself of the debilitating cobwebs. Her skin felt cooler now and she wondered lazily why the man had left her. She must be dreaming, she determined groggily.

"Almighty God, how beautiful you are," he groaned huskily. Bran stared at perfect breasts that reminded him of small white doves, the flat belly and on down past her secret place to well-shaped limbs. "I have never witnessed such pure perfection in a woman, not even—" He bit off, realizing he had almost said "Melanie."

His male body bursting into flames that licked at his groin, Bran hesitated no more, but bent down to sweep her into his arms and crushed her to his hard length, his lips lowering to capture hers in a sweet, lingering kiss. Her lips melted so easily, indeed slack beneath his, that he knew beyond doubt that her actions were abnormal. She was either drunk on something or . . .

"If you are bewitched, Aurora Gregory," he murmured deeply, "I am even more so."

"What—" she began. "Don't understand, please say louder, cannot hear, but you mustn't be bewitched. Are you—who I think—must tell you I am—Aurora. Aurora Gregory. Only me—no one else." She was gibbering.

Bran groaned. "Ahh, sweet little witch. I know who you are now, indeed Aurora Gregory, I've discovered no more illusions about that. You *are* Melanie's cousin, aye, and we should have been met before this. Fool that I am that I did not believe you when first I laid eyes on you, but my dear—I must say you appeared quite the waif in that drabbest servant garb—"

"Drab servant I am not," she muttered.

"Don't I know!" His eyes glowed down over her with fervency. "Lord, but I crave you! I wanted to pleasure myself with you as soon as I saw you glide into the hall tonight—like some magical princess."

Reluctantly Bran brought to mind all the women he'd known in the past—Elspeth Woodville and all the others—the beauties of the flesh; he wondered now if this Aurora Gregory could yet be a fledgling in matters of love. All the others had been experienced . . .

He could feel her sweet breath tickling his shoulder, driving him mad with desire. His eyes snagged on the taut curve of belly. He could easily discover . . .

Bran's long hard fingers slid down her belly purposefully, found their entrance and then probed first gently, now deeper. Aurora cried out softly as the painful searching made her surface from the slowly ebbing fog. Bran frowned down the length of her pure, slim thighs. Aurura's eyes widened in terror. This man was not a romantic figment of a dream she'd been having, not her phantom Fay—but Bran Ravenleigh!

Bran groaned deeply, then crushed Aurora to his chest once again, smothering her neck and hair with feverish kisses. "We must have more time so that I might court and woo you properly. You aren't in your right mind now"—and neither am I, he thought—"and I am certain that you have been drugged by those foul candles, and I would have you in your right mind. Confusion reigns in me now, for I have loved foolishly, more often than not, and would not make the same mistake again. Damn, if only you could hear me, understand me fully—" He snorted softly then as he rose brusquely—"If only *I* could understand . . ."

Bran was reaching for the sark, damning the grinding ache in his loins when he noticed the spot of blood on the bed. He stared incredily. What is this? He ruffled his hair with raking fingers and hadn't a chance to take in the young woman's horrified expression before a warning knock sounded on the door. Once, then again, before it was wrenched wide. There Bran stood in all his naked glory, fully aroused as his passion-hot eyes met those of first his grandfather and then Ida Minter.

Bran groaned and cursed inwardly.

"Aha!" Sir Eric exclaimed with a hearty snap.

"Shame! Dallying with the innocent Aurora

286

Gregory!'' Ida Minter chided as she charged directly
to the bed. There she immediately began to clothe the
naked and shivering girl. A graying brow rose
imperiously as the drop of blood there confirmed her
suspicions.

"That—" Bran growled as he gestured to the bed,
"that is not what you—you both think!"

"Garb yourself, son! We have much to discuss this
night . . . like your immediate wedding!"

Bran, having nothing or no one else to back him,
sputtered in embarrassed rage as he tugged on his
breeches. He narrowed his regard in on his grandfather and the suspicion grew that he'd been framed.
Though he still had a plaguey headache, his brain
had cleared sufficiently for him to realize now that
indeed Aurora had been drugged.

"Why . . . Grandfather, didn't you think I could
get me a wife on my own devices?" Bran ground out
mockingly between flashing white teeth.

"Faugh! I've done nothing, young cock, you've
done it all. Dost see there, the virgin stain on the
bed?" he snorted imperiously. "So, lad, you shall
honor the maid by giving her your name. Better Ro
than someone like that vacuous twit Melanie."

"Aha! I've got you, you devious old man!" Bran
wanted to shout, but the words issued forth in a low
hiss.

With both the door and the window open to
ventilate the room of intoxicating smoke, Aurora
came fully to and stared horrified first at the stain on
the bed and then up at Bran Ravenleigh. Chills of a
foreseen disaster went clear through her as her eyes
focused on Sir Eric and then she felt Ida Minter's

cool, gentle hands dressing her.

Recollection again haunted Bran. Sitting up in his bed, with Ida's gentle hands stroking the black hair that fell in glossy ringlets to her shoulders, Aurora reminded Bran of someone for a moment. Melanie? Again, nay. Who then? For a second in time, he became Fay, and had lost completely the identity Bran Ravenleigh.

"See here." Ida snapped Bran out of his daze as she rebuked, more on the girl's side now than on the young master's, "She has been ravished, see this here rent in her petticoat?"

"Indeed!" Sir Eric choked back a chuckle as he disregarded Bran's murderous glare.

"Oh, would that I were dead!" Aurora finally found her voice to sob. With sheer loathing dilating her eyes, she peered up at Bran Ravenleigh. "I dearly loved another and . . . and now you have ruined me. I hate you!"

Sir Eric felt his shoulders droop and the mischievous sparkle went out of his eyes. Bran gaped down at Aurora, feeling as if he had been kicked in the belly. She had been so soft and yielding in his arms, acting as if she loved him. He knew full well the reason. In her drugged state she had believed him to be another. Mistaken him for—perhaps, then, she was secretly in love with the pirate, and concealed this fact from Strang's enemy now—namely himself.

About to give a rebuff to his grandfather, Bran stepped to the bed instead, having come to an important decision. Also, he had studied her hand for a fleeting moment.

"You shall become my bride, Aurora Gregory," he

said commandingly. Then, "You must. You are a virgin no longer."

With that he snatched up his velvet cloak, shocking his grandfather with a swaggering nod as he strode from the room. But as he went along the corridor, his countenance loomed dangerously dark, swearing by all that was holy that Aurora Gregory would someday fall in love with him. In this way, he would somehow exact revenge, for he had long awaited to savor it. She was now his prisoner of love; and his servants were loyal enough to keep her from fleeing. With his cloak whipping out behind him, Bran descended the stairs and headed toward the door.

"Fay! Fay!" Aurora cried softly, her pounding fists muffled upon the soft bed. "Heart's love, you are forever lost to me."

Sir Eric and Ida exchanged looks of commiseration. Ida shook her graying head, but the older man sighed deeply, much grieved over the sin he'd committed against the young woman whose heart was bound to another.

Sir Eric went in search of the candles and, finding them, swiped the damnable things from the room. He decided he would not return them to Tom who had gotten the candles from an old Indian woman—a Chiskiak squaw—expert in her business of making various herbal candles. Hasheesh with crushed mandrake root made a narcotic more powerful than any potent drink.

Whipping open a window slot midway down the back stairs, Sir Eric tossed the half-burned candles out into the bushes below. "Be gone, Satan's devices,'' he snarled, turning brusquely from the window, and climbed wearily back to his bedchamber, vowing: I shall do everything in my power to make this marriage between Bran and Aurora work. His countenance brightened a bit then. Better little Ro than Melanie Wellbeloved. To be sure, better sweet Aurora than any other. So be it!

## Seventeen

The House convened on June the fifth. Jamestown
was crowded with members of the new Assembly; in
the May elections, Bran Ravenleigh had been chosen
to represent Elizabeth County. Bacon was still
waiting in Jamestown for a commission to fight the
Indians and, discounting Berkeley and the Elders,
most were sympathetic to Bacon and his Indian
crusade. Though under a charge of treason, Nathaniel Bacon had been chosen by the electorate to
represent Henrico County out west.

Bran discovered while sitting in Council that the
governor had promised Bacon leave of absence, but
no sooner had he approved the papers than he
regretted his action, and an hour later he ordered the
high sheriff to halt Bacon from leaving town. Bran
feared for Bacon's safety and surreptitiously slipped
out from the House, cast his wig aside to his
saddlebag, and caught up with Bacon in the
courtyard. With Nathaniel garbed in plain black
garments, Bran recognized the slim man at once.

"Leave by way of the forest and don't look back,"
Bran warned his friend quietly.

"What is it, Ravenleigh?" Bacon wondered, his

deep-set eyes glowing in the semidarkness of twilight.

"The governor has decided that you shall not be permitted to visit your wife at Curle's Neck. Your arrest will be sought."

Worry lines leapt into Bacon's lean, reflective face. "I shall hie to the backcountry, into the Surry forests and round up a band of one-hundred men. We must break the power of the savages for all time. Join me later, Bran?" Nathaniel had almost said Fay, the name used by Bacon and his band of rebels.

"Aye," Bran promised as the slender, aristocratic frame was already moving quickly away from him. By evening, he knew, the guards would find no trace of the stealthy Bacon. This meant full-scale rebellion; nothing else.

Bran would indeed join Bacon later, but for now he repaired to the inn. Come morning would be the Sabbath—his wedding day.

Aurora, her lovely face pale, peered out the window. A thunderstorm was brewing, rolling downriver, and the pale morning sun was half obscured by outskirting clouds. In the glebe of the church, the spring green leaves were very still. The calm before the storm breaks, she thought to herself dismally.

"I pray he never shows," she softly said of Bran Ravenleigh, uncaring that it might be sacrilegious on so solemn an occasion as today. To her this day could never be thought of as sacred. She had been drugged, framed, and now forced into his unholy marriage to a man she would ever loathe.

Melanie arranged the lacy veil to better shadow Aurora's features, fussing with the creamy overskirt embroidered with yellow roses next. She had gifted her cousin with the heavy, cream-silk gown with primrose-yellow underskirt and had even been generous in helping to alter the bodice to fit the smaller bosom. Because of the intricate rosebud pattern of the lacy veil that had been Margaret's own, not one soul could be certain of the bride's mood or what she was thinking. She hung her head as if in quiet meditation. If they only knew the circumstances, Aurora sighed dispiritedly.

"Ro," Melanie began in a hushed tone, "I meant to tell you this before. You needn't think that I'm angry for what has come to pass. I still don't understand it, but I'm so very happy for you. You and Bran make such a handsome pair—"

"Don't, Melanie," Aurora said with strained effort and received a bewildered frown for it.

Aurora shut her eyes, trying fiercely and with much pain to cleanse her mind of her phantom Fay. Her mind labored in vain. She attempted to dwell on other things, like the soothing voice of Parson Trumble, but again it was a hopeless effort. The Almighty had planted a man in her heart and all the angels in Heaven could not remove him. She would rather that the precious gift of her maidenhood had been his, she thought for a wicked moment.

Just as the murmuring congregation thought the bride would be stood up, Bran Ravenleigh entered, dashingly swank in all his finery. The bridal hymn opened up as Bran moved to the aisle and in spite of himself his eyes strayed to the Edwards pew. Aurora, still as a statue, stood beside her cousin with David Wiley on the other side of Melanie. When Aurora and Bran came to the front of the church, his arm brushed hers and she trembled as if taken ill. Bran noticed but stared straight ahead at the minister.

With the long ceremony ended, the vows exchanged, a light touch of lips sealed the couple together in holy matrimony, just as a distant roll of thunder was heard. Arm in arm they turned, passing slowly together through the chattering crowd already milling about the door. Bran bowed to the ladies and made small talk amidst congratulations. After Catherine and Aylmer Tobie congratulated them and moved on, Aurora turned to her new husband. There was a question in her lackluster eyes and he bent his dark head downward.

"Mistress Ravenleigh?" he said, shocking Aurora momentarily with the usage of her new last name.

"I miss Hetty. Is she still at North Creek?"

Sea-gray eyes bore into hers. "I've sent her ahead to Raven Keep—*our* home—to prepare the bridal chamber. We shall share the room from this day onward, my wife." He pressed her arm meaningfully.

Aurora lowered her veiled head meekly, feeling as if she were being spirited away by a stranger. The parishioners, especially the ladies, thought the new Mistress Ravenleigh strangely sad and withdrawn for just being wed to a man as darkly handsome and romantic as a Scottish highwayman or dashing pirate.

The women jostled one another to get a closer look, perhaps even to accidentally brush by the handsome groom. In the crush, the bride's hands made contact with the male hardness of her eager husband. His ardor grew even higher as they were squeezed together for several minutes; Aurora's heightened color was taken for her wedding-day blush.

Her blood tingled with excitement and her skin prickled, her senses coming alive at this first curious touch of man. Wondrous and breathtaking, though willing it not to be, she suddenly felt devilish, seductive, womanly.

Bran bent down close to her cheek, his fingers brushing against her ear. She suppressed the excitement she had been feeling.

"You have a soft milky touch, my sweet lady. You blush most becomingly all of a sudden. What happened to your wheyface of several minutes ago?" he asked with pauses in-between.

"Bran, please, I am suddenly foot-weary. Can we move along?" She kept her hand held safely near her waist.

He chuckled. "Are you as naïve as you appear to me?" Almost sounding bored, languid.

The black fringe of his lashes swooped lower as his lips gently nuzzled an ear, tiny and lovely, set close to her head. Her eyes lifted in an unusual manner, questioning, wondering, before curled lashes, long and dark, veiled her innermost thoughts.

"I know one thing," he said, with lips twitching curiously.

With a slight catch in her breath, Aurora looked up at him, lifting a questioning brow. He seemed to be enjoying himself, but the cat had her tongue. He was easy, and she was nervous.

"What, Bran, did you say something?" She tried to match his mood of airiness.

"The naked, brutal truth, yes. You've a pressing need to make love, just as strong as mine is for you." He took her by the arm to guide her outside. "Don't looked so shocked, love, you'll find that you will be quite satisfied after our lovemaking."

Aurora *was* shocked. Never had a man been so bold with her, and now that he had made her wife did that mean he would never give her a moment's peace? He was already proving how possessive he could be with his arm wrapped about her waist almost painfully, hip grinding in her side.

Melanie, looking pleased about something, walked with David to the waiting Edwards conveyance while Bran guided his new wife to a dainty Arabian mare that stood nuzzling Nimrod with her white, velvety nose. Aurora's own mare, Cupid, had been sent on ahead with her meager belongings to Raven Keep.

Farewells and felicitations were called to the bride and groom as the light drizzle of rain began to fall and the horses moved off, away from the wagons and carts. Bran rode beside his wife, tall and as handsome as a cavalier in his red-plumed hat and black velvet cape, the white ruffles of his shirt falling over tanned wrists. From his high perch he reached over to hand his wife a lovely camlet cloak with demure hood attached to it, and slowed his mount to match the pace of hers. She could smell the masculine scent of him and it clung disturbingly to the soft garment.

"Thank you, Bran, 'tis lovely," she murmured, careful not to ask where he had obtained it as he arranged it around her shoulders.

"It should keep you dry, at least until we reach the inn. The rain will hold us up for a spell, perhaps the night if it lasts." He waited for her to speak, looking over to her slantingly. She continued to ride in silence. "Well, would you rather we kept going on? Or what?"

"It matters not to me, Bran," she answered meekly, her face concealed from him by the deep hood of the cloak.

Bran cussed beneath his breath, his frame of mind dark and brooding. On the road up ahead a rider mounted on a magnificent red hunter appeared out of nowhere. The white mare nervously pranced as she sensed her master's alarm. Bran reached over to quiet the mare, scowling at his wife at the same time.

"Relax Ro, 'tis only Tom Bone, my manservant. Lord, but you are skittish. If you keep it up, she'll throw you," he said sternly.

Aurora finally gave vent to her frustration. "Mayhap she will," she said, watching the servant while he made a sign with his hand and then rode on ahead.

Bran snorted at her reply, his regard too on the servant that would meet them at the inn. Tom Bone was serving as outrider, for there were dark reports circulating that the Monacans had been raiding, coming as far south as the Chickahominy River. He would take no chances; he wanted to see his new wife safe and sound to her new home. Even should they stay at the inn, he would have her tonight!

Arriving at the inn, Bran dismounted and slipped his arm around Aurora's waist to help her down, his unsparing regard never leaving her countenance.

Tom Bone was waiting outside to care for their mounts. Aurora swept a look over to him. She knew him as the man who had held her captive while Bran had gone after Captain Strang that day at the hollow. Something else was tickling her memory. Those eyes—had she seen them lately in a dream she'd had?

Inside the inn, Tom sat at a respectable distance away from the newlyweds. Rachel Smythe brought Bone the rasher of ham and warm buttered bread he'd ordered earlier and then moved toward the table where the newlyweds were seated. Tom watched Aurora's face for her reaction as Bran looked up, somewhat sheepishly, to see the serving wench standing there smiling down at him. Munching a corner of his bread, Tom slid down in his chair to watch uneasily the next move.

"Mutton stew, Bran?" Rachel asked. With a curious glance sweeping over the lovely young woman, she added, "Ale?" She took in their fine regalia. Rachel then smiled knowingly at the man she'd known as lover. "Ah, this calls for something stronger—like wine, Bran?"

"Aye, Rachel. The stew and the wine."

"A rasher of ham and bread for the both of you, Bran?"

"Aye, Rachel."

Rachel curtsied and then sashayed off to the kitchen. Bran stole an imploring glance at Tom Bone, but the manservant cast his eyes upon his half-eaten meal. Rachel had made no secret of their having been lovers, Tom was thinking to himself. He had overheard everything and seen the sultry look that Rachel had turned upon Bran. Again, he waited for the next move.

"I rather thought it meet not to tax your strength further, sweeting," Bran began, his eyes averted from his wife's. "I've decided that we shall stay for the night."

"Aye, Bran," Aurora answered mockingly. "Whate'er you say, Bran." She smiled in affectation, laying the serviette upon her lap in a tidy fashion.

Bran snapped his own napkin up and followed suit. Tom looked on, taking in the scowl in the sea-gray eyes. His master was now catching it for having been such an affectionate varlet, one that had set many female hearts on fire. He wondered just how Bran was going to unsnarl himself out of this one.

The meal was brought to the table by Rachel and another serving wench, and though Aurora was not hungry, she decided she would nibble at as much as she could. After Rachel had laid out the meal and gone back to her other customers, the bride and groom were each occupied in supping. Aurora merely played with her food, though, while Bran plied a good knife and fork. He had just drained his second goblet of wine then raised his third one in a toast.

"To my sweet bride, our marriage and—this night," he toasted, never slurring a word.

Aurora, finding she could naught do otherwise without drawing attention to herself, lifted her full goblet, and merely followed with, "To our marriage." But her hollow murmur belied her words.

Bran's ardent gaze bore deeply, his lazy smile half-teasing and sensual. Aurora was thinking that he must have turned that smile upon a hundred women before her, as he must have done with Rachel countless times.

"Do you really mean that, Aurora?"

Aurora's teeth tugged at her lower lip. She had not a moment to answer, for Bran rose slowly to his feet, drawing her up with him. His next words were just heard by her, so soft and low, but for all the fear and trembling they provoked they might as well have been an explosion ringing in her ear.

To cover up her nervousness and to gain a moment to gather her wits, Aurora pretended she hadn't heard him. She stood so near to him, and with his great height he seemed to encompass her in a warm and private world.

"I am sorry, Bran, I did not hear what you just said," she lied.

"I said—I would be alone with you soon, dear wife. But first, I shall have Tom go out to the horses and fetch some things I've lately purchased from Jamestown, some dainty items that came in off the ship a week ago. One of the female servants will bring the items up to you."

Aurora trembled, damning her coward's heart. "Will . . . you be coming up then soon afterwards, Bran?"

"Of course. Do you think me a fool? Any man would crave to look upon his new bride in a fresh, revealing nightie he has just gifted her with."

She peeked up at her dark-browed husband. "Not so loud, Bran, you embarrass me. You will not imbibe too much more, pray?" She had seen the fire in his eyes, and the drink had begun to fan it into a roaring blaze.

Bran lifted a dainty hand and pressed a warm kiss into the palm. "'Tis our wedding night, sweeting. Forgive me. Now, off you go," he finished in an undertone that only she could hear, "but do not keep me waiting too long. I'm a man of a most impatient nature, love."

Aurora's legs trembled beneath her as she mounted the narrow stairs, to seal her fate, she concluded.

Long shadows crept across the floor as a servant entered the room and began lighting candles in their earthenware dishes. Aurora sat motionless on a bench before a wavy mirror, straining her ears to hear the echoes of her husband's boots come clicking along the hall. She had waited an eternity, it seemed, and still he did not come. Her unseeing eyes wandered to the door. Where was Bran? What was he doing?

The young female servant busied herself in the corner of the scantily furnished room, placing a fresh jug of water on the stand next to the basin. She then went out as quietly and busily as she had entered minutes before.

Aurora again peered at herself in the mirror; the white satin gown, cut low in the front, half-exposed her small white bosom and made her look startlingly ghost-like. But high color spotted her cheeks and her raven hair contrasted against the pristine white fabric. Upon her dainty feet were white satin slippers, and suspended on a thin gold chain about her neck was a diamond heart surrounded by delicately cut emeralds. She had never owned anything this expensive and fine, nor had she worn such rich garments before today. That included the pale blue velvet robe with silver riband ties that lay like a jewel out of place upon the patched and shoddy coverlet on the bed.

*Do not keep me waiting*, her husband had warned. Aurora sighed softly and with a bitterness born of resentment. If she were lucky, he would drink himself into forgetfulness and bed that Rachel wench. But she doubted it, even though she could hear drifting up to her the sounds of merry-making and drunken giggling, accompanied now and then by the lusty bawling of a songstress.

"Oh! Celebrating without me, is he," Aurora shot to her feet. "Well, a merry good night to you all."

Aurora kicked off her fine slippers and slithered beneath the cool covers, blowing out the candle beside the bed in a huff of exasperated breath. Punching and plumping the pillow that smelled musty and was harder than a saddlebag, Aurora rolled over and put her back to the door.

Aurora woke suddenly with a start when the door opened. She did not stir, but lay still as a post. Yet inside, her heart was storm-tossed and she was put in fear as the menacing steps, familiar to her now, came toward the bed. She waited on pins and needles, shutting her eyes tight and pretending to be asleep as the weight eased itself down onto the bed. Warm, hard fingers ran down her spine, taking her breath away. She couldn't help it, and gasped.

"You could not fool me, sweeting." There was a smile in Bran's voice. "Roll over, 'tis our wedding night. Come now, my shy bride, do not be so unsociable.''

Unresponsively Aurora permitted him to fondle her buttocks from behind while he traced feather-soft kisses down from her nape to her shoulder blades. She shuddered. She was feeling so bewildered, she had promised her heart to love forever another, yet her husband was making her come alive, too. What was the matter with her? Was his lusty nature rubbing off on her? The thought angered her.

"Go away, sir, go back to your sin-laden wenches. Can you not see that I am asleep," she stated rather than asked.

"Cease with your children's games, Aurora."

Aurora bolted from the bed, having seized the chance when he released her. She stood facing him with her arms akimbo.

"Why do you not go and fondle your comely wench? You seem to be familiar enough with her . . . Bran," she mocked with a haughty sniff.

Bran leered up at her from the bed. "'Tis a sure sign of jealousy, but I took that badly, wife!"

Aurora snatched up the lacily frilled cap that had been among the items in the large bundle of fine clothes brought to her by the tavern-maid. She fitted the cap around her head with brisk movements and then made to snatch up the robe.

"Just what in hell do you think you're doing?"

"I am going down to celebrate. 'Tis my turn!" She turned her back to him in a huff, meaning to do just as she had said.

Bran chuckled, but there was a dangerous tone in

it. "Are you mad-brained? If you go downstairs as foolish as you look, you'll make a laughingstock of yourself—not to mention me."

As soon as his words were out he moved like lightning, cool fingers fastening firmly about her wrists as he snatched Aurora back to the bed and, with a squeal issuing from her, he tossed her onto her back.

The thick stub of candle he had brought with him squatted in its earthenware dish and the little flame stood tense, as if seeking to reach the stars beyond the low-ceilinged room. Bran rolled over, snatched it from the table and held it over her head, scrutinizing his wife in her white frilled cap that fitted snugly around her head. She stared wide-eyed and frightened up at him as she busily tucked the recalcitrant strands of raven hair back up inside.

"Speak again."

Dark-winged brows drew together in the beginning of bewilderment. "What did you say? Was it 'Speak'?" she asked.

"Softer."

The candle floated slowly above her, and mesmerized, she followed it. She caught Bran staring hard, too, but at her. Eyes, so intense, glowed with a look unfathomable, and she could not help but draw back and gasp at the back of her hand. A strange fear clutched her heart as he continued his studying of every corner of her face.

"Dear God," his breath exploded softly. Again, "God!"

Aurora's trembling fingers slid up to examine her face. "Bran . . . what is it?" She was afraid she had broken out in some horrible pox or something, maybe grown aged of a sudden from the wearying events of the day. "Please tell me. Have I become homely suddenly, from some malady that has attacked me?"

"Nay . . . quite the reverse," he half-choked out. "I—I've never seen you quite so—so beautiful." The candle shook as he placed it back upon the table, then turned back to visibly search her shadowed countenance. "Aye, you take my breath away, sweet." He reached out drawing her into the circle of his steely arms.

Aurora was startled by his emotion. "Bran . . . you tremble."

"Aye," he breathed deeply of her sweet fragrance, the fragrance of bayberry soap.

"Are you unwell?"

"Aye," he nibbled at the slim column of her white neck.

"What ails you?" she wondered, becoming against her will more sensitive to his touch.

Unseen, he squinted one eye devilishly. "Are you concerned, sweeting?"

"I . . . can I be of help? If 'tis a headache I've some herbs to remedy it. Oh, but they are in my saddlebag, that is if Melanie instructed the servant to pack my pouch—"

Now he groaned as if truly in pain, at the same time hugging her close. "Aaah, thou art beautiful, little Ro, my sweet bride," he murmured husky-deep. "You see, my need is great for a soothing balm, but 'tis not an ache of the head."

Aurora came up on her knees, tucking her legs

beneath her. "Tell me then, where does it hurt? Your back? Your belly?"

"Aye," he groaned, "'tis my belly, something I ate perhaps. But your herbs—"

"Never mind them. Lay back and I shall rub the pain from it for you. Remove your shirt," she ordered in the tone of a proficient nurse.

In his haste Bran nearly rent his laced shirt in removing it. He did as she instructed, shutting his lids while he awaited those little hands to perform their magic. As she began to massage, his belly tightened, and he groaned every now and then in making a show of pain he was experiencing.

"Bran! You give off a warmth as though you be a smouldering fire!"

"Don't I know. Lower please, 'tis moving lower," he murmured with fire indeed in his breath.

"You grow hot!" she worried in her maiden innocence. "You need . . . remove your breeches, Bran."

"Aye . . . Aye, to be sure."

As he rose to do her bidding, she properly averted her gaze from looking upon his nakedness. He was back in a flash, thoughtfully slipping beneath the cool sheet so as not to shock her with the sight of his throbbing ripeness. As she began again, with her eyes cast aside, the candle sputtered and then went out, plunging the room into darkness. She paid it no mind but continued to knead the muscled flesh. He groaned even louder and she was ignorant as to his true affliction. Now his hand moved beneath the sheet and found her thigh, emulating the motion of her busily soothing hands. Her flesh quivered where he touched it. Again he moved, now bringing her hands into contact with his proud flesh. She gasped in surprise.

"Oh, Bran, what is it?"

"What is it? *What is it!*" he exclaimed, stifling a peal of laughter. "Sweeting, don't you know anything?" He was quick to close long fingers over hers to hold her there. "'Tis my trusty blade, dearest wife, and you possess the sweet sheath of its pleasure. And now, Mistress Ravenleigh, you too shall know that pleasure." He rolled over to pluck the frilled cap from her head.

"Bran, you are not ill!" She held him off with hands splayed to his chest.

"Aye, but I am. My pain is great, and only you and you alone can ease this torture you put me through. I've waited long enough, Ro, you are my wife now—"

"Bran! I am not ready to do what you ask, even though 'tis my duty as wife," she squeaked in a tiny voice brimmed with apprehension.

"I do not ask"—he paused to lift her nightgown— "I demand! Now, help me remove this plaguey thing off you."

"Nay!" She tugged downward as he tugged upward.

"Hell and damnation! I've tried being gentle with you, tried to warm you. 'Tis too late for your shyness. I shall not heed your protests or tears after this act has begun, sweeting. Curse it! cry now if you must."

"My husband, you do not understand," she did cry,

the tears rolling and splashing on his hands as he knelt on the bed, snatching the gown up. She caught his busy hands in a prayerful gesture. "Pray cease, give me time, Bran!"

He wrenched from her and leapt off the bed, the warm sweat beading on his brow as he went to throw up the sash. Having risen, the new summer moon came in and cast its paleness over the mussed bed. Aurora sat searching wildly for means of escape, tugging at the gown that was bunched up around her waist. She continued to sob as longings for Fay merged with the unwelcome desire she was beginning to feel for Bran Ravenleigh—her husband; and she was troubled as never before. He shan't wipe the memory of Fay from her mind, her heart screamed.

The moon slipped beneath a cloud as Bran returned to the bed, determined to peel off the barrier that lay between them. First, he raked his fingers through the midnight hair, threading them back as he came down beside her slowly. Tresses undulated in soft waves, hair as shiny as the richest silk, which imprisoned a faint, delicious perfume all its own. He took his time in love-play, slowly trying to awaken the maiden flush in her, slipping his hand beneath her gown to cup a small round breast. His breath quickened at the delightful feel of her silky skin as the nipples hardened against his fingertips.

Helpless to stay the sensation, Aurora felt delicious tremors coursing through her like quicksilver, and the wine of budding desire flowing in her veins. As Bran murmured love words into her ear, her hair, the earthy deepness of his male voice seemed to vibrate down into her quivering belly.

"Aaah, Ro, my darling, my beloved," he breathed gently against her moist lips.

"Bran," she choked back another tear, "you . . . love me?"

Out from the midnight-blue clouds the moon stole, flirting down through the tiny window. Bran's eyes sparkled as he lifted his dark head, and Aurora at once caught her breath at the diamond-white brilliance of them.

He caressed her soft cheek, then turned his hand brushing his knuckles along her fine chin, answering tenderly, "Aye, as my own life do I love thee. You are the light that shines to brighten my day. I have loved and worshipped you since first . . . we met." He would say no more, for now.

Her heart pounded savagely, faster as both soft and hard lips twisted gently across hers; and faster yet as his iron length came in contact with her smaller trembling frame. The gown disappeared as if by magic, slipping easily up over her head as his mouth left hers for what seemed merely an instant. Again his lips sealed with hers, his tongue plundering the moist tissues of her mouth, tongue, and lips. The taste of her salt tears and her honeyed lips mingled bittersweet.

Her loins tightened and throbbed and the name was wrenched from her lips. "Bran!" and above her she could see his features cast in relief from the moon, as he slowly lifted his head triumphantly. Her yearning eyes then widened and she was suddenly put to fear as he set to quicken the pace of his

309

lovemaking. She could feel him tense, moving hard and fast between her thighs.

"Ro, little love . . ."

Now he was guiding her softly curving hips, and her hot breath quickened with his as he repositioned her thighs. Of a sudden she was shocked, repulsed, for he was not her gentle, romantic Fay, but a stranger, this husband of hers—a beardless, ruthless lover she knew not. She pressed and squeezed his arms, struggling in earnest now, making little whimpers of fear in her dry throat.

"It needs be this way, love," he said to soothe her worst apprehension of that first initial thrust. "Only for a moment and then you will taste the first joys of your womanhood. I warn you, Ro, cease your struggles now or it shall be all the worse."

"How can this be? I am a maid no longer—"

"'Tis done!" He could not desist.

Taken unawares, Aurora felt a shaft of pain tear through her loins; yet the searing burn of her deflowering was mercifully fleeting, as he hushed her panting cries with raining kisses. He was part of her now as he began a rocking motion, squeezing her buttocks while forcing each squirm of her hips to move in close action with his. Little tendrils of hair moistened with his sweat curled on her forehead. A long shudder of pleasure unbidden escaped from her as faster and faster in a powerful rhythmic movement he strove to go higher, discovering her deepest secrets. Her tender flesh began to burn and ache again as he rode her like a savage, thrusting deeper and deeper, as if he would possess her very soul. His breathing became labored and she gasped in half surprise, half pain, almost shrieking when his proud flesh began its throbbing inside of her. Although she tried to surface, Aurora fell into a dark-like tumbling down a long tunnel.

"Rise with me, love!" he cried out in painful ecstasy.

His thrusts now gave way to a sudden explosion of all the pent forces in him to an agonizing and unresisted end without her. His tempest broke and flooded as her tense thighs finally fell back, admitting the full measure of his release. Leaving her, he collapsed onto his back and lay motionless, brooding at the ghostlike pattern on the floor as the moon and stars came in. When he would have reached the second time for her, she hid her face in the curve of her arm. Bran snorted softly and again rolled away from her, his thigh muscles yet twitching.

After a minute of breath spent, he asked, "What is it, why do you shun me now?"

"You hurt me! But you shan't ever hurt me again."

He groaned impatiently. "It always does the first time. The discomfort shall lessen as you become stretched and yielding, my virginial mate."

"Nay, never! You played me false, Bran, drugged me into this unholy union. What kind of a man are you? If you but truly loved me you would not have tricked me. Why?" she wondered, but Melanie's words came back to haunt her: *Bran Ravenleigh no doubt has bastards strewn about the countryside. He loves a woman like a lord one day and then searches for another the next. Even a comely wife could not*

311

*keep him long at her side.*

"Listen well, my frosty wife," his words stabbed her now. "My conniving grandfather thought you a better match than that slut whom you call cousin. And, as for the blood, it came from the little wound on your finger. See? You've still the mark." He snatched her hand up before her eyes.

Aurora snatched her hand back. "But, still, you cast Melanie aside, she who was to become your bride in the first place!"

"Oho! I had never promised to take her hand in marriage. But you are right about one thing—I loved foolishly, blindly," he said, but his damnable male pride would reveal no more.

"You've a fickle heart, Bran Ravenleigh. You shall never win mine, though husband you be," she muttered coldly.

"Just what do you fear, Aurora?"

"Nothing!"

"Aye, you do. Perhaps you are afraid of nothing but fear, and perhaps you enjoyed the sample of passion that has just transpired between us, but haven't the courage to want more."

"Fear? Hah, I desire nothing from you . . . you unspeakable knave!"

"Just who is this man that makes you so lovesick that you deny yourself the pleasure of surrendering completely to your own husband?"

She turned a deaf ear to the first part of his question and retorted, "I shall never surrender beneath your churning loins!" She put her back to him haughtily.

"You shall, as surely as I penetrated your icy

maidenhood this night. Someday, I swear, you shall beg me to pleasure you, and damn me if you shan't know the full joys of your womanhood. Sleep now, for come tomorrow and all the days thereafter that we are together you shall know my thrust. But listen to this—you'll not know the full measure of ecstasy until you beg for it."

"I shall never!" she choked on a sob. "You are lecherous and—and I hate you, the very wicked sight of you!"

"Sweeting," he began low, "you have but only tasted my lechery this night. Mark my words, Ro, before the year is out you shall open your sweet thighs to me willingly. You'll soon fit me like a glove."

"So be it that you ever rape me, Bran Ravenleigh, but mark you *my* words. I shall be the victor in this, for you will tire of me within a fortnight, and you too shall be blue with cold, and hoarfrost shall grow on your beloved manroot!" She was aghast at her own usage of words, but it was too late to pull them back.

Bran chuckled at her wrathful humor softly. Then, with a suddenly bored and tired yawn, he too rolled onto his side. Before he fell into a deep but restless sleep, he felt an icy premonition wrap itself around his yearning heart.

Horribly exhausted from the grueling day, the new Mistress Ravenleigh felt herself tumbling into a comatose sleep. But first, terribly frightening thoughts nibbled at the core of her weary brain. She was doomed to become a prisoner of Bran's heartless and selfish love. How long would she be able to deny

313

her woman's body its release beneath him? Though she was inexperienced, she knew without a shadow of doubt that her husband knew no rival as a lover. Most important to her happiness: Would Fay forever and ever haunt her, right to her grave?

For now, Aurora knew the sleep of the living.

## *Eighteen*

Frail morning light filtered through the leaded casement window as Aurora, mistress of Raven Keep, put down her needle and blue material while heaving a sigh of boredom. She glanced about the room she shared with her husband; that is, when he was at home.

Aurora had discovered early in their marriage that Bran was not cut out for home life. He had been instantly bored when they arrived home as man and wife. She could hear him prowling in the dark all the first week, and like a restless cat he had finally gone out to roam, just as she had known he would. Late nights of debauchery, she added to herself shrewishly.

What do I care? she thought now. As long as he left her alone, she felt fine. It was only when he came home and *didn't* leave her be that she turned unhappy and nervously bothered—and bewildered too.

Just running her hand over the deep, riotous carving of the Elizabethan bed now caused her to shudder in apprehension. She moved quickly from the bed to lighten her mood, her skirts brushing with a rustle against the rich black-and-red Turkey carpet, finally walking on the polished wood floors that bordered it.

Massive pieces of black walnut furniture in the Tudor style dominated the bedchamber, pushed up against the wall emphasizing the room's vastness—but for the long French chair that was her favorite piece; Bran had known this and moved it into the room before the hearth. The chair was large enough for her to lie down full length to rest if she so desired. It was a daintier piece, decidedly French, with French-green velvet upholstery and a curved back that dipped down at one end and rose high at the other. It was true that the material clashed with the red, but Bran didn't seem to mind all that much as long as . . . as she was . . . happy.

Did he indeed want her to be happy? And was she? She didn't know any more, she thought, a rueful smile playing on her pretty pink lips.

Aurora moved to the wardrobe after having sighted the sleeve of Bran's white lawn shirt sticking out. She could almost picture him wearing it, his jet hair a startling contrast to the whiteness, the sleeves billowing in the wind, the ruffles all aflutter—on the deck of a ship with his long lean legs spread wide, his blue-black hair blown back in a salty breeze, and a golden hoop piercing one ear. She would not be one bit surprised to learn that he had ancestors that had been pirates.

A pulse began in Aurora's throat as she opened the doors on the wardrobe wide and looked over all of her husband's clothes. She felt as if she were eavesdropping on him, into his past, present, and future . . . *future?*

Her hands floated over the deer-color leather leggings; breeches of Osnaburg, doeskin; and waist-coats in puce and buff of brocaded cloth, with silver buttons. Riding clothes. Beneath were high boots, marching in a line and well varnished. Luxuriant wigs of the gentleman, combed, curled to perfection, sat impressively on stands on a side shelf. She continued to feel, pausing on the soft velvet robe of scarlet with black silk neckcloth. Vests, cravats, wigs, garters, and buckles of silver and gold, scarves of white linen, quite sheer, and measuring, she guessed, two yards in length.

"He must have been of noble birth!" she breathed. Of course, Sir Eric had told her that King Charles was a distant relative on Sir Eric's mother's side.

Aurora could imagine Bran in only half of these fine clothes that made up the dandy, arrogant cavalier. All this fancy finery must have been a snobbish hobby with him at one time. He must have taken many mistresses at the Stuart court and watched with wry detachment as they filed past him and made room for the next one in line.

She had in fact seen him in his regalia on several occasions. There had been Melanie's party while her parents had been away: Bran had worn a rich, curling wig that had poured over his broad shoulders, and his lips had twisted in a sarcastic smile as he had entered the house. At what had supposed to have been an engagement party between him and Melanie: Oh, he'd cut quite the dashing figure, a swaggering cock, to be sure.

Now Aurora picked up her skirts, displaying a well-turned ankle. She pointed down to her toe, bustling up her skirts in back, playing the powdered and posturing lady of the court.

"See here, milord?" she boasted. "My high-heeled slipper with splendid buckles and my China silk gown of royal blue with matching silk petticoats? See anything that catches your fancy, milord?" She curtsied, whirled, laughing and dancing about the room in a whimsical fashion.

Aurora stopped as if to face a somber someone. "Ah, yes, André, ready my coach-and-six, I shall take a spin about the park. Now, go and hasten the lackeys to my coach. Of course, bring the Madeira to my drawing room first, and tell milord Ravenleigh—"

"Hist!" Hetty entered with a tray of food and a surprised look. "What are ye doing, luv, spinning about the room and gie'ing yerself airs. I did'na see someone wi' you in here." She poked her head around.

"Oh, Hetty!" Aurora pouted as she flounced over to plop down onto the French chair. "'Twas merely make-believe, having some fun I was. 'Tis a bit boring of late, with—"

"Aha! Wi' yer husband gone, sure. Ye already miss him and his dark brooding looks. Whew! He never seems to be wi'out a scowl when he's here, which ain't much a'tall."

Hetty wore a masklike expression while settling down a wooden tray of crusty bread spread with honey, and hot tea. Sir Eric had been discussing Bacon and his rebels with her, that many planters had banded together to take the field with Bacon. He had left the conversation hang after that. And where, Hetty wondered now, was Bran Ravenleigh just

318

when Bacon was marching again?

The threat of civil war that had hidden like a poisonous snake in the grass now slithered out and lifted its head, prepared to strike the deadly blow. Nathaniel Bacon had crossed the boundary into civil war and rebelliously took charge of provincial affairs in Jamestown while Sir William took to ship, across the bay to the eastern shore.

The Indians that had been raiding as far north as Middlesex and as far to eastward as the Great Dragon Swamp, now had become enemy to Berkeley as well as Bacon. No one family in the colony knew who was friend and who was foe, and even the friendly Indians were being murdered. Now Bacon's rebels plundered the Pamunkey camp of its pitiful booty and returned to the James with close to fifty Indian captives. Up in Henrico County whole families had been wiped out by the savage Monacans. Just who was savage and who was civilized, and who was rebel, Bacon or Berkeley, it was hard to guess. . . .

It was a dark and long-bearded figure that rode his unflagging mount westward through the forest, blood staining his buckskin-clad thigh and trickling down into his tall boots. Tom Bone rode quietly but concerned beside his master, noting that Bran was quite woozy from loss of blood by the time Raven Keep was reached.

Painstakingly and frequently Tom had bandaged the thigh, but the Indian's blade had slashed deep. The Indians were poor shots, but they could wield their old-fashioned weapons with ease in a sneak attack.

The wolfhound barked once, then settled down. Sir Eric was already nodding in the great oak chair when Bran and Tom entered, with the manservant assisting the wounded man to the crimson-cushioned settee. Sir Eric came wide awake, seeing his grandson stretch his long, bandaged leg out stiffly in front of him, while Tom bent over to remove the bloodied rag with a swift but careful motion of his knife. Next he slitted the breeches in a swift upward slice and Bran grimaced once.

"Blood of Beelzebub!" Sir Eric shot up and came to stand before them. "Ah-hah! Chasing savages again, eh? Serves you right, son, you should stay at home where you belong with your newly wedded bride!" he snorted but worry lines crept into his seamed face.

Cuffee and Mr. Minter entered the Great Parlour just then, each carrying clean rags and earthenware bowls of fresh water. They had been alerted to the urgency of swift action when first the manservant had entered the house with the young master leaning against him, one arm slung about Tom's strong shoulders.

"Newly wedded bride—" Bran gritted between his teeth as Tom bathed the deep cut—"yea, of nearly four months you mean. By the way, how is she?" He put his head back on the settee and stared at the high, timber-beamed ceiling.

"Hah! Lot you care," Sir Eric chided. "You've not seen her in over a month's time again. She could be a bride of only seven days for all that you've kept her company. Well, how in the world did you manage to get that?" He indicated the swelling gash with a waft of his hand.

Bran chuckled lightly. "I had some help, sir, 'twas not easy, though. The old Indian was quicker than a blink, that is for damn sure. So, you did not answer my question?"

"As fine as a deserted young wife could be. Guess she'd be bored half to death had you not sent those fancy materials here six weeks back. She's been busy enough sewing herself up some pretty dresses. Her heart ain't in it or anything else, though," Sir Eric ended, wearing a look of sore regret. He turned to Minter then. "Go and fetch the little bride down here, tell her that her roving husband has come home—for a visit." He tossed in the latter as a taunt directed at his grandson.

Having imagined his wife in the black embrace of loneliness, Bran's conscience now chafed sorely. He fingered his long beard, then spoke tersely. "Nay! Not now. Later will I see her." He grimaced next. "Damn, Tom, you're about as gentle as a prickly porcupine mounting its mate!" he snapped with sudden irritation.

Tom loosed a chuckle. "Least we know where your healthy thoughts are at, master." But he tried to be more gentle as he finished cleaning the wound. "Looks bad," Tom added as he rose to stand. "Might be getting infected. We might have to apply some poultices if it doesn't go down in awhile." He unbuckled Bran's belt and set it aside for him.

"We shall see," was all Bran said as he took the cup of strong sack that Cuffee offered him. Then he shut his eyes and with a deep sigh leaned back.

It was apparent that the young master would be left alone to rest a spell, so they began to file out the door. When the wolfhound whined to be let outside, Sir Eric himself went to walk him. Bran reopened his bloodshot eyes, calling Minter back.

"I would like to shave and then bathe, Minter. Could you see that the bath is readied in my old bedchamber upstairs?"

Minter was slightly taken aback by the request that was more a plea than an order. He inclined his slim face. "Of course, Master Bran. Would you like your supper warmed now or later?"

"I shall rest first, then have Cuffee prepare Tom and myself something. Where is my wife, do you know?" he asked wearily, again shutting his eyes.

"Pardon? Oh, upstairs, resting after the evening meal." Minter peered at the man strangely, recalling that Sir Eric had already informed him of her whereabouts. "You really should get more comfortable, young sir. Could I perhaps help you upstairs now, with Cuffee's help?"

But Bran could not hear the servant; he was already in the land of nod. Minter stole quietly to the door, placing a finger over his lips when Harris appeared there and was about to speak. Steward Harris followed Minter down the hall, conversing softly with him.

Wild, nightmarish, vaporous dreams swam in Bran's head. Below the winking stars in the velvet sky dawned a savage orange glow, bursting, blooming, restless to consume the warehouse . . . the place he had burned several months ago. He stood there, wondering why it was happening again, as the dancing, leaping, groping tongues of fire melted the warehouse . . . Strang's pit of evil and ill-begotten goods. From the smouldering ashes stepped a raven-haired beauty, afire from waist to foot, bearing the remnants of flame as she floated toward him . . . *Aurora!*

Bran moaned and thrashed about on the settee, groping toward the advancing figure to beat out the flames of blood-red. It was useless, he couldn't reach her! Her lips formed the words "Help me!" but again he was powerless to reach her. In the background stood the pirate, his lips split in mocking laughter. Bran reached out as though he would rend the man in two, but the slender frame vanished behind his wife, leering up from her feet with a face of fire. Gnashing his flaming teeth, the pirate retreated to a dark ship, vanishing into the murk of a black sea.

Aurora cried out to him: "Bran, help me—help! Put the fire out, Bran!"

Bran felt himself hurtled forward, but then stood back watching his form reach Aurora just as a ghostly, blood-red mist was rising to engulf her. He saw his twin reach down and bring up the herb-pouch, and scattering the bright leaves about, he doused the flames and mist in a sparking crackle. She was now whole, gowned in white-and-diamond brilliance, and he went forward in slow-motion and entered his own form again. Like white velvety snakes, her arms reached for him and in his dream he felt the tightening of his groin as they came together beneath the cedars in the lane. His hands slipped beneath her hips, drawing her up to him as he opened her thighs and entered. She arched against him, then moved back, matching his rhythm and giving. Giving! Thrust for thrust. She moaned: I love you, Bran! The pulsating warmth in his being gave way as the final stroke exploded between her yielding thighs and she met him all the way, reaching the stars with him. Suddenly she was slipping away from him, then fled, crying: I am not Melanie, not Melanie, nay, I am not fair-haired.

Bran came awake with a feverish jolt to his senses. His eyes glowed insanely bright as he tried holding onto the dream that for awhile had given him pleasure beyond comprehension. Aye. Nothing but a dream. He battled with his wits and tried fiercely to recall every detail about it. But now it came and went in flashes, some parts as elusive as a spring butterfly. He felt his breeches sodden with the seed of his passion and cursed out loud. He shook his head, damning the throbbing pain in his limb. Looking down, he was all but shocked at the swollen size of his wound.

"Minter!"

Upstairs Aurora stirred in the huge red bed, then sat bolt upright. She searched the room visibly, as if she expected to find someone standing here or there. Then she realized what it was. She could feel it, sense the presence reach out to her as if he stood right here beside the bed. Bran had come home.

Since she had become Mistress Ravenleigh, for weeks at a time she had not been bothered by his commanding presence. She could almost have found a peaceful and monastic existence here at Raven Keep if he'd chosen never to return. But now he was back and she must brace herself for what was to come. She would have to share this bed with him and suffer a near re-enactment of their wedding night.

Several gay dresses lined her wardrobe now. She had added another purple satin, one of blue silk cotton, some trimmed in lace and threads of gold as befitted a princess. There were linen smocks and silk cotton smocks, petticoats green-trimmed in lace, some black, some yellow, one cloudberry. But she didn't care much for the carnation-red petticoat. Melanie would love it, and so she decided that her cousin should have it next time she saw her.

Besides the jewel-colored materials, a bundle of accessories meant for inclement weather had accompanied them. It was only proper that she had thanked her husband for the lovely cloths and other items the last time he came home. But he had wanted something more generous than verbal thanks.

Bored and wanting for something to do after she had completed several dresses, Aurora had gotten the bright but dangerous idea to search for the treasure. She had studied the map while out riding; she was certain that the treasure was buried on the ground of Raven Keep. It had to be. There was a faint drawing on her half of the map and, after a thorough study, had found it to be very similar to the house she had become mistress of. Still, she had decided it unwise to put her half of the map together with the one in the chest. She guessed that that would only have aroused suspicion should someone—like Bran—find it all of a sudden magically whole. Only when she went out riding did she take both halves with her, then replace one back in the chest.

Once she discovered the treasure—and she had said

to herself repeatedly that she would, even if she had to dig and dig strenuously for days—there would arise the problem of what to do with it. Turn it over to Sir Eric? Bran? So, rightly she had discovered the half in Bran's bedchamber, and rightly he should be the first to learn of its discovery. Though terribly exciting to unearth a treasure, she cared not for material gain nor earthly riches of any sort. All she had desired out of life was lost to her forever—to love and be loved, mutually heart and soul. She could not count on her husband's love. His was the kind of love that was here today, gone tomorrow. He had already made that quite clear to her by staying away for long periods of time. Too, what he did while away was of no interest to her.

What was of continuing interest for Aurora to unearth was why Mr. Wellbeloved had had the map in his possession. Something told her that every day she inched nearer to the answers; there dwelled more than one mystery in this Keep, she had come to realize. Also, she had become cognizant of the fact that Sir Eric kept knowledge of many secrets locked up in himself, as did several of the servants. Yet of all of them, Bran was the most mysterious of all. She shivered now, wondering what would happen when all the ghosts emerged from out of the closet and into the light of day.

Hetty entered just then to help her mistress change into a fresh dress. Despite all her efforts to be animated, Hetty knew it was all a front on Aurora's part. How sad in heart the lass really was beneath her bright semblance, she ruminated. The lass was going through an important change just now, one that would affect her future, the Scotswoman knew.

"Yer husband's come home, luv." Though Hetty was often given to thoughts of wonderment concerning the hasty marriage, she never once questioned.

"I knew, Hetty."

"How—did ye know? He's not been to see you."

"I can always tell."

Hetty lifted one thin eyebrow. "Do ye also know he's been hurt?"

Aurora stood motionless, but her insides were in turmoil. Hetty studied the young woman, scrutinizing the heather-dark eyes reflecting the candle flames. A haunting torment stirred in the depths of them. Her complexion was as pale as a magnolia bloom and her cheekbones had become more visible in her new gypsy-like thinness. In the past weeks, nay months, of near fasting Aurora had come to look even more gorgeous and willowy. Even more enchanting, she had taken to wearing her hair in the mode of court, with her hair piled up on her head while one long ringlet caressed her shoulder as it trailed downward.

"Where is he, Hetty? I must go immediately to him."

"He has his servants wi' him, luv. He'll soon be bathing in his old chamber. Oooh, 'tis a bad wound, Ida Minter said. I hae not seen it, but she thinks it might be festered."

"Oh!" Aurora exclaimed. "He must not bathe. Hetty, fetch me the pouch of herbs, the yellow ones I gathered this summer. Go and tell the servants to light a fire in the grate. Find the manservant Tom Bone and tell him that I shall need a steel knife.

Hurry, I shall complete my dressing," she said quickly, then peered down at her rumpled dress. It was an old one. "Nay, I shall stay as I am."

Hetty blinked fast as the orders flew at her, but finally realized what her young lady was up to. Aurora had healed the sick and the wounded many times before this. She had one time gone into the woods near North Creek, gathered, and burnt ant eggs, let them cool and then applied them to the sick eyes of a young boy. He had almost been blinded by the milky-white film that had grown over his eyes, but after Aurora had completed this procedure he had regained his sight and was again as whole as before.

Bran wore his hair clubbed with a dark riband at the nape of his neck and his beard had been removed. He was naked to his waist and his wounded leg was stretched out toward the crackling log. Servants rushed to and fro when his wife entered the chamber, her eyes filled with concern at the thigh that was swelling horribly. If he noticed this concern as she came over to feel his forehead, he gave no outward indication of it. But there shone a feverish gleam in his eyes, making them flash like blades in combat.

Aurora straightened from examining the long flaming-red gash that ran the length of his lean thigh. He made no move as she ordered the servants around.

"One of you fetch him strong drink." She then turned to Tom Bone who had been eyeing her coolly, curiously, without emotion. "Tom Bone, have you brought a good steel blade?" she asked brusquely, reminding him of a proud Occaneechee squaw he had once known. He had noticed too, that the lady walked with the straight-backed gait of a woman of the woods.

Could this be the same young woman who had trembled and quailed in his grasp? Tom wondered. He answered her now.

"Yea. He will not need much more drink though, mistress. He has already had a good deal of Canary and sack to drink." He handed her a short knife, his eyes never leaving her flushed face.

Bran finally spoke up. "Do as she says, Tom, she's the physician here."

"Aye," Tom smiled feebly. "But do not speak of porcupines at this time, master." He slanted his regard in the direction of the mistress who was at the hearth, indifferent to his cryptic statement as she readied her articles of the ancient healing art.

Tom thought he was beginning to know her quite well. Nurtured in the woods where there had been many comely squaws of friendly tribes, he had come to know the ways of woman. Especially those who held a fancy for one man, be he a young warrior, a chief, or a colonial as he'd been before going off impulsively to England. There, because of a petty theft, he had become a bondsman. Bran had already made him a free man, but Tom chose to remain servant to his master and friend. His wandering musings now came back to the mistress. She had spoken the name Fay with love in her voice, though she had been drugged. Bran was Fay. Therefore she loved her husband, though wasn't aware of this yet.

How had they met? It could have been that Fay happened by North Creek when she was out riding or walking. What she had not then and did not now realize was that Bran and Fay were one and the same. Brian had said she loved another, trying as he had unsuccessfully to conceal the pain in his eyes. I must not intrude, Tom warned himself. They would someday learn the truth. For now their love was new, though blind.

Aurora was withdrawing from her pouch dried leaves which she crumbled to a powder into a small bowl containing a yellow, sticky-looking salve. Tom nodded, having seen this done before by a medicine man. But that was as far as his knowledge went. As to which herbs had medicinal properties he was totally ignorant. The lady must have had contact with someone, Indian or otherwise, used to healing with herbal concoctions.

One of the servants entered just then, having gone to fetch the strong drink ordered by the mistress. Bran tilted the potent brew to his lips, and some of the stuff trickled down his chin and onto his hairy chest. He wiped at it with the back of his forearm, keeping his blurred vision trained on the back of his lovely, busy wife. He grinned wolfishly, as if some nasty thought had entered his mind just then. Now his gaze softened, and he spoke low, impulsively in his feverish state.

"Why can't you see it in its true colors?"

Before Aurora could catch his words, Hetty had stepped in between, cutting off his stare to his wife's back.

"What was it ye said, sir?" Hetty tossed the question to Bran before he could repeat it.

"Eh, hell. Forget it," Bran slumped further down,

330

wishing everyone but his wife would vanish from the room.

But it wasn't to be. A pot of water boiled over the grate, and Aurora held the blade submerged until she felt the hilt grow hot in her hands. Steadying herself as she knelt beside his leg, she gave no pause for her own fears to surface, but deliberately inserted the blade into the already crusting gash. Bran stiffened but once, then settled down. First a thick yellow substance began to ooze out, and then after several breathtaking minutes, clean red blood followed. Bran mercifully began to nod sleepily as she applied poultices that steamed over the sickly colored slash.

"Ohhh," Ida Minter finally broke down, unable to stand any more sight of the blood and gore and slimy yellow liquid on the rags scattered about her feet.

"Here," Hetty said from her stance at the door, "I'll help ye out the door. Dinna faint now." She rushed forward and, with Tom's aid, brought the servant down to the kitchen for a tot of rum.

Bran tenderly clasped the wine jug to his chest, alternately frowning and smiling at sweet dreams and nightmares. He raised his voice once with unintelligible words flowing forth and then settled down, murmuring in his fitful dozing. His eyes merely slitted open now and then, catching a glimpse of the blurred vision of a young woman kneeling beside him, her small breasts brushing his thigh sensuously. His dream, in a sweat and a fever, brought him on a journey back in time. He dreamed of hair as black as midnight.

"Tadewi, wind-maiden," he muttered. Then he saw a vision of hacked-off hair. "Rachel, what has happened to your hair?" He reached out carelessly to fondle the single curl that lay upon the woman's shoulder, but his hand was thrust aside in a gesture of annoyance and a burst of anger.

Aurora then swore for the first time in her life—"Bastard! Keep your bungling lecher's hands off me!" With all due haste, she rose swiftly and fetched the bowl of herbal salve from the hearth.

Tom Bone entered just then and was taken aback when the bowl was thrust into his hands abruptly and carelessly. Aurora's eyes were eclipsed by a dark and overwhelming resentment as she brushed airily past the bemused manservant.

"I am finished here!" she snorted, then waved her hand negligently toward her husband, while addressing Tom Bone. "Apply a few more steaming poultices and then pack the wound with that stuff. Mayhap you know how to bandage a wound?" She paused a moment with her hand grasping the doorknob.

"Aye," Tom answered, wondering what had caused the angel-like temperament to turn ill.

Before whirling out the door and into the hall, she tossed with pique over her shoulder, "Inform your master when he awakens to sanity in the morn that from now forward I shall share the little room with my maidservant, Hetty. My actions shall be justified when you tell him that he spoke foolishly and rashly in his febrile sleep. All you need then do is mention the names of Tadewi and Rachel. Though only God knows how many others he has worn on his sleeve and bedded!"

Tom Bone stood with jaw unhinged, as in going

out she gave the door a good slam. Heaving a deep-felt sigh, Tom stared down on Bran's dark head and still steaming thigh which sported a cloth that had been slapped carelessly and angrily across it.

"Fool," Tom muttered, shaking his head. "Like a ready stud you have mounted too many mares. Alas, you must pay the price, master; the pleasures of lust have finally caught up with you. Like a fat man, you could never push yourself away from the table. Now, fine cock, you will have to beg on your hands and knees for sustenance."

# *Nineteen*

Riding through the forest to the joyous song of water playing leapfrog over the rocks in the stream, the beauty with pale velvet skin enhanced by hair as black as smoke, felt for now great pleasure in her abandonment. Aurora sat sidesaddle on her second favorite mare, Elektra, a wedding gift from her husband. Her father-in-law had named the white horse for her, since the mare was offspring of the stud Agamemnon.

Had there ever been a more perfect day? she wondered now. She had chewed a mint leaf and her fresh clean mouth made it seem like she breathed in of the woodland. She felt in harmony with nature, the dull green of the towering pines, the sun-kissed grapevines growing in wild profusion, thickets of red and pink raspberries, tangled brambles, the blue sky patched high above, and fresh waters running through the woods. A bandit-masked raccoon peeped out at her from a jungle of green thicket and Aurora's laughter tinkled musically as she waved gaily at the funny little character.

Whatever Bran would think of her disappearing so early in the day disturbed her not in the least. If he even stirred from his old chamber where he'd spent the night, with his painful wound, not to mention some distress from a hangover, it would be a small miracle.

Of all the times she had been out riding either Cupid or Elektra, she had seen nary a soul. Not one Indian, nor any neighbors, nor one person who dwelled in the forest, not even a masked man . . .

"I must cease!" Aurora chided herself severely. Dreaming of Fay was painful, and though she would love him secretly through all eternity, he was now part of her past. She was Mistress Ravenleigh now, and for whatever their marriage was worth, she should take steps to make it work, even though she felt somehow that Bran had downgraded her life.

"I shall make the most of life, come what may. I shall find peace and cease to be a sorry figure. I shall! I shall!"

The voice of determination, instilled in woman since the drawning of time, now echoed down the wooded lane. As she cantered toward the leafy door in the forest, Queen Elizabeth's words rode with her: "I know I have the body of a weak and feeble woman, but I have the heart and stomach of a King. . . ."

Of clouds there were few today, though there had risen a late-summer storm nearly every afternoon for weeks. Cantering toward her destination, Aurora felt inside the pocket of her belted rail for the map. Before dismounting at the hollow, she sensed a fleeting moment of déjà vu, and sat on her horse, unable to move. The pine-smelling evergreens in back of her seemed to have eyes, and the woodland birds whistled to her tentatively: *Remember*. What was it that she should be remembering? Eyes, in the looking-glass of time, the mystery of the past trying to reach her.

Aurora spun about then. Had someone been tracking her? Time seemed suspended as she waited for something to happen. She shrugged now, finding it ridiculous and possibly just her imagination, and dismounted.

Aurora pulled out her map, studied it as she had done a hundred times before while matching the Ravenleigh half with hers. Her head bent studiously over the parchment, she paced to the rim of the hollow until she reached a clump of small trees.

"Oh, this cannot be," she said aloud. The trees—if that's what the mapmaker had been signifying— would have to be ones that had known the passage of time. Not these saplings. There was a mistake here, but there was no other hollow one-half mile from the house. It had to be here.

Perhaps if she walked east . . . There *was* a huge, lone oak tree. Lone! There was only one, whereas the map showed a line of three.

"Oh!" Aurora exclaimed her futile hope. "I cannot read a map! 'Twould take an expert to figure all these signs!"

Suddenly a huge shadow fell across the map, a shadow that she sensed was more ominous and angrier than a thunderhead. She spun about and found herself looking directly at the huge barrel chest of Nimrod, her husband's great brown hunter. Up, up, she lifted wide eyes to meet with the dark countenance that scowled down upon her from beneath dark brows. Sliding down from his mount, there could be no mistake as to the pain Bran was feeling from his wound as a grimace crinkled the corners of his eyes and his teeth gritted together hard.

"What have you there? Don't try to hide it behind your skirts, Ro. I've already caught your furtive actions to conceal whatever that is from me."

With the speed of thought, Bran reached out to check her hand from tucking the parchments deep into her rail. Aurora had backed up, but like tongues of flame licking out, his fingers squeezed her wrist and easily snatched both parts from her now limp fingers.

Putting the pieces together and scanning the whole, he lifted his gaze; his control seemed to simmer just below boiling point.

"So, my busy mate, you have taken to stealing from your husband's belongings? And, by the way, how came you by this other half—the one I've searched high and low for and now find in my wife's possession?"

Though Aurora had never seen him so coolly angered, an anger she would normally cower beneath, Aurora squared her shoulders, and with brave face she spoke, cold measured steel in her woman's voice.

"'Twas a bequeathal from Mr. Wellbeloved. On his deathbed he placed this parchment at my disposal, mine to do with as I choose."

Narrowing an eye, Bran spoke with a measured clip. "Why should this man, on his deathbed, choose to present this half-map to you and not to his loving spouse?"

She shrugged. "You know the answer to that as well as I do. All he said to me was that 'Riches await you, as does . . .'"

"As does what? Tell me!"

"Love."

Bran snorted. "Love?" He looked aside, then back to her. "And have you found these treasures? Hmm?"

Aurora chose to ignore the half of the question that was a puzzlement her own mind had not yet solved. "I've searched for the treasure, aye, 'tis true, but have discovered nothing save this place, this grave of riches I care naught for. 'Twas only the adventure, the thrill of discovery—the desire to discover something, anything, has always dwelled in me, has been a flame in my blood since first I became aware of myself as a human being."

"Perhaps"—Bran paused in search for the word to put exactness to her meaning—"Aye, it could very well be, Mistress Ravenleigh, that you are blind."

She blinked up at him. "Blind? Ho, how can that be when the Almighty has given me eyes with which to see?"

"Aye, God-given power of sight. But what of the heart?"

At that, Aurora abruptly spun about to walk across the moss and grass, and snatched up the trailing reins where Elektra had been contentedly cropping the lush green blades.

Bran stood bemused at her brand-new attitude and her spunk. The treasure—he scanned the hollow visibly—aye, it was here somewhere. He peered up at the sky. A storm was brewing, already dark scowling thunderclouds threatened to spill. This was not the time to be searching—for love or gold.

"Ride with me back to the house!" Bran called across the rim as Aurora mounted up.

Whirling Elektra about, she spiked her heels into the muscled flanks, tossing over her shoulder. "Sir, are you ordering me?"

"Demanding!" He tossed his tall frame to Nimrod's back, forgetting the plaguey wound.

"Are you?!" She was off, her retort underscored by lightning-flash followed by a clatter of thunder and pelting raindrops.

*"Aurora!"*

To put distance between them and reach the house before her angry husband, Aurora defiantly urged Elektra to gallop faster. But the dainty-limbed horse was no match for the great brown hunter. Eating up the distance she had put between them, Bran had to ease up a bit to check Nimrod from racing past her.

"Slow down, or else you can minister to my wound again should it open up!"

As far as Aurora was concerned, that did it. She reluctantly slowed Elektra. She would not care to be caught in his less than gentle embrace, for it would come to that today should she allow him too near her behind closed doors. She would surely be in for quite an interrogation if shut in with him. She just wanted to be left alone in the little room, where she had just that morning moved the rest of her belongings. Hetty was by far more cheering and less demanding a roommate than her husband.

Soaking wet and feeling like a cat rubbed the wrong way, Aurora dismounted and hoisted her nose in the air as Bran reached out to snatch up Elektra's carelessly trailing reins. She would not even look her husband's way, but directed her gaze toward the door.

"Go inside, to our room. I'll join you there as soon as the horses are stabled."

"I mean to do just that. Do you take me for a bloody fool, to stand out here in the damp air awaiting your escort into the house? I am quite capable of finding my own way, sir, to *my* room!" She lifted her skirts with a snap of her wrist and walked around in back of the horses.

"We shall see about that!" Bran called over his shoulder as he viciously kicked Nimrod into a surging trot. Elektra whinnied at this injustice to her soft mouth, but then craned her rain-plastered neck to follow behind meekly.

"Oooh!" Aurora ejaculated resentfully as flying mud from Nimrod's hoof struck her smack on the cheek and slid unpleasantly down her neck into her bodice. Scooping up the excess from her cheek, she angrily flicked it from her palm, guessing that Bran had purposefully done it to make her entrance into the house less than dignified.

Inside, the house was quiet, and thankfully there were few servants about as Aurora slipped up to the little room. A dropping of her chin and a lifting of her brow brought to life the astonishment Aurora felt as she gazed about the room now empty of her belongings. Pressing her lips together knowingly, Aurura spun from the room to go to the great bedchamber.

"Ah, come in sweeting, I've been waiting for you."

Again astonishment registered upon Aurora's countenance as she beheld her husband stretched out comfortably upon a plush chair.

"I must be hallucinating. How did you appear so

fast?" Aurora slipped into the room nervously, staying close to the door.

"Magic. 'Tis called materialization. I can appear anywhere, any time, umm—quite unexpectedly," he said, squinting over to where she stood. When she showed no reaction to this he sighed wearily. "Ahh, but it taxes myself to the limit to perform such remarkable feats."

"Of course, 'tis worthy of notice! And I suppose you materialized all of my belongings into this chamber, also remarkably?"

"Naturally, haven't you heard of magicians who can move things from one place to another—even their own forms?"

"Humbug hocus-pocus! I've only read of the ghost in Shakespeare that materialized before Hamlet."

"Ah! But I am flesh and blood and bones and—" He was suddenly cut off.

"Alas, I suppose you can also materialize all your wenches into your bed—like Tadewi and Rachel?" She cocked a dark eyebrow.

"Merely flowers of the past. They mean nothing to me now." He waved his hand above his head as if to wash them from memory.

"Flowers? Huh! You've collected quite a bouquet of these flowers in your lifetime, sir. Who might your latest flower be in your bed? Or do you pride yourself on collecting an assortment and using them until they are well-trodden?"

Bran smiled crookedly. "I've only a single rose that is supposed to be my loving mate, but she's proven to have the sharpest thorns of any in my bed of roses."

Aurora snorted through her pert nose. "Sir, if you

are a rose, then you must be a black one indeed!"

It was as if the thunderclouds had moved into the room and swept Aurora out the door with them. Tossing up his hands in the hot air she had left behind, Bran watched her exit into the hall.

"What the hell do you want—a sin-offering?" His belated words pursued Aurora to where she very nearly collided with her cousin who had been standing, seemingly, outside the door prepared to knock.

"Melanie!" Aurora was genuinely surprised, for she hadn't heard from her cousin in quite some time.

"Didn't he tell you? He sent for me."

"Who?" Aurora wrinkled her brow in her cousin's face.

Melanie's regard shifted from Aurora to the door that had been left slightly ajar. "Who else? That was quite some spat you just had with *him*." She tilted her blond head sideways.

*Him*, Aurora thought with boiling blood, could only mean her husband. Well, Melanie, you can be his next flower, she added silently to herself.

"Why, cousin, have you been rolling in the mud again? You haven't done that since you were this high." Melanie held her hand three feet from the floor. She watched then as Aurora whirled away like a ballerina performing a pirouette. "Where are you going? You haven't even welcomed me yet!" Melanie called with a smile in her voice at her cousin's back moving down the hall briskly.

"To bathe!" was shot back—"In very cold water!"

"My, yes, to cool off." Melanie might as well have said it to herself, for she stood alone now, but for the soft cursing drifting out to her from behind the cracked door.

Sharpening her claws, Melanie went along to the room she'd occupied before. Perversely excited after eavesdropping on the "happily" married couple, Melanie thought *why not?* She had quarreled with David anyway. Now that she was here, why not have some fun, after all. She had been bored for too long.

Aurora stared from the window, pressing her cheeks on the cooling glass, as she gloomily studied the wet bricks of the high chimney stacks, counting them for something to do. Not even the afternoon rain could wash away her sunken state of depression, greater than that which she'd undergone in the past.

As usual these days, she kept herself locked up in the great chamber when it was raining. The weather seemed to be keeping pace with her moods, which were gloomier than the gray clouds that shrouded the Keep. She stayed here, and Bran stayed in his old bedchamber, but for those times when she watched him from the window as he was leaving the house. He was always garbed in impeccable black with white lace peeping out and falling over those sun-browned hands. He wore his hair longer these days, drawn back and tied at the nape of the neck with a black riband. Even though she had hardly spoken to him or sat down longer than a half an hour at the dinner table across from him, she sensed his strange possessiveness reach her like tentacles snaking along the hall and into her room.

August had waned and now September waxed. Melanie came and went, and now Aurora wondered at this last visit, which had been so far the longest. Melanie seemed to spend more time with Bran than she did herself, sitting up together into the night so that when they finally retired Aurora would wake up to the sound of laughter out in the hall and their good-nights to each other. It was as if Bran lifted his voice at those times, with the sole intent of waking her and having her hear him.

No more was said about the treasure map. What did she care if he had confiscated the half that belonged to her? She cared no more about the piece of parchment than she did about Melanie's and Bran's new intimacy. But of the few days out of the week that Bran was home, he seemed to make the most of each moment by spending time entertaining Melanie. Aurora had become his wife only in name; there was nothing else between them anymore.

Bran never sought her bed anymore either, and it was just as well. The last time had been over two months ago. She had been horribly frightened to feel the power he'd had over her as he searched out the hidden secrets of her body. He had entered the bedchamber when she had been reclining on a long French chair. . . .

He had been smiling—a smile that was the cruelest she had ever seen on him. Black of hair and lean of jaw, Bran Ravenleigh had been like a total stranger to her. He grinned then, looking like a pirate or an English highwayman, enjoying himself hugely. He started toward her again, and Aurora felt her knees going trembly as she tried to sit up.

"Are you afraid to be alone with your husband, milady?" he said mockingly.

The fire in the hearth matched the wild heat that had started in her loins and her limbs; against her will her body was shaken by his nearness. She stared at the Turkey carpet on the floor when he came to stand before her.

"Yea," she said, finally.

"Faugh!" Bran said, in cool humor. "Don't alarm yourself, sweeting, I shall be quick in taking my pleasure."

He then put out his hand to snatch the bodice of her dressing gown open, his big fingers resting hot and hard on a quivering nipple. Very unceremoniously he then bent down, slowly, and scooped her up. The pupils of her eyes dilated until only a rim of deep purple showed around them. He parted her lips suddenly with a ruthless kiss, his open mouth ravaging them until they were swollen and trembling. He lifted his head.

"I shall never love you, Bran!" She saw the flash of fire in his eyes and regretted her heated outburst instantly.

"I see," he returned drily. He stared into the little face that had gone very white after the kiss. "Afraid, sweet wife, that I'll make you hot all over again?"

"Nay, I am not!" she lied.

"Oh-ho, yes, you are. You're afraid all right, so frightened in fact it makes you sick and trembling all over," he said, his voice hoarse as a flush of intense desire stole over his darkly handsome face.

"I said nay," Aurora whispered, keeping her eyes cast downward, "because I shall not allow the horrors you put me through when—" She couldn't continue.

"When I touch you and make your flesh scream and come alive?" His scowl deepened as he went on. "I can feel the wild pounding of your blood when I take you, look into your eyes and watch them grow dreamy and languorous. Ahh, I shall melt that tiny flame of rebellion in you, milady!"

"You shall not!" Aurora pounded on his back as he bore her to the huge bed.

"Aurora, I warn—"

She fought to escape him as he pinned her down, her feet and ankles scissoring and giving glimpses of white flesh as he looked down. His cavalier boots made a dull thud, first one and then the other as he peeled them off, still holding her captive. He worked over her then until she had only her chemise on. The dressing gown was off now. He slid the chemise up to her waist, feasting his eyes on the thighs with skin like snow. His hands kneaded the softness between them. His breathing grew harsh as he saw the place that was as soft and pink as a tiny rosebud.

"Lord, you tease me until I pant so hard, Aurora my darling!"

"Oh, wait, Bran, wait!"

"Only say the word and you shall know the most glorious secret of your womanhood. I'll pleasure you to your heart's content, all through the evening. Say it, my darling, that you want me over and over, cry out that you desire me. Me! Bran, your husband! No one else! Damnation! Say it!"

"I—I cannot!"

He waited no longer but spread her apart with his hands and gave a low cry as he thrust between her legs, spreading her wider until an exquisite sensation of pain drove like a sword blade through to her belly.

"Quit, Bran," she panted and sobbed. "You—still hurt me—"

"You," he muttered thickly as he rocked more gently, "you shall know no more pain after a few more joinings . . . I promise."

He continued to love her, soothing her with low spoken endearments and gentling hands. A warmth was spreading through her loins, and then, almost in the last throes of utter surrender, he burst inside of her hotly. He was looking down at her wide and frightened eyes when he surprised her by withdrawing quickly and rising to his feet. He dressed bursting with a haste to be gone from her. He turned back to her from where he stood at the door.

"Someday, Aurora, I promise you shall desire *me*."

It had been a battle she had almost lost in holding out against him. She had thanked God that he had been the one to bring the act to an abrupt end, after he'd obtained his pleasure. She could almost hate him now, for he had caused this gnawing in her groin that was ever-present and found no fulfillment.

Then. He was making her suffer! He had planned it this way! And now he faced her with that frosty exterior of his. But his cool gray eyes, curiously at times, seemed to be saying: "You're mine, Ro, I possess you!" Her innermost secrets seemed not to be hers anymore. Just what end did he hope to achieve? What kind of games was he playing? Perhaps he had it in mind to divorce her and marry Melanie? But this didn't strike logic, not when she brought to mind the fact that she had been framed into this marriage.

"Was it because he knew about the map, and wanted the assurance of obtaining it by becoming closer to me—through marriage?"

Aurora left the window and went to lie down upon the huge, lonely bed. There were too many questions her body and mind were asking her, and not enough answers. She closed her eyes then to seek what comfort she could find in restful slumber, praying that when she awakened she could meet the rest of the day with renewed strength. Perhaps she would even take Cupid out for a ride.

A white horse stood, sedately cropping late summer grass. Birds, mocking each other with chirps and chatters, took to the air at the sound of twigs snapping sharply. One stayed, then it too took wing. The sun slanted through a copse of gnarled oak where a lonely figure in a gray cloak walked. Her path weaved in and out of the trees as she wandered to the river's edge, a small breeze flirting with the hood of her cloak and tinting her pale cheeks pink.

Emerald and gold of late summer surrounded her as the sun kissed her sweet face intermittently through the swaying branches. Dew from the grass clung to the hem of her dress and cloak and shined the tips of her leathern shoes. The air smelled sweet and felt crisp here.

She tried not to think but just to feel. Silence hung over her until a raven called a *tok* from the woods in back of her. She glanced up sharply. Then quiet again; it was so peaceful near the water's edge. Her mind was far too preoccupied with nature's beauty to notice that someone had come up stealthily behind her and stopped before a fallen tree.

"Aurora."

She was calm. She hadn't been startled to hear the deep voice. The mirrored sun on the water blinded her for a moment and she moved a fraction of an inch. He stood closer now. She could almost hear him breathing.

*Do not look at him,* she told herself. He does not want you to.

"Are you real?" she breathed the question, without moving a muscle. "Or are you just a figment of my imagination?" She said this last to herself.

The clothes he wore she knew, even without looking at him. A horse neighed from the woods, close by, and Cupid called back. The voice behind her was deep, barely audible.

"Only your fear of reality stands between us, my love."

He had said the words cryptically, his hot breath stirring strands of black hair coiled at her flushed cheeks.

"Please do not call me that," she said.

The voice went deeper yet. "Why? Is the privilege reserved only for another?"

He stood so close that she could feel his male body heat. But was it her own heart she heard pounding just now so strongly? Or were the two combined in a tortured and loving beat?

"You must go away now . . . you confuse me horribly, so much that I cannot think straight . . ."

Her hand fluttered across her brow and she wavered on her feet.

"Who do *you* love, Aurora Gregory?"

She leaned weakly against the tree for support. Her hand clutched the cloak over her pounding heart.

"Do not torment me, Fay. You must know that I am no longer free to—Go away, pray vanish from my heart forever. Please!"

"Aaah, but that is not your desire, Mistress Ravenleigh. You want us to go on forever, a stolen kiss in the wood, a passionate fever in the blood. You love *me*—do you not?"

"I release you from my heart and mind forever, renounce you, phantom! Go and never return!"

*Lies, lies! I shall love you forever and ever,* raced through her mind again. *But it is too late. This cannot be.*

"You can wipe me from your mind and heart that easily?"

Aurora shivered. He sounded angry, menacing. But had she detected a note of pleading in his deeply resonant voice? Or a demand?

"If—if I ask you to remove the disguise, will you do so? For me?"

He placed one gloved hand on the tree, as if to imprison her. She swung her eyes to the leather spread on wood.

"Someday, love, you shall do that yourself. But not—not just yet."

"Please!" She struggled inwardly to turn and see him up close, in the light of day.

"Don't," he warned, stepping back.

His hand lifted, and she whirled to face the phantom.

He . . . was gone! How . . .

She fainted dead away.

When she finally came to, Cupid loomed above her nudging Aurora with her velvet nose.

A dream. He had to be—after all, he had never made love to her. Only a real flesh-and-blood man could do that.


"Bran, are you in there? Could I come in please?" Melanie knocked on the door to the bedchamber, waited, then tried again. "Bran—?"

The door was whipped open suddenly, unceremoniously, and there stood Bran in a state of reckless attire, his usually neatly combed hair falling in thick black waves over his forehead, his usual garments of gentry replaced by a leather doublet and breeches, the shirt he had on beneath the doublet of a warm tone of brown.

"Nice . . ." Melanie purred, seeing the riding boots of the finest Cordovan leather that stood waiting beside a chair. "Are you going out for—umm—a clandestine meeting in the woods with a pretty squaw? You are so roughly handsome this late afternoon."

Unsure of herself at first, Melanie then impulsively leaned toward his mouth, trying to press her lips to his in greeting.

"Hmmm . . ." Bran murmured. "Do I detect the odor of sour grapes on your breath again? Shame, Melly." He set her from him before the kiss had

351

been accomplished.

"You have a limited sense of humor today, milord?"

Employing her feminine tactics, Melanie brushed past him, her buttocks swaying while, quite at home, she walked to the bed, sat down upon the edge, and kicked out a dainty leg while humming a sailor's ditty.

"Only when the spirit moves me am I inclined to be witty and entertaining," Bran said, shaking his head and smiling roguishly as he quite unthinkingly shut the door. He felt safe enough with Melanie who had become his "sipping partner," though he had to admit (only to himself) that there were two strings to his bow. Besides, he was used to coarse, blatant women, and Melanie was very much like Elspeth Woodville, less the fact that the lady of the court had been his mistress.

Then Bran stopped himself short as he bent down to pick up a boot and seat himself to pull it on. There was something different about Melanie now. Or had it always been there, just now ripening? Her sparkling eyes seemed to be saying, "Playing at silly games is over. It's time for the real thing." He could take it from here, or leave it. He could . . . forget it, that's what!

"Melanie"—he chuckled to conceal his unwelcome, wicked ponderings—"Why don't you fetch us a bottle from out of the cupboard over there. We'll have one for the road."

"Are we going somewhere, Bran?" Melanie rose to slip the bottle and two silver cups from the cupboard, returning to pour at the small table next to the bed.

Bran watched mesmerized as she came to him with that sensuously flowing gait, telling himself that she didn't affect him in the least bit. But damn, she did! She was *Pleasure*, nothing else. His conscience chided: *Forget it! You've a wife now!*

*Sure,* he answered back, *one who loathes me, and every time I look at her I become all raw nerve ends, hot one minute and then cold when she leaves the room.* As the days totaled up, she became to him more beautiful, more desirable.

*Lose yourself in this vixen Melanie!* the demon on his shoulder urged. *Take advantage of this and enjoy yourself to the full!*

"'Tis driving me insane!"

"Bran," Melanie smiled knowingly, "you haven't answered me yet, darling. Are we going somewhere?"

Melanie reminded him at times—like now—of Aurora, in countenance if not in manner. He shook himself now. "I am, but you, Melly, after one little drink, must do me a favor and tell my loving wife that I shall return in a few days." He sighed. "Though I doubt that she will even miss me one small whit!"

"Poor baby," Melanie crooned. "You would have been better off taking me for wife. We've much in common. Alas, you and *she* are opposites." Melanie grazed his thigh with her leg in handing him a silver cup.

Bran looked up, narrowing his lids speculatively. "You say that as if you're feeling sorry for me. I can quite take care of myself." He tossed down half the contents of the cup.

"Doesn't that get to be a little boring and lonely, taking things into hand yourself?" Melanie half-teased.

"Melanie. Tsk, tsk, you should know me better than to even suggest such a thing." He applied his full attention to shining the tips of his tall boots.

How close she had come to the truth! He'd almost had to resort to such shameful activity. That which he'd never done in the past. There had been no need to, he'd always had his mistresses and wenches.

"My, it's warm in here," Melanie muttered, lifting her arms behind her neck, the movement bringing her breasts up and pointing out.

Caught by the sight of the lovely beauties, Bran, unshaken at first by Melanie's subtle seduction, now felt a spasm tense his groin. He had been too long the monk!

"Wet the other eye, Melanie," he said as he held out his cup to be refilled. She did as he asked and poured him another after having fetched the bottle.

"The last one," Bran continued. "I must watch it that I do not overindulge. I've much business to be about." Like meeting a half-blood by the name of Savage. Rufo, whom he had come to know and trust, promised to keep up his vigil day and night in the hollow, safeguarding the spot. Bran had not tried digging up the treasure he knew was there, for to do so would lose him his chance of getting his man—or men.

Melanie bent over Bran all of a sudden. "Kiss me, Bran. Just once, come on," she said in an easy, breezy manner, all giggly. She then flipped her hair flirtatiously over one shoulder, bringing a long, loose wave close about her face, the bright cloud highlighting and framing her delicate features.

Bran's jaw clenched in irritation. Whose face, like the fairest rose, did he in every place envision? Whose voice, so soft and honey-warm, seemed a thrill of pleasure? Whose name, heard even whispered in the wild of the woods, did tug and work the strings of his heart? She was his queen, he her bumbling slave. Beloved Aurora, frosty wife, she had ruined him for other women!

*Damnation, I'll not kiss her rosy butt the rest of my life!* He'd take his pleasure at his will and be damned with *her!*

With that burning in his brain like a bold imprint, Bran stood all at once to pull Melanie into his arms, delighting in her sensuous female sweets. Melanie murmured her pleasure, smiling lewdly at this sudden change of heart wrought in Bran before he kissed her, his tongue then pummeling her hot mouth, his teeth bruising her soft, parted lips. With Melanie pressing her breasts hard into his chest, her arms wound tightly about him, Bran soon felt the demanding movements of her luscious hips. Loosing one hand from around his neck, while he bent to kiss her throat, Melanie trailed her fingers into his breeches and below his naval, finding him ramrod-stiff. The comparison to David was shocking, in fact she had never before known such a wealth of manhood was possible.

Her fondest desires were to be realized, Melanie thought greedily as his body shivered with the heat of long unquenched passion. He was all hers now, and she didn't care if Sir Eric himself were to find them locked in an embrace. In her mind, they were beyond the point of no return. Her buttocks beneath his hand moved rhythmically, tantalizing him to the peak of sensation, and just when she thought he would lead her to the bed, he surprised her by snatching up her hands and pressing them gently but firmly to her desire-flushed cheeks. His lips twisted tautly as he seemed to force the words from them with a deep male groan.

"You are a damnable temptation, but you see, I must apologize for the first time in front of a woman. My heart and soul just wouldn't be in the few minutes of pleasure we could give each other, Melanie, and you would know my thrust but once— never again."

Slow to believe this Melanie said, "What are you saying?" But still she thrust his hands from her face and glared back at him. "'Tis true, you don't mean to—why, then, did you send for me to come here, Bran, twice? You want me, your body cries out to me."

"I'm sorry, Melanie, 'tis all for another this, my desire."

Melanie pouted. "I care nothing about this heart and soul you speak of. The body is the ruling force here, nothing else!"

Melanie watched him closely for his reaction to what she had to say next. She peered down at her tangled hands first, then up at him again. Her eyes burned like embers in the hearth.

"You love *her*, Bran?"

He began low. "As I love life. She's in every breath

356

that I take. She is my joy in this beautiful world, my hopes, and my dreams.''

"Oh." Melanie swallowed hard.

"Melanie"—he shrugged—"I'm sorry."

"Of course!" she replied bitterly.

"She is also my wife!" he started angrily, and then he sighed. "I—I never meant to lead you on, but I guess I did just that. For her, to make her wake up, perhaps by making her jealous. It failed, miserably!"

"And you"—Melanie laughed shortly—"you thought at one time that I was untouched. The joke would have been on you, my dear lost lover Bran."

"You hadn't fooled me, my dear, only your cousin accomplished that." His witch in the mist—Aurora.

*"Her*. She has always gotten what I've wanted!"

"Damn it, Melanie, that is a lie. You know it as well as I do."

Pitying her, Bran stepped back from her as a look of total rejection stole over her countenance. He wouldn't tell her that he had hoped by summoning her here that David Wiley would accompany her. He was after the man, but Wiley seemed to be avoiding meeting up with him again.

Now Bran reached out to tenderly stroke the blond, disheveled head, but her body was rigid, her eyes sparkling with unshed tears of defeat and frustration.

It was thus that Aurora found them as she stepped tentatively into the room.

"Bran, I am sorry to disturb you, but I have been searching the house for Mel—"

As the well-loved presence stood in the threshold, Bran had taken in her surprised shock that switched immediately to a cooler, composed manner. Never would Bran learn that as he had turned, giving his wife a full view of the breathless, bosom-heaving woman, there also had been no mistaking the now half-firm outline against his breeches that displayed his lust.

## Twenty

"Aurora, cousin dear, you were looking for me?"

"Not anymore," Aurora returned. The truth of what was going on here came to her again: Of course! Her husband had asked Melanie here merely for some diversion. Lord, he was a roué.

"Oh? Why is that, Ro, that you aren't looking for me anymore?" Melanie asked, slanting an openly covetous look toward Bran.

"Because—I have found you, that is why," Aurora quipped.

In the deep silence that fell over the room, Aurora looked from one to the other, her face an image of knowing what was what, as Bran wretchedly read it, and Melanie looking like the cat that swallowed the mouse whole.

Hetty broke the stifling silence as she stepped into the room from the hall. "Ah, here ye are, luv. I've been cleaning out the room, what do ye want me to do with this thing, luv, I mean *mistress?*" Hetty hoisted the pantherskin high in the air, pinching her thin nose. "Whew! There's a smell of the wild in it."

Bran studied the familiar fur and then watched his wife's reaction covertly, closely.

"Hetty!" Aurora rushed to receive it into her

trembling hands. "Where did you find it?" she asked, knowing well where and covering up her embarrassment.

"'Tis yours?" Hetty blinked her disbelief at her mistress.

"Aha! I remember that horrible stinking thing!" Melanie put in, moving forward to place her hand possessively upon Bran's arm, from which he abruptly removed her clinging fingers.

"Be still! Say no more," Aurora snapped smartly. She then turned her full attention to smoothing and caressing the pantherskin, her starry gaze lifting to Bran who watched her from beneath heavily lidded eyes.

Bran then went to pour himself two fingers of a more potent libation than before and then sat down, gesturing with his goblet at the pantherskin.

"Where did you get it?"

Instead of answering him immediately, she glared threateningly at Melanie and the cousin was so shocked that she stepped back in alarm, splaying a hand over her chest.

Aurora stuck her fine chin in the air. "I found it . . . in the cedar lane at North Creek. Why?" she asked, fighting back the stinging tears.

Tenderly, Bran answered. "It seems to hold some special meaning for you, am I correct?" His eyes glittered strangely.

Melanie whirled to face Aurora, singing in a high voice before her cousin could speak. "And so it does," she paused as the threat came her way again visually. "Well, it doesn't matter. So, it seems I'm unwanted here, so I'll be downstairs to dinner should you happen to want me for anything more.'' Half of her sentence seemed directed toward Bran as she breezily brushed past the maidservant.

Aurora made to follow Melanie out the door, but a halting word from her husband stopped her short. Without even looking at her then, he dismissed the servant whose eyes had taken in the strange goings-on and hadn't liked what she had seen one bit.

"Tell me, Ro, what does that thing mean to you? Mayhap it belonged to your lover?'' He tensely stayed where he was, not being sure what he would do if he got too close to her. *Not yet*, his mind said.

Aurora worried her fingers in the black fur. "Truly, 'tis not mine to keep. Not any more. I was going to have one of the servants return this to the place where I first discovered it.'' Her voice ended on a caressing note.

"I shall be going that way''—he cast a narrowed glance about the room—"tomorrow. Would you trust me to return it for you, my sweet?''

"Aye,'' she answered half-tearfully, then, after placing it gently on the bed, turned to go.

"Aurora''—Bran was to halt her again, but only heaved a deep sigh—"I know not where to begin, so it is better to leave words unsaid—for now.'' He measured her mood with a mysterious glint in his look.

At first cocking her head at him in bewilderment, she then said, "I understand. I always understand, I guess,'' then went back to the lonely bedchamber, as the hours were now waning on toward the evening.

Awakened by a nightmare, Aurora struggled

upright on the bed, unaware and uncaring that it was the dead of night. Sweat drenched her nightgown. In the dream, Bran had been her lover and Fay her husband. They had been fighting and there had been blood covering both their faces. She lifted a shaking hand to feel her tearstained cheek. What had the dream meant?

Shivering in cold horror, she drew the coverlet closer to her breast, her own silent scream yet ringing in her ears. She gasped at the back of her hand then. The edges of a tall figure standing before the glowing embers of the hearth were delicately blurred. Whoever it was that stood there so deathly silent had entered with no sound of tread or word. Or had she been sleeping? And was she still dreaming?

"B-Bran?" she inquired with a quiver. "Is it you?"

Without answering her, he came on noiseless stride to stand before the bed. With his back to the small fire in the hearth, his features were indistinct. But now she found her eyes fixed on the flowing garment draped about his shoulders. He was caped. Her heart picked up a crazy thudding.

"You have had a nightmare," came the deeply muttered statement. The dark head turned slowly toward the window. "The night mists have come, and there is a full moon outside."

Feeling hot and faint where she sat with legs tucked beneath her, Aurora cast a quick glance toward the window and then back to the caped figure. She wet her lips and then parted them as if to speak, but no words issued forth. The sweat-dampened nightgown clung to her breasts and between her thighs, but she never noticed the

362

discomfort. All she noticed now was that he was easing his weight down to sit on the edge of the bed. Suddenly she saw it, as the moonbeams poured through the window and across her bed. He was masked!

Long fingers reached out and at first she drew back, then allowed them to come and thread through her hair. Her eyes closed automatically as peace, not fright, touched her in a curious way—a sense of some dearness. Her lips parted moistly and her eyes merely slitted open to watch him, as if in a dream. A slow smile touched her lips then. Aye, she was dreaming of Fay. She wished she would never have to awaken from this fantasy.

"Your hair, sleek and beautiful," he began low, "haloed by dark fire from the glowing embers, looks like a curved bridge for angels to play and dance upon and then disappear down into the deepening colors beneath it . . ."

His warm hand palmed a shoulder her damp nightgown had slipped from. Following it, he bent to kiss the hollow at her collarbone. A low moan escaped from her lips as delicious tremors washed over her. Her eyes were closed, and her lashes looked very long and sooty against the pale, tear-stained cheeks. She was so filled with sudden desire that her woman's body, soft and supple, prepared for love, began to tremble. But still she did not move invitingly. Kissing her tenderly on the cheek, the phantom pressed her back to the pillow and then he moved to rise.

She pulled him back to her, pleading softly. "Fay, do not go. Stay . . . please? I am so lonely."

The moon slipped beneath a cloud as he bent over her, his voice barely above a whisper. "What is your heart's desire? Say it and it shall be yours."

"Fay! My phantom love!" Her husky strained voice told him what it was she desired, what she ached for most in this world.

Aurora welcomed him with open arms, feeling the heavy hammer of his heart coming next to the tripping of her own. Then silently, magically, the nightgown came off over her head. In a blur of movement he tossed off his cape, nothing else. The vizard remained, as did his clothing. An intense heat overwhelmed her as his fingers worked between them at his belt, then slipped behind her easily to grip the softness of her thighs to guide her in her first effort of loving with abandon. His masked face lowered a measure to capture the sweetness for which Fay's throbbing lips were searching. The kiss was deep, fully tasted.

"Fay! Fay!" she whispered into his mouth, then cried, then rose breathlessly, clasping his hips to her narrow ones.

Mounting her, he nudged her legs apart with a knee and, hard and hot, he entered the honeyed cup. She invited his thrusts farther and farther into her, until the flame rose and heightened to wildfire, spreading scorching tongues that bound them together and licked at their bellies and loins.

In a passionately crazed moment Aurora reached out to tear at the mask in a desire to see her dark lover's ecstasy. But the longing was quelled as he gripped both her wrists painfully and thrust them high above her head, imprisoned in one of his hands.

"Nay, my love. That," he went on hoarsely, "must wait a little longer. You must use your heart to unmask and see me true."

"But," she moaned beneath him, "you are not real, you are a dream—a phantom!"

Seeming not to hear her, he continued in a new and painful ecstasy, the thrusts coming bolder yet, and Aurora cried out as she clutched and strained against her phantom lover who brought them up, up, and ever upward, to that mutual bursting star where they rolled over once, twice, in slow-motion and faster and faster still, mounting to an explosive orgasm. Coming to a rest, they spun down to a soft bed of cloud, with her head resting upon his shoulder and one of her willowy legs still thrown about, clasping his hip, which was still locked with hers. The moon spun in with mist-silver streamers and bathed the rumpled bed in its paleness.

Abruptly he was off the bed, hitching up his breeches as he stood towering above the sprawled figure that couldn't move for all her hurtful confusion that he could be done with her so carelessly. She watched with pain-filled eyes as he swept up the tossed aside cape, and before turning brusquely away, he spoke deeply, with low timbre and a mockingly cool manner.

"A wonderful dream, *Aurora*, but should the seed I have just now planted in you bear fruit—what then?"

Aurora struggled up to a sitting position. Her tangle of raven hair made her look very young, like a lost little girl. The slits of glittering eyes studied her hard for a few more seconds, then, in a swirl of black cape he was vanishing toward the door. Like a phantom of the night.

Yet feeling indeed the hot seed in her belly, touching the tender flesh he had just quit, Aurora lifted her head and did a most fantastic thing. She smiled. Radiantly.

From beyond the reaches of the Keep, the gay trilling of a woodland bird was carried forth on the wind.

Filled with a deep contentment, Aurora had fallen into an exhausted but not unpleasant slumber, dreaming this time that she was cuddled against the long and naked and lean frame of her lover. Now, as her lashes fluttered open dreamily, memory came flooding back with a sense of joy and tenderness. Thrusting her bare feet impudently out of the carelessly tossed covers, she opened her dewy eyes fully and noticed, naturally, that the pillow next to hers was vacant of his dark head. It didn't matter. She breathed in with delicious remembrance, stretching luxuriously with the stimulating scent of male yet clinging to her softly bruised flesh.

Outside, the wind was in competition with the sun as autumnal leaves were sent scudding past the window like a flock of colorfully dressed children chasing each other. The sun's rays flooded the room as Hetty entered with a hum and a breakfast tray. Soft sunlight had glinted momentarily on the bold purplish imprints on the delicate curve of Aurora's hip and she reddened slightly, having been caught studying herself; but Hetty, hiding a secretive smile as she set down the tray, merely kept up her humming tone.

Covering her lower half, Aurora sat up, wearing a listening expression.

"Hetty, what tune is that you are humming? 'Tis lovely." She reached for a maple-sugared wafer from off the tray.

"'Tis an old, old song of a magical love story . . ." She continued to hum.

"Mmmm," Aurora murmured absently.

Through half-shut lids, Aurora's sunshine-on-heather eyes swept mistily over the bed as she seemed to purr more than speak. "Where is my husband?"

Hetty frowned, then collected herself. "Didn't ye know? He's gone off with that Tom Bone, them both in buckskin breeches, bucklin' on short swords when they went wi'out early with the chirpin' of birds. Ye've a strange man, luv. He goes when that Bacon and his rebels stir up trouble. Do ye think he's one of them?"

The violet eyes veiled with deep thought. Melanie had once said something of this nature. He did leave all of a sudden, again. It was as if he always had an important appointment with danger, always being summoned during the wee hours and then indeed was vanished when she awoke. Munching on another wafer, she stared at the cold gray ashes in the hearth. So be it, then. If she had to choose between siding with the rebel or the governor, were she a man instead of a frail woman, she would have ridden with the younger man. The "Great Rebel" as he was famously, or infamously named.

Of course! That would accout for Bran's horrible knife wound. He had been fighting alongside Bacon, with him when those Indian captives were herded to Jamestown. Sir Eric always knew the latest gossip dealing with the rebellion. How he obtained it so quickly she couldn't even begin to guess.

"Yer father-in-law loves to gossip, sure, like a woman. He tells me right after his grandson goes out, as if he's proud o' it, that Bacon's marchin' back to Jamestown this very minute, bold as a cock atop a hill scrappin' fer a fight. Yer man's more than like wi' him, that rebel!"

Aurora bounded gaily from the bed, all light-hearted despite the talk about rebellion. She went to flip through her wardrobe for something pretty to wear. That was how she was feeling this morning— feminine and pretty.

"If Bran is with him, as you say, then surely he also is a rebel. 'Tis a just cause he sides with, Hetty."

Stepping back with a light graceful step, Aurora held against her bosom a fair, blue-violet gown that had been dyed with indigo.

"Whew! Yer fine husband's an outlaw, now luv, no less. Do ye not care that he murders poor Injuns, most like their wee ones, too? The good guvnor's going to hang him, yer husband, along with the lot of them, as sure as yer hair is black!"

When Hetty caught the little gasp in Aurora's breath, she smoothed over, "Aye, ye do love him surely."

Aurora collected herself then and there. "Hetty, the

good farmers up north are also being ruthlessly murdered. The ill wind that has spread throughout the colony had its beginning when the savages began killing those on the border. Nathaniel Bacon seeks only to stop the heathens from spilling brethren blood. Rich and poor alike have given Bacon thanks for his caring and endeavors for their preservation. Among Bacon's followers and supporters are some of the most prominent men in the colony." Aurora thought of Bran, but didn't say it aloud.

"Ye know how the servants hae been saying that the rebels nearly killed the guvnor. They call Bacon and his followers, Tagg, Ragg, and Bobtayle!" Hetty could not help but loose a half-chuckle.

"A scare that, yet at the time the governor granted Bacon the commission he wanted. Sir William talks rebellion while Bacon had merely peace in mind all the while. The Baconians do not think themselves engaged against the king's authority, only against the Indians. This said by one of Bacon's own lieutenants, John Goode, Sir Eric has told me. I believe that the future shall look back and see that this rebellion settled once and for all Virginia's Indian problem, and that it will become something merely reminisced about. Bacon, I foresee, will be celebrated in verse and song down through the years."

Hetty tossed her pert cap askew. "To be sure! The maidservants gossip downstairs that Bacon's soldiers hae a reputation as being romantic as Scottish bandits. They be singing about him and his band already. If that don't beat all hollow, I'll eat me nightcap!"

Aurora heaved a sigh. "'Tis just what I have in mind. I am famished, Hetty. I would forego breakfast and have lunch. What is being prepared?" she asked, busy plaiting her hair into a long thick braid.

"Ugh! Ye look just like an Indian squaw, luv. Why do ye that to yer hair?" Hetty cocked her head sideways.

Aurora slanted a sly look in the maidservant's direction. "An Indian, hmmm?"

"Ye be makin' yer point, luv, so hush up yer eyes. There be goodness and beauty in all folk, Indian or white. The Almighty loves each and every one of us and we be all equal in his loving eyes. We should all do as he bids us to and love one another as brothers. I guess this old earth canna ever be free of wars, as long as man nae can get along," Hetty sighed, smoothing her rail before being about her business, going downstairs to set a place for her mistress.

Aurora went down shortly to a light lunch, which Hetty herself served to her, and then she returned to her—and Bran's—bedchamber. She sat down on the edge of the bed, smoothing the old, but lovely, scarlet coverlet lovingly with her hand. Her eyes misted over as she recalled what had passed in the night. She shivered and perspired between an ague of pain and a hot fever which threatened to consume her completely as she felt the renewed desire licking at her insides. She looked toward the leaded casement window to see the mid-September day smiling in brightly at her.

"I do, God"—Aurora bowed her dark head—"I do

solemnly promise . . ."

Drums were beating out the thrilling rattle-thud-thud when Bran and Tom neared the "French work," which was being dug as a counter fortification and for siege against the capital. They found Bacon desperate, the soldiers filled with bitter anger. They pulled their mounts up, listening.

"Come on, my hearts of gold," Bacon harangued the men spiritedly, "he that perishes on the field lies in the bed of honor."

Bran immediately noticed that Nathaniel's face was pinched and pale, his thin fists were clenched, and he looked wearier than ever, but for all this there was still fire in his dark eyes. Bran realized that their leader was already readying his army to attack the city, where the governor and his men were being confined firmly under siege by Bacon's soldiers.

For a moment Nathaniel failed to recognize the two who had ridden in. Then he laughed warmly, beckoning them both over to him. Wearing a coat thick with dust, Bacon greeted Tom and then faced Bran squarely.

"We have Berkeley imprisoned, Fay, and we shall chase him out of Jamestown," Bacon said confidently.

Bran dismounted, asking, "Will the militia try to strike our line?"

"Methinks at dawn he shall try—if he dares!" Bacon went on heatedly. "He has over six hundred men, but alas, too many to feed."

"Aye," Bran rubbed his chin which was already

371

black-stubbled. "He must attack, or else send his starving men back across the neck. I see we've already our night's work cut out for us."

"What's that, Fay?" Nathaniel wondered out loud.

"You'll see. There will be found much pleasure with the terrors that we shall inflict upon Berkeley's pickets come midnight. By morning they shall all have a bad case of the jitters!"

"You shall need a wink or two before dawn, my friend," Bacon advised.

Bran chuckled grimly. "Does the wicked find any time for rest, good Nathaniel?"

"Heh-heh," Tom Bone chuckled, rubbing his hands together for the fun to come.

Again taken ill by some strange malady, Nathaniel rested fitfully in his headquarters that night amid the whooping excitement of the camp. Bran and his chosen men made more clamor than one hundred wild Indians. Nathaniel learned in the morning that Bran had the men fill some gourds with powder, stealthily snake close to the governor's nervous and terrified lookouts, and toss the "loaded" gourds into the campfires—which added immensely to the ruckus. Well after midnight, Bran led them as they loosed with butt-slaps a pack of the Pamunkey Indians' captured horses into the enemy lines and caused the pickets to fire blindly, insanely, into the dark, completely—much to Bran's relief—missing the beautiful, thundering beasts. It was an eerie campfire sight, as they shot above the horses' riderless backs. The enemies' camp was a shambles come morning, but the Baconians had been gay as well as fierce and had enjoyed immensely the terrors they had inflicted upon the milita in the village.

Several of the governor's ships stood ready with their guns, out in the bay. The captain of one was none other than Javier Strang. He had more heard than seen the attacks of the night before from his ship. Helpless, he had watched, with detached interest. He had recognized his enemy, though, through his spy-glass; the tall man had moved with an easy trot, like an Indian, on the fringe of firelight. There was no mistaking the pantherlike man who for several years had stalked him. The masked man whom he had discovered too late had burned down his warehouse, like a stealthful Indian, attacking on a moonless night. Bran Ravenleigh. Also, he had learned, Ravenleigh was known only by a few as Fay—*the Raven.*

It was hard to see much in the misty half-light of dawn now, as Captain Strang peered through his sailor's glass. Berkeley's force was beginning to move, and Berkeley himself was shouting encouragement to his men. Strang gave the order to open up the gun ports of the ship. He could see Bran Ravenleigh yelling defiantly as he checked the priming of his weapon, then peered through his own glass. The mist was lifting steadily.

Bran frowned, lowered his glass, then peered again at Captain Strang. He cursed.

Bran lost no time. He aimed his fusil on a prayer and miraculously and with deadly accuracy he met his mark. Looking through his glass again, he saw that the pirate was wounded. Blood trickled down his neck; his left ear was missing. Bran smiled grimly. He had stung twice. Strang, though a bloodied mess, was curling his lip in a nasty snarl. He could be seen to curse, ordering his men to throw shot in Bran's direction. But, to Strang's misfortune, the attack suddenly halted.

Bran, too, lowered his fusil after ramming another shot home. He could have fired and killed Strang. Now the pirate's ship was moving away, going to deeper waters in the river. Berkeley had retreated with his wounded, having lost all stomach for the fight. Bacon drove the militia back. Despite their superior strength in numbers, Berkeley's forces were badly beaten. Sir William was forced to abandon the citadel as Bacon's men continued again, now rattling shot off the housetops.

Sir William Berkeley took ship and sailed back to Arlington. The town was abandoned when, six days later, Bacon entered Jamestown. He waited until nightfall to destroy the village. He set fire to Virginia's capital, burning every building within its walls. The Statehouse, wharves, mansions, and every inn went up in smoke, the flames dreadful against the night sky. Bacon did not even spare the church, which he torched himself. The records of the colony were the only things preserved. Bacon had planned to leave Sir William not one quarter to use as base. He had executed this with the expertise of a shrewd general.

Nathaniel Bacon had planned also to finish the great fight against the Indians, but first he feasted hugely with his men at the governor's mansion,

Green Spring. When Bacon set out to take his army to Gloucester County to plunder the loyalists' estates, this was where he and Fay parted company.

Bran had first told Tom that there was a certain pirate that they must track. They would know him by his blood and destruction.

Bacon's troops became so preoccupied with plundering the houses, taking whatever precious goods could be found, that Bran and Tom were mildly sickened by the scenes. Nathaniel was burning himself out, afflicted with dysentery, drinking overly much, the long swamp marches taking their toll on his health. Bran foresaw that this would be the last he would see of the "greatest rebel Virginia had ever known."

Bran was in low spirits when he and Tom left Warner Hall, which Bacon had seized as temporary headquarters, but Bacon, on the other hand, was ever the good-humored comrade and bade his friend farewell. If Bacon had fears, he never displayed them. When Nathaniel died—his rapidly failing health attested to the inevitable—the rebellion would die with him, Bran concluded.

"It seems to me," Tom was saying as they cantered toward the forest, "that the gods, or devils, meant for you to meet Nathaniel and be at Jamestown at the same time your enemy was there. I think you were never meant to be a rebel, master, you were just at the wrong place at the right time. That is all."

"You mean that I have played this part for naught?" Bran laughed tersely. "Nay, Tom, none of us were rebels back there. In fact, Berkeley was the rebel! Nathaniel would heartily agree with me that our sole purpose was to drive back the Indians. It was our right to guard the lives of our brethren."

"You are not an Englishman anymore, Master Bran."

"We are Virginians, Tom, Americans!"

"Aye."

## Twenty-One

Jamestown lay in charred shambles as Bran and Tom rode through the blackened ruin. Their half-empty stomachs made their senses keen, for they had only nibbled on jerked beef and dried grapes from their pouches. They passed through the village silently, just as a light drizzle began to fall, which made the powdery ashes cling damply to their horses' hooves. A keen intuition was dragging Bran toward Rachel Smythe. It told him she would have fled Jamestown and headed for the next nearest inn to look for work, or lodging, in one of the scattered settlements along the James.

"Could be the devil has bled to death by now," Tom dared to say out loud.

"I hope not," Bran said meaningfully.

"Aye," Tom agreed. "You would be cheated out of seeing the bastard draw his last breath."

They reached the settlement just as a hazy, rain-sodden dusk was gathering. As they drew nearer to the inn, they could see a hulking gray shadow out in the creek. Captain Strang's black sloop! Tom whistled at their good fortune, at the same time fingering the French hatchet in his belt.

In the half-gloom of the courtyard, Bran's handsome face turned suddenly sharp, and hardened. His heart beat faster as it always had done when he thought of the callous murderer, Strang. Tom knew exactly what his master was thinking. There could be no peace in his mind until the pirate met his death.

"Tom," Bran said low, "take the horses and conceal them in the pines over yonder. Wait. You know we'll be outnumbered. Are you ready?"

Bran returned the gesture then, as the servant grinned in anticipation of the long-awaited fight.

Alone now, Bran crept pantherlike up to the tavern and peeped through the shutters. He counted eight men in the public room and three wenches. All were well into their cups, but the wenches looked disheveled and done in. Strang was nowhere in sight. Without warning, one of the burly sailors stretched out a long, hairy arm and snaked it around a girl's waist. He buried his bearded face in the dark-haired wench's ample bosom, cupped a pendulous pear toward his lips and surprised her by biting the pink aureole. Her pitiful cries went unheeded as he thrust her upon the outthrust knee of another sailor and lifted her skirts unceremoniously.

Bran let his stare lift to see another wench bearing a tray containing mugs of wine which soon were snatched up by burly fists. She stood mesmerized, looking sickened and helpless as the bearded sailor copulated with the struggling wench against the seated man. Soon that sailor too joined in the one-sided pleasure.

Bran shook his head at the tangled mass of heaving, straining bodies, the girl's limbs like flailing white snakes trying to escape the bruising and pounding. Bran felt rather than heard Tom come up behind him. Tom took a look through the shutter and snorted softly, his lips folding together in a tight line.

"They have the habits of rutting pigs from the swamp. I'll bet their urine even reeks of evil, like the wolf who has fed on carrion," he muttered. Then, swiftly and easily, his fingers loosened his hatchet from its fringed bag as two of the sailors stumbled to the door leading outside.

The door was flung windward, and the drunken sailors tripped into the courtyard and began urinating against a tree. They stood side by side, sharing a lewd joke. Both were bearded, after the Spanish style. They never noticed it when the wind nudged the door almost shut. Even more to the advantage, they never knew what hit them as together Bran and Tom attacked stealthily, silent as two big cats.

Soon, bloodied sword in hand, Bran quietly rolled the still body into the shadows with the sole of his boot. Tom did the same, cleaning off his hatchet on the dead sailor's coat. Bran hastily snatched up their weapons and concealed them in a thick bunch of yellowed grass.

"The odds have changed, Tom," Bran whispered, sheathing his stained sword.

"Two down, six to go," Tom muttered.

"Nay, seven. You forgot, friend, Strang is in there somewhere, too. No doubt tumbling Rachel Smythe against her will. I know she is here; those three wenches are from Lawrence's where they all worked together before the inn was burned to the ground."

"Where is the proprietor, do you think?"

"No doubt floating in the creek with a knife buried in his back. I would not put anything past these stinking vultures!" Bran hissed.

Returning to the window, Bran and Tom exchanged grins of great satisfaction. The pirate was seated at the table, leering at Rachel's back as she went to baste a saddle of mutton at the spit. The glow from the hearth cast every feature of Strang's swarthy countenance into high relief. And there it was—the blood-crusted bandage over the hole where there should have been an ear. He smiled cruelly, wolfishly, as his mates continued to take their turns on the swooning girl that was now spread-eagled on the top of a table. The pretty wench's lips were cracked and bleeding and her breasts were bruised the color of purple plums.

Bran could detect a slight, sweet similarity to Aurora in the wench. That did it! Bran lifted the hilt of his heavy military rapier from its sheath and the long blade followed. Tom touched his arm and shook his head in a warning not to be too hasty. Tom's voice was barely audible as he spoke.

"His evil is so deep it's like Hell itself, master. But still the man is dangerous, more than any Indian you have fought and slain. Look, his men work on the wench, but still have their swords ready at their sides. We must wait until two of them have drunk themselves under the table. The captain is an expert swordsman, and so the others look to be."

Bran shivered passionately. "This blade of mine cannot wait to be buried in that villain's heart— Berkeley's pimp! Strang's greed helped to breed rebellion in Virginia. He murdered my uncle, my own flesh and blood!'' He took a deep breath and, when he looked ready to explode, hollered at the top of his lungs, "You son of a bitch Strang! I am waiting! Now!''

A loud clatter sounded and a mad rushing all at once livened the tavern. Heavy benches were overturned, and one of them pinned the pretty wench that had been repeatedly mauled and raped. The door crashed wide, and Tom tripped a roaring, cursing sailor as he leapt out of the doorway, then fell flat on his face. Rachel ran outside, knowing who was out there. She had not been able to tell anything by the bear-like roar, but all day she had been using her mind to draw Bran Ravenleigh to her and the wretched wenches.

Then Strang himself stood framed by the wood, wielding a rapier, the gold on the scabbard shining. His black eyes glinted beneath the rising moon, narrowing dangerously as he looked first at Bran Ravenleigh, who stood coolly challenging him, then to Rachel Smythe, who backed up slowly with both fear and rancor in her eyes.

"So," Javier began, "you have betrayed me, bitch. You have sent for your handsome lover, eh?'' He gave Bran his undivided attention then as he waved his weapon. "We have finally met face to face. You hate me very much, I know. You have burned my warehouse and shot off my ear not long ago. You think I killed . . . Jason Ravenleigh. I did,'' he stated bluntly, his eyes burning coals in his face. "Wait, before you *try* to kill me, I have more to say. You see, Jason had a map that belonged to my grandfather. How he got it, I do not know, but there was a servant who knew this. He worked for your father. *Si*, your father. Jason Ravenleigh was your father, this servant learned and told me long ago. Now you have more reason to kill me, eh?'' Javier knew he had thrown Ravenleigh offguard.

Now Tom Bone shrilled a terrifying Indian war whoop, and Captain Strang, startled though he was, was ready by the time Bran lunged in with his rapier.

"Indeed, I shall kill you, half-Spanish pig!" Bran snarled as he stepped back, lightning fast, to avoid the pirate's quick, neat thrust. "You lie! The map belonged to Derek Ravenscar, dog!"

Like most sailors, Strang was skilled with the blade, but he could not slash furiously enough, for Bran sidestepped the lunge every time. Strang tried in vain to get his blade in for a slash at the legs of his opponent, but Bran's point scraped his throat and brought flecks of red to the soiled lace collar. Then Bran's point flicked a button from Strang's brocaded sleeve. The pirate flinched, then grinned at this.

"Why did your father leave you when you were a babe, eh? You were too ugly a bastard to look upon?" Strang taunted. "Aha, I like to fight with an angry man. It makes the fight more the challenge. You will die soon, lad, so you must make this last one your best, eh?"

Strang lunged expertly now, but soon noticed that his opponent's body was hardened by battle and he moved quickly, much more than any expert swordsman he had ever dueled with. Here was the opponent he had long awaited. True, he had avoided Ravenleigh like a coward, but now there was much pleasure to be found in the heat of the battle. What he didn't like was the Englishman's silence. It was eerie.

The moon steadily climbed and the water of the creek stirred and glittered beneath it like molten silver. Tom Bone was holding his own for the most part, and had finished off four of the sailors, with some aid from the wenches, who had held back two of the sailors by heaving a keg over on its side and sending it spinning and crashing into their legs.

"Friggin' bastard!" said one of the sailors as he tried in vain to gouge out Tom's eyeball. He was soon impaled to the building, and Tom found his hatchet and buried it in yet another skull.

Now, as Bran's weapon swept up, Strang slashed expertly in warding off the blow and ran his blade halfway through the ball of Bran's hand. Still Bran held his tongue as he stepped backwards, though a lesser man would have screamed out with pain and rage. The swords crossed again, clashed, spun madly as if locked together, then flew in a slashing exchange. Stepping back again deftly, Bran faked a slight slip of his foot, bringing Strang forward for a thrust at Bran's heart while he dropped to one knee. Momentarily, hateful eyes clashed together like fighting steel, and then Bran's blade-point skewered Strang as he applied the force of his charge to drive the steel home.

"Now, may your black soul rot in Hell," Bran breathed with a hiss.

Strang bubbled his words forth with a fleck of red foam. "You . . . bastard!" He jerked at the hilt with trembling, already bloodless fingers for a moment. Then he shuddered. He was dead.

While Strang's soul sped swiftly to its dark

destination, Tom was battering a face, which was already homely, into a bloody pulp. All the sailors were down at last. Their bloody figures writhed convulsively then joined the journey with Strang, wearing noses smashed flat against bloody puddings that had before been faces. Tom had given no quarter. He was a ruthless fighter.

Before Bran and Tom took their leave, they stowed the bodies on the ship in the creek and freed the sloop to drift downstream. Then they went inside to check on Rachel who had gone upstairs with the other girls. The pretty one that had been ravished severely was going to live, Bran was sure, as he picked her up carefully and laid her across a bed. While Rachel tended the wounds, bathing the girl gently, she informed Bran that she would take over the tavern as proprietor. Strang's men had indeed knifed the former owner, Thompson, to death.

Downstairs, Bran sat with his long legs stretched out in front of him, a cup of sack dangling from his loose fingers. Tom stood with his back to Bran as he gazed thoughtfully into the dying embers in the hearth. Jason had been Bran's father—would his master believe this? This revelation must be a soul-searing torment in itself to Bran. What was he thinking now? Tom wondered.

As Tom remained silent, Bran had a notion of what would put an end to his pain-filled wondering. He came to a conclusion swiftly then. If Jason had really been his father, Sir Eric was the only person who could confirm this. With that thought, Bran rose and Tom followed him out the door.

\*　　　\*　　　\*

Rainy winds huffed against the exterior of Raven Keep, as the first of October brought a new chill in the vast corners of the hall. But a hickory fire blazed in the hearth, cheery and warm; nearby sat Sir Eric, with a mug of foxgrape wine. Beside him on the floor, Duchess was acting nervous, whining, her eyes rolling, her ears pricking up now and then at some outside sound humans could not hear. Aurora paid no mind to the wolfhound, pulling her shamrock-green shawl tighter about her shoulders as she stared reflectively into the fire.

Aurora wore a gown of dusky rose with a petticoat of the warmer homespun. Her hair was covered with a little cap of quilted calico, the longer waves allowed to cascade down her back. In her lap rested her old Psalter, but she hadn't opened the book once yet tonight.

The old knight reached for his mug, then patted the wolfhound. "What is it, girl? Someone coming, eh, girl?" He was thinking of his grandson, but when the hound settled down again, Sir Eric shrugged back against his chair.

"It could be some of the militiamen again, Grandfather," Aurora said softly, having gotten used to calling him that.

"Not again, I pray! Our cupboards and cellars are near bare," he sighed. "The ships are long overdue, Harris said just this morning. Pirates flourish in many a hidden inlet, and the incoming ships must have been forewarned and turned about at the river's mouth."

"We still have ground Indian corn and dried apples aplenty in the larder," Aurora reminded him.

"And there is always fresh meat to be had."

"Sure there is. But the servants are afeared to go out too deep and hunt in the forest. And man cannot live by meat alone," he said, grinning at this twist and seeking to liven their melancholy mood.

"No laughing matter. It shall be a hungry winter for all, Grandfather. The rich and the poor alike." For some odd reason she thought of Melanie upstairs abed, afraid to go home because of the threat of roving Indians (she had adopted a great fear of the savages), she had all but abandoned North Creek.

"Anyway," Melanie had said a week ago, "'tis so lonely with only Aunt Bertilde there. I'm afraid of ghosts, too, Ro, and more than once I thought I heard Mama and Papa walking the halls, heard their voices as if in low conversation. And David, his visits were so rare. Damn him!"

"Damn!" Sir Eric was saying at the same time Aurora was reflecting back. Now he apologized swiftly, but his granddaughter-in-law only smiled affectionately. "I was thinking . . . if my grandson was here we'd have plenty of meat, and sacksful of grain for bread, too. He tracks and brings down meat as fast and skillful as a fleetfooted Indian. Faugh! And him born an elegant and arrogant English cavalier at that. You'd think he was born a wild Virginian now, instead, the way he runs around in leathern breeches and comes home with full black beard, his countenance like a dark Rasputin!"

"I have never seen Bran in a beard . . . mayhap, oh yes, he would look very handsome indeed. He would look the image of—" She halted as she stared pensively into the leaping flames to picture him. Her lovely eyes softened as the sadness left them. He couldn't be angry with her, she wouldn't let him be!

Sir Eric went on as if she hadn't even spoken. "And, egad! when he comes home he reeks of woodsmoke, horse, and sometimes wild blood, aye, if he's made a kill. Sure, he'll bring fresh meat home, he knows all the plantations have been stripped these past several weeks to feed the militiamen—and the rebels!" He reached for his wine again, but looked across to her in surprise. "What's the matter, sweet, you suddenly look as if you've seen a ghost?"

"'Tis nothing, Grandfather. I just feel a bit tired, that's all."

Aurora rose to retire, but first walked over to brush a kiss on his wide forehead. In her usual flowing gait, she walked from the hall but beneath her skirts her knees trembled. What if he had been hurt again, or worse yet . . . she just wouldn't allow herself to dwell on such disaster.

Sir Eric began to worry again. The coffers were draining, too. Tobacco was scarce after the many droughts and high taxes (Berkeley again) had put a hole in their funds. All they needed now was a miracle—a treasure. He chuckled at the absurd thought.

His ruminations went darker as he bethought himself back to when he had sent his own flesh and blood from his breast. Jason, his own, once a wild young highwayman, that had been murdered in this strange New World. Was it his own fault? Why had he never told Bran? A coward? Damnation! Why? Was it too late to tell him?

Sir Eric nodded in his deep-cushioned chair. The

house was so very silent, it made one's flesh creep. The wolfhound shot his head up once and then settled down. The old man's eyes closed. Jason's image haunted him as he dozed, then slept hard.

Aurora awoke at midnight. Strangely, her heart was pounding as she floated to wakefulness, seeing a candle flame floating toward her. Was she dreaming? But she watched it come nearer—nearer. She rubbed her bleary eyes. The hair prickled on her scalp and her blood froze.

Someone laughed softly down at her. An evil sound.

Aurora snatched up the coverlet to fold it over her breast. He inched closer, his knee bumping against the bedstead. *He.* She could make out a man's pale-complexioned face floating above her. She gasped at the bloodless and bodiless face of . . . David Wiley!

"What—what are you doing here?" The words came out slowly as she felt her flesh crawling.

He bent down to find a wrist and grasp it, but she shrank back from him.

"Be warned, say nothing of this to anyone," David muttered.

"How did you get into the house?" Her voice turned stony after he shrugged leisurely. "Get out, before I scream. This is my"—she paused—"*ours*, my husband's and my bedchamber, and you've no right being here in this house. You trespass, David Wiley. No one invited you." She shrank back further as he again leaned forward to hiss into her face.

"Holier than thou, aren't you, Ro," he gave a low, sardonic laugh instead of a question. "You are a little bitch, you know that?"

Aurora straightened her back against her pillows. "I shan't be afraid of you, David Wiley. Why don't you just tell me the purpose of this late-night visit and then be gone? You place yourself in much danger should my husband return home and find you in here."

"You should know by now what it is I want, you're supposed to be so intelligent," David sneered above the flickering candle.

Aurora began to tremble with anger, not fear. "Melanie is here, so it is not pleasure you seek from me. Shall we play guessing games—or what?" A black-winged eyebrow could be seen to rise.

"The map."

Aurora slanted her head and whispered, "The *what?*"

With the candle still held in one hand, he reached forward fast with the other to twist her wrist hurtfully. Her nostrils flared at the nauseating touch of him as she tried wrenching away. This only drove him to squeeze tighter, like a crushing vise. There was no denying the insane strength of this man. She couldn't help it, she cried out finally. He eased up a little.

"If you don't give it to me, you won't live to see morning," David threatened earnestly.

"And if I do not live, David Wiley, then you shall never have it," she said smartly.

"What does that mean?" His words, each one, were like a hard slap.

"It means . . . that it is not in my possession at the time. By the way, how are you so certain that there

389

ever was a whole map in my possession?" Oh, no, Lord, a slip of the tongue!

"I'll tell you how." He smirked knowingly. "Melanie, she told me you had a bit of parchment the old man Wellbeloved gave you on his deathbed. It didn't interest her much, but I knew what it was and who Elvy Wellbeloved really was. You see, to a brokenhearted man the map didn't have much meaning, so that's why he tore it in half, sort of in a tormented rage, and carried only one part with him. It was sort of a broken symbol to him, crazy as he was. That other half is in this house somewhere—"

"And?" she broke in softly, blinking up at him in innocence.

"And you have free roam of the house. Don't tell me you haven't tried to piece it together by now? Hah! I know you can produce the *whole* map"—he paused menacingly—"and if you don't, hmmm, I've a better plan, foolproof, one that might hurry you up a bit."

Aurora looked and was confused. She thought for a moment, then found her voice; it exuded a strength she was not feeling.

"Go on, David. I am not afraid to die, alas, not anymore," she said half-truthfully. It all depended on Bran, she thought painfully, whether she wanted to hold on to life or not. Oh, where was he now? She needed him so!

"It's not you that will die, sweet Ro, but, hmmm, someone you cherish very much."

With that ringing in her ears, David left her bedside, his wavering shadow moving toward the door.

Aurora stared wild-eyed at the pale glow being swallowed up by the closing door. That man, uglier to her than any human being she could think of, had, finally, as she had always known he would, become a threat to her and her happiness.

Tremblingly Aurora lay back down. Lord, what now? Bran had the map in his possession, locked up she knew not where. She really did not need the map; the exact location was etched in her mind. Could she get David to believe this? Could she get him to the hollow . . . before. . . .

# Part Three

## Somewhere in Tomorrow's Mists

## Twenty-Two

A log stirred and hissed, tossing up sparks from the grate just as an embracing flame licked it with fiery tongues.

A tall, dark man stood warming himself before the hearth, an elbow resting on the mantel as he smiled down at the old man who grumbled in his slumber. Sir Eric's chin nodded on his chest and suddenly he was startled awake. Wary for some reason, his eyes opened the littlest bit. His eyes widened next as he took in the masked and cloaked figure standing there so casually and with an unreal look about him.

"Jason!" he croaked, gripping the arms of the chair until the bones lifted in his long hands.

The dark figure remained silent, indeed most unworldly.

"Jason, my son, you've come here to haunt me. A phantom, no less!"

Bran feared for his grandfather expiring of a heart attack. He at once proceeded to peel off the disguise, starting with the vizard, then the rakish cavalier hat, and finally the cloak, which he whipped aside with a wide-sweeping flourish of his hand.

"Huh?" Sir Eric blinked in astonishment. "That you, Bran?"

Bran pushed himself away from the mantel, tossing both arms wide as if presenting himself to his grandfather for the first time.

"'Tis me, in the flesh, uh, your grandson. Not Jason. Do I look so very much like my father now, sir?"

Sir Eric sputtered and flushed. "Woe betide! You could've scared this old man to death, nearly did. So"—He puckered his lips into a fine line—"now you know."

Bran's eyes were kind and understanding, smiling through the black fringe of his lashes. "I discovered the highwayman's disguise long ago in Jason's trunk"—His words hung in the air, as if that explained everything that his grandfather should have long ago. He was sparing the old man the pain of not having done so.

Sir Eric beckoned for his grandson to pull up a chair beside his. Thus began a long and serious and draining talk, man-to-man between them.

"So," Sir Eric said in finishing, "I am a stupid old man. Can you ever forgive me for not telling you that Jason Ravenleigh was a robber and a heartbreaker—especially who he was?"

"You are not an old man, sir. When I entered the hall you were grumbling and cussing in your sleep like olden times—when you were a young and vicious knight," he chuckled warmly.

"Hah! I'm still vicious, too," Sir Eric regained his composure, slipping into his usual mock-grumbling role. "You got some pecker coming here! Your name went on the hangman's list last week."

"Sure, and it's proud I am to be in honest

company, sir," Bran said, unbothered by the warning. "I shall not be recognized, especially not with that on." His eyes twinkled as he indicated the disguise, which had been tossed carelessly onto the settee. "You see, Berkeley's men will look for me upriver, never here. That is, if they even suspect me as being a rebel. How is my wife?" he blurted suddenly.

"Huh? Oh, better than the other times you left her. There is a new charm and confidence about her, if that's wholly possible. Yet at other times—" He bit off at once.

Bran sat straighter in his chair. "What do you mean? Is she unwell?" Silver eyes looked worried.

"Like tonight. She seemed upset about something. She said she was only weary, but I read otherwise, Bran. Could it be she's—uh—you know?" His eyes sparkled expectantly.

"With child?" Bran shrugged then, but felt warm all over, a certain tenderness flowing through him at the thought of Aurora bearing his son, or daughter. His last words with her echoed now through his brain. *If my seed should bear fruit . . .*

"Well, then," Bran began, concerned, "you did not mention that my name went on the hangman's list?"

"Nay, nay, nothing like that. So . . . how *did* your name happen on the list? Berkeley didn't find you out, did he?"

"No doubt Strang had my name put there. During the battle at Jamestown our enemy was unlucky enough to lose his right ear."

"Aha! You have got him twice now, stung the evil bastard where it hurts. He'll no doubt be coming after you now, eh?" Sir Eric appeared excited by the prospect.

"Where he is at right now, sir, he shan't be coming or going anywhere—ever."

Sir Eric lowered his whitening head, as if in prayer. When he finally looked up there was much sadness bleary in his eyes. "I should be rejoicing. Hah! Instead I'm . . . Bran! You knew before you came here, didn't you, lad?"

"I did," Bran sighed feelingly. "It was the pirate himself who let me in on the secret of my father. Hell, I never even guessed all these years."

Bran turned, swept up the clothes in his arms, then made his exit slowly from the hall.

Dry-eyed for now, Sir Eric heaved a man-sized sigh. He lifted his weary frame from the chair. Duchess stirred, then stood to shake herself from nose to tail in a crazy little dance. The old man bent to pat the wolfhound, and she rose higher with her back to accommodate the human's tiring gesture of affection.

"Heh-heh, you're smarter than me, old girl. You never stirred once. Recognized him right away, mask and all, didn't you?"

Duchess bathed the big hand affectionately and padded after him to the stairs. It has been a long day, Sir Eric thought wearily. But an even longer night.

Bran stood at the foot of the bed as quietly as possible. The embers were so low-burning that he could not make out her features, only her midnight hair melting into the darkness at the head of the bed. He had wanted to be near her before he must be away again, just to feel her presence. He stepped back swiftly as she stirred. His boot struck a slipper or something on the floor and sent it scudding, the slight sound deafening in the silence of the room.

Aurora twisted around as she sat up in bed. "Go away! Why did you return tonight? This is not the time of night to come creeping in here like a thief. Aye, you are a thief! Do not come near me again—I find your touch loathesome and I shall not speak to you until the morning dawns bright! Go!" She rolled back into the coverlet.

Bran slipped back out to the hall and shut the door softly behind him. He stood there for several awkward moments, his thoughts dark and tumbling over themselves. She still hadn't opened her heart to see. Would she ever see the light?

He shook his head in a new bewilderment, then strode soundlessly back downstairs and outside to find Tom Bone.


Broodingly Bran held his fusil on the pommel of his saddle as he rode beside Tom. They slept each night beneath the cold stars that peered into the deep patch of woods, enjoying the rest as best they could with the wild beasts howling and hissing and screaming around them. During the early morning hours they prowled like wolves themselves with hunger in their bellies, stopping only long enough to hunt for small game. They had left fresh meat and fruits of the earth back at Raven Keep, enough to fill the larders for weeks.

Now they increased their vigilance when approaching settlements or when moving across rebellion-wracked plantations. The men of Berkeley's company were scattered along homes on the James, but usually the watch avoided men in buckskin after dark because such men were bordermen and dangerous, especially a masked one.

In late October, when Bran and Tom rode into Bacon's camp, they heard the drums that were being beaten upside down. Bran knew then that Nathaniel Bacon had breathed his last. The rebel leader had been buried secretly the night before, but the news of his death was already sweeping the colony like a fleetfooted messenger. Bran learned that his body had been buried in the waters of the York, weighted down and lowered into the deepest place his men could find.

"Bacon . . . dead," Bran muttered, hardly able to believe it yet.

"It is true," Tom replied. "I, too, saw it coming. He rode hard and never took his rest. His frail body could not forever match the fire of his spirit."

They looked up as the orange-red sun was rising in the east, casting pale rays over the camp, which lay in quiet mourning. Already the followers of Bacon were splitting, first signs that the rebellion would rapidly disintegrate. Bacon had long before begun to lose control of his wild frontiersmen, those who had seen no reason not to plunder and rob the rich supporters of their enemy.

"Berkeley will waste no time now," Bran determined. He was also silently determined that he would not become a prisoner of the governor's men.

"Hell, the governor can't punish the whole colony that joined hands to fight a corrupt government!" Tom exclaimed.

"Indeed, he'll try," Bran answered with a heave of tired shoulders. "And the slaughter has only just begun. Soon the prisons shall be full and the public hangman busy."

"We should away, master, far away by nightfall. We are outlaws now, like hundreds of others."

"Aye, only because we had fought Indians, high taxes, and voted for the Baconian laws. Tom, before we go I must seek out the second-in-command. Ingram is here, and he alone can hold some of the frontiersmen in ranks. At least we can try to keep some of the rebel bands from roaming about and send them back to their families. If we are lucky in halting half of them from wantonly plundering, half of them will live and never be found out. I shall surrender, but only when King Charles sends English troops and a royal commission to investigate. Order must and shall be restored to the Crown's most valuable colony."

"Who will tell the king to send troops before Sir William completes his orgy of revenge?" Tom scratched his bearded chin, looked slantingly to his master. "Who . . . will be brave enough to send this message . . . ?"

Bran merely lifted a black eyebrow while spurring his mount into a gallop through the camp. Tom's horse snorted, eager and pawing to follow in Nimrod's wake, but the manservant hesitated as he sawed on the reins. A strange tingle ran along Tom's spine. They should return soon to Raven Keep. He had a premonition that there was going to be trouble there. He dug his boots into his huge horse and flew like the wind to catch up to Bran.

\*　　\*　　\*

The harvest moon had waxed and waned; the nights were frosty now. Only a few remaining maple leaves clung desperately to the barren branches; the others had been laid to rest, creating their own blanket of golden flame and crimson and light tan. Raven Keep was one among a handful of plantations that had not been raided by savages or border outlaws. For now, the household breathed a sigh of relief.

A fire crackled in the hearth across from where Aurora sat at the foot of Bran's bed, her legs tucked under her, her green shawl cast off carelessly onto the Turkey carpet. She had been rummaging through the leather-bound chest for an hour, in search of the map her husband had taken from her. Just as she thought. It was not here. She had discovered a journal though, having belonged to one Derek Ravenscar, and the pages had been holding her engrossed for a half an hour now.

Her eyes went from violet to deep purple as the emotions she was experiencing altered the hues. Too, her eyes widened, then softened, and finally, her tears, trembling on her cheeks, fell to wet the pages she had been turning.

Aurora lifted her head and stared into the hearth where the flames were changing colors, going hypnotically from magenta to orange to hot white. She felt lifted, caught up in what she had been reading, and tossed back in time. She felt the deep magic of love cast its spell over her. Love, that great mystery of life, was making itself known to her as never before.

"Rawnie and Derek," she breathed a sigh, pensively. "How they loved and laughed and gave unselfishly to each other."

One of the mysteries had begun to clear while she had been reading. The once infamous Derek Ravenscar, that buccaneer of old, had changed his name after his beloved Rawnie had died. The memories in this old house must have been too painful for him to bear, even his own name, and so he had become Elvy Wellbeloved and had stolen away from all that he had once so cherished.

If only she had known all this while he was still alive, she could have comforted him more. Poor, poor Elvy. He had been a broken old shell of a man.

She had come by the truth while studying Derek Ravenscar's journal. It had come to her in a flash—"I know this man!" She had shared with him his adventures as if she'd been with him, riding the decks of his pirate ship the *Raven*. The name of this plantation, his ship, she had woven all together and come up with yet another revelation. Derek had been Bran's kinsman! He, Derek, had been Sir Eric's cousin, but a poorer relation of the nobler Ravenleighs.

Aurora wanted to rush downstairs right now and tell Sir Eric all that she had learned. Still, it might come as a shock to him, she thought next, and decided to have Bran tell him everything she knew—in time. But she hoped Bran would not think her the snoop for rifling through his belongings. She had to be certain first that he would understand.

Why Elvy, Derek Ravenscar, had married Melanie would forever remain a mystery to her, as would his bequeathal of the parchment. But fate seemed to have a finger in it, bringing them all together with its mysterious force.

"Now that I have unearthed all this, I must now not allow David Wiley to get his greedy hands on that treasure!" She tossed her dark head vehemently.

But how? How indeed could she keep David from carrying out his threat to murder her husband if she failed to get that map for him? The map seemed to be more of an obsession with him than the treasure itself. He must have been hunting for a very long time. She didn't need the map, of course, for she knew approximately where the treasure was hidden. She realized she was stalling for time. Now she must think of something before Bran returned. God! What?

"Yer still poking through that old stuff?"

Aurora whirled, stuffing the journal beneath her skirts. "Hetty! You very nearly gave me heart failure."

"Just wanted to know if ye wanted some of yer favorite sassafras tea to warm yerself." Hetty cocked her head inquisitively, causing the lappets of her white mob cap to brush her shoulder.

"That would be nice, Hetty. I crave you bring it to the great bedchamber, though, as I am almost done here."

Aurora busied herself then with peering and poking through the old chest, and Hetty got the message.

"Sure hope the young master won't be getting worked up over ye nosing around in his belongings. That one has the blackest temper me eyes and ears have ever witnessed," Hetty sniffed as she went to prepare the tea.

Aurora smiled but did not glance up even as the door closed. She put the contents of the chest in their neat former order, and the journal back where she had first discovered it.

Back in the great bedchamber Aurora was changing into a warmer dress, dark magenta velvet with stomacher; the lovely gown complimented the ebony in the ringlets that tumbled down her back. Her only other ornament was a burgundy riband which swept the front part of her sleek black hair back. Her cheeks were stained, not with Melanie's rouge, but with the natural flush of love.

"Fay," she murmured husky-sweet. "Fay and—"

"Here ye are! Nice hot tea to warm yer pretty insides," Hetty announced, as she swept unceremoniously into the room with teapot and cup positioned atop a pewter tray.

"Hetty!"

Hetty lowered her head sheepishly. "I be just worried about ye, luv. Just keeping an eye out for yer welfare, canna see that?"

"I'll say you are. You have been creeping up on me everywhere I go in this house. Do not worry about me, Hetty, I am just fine," she told the maidservant as she poured tea for herself. She could do without Hetty's vivaciousness just now—when she wanted to be alone with her thoughts.

"I know, luv, but ye seem so far away, as if ye aren't part of the world and the people around yerself."

Hetty began to busy herself with tidying up the room, keeping her eyes averted as she spoke again.

"Who is Fay, luv?"

Almost spilling hot tea on her lovely gown, Aurora whirled. "Why do you ask?"

"I heard ye say the name many times. Sometimes in yer sleep when I come in to check on ye lately, and just a minute ago ye said it again. That name be spoken in Ireland and in the Highlands," Hetty left the bait dangle temptingly.

Aurora took a step closer to the maidservant.

"Then you know what the name means? Hetty, I can see that you do, tell me! Please, what does it mean?"

"Whew! Ye've said it half a dozen times. Why do ye not know yerself the name means 'Raven'? 'Tis a waff name for bordermen and wanderers, those turned highwaymen that take to the English roads and take what they can from the rich. There's an old Irish legend of a handsome highwayman who rode down from the highlands, stole the heart of a young princess. She was adorned with fine clothes and beautiful jewelry, but he dinna take these—only a kiss. 'Tis said she died wi'out her heart, he never gae it back to her. His name was Fay, and he was the first of the robbing ravens. Some folks said he was able to take a bird shape—a raven—at will and fly away from his pursuers."

It came to Aurora again, as it had that magical night, again and again, softly, like the oscillation of sunset, stirring, stealing through the trees.

How foolish of her to have been so blind all this time. But then, the poets said that love is just that. There had been a feeling all along, just as she had experienced while studying Derek Ravenscar's journal—"I know this man. We have met before."

From the edge of the bed where she had sat to ponder deeply, Aurora now glanced up. But Hetty was not waiting for an answer to her question as to who Fay could be. Later perhaps, but not today; they shared a silent understanding after Hetty had told her story of the young highwayman.

"Ye'll find all yer answers, luv," was all the maidservant said as she slipped out of the room.

Aurora stared at the closing door and sighed wistfully. There was only one thing now that could make her feel whole: that her love would not be shunned, but be returned as eagerly as she was now willing to give it. A blithe spirit entered her. What could stand in her way?

That night David Wiley came to visit and dine with them. His character was as mendacious as ever, and Aurora had the strangest feeling that he had never left the house that night he came creeping into her bedchamber like a thief, but had hung around and possibly hid himself in Melanie's chamber without anyone knowing it. All he would have had to do was slip out back and pretend to arrive by the front. It could easily be accomplished, for no one in the house paid any mind to whether one had come by horse or foot. The mounts of visitors were usually led out back by the lads working in the stables and sheds.

It was no wonder why David Wiley crept around like a thief. He was indeed after something that didn't rightly belong to him. She had the feeling, too, that David, no matter how dangerous and venomous he was, would rather not be here when her husband came home. His eccentric actions whenever a noise or movement in the hall was detected bore testimony to this. What had he in mind next, she wondered, and what part did Melanie play in his evil scheme?

After the oppressive dinner and suspenseful silence around the blazing hearth afterward, with Sir Eric unusually vapid, Aurora sought the even less comforting confines of her bedchamber. Vacillating between emotions all day had drained her. She was lonelier and emptier than ever and knew full well the reason why. She had not seen Bran in over a month this time. What she had denied in her heart before had all changed now. In truth she had always wanted him near; she wanted him now, and there was a burning ache of desire inside as she crawled into the cold, lonely bed.


Down the hall, in Melanie's room, David pressed the woman's lush figure against the bedstead. His hard fingers coiled about her neck as Melanie squeaked out a protest of pain.

"David, what are you saying? You must be insane!"

"I mean it. There is a treasure map and she, that icy little bitch, knows where it's at. Don't you remember anything? I told you there was riches to be had and damn it! I meant it. Now, if you just do what I say, it'll all fall right into our laps."

"How did you come to learn about this map?" She breathed easier as David relieved her of the pressure of his cruel fingers.

His eyes glittered like sapphires in the snow. "The bit of parchment that was the old man's? Ah! You recall. Now, I don't think she needs that map, your cousin's got it all up in her little head," he concluded, as he tapped his skull.

David paced the room, then halted to glare at the dumbstruck woman across from him. "But, you see, I have to feel that damn map right here"—he tapped his palm—"in my own hands!"

"This time, David Wiley, you had better be telling the truth. I don't want to be sticking my neck out because of some stupid whim of yours that there is a treasure buried somewhere. My cousin's husband can be very unsympathetic when it comes to a woman's greed, much less theft!"

"It's no whim, I tell you. It's there. I know it! Now, be a good bitch, come over here and sit next to me. I'll tell you my plan. . . ."

Aurora floated slowly to consciousness and was startled to sense a presence in her room. Next she thought it could only be David Wiley come to threaten her again, and she steeled her just wakened body to this. Lifting herself upon an elbow, she blinked the sleep from her eyes.

"Go away, David Wiley. You had your chance to speak with me during the day—"

"Ro! Wake up, I must speak to you."

"Melanie? I am very much awake. What is it? Pray, why do you sound so alarmed?" Her head jerked aside then at the hiss of a turning log in the grate. She placed a hand over her heart; Melanie's countenance had suddenly illuminated and made Aurora's blood run cold. "You look like death. What has happened?"

"It—It might be just that, Ro. You see . . . Bran has been hurt," Melanie said shakingly, stepping back as Aurora leapt swiftly from the bed in a white blur of nightgown. She halted questioningly.

"Uh," Melanie began, "he can't be moved in his condition."

"Take me to him, Melly!" Aurora cried as she whirled around Melanie, already lifting her nightgown as she rushed to the wardrobe.

Her lower lip curling complacently, Melanie rushed over to aid her cousin with the fastenings of her woolen dress, her own fingers clumsy but overlooked in Aurora's haste to reach her husband. When that was done, Melanie reached into the wardrobe and pulled out a camlet cloak and hood. Aurora swayed where she stood as she was helped into the toasty-warm outdoor wear.

"Be calm, Ro," Melanie tried to comfort as she tossed an arm about the shivering, cloaked shoulder. "We'll reach him in no time. David awaits us outside with the mounts. He has saddled your Elektra. We must be quick and silent when we go downstairs. We wouldn't want to alarm the whole house. Come on, and stop trembling like you've caught the swamp fever, Ro!"

Aurora never hesitated once, nor did she think that David was up to no good. Later on she would recall that her only concern had been for her husband's injury.

Downstairs Duchess barked in a questioning way as the cousins paused at the door before hurrying outside. Tremblingly, Aurora patted the wolfhound's head and Melanie released a sigh of relief as Duchess

410

went back to her place before the huge hearth in the hall.

Bathed in moonlight, David stood outside with the three mounts. The only sounds to be heard were the jingling of bits and the brief blowing of the horses. Elektra whickered a greeting upon seeing her master, and David clapped a hand swiftly over the velvety white nose. Elektra's huge eyes rolled at this constriction as she tossed her head in defiance at this strange who handled her none too gently.

Aurora rushed to the ghostlike mare, speaking soothingly to settle her down. Elektra responded at once, lifting her dainty head to nibble playfully at her master's hood.

Wasting no more time, David helped Aurora up onto Elektra's back, then turned to do the same with Melanie. No one had uttered a word yet, but David realized he must warn them of a danger he hadn't counted on himself, so he spoke in a hushed tone.

"We'll have to keep our eyes and ears open to the slightest sound. Earlier I caught sight of a half-breed sneaking around out there in the trees. This is not the first time I've seen that one. Don't know what he's up to, but he might be scouting for the Monacans, or worse yet, the Susquehannocks." David kept his line of vision trained on Aurora as he went on. "The Indians have been raiding plantations, have come close to the James ever since the rebellion started and Jamestown was burned, you know. There's lots of dangers lurking about, not just Indians. Keep to the wagon path and don't stray. We're in this all together now, and remember, Ro, if anything happens to you I lose my chance of getting my hands on that map,"

411

David added as an afterthought, but his eyes were hooded narrowly.

Unconcerned with David's greed at the moment, Aurora cast a worried glance over her shoulder at the shadowy black bulk of the house, praying that what David had said about raiders and Indians would not befall Raven Keep. Anxiously she looked ahead, her eye trained on a moon-sprinkled clump of cedars, wishing they could ride faster.

It came to Aurora in a rush. Had David hurt Bran himself and was he now leading her into that same trap? And where was Tom Bone? With Bran? If David had indeed hurt Bran, was he instead regretting his misdeed? Very unlikely for David to regret something he had done.

She had a strong feeling that the terrors of the night had only begun.

## Twenty-Three

Diamond flakes of moonlight played on the surface of the river as they neared it, the old tangled path having taken them down to it in a matter of a half hour. It was slightly breezier here, and the early November chill was already taking residence along the banks and open spaces near the river. Aurora felt the swooping wind nip at her cheeks and curl up the edges of her woolen cloak, but she paid it no mind. Her only concern was to be at her husband's side as soon as the Almighty would allow. It did not even strike her as unusual when her line of vision snagged on the sides of Melanie's mount, where her cousin's packed bags bulged out hugely.

"There it is!"

David's words blew back in the moist gust sweeping from off the river. Aurora could see the *Enchantress* up ahead, the sloop Sir Eric had told her briefly about in one of their long and refreshing conversations.

*Bran! I am coming! I love you!* Aurora's heart and mind screamed, while her white lips were frozen shut in fear for him.

No torches lighted the *Enchantress*'s deck, no sign of human life could be seen anywhere aboard. *No human life.* She gulped hard on that thought. *Oh, Lord, let him be safe and alive!* Aurora nudged her mount to catch up to David's. Remembering something, she reached into the inner pocket of her cloak to make certain her bag of herbs was still there.

"David. Where is my husband? I see no one. Tom Bone should be there waiting for us—"

"We'll dismount here, by these trees. Go aboard then!" was all he said.

While David was helping Melanie down from her horse, Aurora dismounted and tied Elektra's reins to a limb. The trees hugging the banks made a lonely creaking—as if in mourning. Her heart started beating more quickly as she walked woodenly to the sloop, and a faint unease began to penetrate through the agonies of suspense in her mind. Something was amiss here. It was all too quiet.

Once they had come aboard, David proceeded to light a torch. His back was turned to her, and Aurora thought he was moving too slowly. Melanie was standing just behind her, motionless, as if . . . as if holding her there, keeping her from—David turned about then, with an evil cast to his blond countenance. The torch in his hand was lifted higher and Aurora stared, mesmerized by the sudden glare, before her eyes fell to the cabin door. It seemed to be saying to her, *All who enter herein shall find terror.*

Aurora couldn't stand it any longer. She all but leapt to the latch and wrenched the door wide. One sweeping scout told her that there was nothing here, nobody, but a damp cabin and nearly bare but for a canvas bed, a few books and a logbook, a chipped water basin. All belonging to one . . . who was not here.

One thought reverberated: *With all my soul, I loathe David Wiley*.

Whirling about to face the watching pair, Aurora suddenly realized the full significance of them bringing her here. She gazed at them both, stricken with the weight of their deception. Especially Melanie's.

"Bran is not here," Aurora stated, while Melanie reacted merely by rubbing her hands together briskly after she had removed her kid gloves and held them up to receive warmth from the torch.

The evil pair, Aurora thought, analogical with each other and the hissing flame. Both cast in a red glow, with Satan's torch.

Melanie and David stepped into the cabin, pressing her back farther into the room. If she hadn't moved, Aurora believed they would have walked right into her, knocked her down, stepped on her. They looked that intent on getting their own way, even to the point of torturing her. No doubt that would come next. All for a bloody two bits of parchment!

Aurora almost burst out yelling shrilly, like a shrew. What if there just happened to be no treasure? She wanted to cry, she wanted to laugh. She stopped herself. She wanted to live. She wanted Bran.

Squat, greasy candles were lighted. Then it began. All night they seemed to interrogate her. At times Melanie resorted to pleading while David came close to being physically violent. He raised his fist to her face often, but Aurora kept staring dazedly, unflinching. It was Melanie who finally slapped her, several times, until David, ironically, stepped between and

415

put a halt to it. He didn't want to mar such a lovely face, he said, even though inwardly the desire to shake her until her pretty teeth shattered was quite a temptation. Melanie had stepped back, pouting and sipping from yet another wineskin she had brought along. David snatched it from her and took a long pull of the wine while Aurora was left nearly drooling of thirst.

David and Melanie munched often on cold meat and hard bread, but again, Aurora was given nothing, nothing but more questions, fired at her before she had a moment's rest in between. They took turns interrogating her; their intent was to break her.

Aurora, though weary, hungry, and chilled to the bone, was faring better than they were. At least her head was clear, whereas Melanie was hiccoughing, staggering, her speech thick with unintelligent words. And David was comfortably drunk himself.

"Here, gimmee that"—David grabbed for the wine—"you're already foxed!" He tossed a half-eaten leg of wild turkey over his shoulder carelessly.

For the first time, in the wee hours of morning, Aurora was actually seeing what they had been eating. Meat! Wild turkey! That must mean that Bran had been home. She stared at the wastefully scattered pieces of bread then. Indeed, Bran had brought home supplies for the larder. When? How had she missed him? She hung her head then. It had been Bran and not David who had come to her room that last time and she had sent him away.

"You have that map memorized. Let's have it!" David was saying again, as he had time and again until it became a monotonous hammering in her head.

Aurora's willful silence was getting to David. He was as pale as ashes and his eyes were glassy, but the girl with the disheveled hair was beginning to attract him. By God, she had spirit! He was beginning to wonder if he could ever break her. But how much more could Aurora Ravenleigh endure? Ravenleigh. His eyes had been continually drawn to the logbook. Perhaps there was a way. He went to pick up the logbook and made much ceremony of dangling it before her eyes before he opened it up to the first page.

"Hmmm, Bran Fayette Ravenleigh. Mighty handsome name, eh? Bet you'd like to see him again? I wonder if you ever will though?" he taunted cruelly, his drunken and lascivious gaze wandering between the folds of her cloak, as if undressing her would be quite a pleasure.

Aurora sat stunned. Her heart was suddenly torn and she was feeling quite ill. A figure of wax would have been more alive than she was at this moment.

Bran Fayette. Bran! Fay! Echoing in her brain. Too late, Bran, too late for love! There was a weeping sadness inside her. She was drowning, spinning downward into blackness. Something had hit her; she was on the floor; smothered by the full length of a body.

"David, what are you doing?"

David moved upon the whimpering, shivering, lovely form of woman. He had never wanted one as much as he did now, feeling the tragic vulnerable

417

beauty writhing beneath him. David began roughly to undress Aurora while Melanie looked on in befuddled shock, mesmerized, as her violet eyes roamed over the soft curves, the small uptilted breasts. She felt a primitive urge rise in her, a lust beginning to burn in her loins, while David fumbled at the buttons on the front of his breeches.

"I'm going to ride you and break you," David panted. "Come on, fight, show me some spirit again!"

Melanie came to her senses, walking around the erotic scene, quite spellbound by the beauty of Aurora in her glorious nudity, all disheveled and wild-looking with her midnight hair streaming out on the rough flooring, her face like alabaster, her eyes staring unseeingly, like limpid pools of stillness. Silent. No fight left in her. Almost like she was . . . dead.

"David!" Melanie finally shrieked. "You go too far!"

David gave a short laugh and sneered up at Melanie while his hands continued to explore the silken flesh, going lower and lower until Aurora stiffened, giving him a token of his wanted response. He kept his eyes glued on Melanie all the while, as if he were deriving some sadistic pleasure at having her look on. But David did not notice the tears that sparkled in Melanie's eyes, he was consumed only with a new lust for the beauty that lay so still under him. He knew Aurora's game and he was biding his own time. Making love to a lifeless doll was not what he had in mind. Too, he had other plans.

"You—You hurt me," Aurora whimpered as David pressed her into the boards, making her backsides ache horribly.

"I mean to hurt you, and do more than that. Don't you think I should be rewarded for all my trouble?" David prodded between her legs, then cursed beneath his breath.

"David! S'enough!" Melanie's speech was slurred but still lethal.

"Have another drink!" David shot over his shoulder, preoccupied.

"Don't wan' more drink, David," she whined his name. "I wan' the treshure!"

On and on they argued until the silver mist of dawn crept beneath the cracks of the door, until Aurora thought for a surety she was dying, with David's full weight against her own frail woman's body. Everything was becoming increasingly nightmarish with her pinned helplessly to the floor and Melanie above with eyes hot and burning with intense jealousy. She began to pray for a miracle to free her from this horror.

"Hah! You pash yourself off as a man?" Melanie giggled tipsily, drawing herself up to her full height. Eyeing Aurora, an insane jealousy went coursing through her body as never before. But it was to David she directed her spiny barbs. "Can't make it, can you, David? R'member what happens when you drink overmuch, eh? Should see Bran Ravenleigh's when he's only had a few—'tis bigger than yours an' Rodney Quick's put together. Aye! Rodney, does that make you jealous, love?"

"Melanie"—David sneered—"Melanie, the whore.
I don't know what I ever saw in you!" His blue-hot
gaze roamed over Aurora as if she were now the only
woman in the world. He lifted his head to Melanie
again. "Hell-hag! Go out and get the horses ready,
give them some grain from my saddlebags. Hurry, we
haven't all day. It's time we move on before
Ravenleigh comes and finds us here."

Melanie's voice rose to a screeching volume.
"What! I am no slave, David Wiley. You won't get rid
of me so quick, so you and your sweet captive there
can—" Melanie twisted her head around toward the
door. "Did you hear that? What's that tapping?"

Without their knowing it Aurora had passed out,
right there on the floor beneath David, after she'd
heard Melanie reveal how familiar she had been with
Bran. Now she came to, and with inhuman strength
she heaved David's dead weight from her with one
gathered shove that sent him rolling into Melanie.
Her cries of rage bounced off the close walls as she
rose with cloak and skirts and splayed herself against
the bulkhead. She could not halt the words that now
spewed forth like a bursting dam from her lips.

"Ohh! I remember now. In the hollow . . . Captain Strang . . . he told me to forget what I had seen.
My own stepfather murdered Jason Ravenleigh . . .
and you, David, you helped him! You! It was you!"

Aurora screamed then at the top of her lungs until
David leapt in front of her and slapped her
repeatedly, until her head snapped back and forth,
the blood from her split lip trickling down her chin
and onto her naked breasts. Aurora backed up with

hate-filled fury glowing purple in her eyes. David stared at her wildly; he had never witnessed such hate and beauty and wrath all wrapped up in one small woman.

Overcome with desire once again, David snatched Aurora to his chest, almost forgetting what had brought them to this place. He could taste her blood as he attacked her with hot kisses and fumbling, feverish hands, but now she struggled with an insanity born of raging fury. He will not have me! her mind screamed. The treasure matters not anymore. No man in the world would ever possess her body and soul, only Bran, her husband, could accomplish that.

Aurora pushed at David, shouting, "In the hollow! 'Tis yours, all yours—the treasure! Ohhh, remove your filthy lecher's claws from my flesh—now!"

David lifted his head from a nipple he had been having a hard time capturing with his suckling lips. He stared at her hard and fast.

"What?" he asked, very softly.

"You heard me, reptile! Now release me, and have your bloody treasure and your Melanie. Huh, she's no cousin of mine, but leave me free to go to my home, pray, now!"

A scream was heard, sounding muffled. David scoured the cabin over his shoulder to seek out that blond form, but she was nowhere to be seen. The door had been left ajar and Aurora lifted her hot, teary eyes to it. Something was about to happen, she could feel it and her eyes widened further. Death lay waiting beyond that door, like a black beast with horns, panting, with red tongue lolling out, ready to spring . . .

"Help me! David!"

The scream shivered through Aurora with its bloodcurdling pitch. The flapping of huge wings was heard along with the strident cry of a bird.

*"Daviiid!"*

David elevated a pale eyebrow, finally wearing a listening expression. With biting fingers still grasping Aurora's soft shoulders, they stood entranced for another hair-raising moment before ardor-fuddled David finally, but hesitantly, brushed by Aurora, reluctantly releasing her.

Alone now, Aurora scrambled into her torn clothes. Now that she had finished dressing, she found herself frozen to the floor. Something horrible was happening to Melanie out there, she knew.

In another moment, not knowing quite how she had come to be outside, she found herself staring in horrible fascination at the scene before her. David just stood there, uncaring or afraid, she knew not which, plastered against the bulkhead, while Melanie went screaming at the top of her lungs to the rail, her arms flailing above her head while the huge raven relentlessly pursued her. She went spinning past David, garbling a scream in her throat as her eyes begged him to help her, off the deck, as if lifted bodily and heaved into the icy water of the river. She was enveloped in the dawn's silver mist, which crept across the water. The bird returned to perch upon the rail of the sloop, with a sharp metallic *tok tok* directed at David, as if scolding him. David hastily drew back his foot, Aurora having completely missed the furtive movements.

"David," Aurora sobbed, "help her."

But it was a futile plea, she realized, as Melanie disappeared forever from sight, stolen away by the merciless current of the Chickahominy.

Now Aurora knew a terrible dread as the bird of prey sat the rail, eyeing her with its keen sight, unblinkingly, seeming to mark her as its next victim.

Backing up, ever so slowly so as not to excite the raven, Aurora splayed herself in front of the small opening, her heart slamming violently within her breast. She felt rather than saw David inch his way toward her. He hauled her by the wrist to him until her shoulder rested protectively over his chest, using her as a shield. Aurora had a moment to ponder that indeed none of what was happening seemed real and sane. A horrible fantasy!

"Stay as you are, Aurora," David warned in a shaky whisper. "Listen, he's trying to talk, he's trained."

Aurora gazed curiously, strangely unafraid, suddenly, as the lustrous black feathers, ruffled by the wind, displayed a purplish-blue iridescence. Another *tok* sharply issued forth from the raven, followed by a guttural croak.

"See, I told you," David hissed in her ear. "He's trying to say something. That bird, for some reason, doesn't mean to harm you. The stupid thing is after me, I can tell, just like it was after Melanie," he lied. "Don't you see, it's a raven from the Keep, I seen them there before. They belong to your husband, I know that now, just like some people keep killer hawks."

"Nonsense, David, birds cannot talk, and . . ." Her head began to spin crazily as she reflected back: Hetty had said that the legendary Fay was able to take a bird shape at will. She heard David go on now as if from afar.

"Birds can talk, ravens can mimic some human words, and some ravens live to years totalling threescore," David gulped as the bird now began to eye him maliciously.

Recollection of the raven that had once saved her life in the snowstorm, that indeed had spoken, made her stare now, awed as the raven exercised his lustrous wings, displaying proudly a wingspread of more than four feet as it canted a ruffled head, gurgling at Aurora.

Gripping her arm, David spoke as softly as possible so as not to alarm the raven. "Tell it to go away, Ro. It knows you. It'll go for you. Damn it! Tell it, or I'll break your arm!"

Aurora almost swooned against David then. Bran had once said that he could materialize . . . He couldn't be . . . God in Heaven, she could not accept that, it was all too incredible!

"Sh—Sh—Shoo—" Aurora stammered at first, then found strength rising in her voice. "Shoo! Oh, please just go away! You frighten me!"

Sagaciously and with a harsh cry sounding, the raven took wing, but first it seemed to have given David the evil-eye, promising future harm to his person. Heavily, the raven lifted itself—like a symbol, Aurora thought, of dark prophecy smeared against the bleak horizon.

All at once David returned to his former lecherous self. Aurora had been watching the raven's flight; now she felt David watching her. Her flesh recoiled at his nearness, and though she had feared that great bird, she was now wishing she rode upon its feathered back.

"Ahh, now we're alone, my lovely little captive. How I ever preferred Melanie over you—I must have been insane," he breathed hotly down her neck.

"As you are now," Aurora said weakly, her eyes closing, her teeth chattering from cold. She then collapsed onto the deck in a motionless heap on her knees, where David had allowed her to fall.

"Ah, well," David said shrugging, "you'll do me no good if I take you now. I like a woman to have some life in her, and you're as lifeless as a half-drowned kitten."

*Drowned,* Aurora thought. Poor Melanie, riding to her watery death; it must have been horrible to die like that. But Melanie would never wake to relive the experience.

"Get up," David ordered. "Fetch your cloak, we're going for a ride. To this hollow where you saw me and Captain Strang, if I heard you right?"

When a cold silence persisted, David lifted her forcibly up from the deck and dragged her along while he fetched her cloak. Without another word from him, she was shoved from the sloop. Her foot plunged momentarily into the cold water, then she was lifted just as unceremoniously onto the long wharf that led them away from the moored *Enchantress*. A high-buckled shoe made a squashing sound as she plodded back to her horse, every ounce of her will being taken to move one foot in front of the other.

It had rained during the night, and moving noiselessly down the trail's slot among the dripping trees, David slowed his pace, then dismounted when they had reached the rim of the hollow. Aurora wavered in her high perch as David reached up to lift her down, his male form pressing her along his length.

"I pray you not do that," Aurora pleaded, but uselessly, as he began to caress her thighs, first gently, then growing roughly intimate. Her heart cried out for Bran, though her lips could not form the words.

David murmured thickly into the damp strings of her hair. "You remind me of a pretty Indian squaw I had once. She was good, wild as a summer storm, and I'll bet you are too. We'll dig up that treasure, and then I'll take you away to England with me and we'll be rich there! Would you like that?"

David's blue eyes shone with a sickly yellow cast to them, a lunacy lurking in the dilated pupils. Aurora shivered with a passionate hatred and, gathering what strength she could, spat in his face. A great reward was reaped as Aurora watched the pale countenance registering shocked surprise. Her tongue lashed out before he could react further.

"I despise your evilness. I have always loathed your mere presence, and you shall never have me, David Wiley. Go with you to England willingly? Hah! I would rather sail on a ship with a pack of yellow-eyed rats!"

"Good, I like your spirit!" he snarled, but just the

same slapped her hard across the face.

Aurora felt her head being snapped back and bouncing off Elektra's padded ribs. She slithered to the ground then, as he went to take down a spade from his mount's back. In the other hand he suddenly held a wicker-bound jug to his lips and drank greedily. Aurora watched him through the haze in her brain and wondered why she hadn't sighted the stout digging tool before now.

Off to the right of the eye that was beginning to swell, she caught sight of Melanie's mount catching up with them, the long reins trailing on the ground forlornly, the saddlebags' leather creaking, as if in mourning for the one who had packed them the day before.

David returned to her with sauntering stride, a length of hempen rope dangling from his long and cruel fingers. Aurora met his eye with a sneer of utter contempt as he bent over her, his breath reeking of Canary wine.

"Now I must bind my beautiful captive," he taunted with a deep chuckle.

"You *are* insane, without a doubt," she barely gave utterance to the words.

But David had heard, and he stopped to slap her heartily once again. It was by no accident that he brushed her breasts as he completed tying her hands behind her back. Though she longed to bite into the arms that persisted with their familiarity, she held back the urge by sheer willpower.

Before Aurora slid into blessed unconsciousness, she heard a loud, harsh call, and rolled her head on the pine tags to see the raven again, this time perched on a pine bough above her. David must not have heard the bird's *tok* then, for he kept on poking his spade in the spongy morass of the hollow. He was on the far side now . . . in the vicinity of . . . a huge, lone, ancient oak treee. . . . The raven spoke again. . . .

## Twenty-Four

At last, the coma of exhaustion abating, Aurora was awakened by the thunderous flapping of huge wings. At the same time she saw the bird winging through the mist that now enveloped the hollow, she sensed a powerful presence standing immobile behind her. Thinking it might be David, her flesh crawled in horrible anticipation, and she struggled into a bowed sitting position.

A movement to the left caught her attention. *That* was David, laboring at the distant edge of the hollow with a spade. Then who . . .

Aurora looked up in surprise, crying out softly at the pain it caused in her cramped neck. She caught her quivering bottom lip in her teeth. Her chest ached horribly. A figure loomed there, not far behind her.

In sweeping dark raiment he had appeared suddenly, phantomlike, his wondrous magical power reaching out to her. He moved a little, the motion graceful, so that he scarcely seemed to be moving at all.

Aurora waited with bated breath. He seemed to be silently perusing the scene, the slits of eyes sliding to the far side of the hollow and back. His lips were set in a cool and ominous line.

She shivered in the thickly gathering mist about the hollow.

"Fay." She breathed the name like a sigh, pure joy lighting up her deep-violet eyes. Again, "Fay—"

Aurora felt as if she were just now awakening from a long long dream. It was all coming together.

There was a faint whisper of wind aborning as he came to her, slowly, almost menacingly. He said nothing as he bent to take her firmly by a shoulder, and reaching behind her, he brought a knife up in his other hand; the sharp blade sliced apart the bonds that had imprisoned Aurora's arms stiffly behind her back.

At the silvery, unreadable look in the mask-darkened face, Aurora's eyes widened and there was a tingling in her breasts, making her nipples harden. He saw them, as if they sought to protrude through her bodice. The look he wore now took her breath away.

A voice out of long-ago brushed her dizzied brain, and she looked up just in time to see a darkly bronzed Indian, coming catlike up behind them. He seemed to flow with the swirling mists as he halted before her.

Aurora peered up at the tall figure and the long, horselike face. The words clogged in her throat as she tried saying his name.

"Ru—Rufo?"

He nodded, the feather in his hat stirring in the wind, his long hair sweeping his broad shoulders. She noticed that he still wore the same battered hat.

"Little Ro. You remember. I have watched you

from afar, many times. This time, when you left with 'white eyes,' I went in search of your husband. I see you have been hurt"—he moved a hand toward the split lip and bruised cheek—"I could not help you this time. I would have killed him for you—"

"He is mine," Fay said tersely to Rufo Savage.

Aurora was only slightly aware of the Indian's brown hand hovering near her bruises. She felt the same rush of warmth in her heart that she had known as a young girl for this man who had been soft-spoken and quick to smile for her.

"Aye. White eyes is there," Rufo said inclining his head toward the far side of the hollow.

David Wiley had not yet detected their sudden, stealthy appearance. Too, the trees and the mist and the grazing horses blocked them from view.

There was the soft tread of moccasins and when Aurora tilted her head back up, Rufo had vanished. She looked farther and noticed a lone man mounted silently, a sentinel astride a huge chestnut horse. Man and beast seemed carved out of stone. She knew he was Tom Bone. Then Tom, too, slipped back into shadow.

"Are you hurting?" the velvety soft voice stirred her hair with its breath.

The light was continuing to fade, and clouds gathered fast as Aurora's regard slid to Fay who was hunkered beside her. As she stared, their gazes locked. His was cold, frightfully so, and she could not fathom the reason nor judge his mood. His eyes must have narrowed, for the high points of his cheekbones crinkled with sun lines.

Aurora shook her throbbing head, feeling as if

she'd just met some dangerous stranger. Indeed, she did hurt, the tissue of her frail body bruised. But why couldn't she speak to let him know this?

Finally he stood, dragging her carefully up with him. She could smell the saddle leather, the sweat, and the woodsmoke on him. It clung to her sensitive nostrils, making her head spin crazily. He had been riding long and hard, she could tell, for he appeared leaner to her, trail-weary and hardened by the elements. Dangerous. He was as she had seen him before—long ago. A tall masked ranger of the woods. A Virginian. But now he was so cold and unanimated that it was almost as if he despised the very sight of her.

Why? Why was he doing this to her now? Now, when she knew him. Or had she ever really, *really* known him?

God, how she wanted to reach out and touch him! Hold him! Feel his long hard length crush her in a smothering, loving embrace. Why did he seem to be waiting for something to happen? Then, she sensed a struggle within him—as if he were in conflict with another side of himself.

Aurora swooned toward him, grasping for his cloak-draped arms.

"Fay . . . Fay, don't you know how much I love you? Can you feel that I want you to hold me? Darling! Hold me. I need you!" she sobbed, tripping on the hem of her sodden skirts as she rushed to him.

The eyes, glittering as coldly as ice-chips, swooped down over her while he set her firmly from him. He could see the instant hurt in her heather eyes, making her look like a small wounded animal. He almost reached out to capture the forlorn tear that was sliding down her cheek.

There suddenly intruded the rumble of thunder in the distance. Along with it, Aurora sensed the tightening in his tall frame.

"Fay—*please*," Aurora said.

"You didn't want me to hold you before—" He halted the sentence between flashing white teeth, his tanned face in deep contrast with them.

"Before?" she wondered.

"When I came to your—our—" His eyes narrowed over her shoulder.

Aurora had no time to frown her utter confusion, for David Wiley had spotted them and his strides were long and vicious, eating up the distance between. In his hand he clutched the spade, wielding it like a weapon, his taut knuckles white against the dark wood of the promisingly dangerous tool.

"Stay away from him, Fay, he will kill you!" Aurora cried. When he glared over to her, she said softer, "He is insane." She pushed back her tumbled black hair out of her eyes, the contrast of the strands startling against her face that had gone white as a sheet.

"Damn!" rebel Fay growled low as his gaze first raked over her and then David.

Her eyes went dark purple. "Oh! You do not think that David and I—we planned—Oh! Fay . . . no!"

"Cease with calling me Fay! Wake up, Aurora, or will you forever be blind!" His voice had snapped like a whip, draining the question from his words.

As he came to a halt in front of them, David's deep blue eyes sliced through the tall, darkly dressed man.

His voice drawled out gratingly.

"What do you want here, ranger? You hiding from the governor's men—in that mask? Hell, I just bet you are!"

Aurora stared between them, catching a feverish excitement that she would rather not feel at all. A sick core of fear lay heavy in her. She bit the knuckles of one hand, forcing back the taste of bile rising in her throat. They were going to fight—perhaps even try to kill each other!

"So, David Wiley," the ranger began, "we meet again. Do you have a weapon?" Directing his gaze to the spade that David clutched.

"Wha—?" David blinked in confusion. "Am I supposed to know you? I've no quarrel with you, but if that's what you want—"

With his sandy hair falling over his forehead, David clutched the sharp-spaded tool, curling his fingers tighter about the length of it.

The ranger avoided the question, guardedly keeping Aurora in the periphery of his vision. He went on to ask a question of his own, with the intention of not waiting for an answer.

"You murdered Jason Ravenleigh—or perhaps you were just an accomplice, would you say? Either way, 'white eyes'"—he shrugged casually—"you are soon going to join your evil companions in the vast caverns of Hell. I am sure there is plenty of room there for your kind, David Wiley!"

"Just what in the world you think I am, or who you are, ruffler, I don't give a damn. I've got work to do, and you're wasting precious time of mine," David snarled.

The ranger wore a waiting look. David now brandished the spade like a weapon, trying to scare the masked man away.

"I could damn easily plow this cold steel into your guts!"

"No!" Aurora screamed.

"Aurora—get back!"

Aurora stepped back at Fay's sound of warning, and the silky mane of Elektra blinded her momentarily as it blew around her face. The smell of horseflesh and sweat was strong, but not so much as was Fay's musky odor, primitively savage, ready as he was, she knew, to attack his foe.

Reaching behind her cautiously, Aurora snatched up Elektra's trailing reins. Just as she was struggling to mount the snow-white back, a strong arm encircled her about the waist at the same time as a sudden rush, like wind, came to halt momentarily beside her. In a blur of movement, the reins of Aurora's horse were snatched from her, and she was lifted up bodily behind the warmth of a muscled body.

The forestland swam in greens and browns and autumnal colors around her as Tom Bone led her away from danger, hoofs drumming on the turf and with her clutching his back for dear life.

David slowly took a step backward, watching with mouth agape the lightning fast action. He had been so engrossed in watching Aurora being whisked away that, in the next moment as he looked down, the spade, his only weapon, was lifting as if by sheer magic from his slack hold. Powerless to do anything, David blinked in startled confusion as the black snake of a whip uncoiled, and his spade was unceremoniously dropped with a dull thud—luckily at his feet.

"How—just how in hell did you do that?" David watched the long length of whip, seeming only to brush the ground like an elusive butterfly, hiss back to its owner.

David saw eyes that glittered through slits in the mask—with the feral hunger of a hunting wolf.

"Worries you, does it?" said the masked face.

"Me?" David snorted through a fine-boned nose. "Huh!" was all he added.

"Retrieve your weapon, David Wiley, for 'tis the only one you've got to defend your scurvy butt with"—a corner of the ranger's mouth curled nastily—"Now!"

Blue eyes glinted just as coldly as silver ones.

David let laughter well up wickedly from his throat.

"You dirty bastard. I'll chop that old whip of yours into little pieces!" The spade was already back in both his uplifted hands.

The ranger bowed his head invitingly, arrogantly, and from some almost forgotten memory, David called up the timbre of the man's voice. He couldn't decide just whose it was, but it was beginning to make his blood boil that the man kept his identity hidden from him so well.

"I can smell you from here, ranger, you haven't washed since the moon of ripening corn. Just *bet* you know what that means. You look like you've been shacking with filthy squaws all summer. I don't care how bad and ferocious you look, you don't scare me none. You're just getting under my skin. You know? You and me are kind of alike. I've had to sleep and eat on the road, wherever I could''—he laughed with a rumbling sound—''but no more. I'm going to be a rich man, ranger, and no devil, not even a nasty-looking one like you is going to stop me!''

Only the wind made any sound now as the ranger caressed his long black whip with black-gloved fingers. Even his hair was black, Wiley noticed, and his clothes.

''You have been after this—ummm—*treasure* a long time, hmm? 'white eyes'?''

''How in *hell* do you know everything?'' David said scathingly.

''Never mind.'' Bran shrugged. ''But let's just say that we've an old score to settle. Let it go at that—'' He was thinking of a new one, having to do with his wife. No one, but no one, took away what was his.

Bran lifted his shoulders again in a casual shrug. He was in no hurry.

David snorted, then nodded in the direction the other man had taken Aurora. ''Think you ruined my sport for the evening and many to come by taking my woman away? Huh!''

''*Your* woman?''

''Sure,'' David returned. ''I'll get her back, but first I'm going to get rid of you and then your sneaky friend, ranger!''

''I'm waiting.''

Unprepared for the sudden sound and lightning movement, David heard the whip crackle ominously in the air twice before it snaked out. *Crack! Crack!*

Spontaneously David chopped the blade down, his

motions like a madman, a true raving maniac who sputtered and cursed while diving at the same time toward the spread-eagled legs. He came up, awestruck, just inches below the ghastly whip.

Casual and cool, the taller man merely stepped back, the weapon of rope and leather entwined, slithering on the ground back to its owner, as if it were a pet snake.

Recovering, David crouched low, wielding the spade like a lance as he hollered a war-cry and lunged toward the ranger's middle. Expertly the attack was sidestepped, but David kept charging, unable to pull himself up, until the tip of the spade struck the bole of a dogwood tree. The impact jarred him but he paused only long enough to shake his doddering head and clear it.

This time, an inhuman cry matching the savage whoop of a Monacan, rent the misty hollow, and the whip wrapped itself, as if it were a living thing, about David's waist, crisscrossed with the flick of a dexterous wrist and fastened securely. The spade had been sent flying free of David's grip and now he bent over in trying to retrieve it, but the leathern weapon was so tightly coiled about his waist that a jerk of the whip from its master found David's legs slipping out from beneath him.

Even with his hands out to break the fall, David fell flat on his face and torso, his breath escaping him in a great whoosh.

As from afar, David heard a shrill whistle, and a moment later sighted through his dazed eyes a huge hunter. The horse reared, making his silver ring bits jingle as he pawed the air, before galloping hard toward David where he lay. He cried out in alarm, almost certain that his skull would be crushed by the thunderous flying hooves. A breathtaking second before, with powerful muscles rippling at flank and quarter, the hunter veered off to the right and slowed to a skidding halt.

Though David watched as the ranger slid a booted toe into the iron stirrup, nothing registered in his brain but the creaking of saddle leather as the enemy mounted up. The whip was drawn in greater tautness about his already pain-filled middle.

A sudden gust of wind swooped into the hollow, lifting the glossy mane and tail of the high horse. Now, peering up into the face of the tall, masked man seated ramrod straight on his pawing horse, David took in the cold, emotionless concentration in the mirrorlike gaze; and it would have sat easier on his mind if the silver eyes had registered murderous intent or even hatred. But there was nothing there—only that frozen, blank expression.

Squirming for dear life, David tried one last time to reach his weapon, as he intended to slash at the prancing forelegs of the horse. All he succeeded in doing was to flop like a fish on his belly when a tug of the whip began to drag him. He couldn't believe this was happening and he looked up one last time to see in stunned disbelief the mask come off with a swipe of the long, cruel fingers.

"You were not curious, David Wiley?" Ravenleigh said coldly.

"You!" David croaked.

David knew his tormentor now that dragged him mercilessly over the ground, faster and faster as he bounced off jutting rocks and roots and brush. His blood stained the turf, and his screams of pain and rage were sent echoing across the hollow. He held tight to the whip with both bleeding hands, unconscious that this only heightened his torture.

Beneath the mostly barren branches of a tree, Aurora turned deathly pale in her seat behind Tom Bone. Emerging from a mist which lay about like transparent veils, a rabbit was hopping across the hollow, impervious to the danger in its path. Holding her breath, Aurora then released it as the rabbit scampered away to safety. Holding a hand to her throat, something in Aurora snapped as David's death approached with impetuous speed.

It came to her in a twinkling: Life is precious, even to the worst of humans. David's life could be spared, just as the little creature's life had been.

"No . . . no more!"

The feminine shriek reached him. Consequently Bran slowed Nimrod to a trot, unmindful of his bloodied victim, hearing only the anguished cry from his wife's lips.

Though it was mist-clouded everywhere, his quick-silver eyes sought and found her. Tom had wrapped an arm about her waist to keep her from falling off the high horse. She was bent over, with Tom brushing her hair from her face as she retched violently.

Finally, collapsing limply onto his battered face, David was released from his world of torment, even though Bran would have rather ended it here and now by finishing Wiley off. He prayed that he was not making a big mistake by letting him off so easily.

"Begone, and never come this way again," Tom warned.

The Indian that had seemingly stepped out of nowhere met Tom and helped set Wiley on his horse while Bran and Aurora hung back. His countenance had softened only a little when he had swung a dark woolen cape about her shoulders. That was all. He was quiet, frighteningly so.

David had suffered a few broken ribs, his nose was a bloody pulp, but miraculously he was still able to sit his horse, somewhat at a tilted angle, and ride away.

As David rode off into the oncoming night, toward the empurpled woods, he glanced back once through swollen lids. With painfully stiff movements, he turned himself toward his destination. He cursed the vilest of words on Ravenleigh's head. But no one had heard him.

## Twenty-Five

The sweet smell of rain had been in the air, until now the first drops were beginning to come down, seeming to mutter in their pattering voice that others would follow to drench the earth.

At Raven Keep, Aurora and Bran were met with cries of relief, mingled with great concern over what had taken place since the mistress disappeared so mysteriously the night before. Sir Eric was blustering about as they entered, and Bran wordlessly began to carry his wife up the stairs.

"God's nightgown!" Sir Eric moved forward.

"Not now, sir!" Bran said.

Halfway up the stairs, the lower half of Bran's face went into shadow, and it was as if he weren't unmasked to Aurora; and her violet-dark eyes touched on his jet hair, his silvered eyes, the sensuous curve of his lip, and his aquiline nose. To her at this moment he was so painfully handsome and dark. And—cold.

Is that why she felt like crying just now? Was it because, though he carried her, he seemed to cold-shoulder her? So near, and yet—so distant.

He kicked the door open, never putting her down until he reached the bed. The fire in the grate was crackling merrily, tossing a glow of warmth through the bedchamber. She could hear his thunderous heartbeat, making her want to snuggle closer to the hardness of his chest. For some reason, her woman's mind told her, it was better for now if she did nothing. But for how long could she stand his aloofness?

The thunder grew louder, and the windows rattled violently, seeming to match her husband's indifferent mood. Dark and leashed and quietly violent.

"Would you like to lie down while a bath is being prepared for you?"

He set her down on the edge of the bed, his hand absently lingering on her back, coming in contact with a sore bruise through her torn dress. She flinched and drew back. He swore under his breath.

Aurora's lips had moved, shaping the answer to his question, but the words would not come. As if she had indeed spoken, he now nodded and strode toward the door.

"Bran—" she said softly, to call him back, but he was already closing the door against her plea.

Had the world ever seemed so bleak to her? she wondered, gazing at the flames and tossing sparks illuminating the hearth. The warmth should have seeped into her bones by now; then why was she shivering so uncontrollably?

She knew what it was. How could she live out her life knowing she loved a man who didn't love her anymore? Oh! Had he ever really loved her? Had he ever loved Melanie or any of his past loves, she had been about to question herself.

*Wake up, Aurora,* he had said to her in the hollow. Fay. Bran. Suddenly there was no separating the two of them in her mind. Was that his desire—that she see him as he truly is and not as some romantic figure she had fallen in love with?

Aurora wrenched herself about and leaned forward to pound on the pillow. Her lip bled as she bit into it until she quivered in frustration. A mist of tears swam in her eyes, causing the bed and everything about her to seem underwater. She sniffled and dried her eyes.

How long ago was it? She had thought herself to be foolish to have been blind for so long. I am not *blind* anymore! Why when she had known Bran as the masked man in the hollow—why had she called him *Fay?* Why not Bran . . . her husband . . . ?

Why hadn't anyone come to prepare her bath? She wondered wearily and dully. As if in answer to her question the upstairs maids and the lads bearing steaming buckets of hot water entered. Very gently, after the shy-faced lads had drawn her bath, Lucy and another maid undressed her and helped her to the tub.

"Hetty—" Aurora broke off, as if it was too much of an effort to speak.

"She be coming in later," Lucy said, dipping a sponge cautiously into the water.

"Later?"

"Aye, mistress. She took ill while you was away. She had a cold to start, and so 'twas too much for her these last few days, so she's been abed. She says to take good care of her lady."

444

*Lady*. Hetty used to call Deana her lady. And now she, Aurora, was a woman. *Woman*. The word had a nice strong sound to it.

Yea, I am a woman now, she told herself.

Though she was wearier than she had ever been, Aurora exulted in the strength that began to flow into every part of her. All her senses sharpened and quickened. She looked down at her milk-white breasts, on down to the raven patch between her legs, long limbs for a small woman. She had forever shed the innocence of her maidenhood—then why didn't she act like a woman? Is that what Bran wants me to do?

Of course. He wants *me* to come to *him.*

Aurora quailed at the thought. How could she do it? That seemed such a wanton and brazen move for a woman to make, to prove that she loved . . . even though she was his wife.

"I shall think on it," Aurora murmured absent-mindedly.

"What'd you say, mistress?"

"'Twas nothing, Lucy. I am ready for bed now." Aurora stepped from the tub, wrapped immediately in a fluffy linen.

Lucy clucked her tongue softly, seeing all the bruises that covered the mistress's softly feminine form. And him, downstairs in his cups, not seeming to care one bit that his lady had gone through being kidnapped and treated ill. Almost *killed*, it was gossiped belowstairs already. She could never have lived through it herself. The mistress must be stronger than she appears to the naked eye.

445

Thunder rumbled while wind howled around every corner of the Keep. Even though it stormed outside, there was a cozy feeling of warmth wrapped about the mistress, with her hair softly flowing about her shoulders, in her snug nest of bed.

"Would you be wanting more than the tea and corncakes you just had?" Lucy popped back into the room after having gone out with the soiled linen and returned.

"I am just fine, Lucy. Thank you, and close the door when you leave, please?"

Many faces flitted through her dreams an hour later. Melanie; David; Fay. She was home, home at last. Fay and Bran were one. Her lover, her husband. *You must use your heart to unmask and see me true.*

She must not have been asleep for very long, because the fire at the hearth, still bright and cheery as when she had taken her bath, met her gaze as she sat up in bed. She glanced about the room, then riveted her gaze back to the hearth. He hadn't been standing there a moment ago. His tall frame was now silhouetted against the orange and magenta flames.

A clap of thunder sounded just then, but the house was too sturdy to tremble—as her heart was doing just now.

He must not have heard her stir, for he stayed as he was. Had he actually spoken those words of gentle command as she awoke, or had they merely been part of her dream?

Suddenly Aurora realized that she was naked, the spill of scented black hair all that she had for covering her body. . . .

Just as she was about to lie back down, deciding to feign sleep if need be, he turned. His storm-dark eyes never left hers as he came to the bedside, wearing nothing but a claret-red robe and silk trousers, his easy stride reminding her so very much of a graceful animal. A panther. A full tide of delicious thrills washed over her as he continued to run a penetrating gave over her, from bust up, where the counterpane lent her no modesty. She couldn't know, though she was slightly bruised, that he was thinking she looked to him like gold-tinted alabaster.

A lovely nightgown, she noticed looking aside, was draped over a chair. Trimmed with ivory-colored lace at the bodice and in a waterfall at the wrists. He had brought her another gift. How sweet of him! The next minute her world came tumbling down.

"My grandfather has gone through a lot of haggling to get that for you," Bran began, gesturing to the dainty bit of sensuous nightgown. "A woman who had been burned out of her home in Jamestown finally gave in, after Sir Eric flashed some pretty coppers at her. You are lucky, it is not even smoke-stained, and you should be grateful."

"I am," Aurora said in a tiny voice. "But I—I thought that you—"

"You thought that that was from me, I suppose? Well, for me . . . to purchase something as expensive and revealing as that for a woman . . . first she would have to come to her senses, and next be a wife. I mean not only in name, either."

"Why you—how can you come in here and

447

verbally abuse me! When you know already 'twas quite an ordeal I had been through! You are arrogant, insufferable, insulting and—and—Oh! I cannot think of another word!" She tossed about for something to throw at him.

"That will do, you've already said enough, my dear, 'tis quite plain what you think of me." He turned on his heel. "I have known for a long time now that for you to come down from your dream-world would require a miracle," he tossed over his shoulder. He ducked when a flying slipper neared the back of his head.

"You cad! You lecherous rogue!"

"Beware, Aurora, for when and *if* you come back down to reality, you may just find the world a dangerous place to live in. The big lad lecherous wolf might get you!"

"You—you started it, causing me to fall in love with Fay—not yourself!"

"Faugh!" He reverted back to his courtly speech. "I never made you do anything of the sort." He turned to face her from across the room, his eyes blazing silver sparks. "*You* said the name Fay every time we made love. *You* said, 'Fay, I love you' in the hollow. Fay was merely an agent—of me!"

"Your name *is* Fayette!"

"Let me correct you, sweet, my *middle* name. I am Bran—Bran Ravenleigh. The sooner you get that through your thin skull, the sooner we might become man and wife. Might!" He strode to the door. "If by then it is not too late."

The remaining slipper struck the door just as he

448

was closing it. The slipper fell to the floor, and Aurora stared at the shadowy object of her spent fury. She felt even more miserable now, and it was all his fault, the cur!

His biting and wounding words left her shaking with the recollection of *You must use your heart to unmask and see me true* pounding through her already aching head.

Gratefully, a much wanted languor stole over her and she softly cried into her already damp pillow. Tears, tears, and more tears. Why was it that woman spent half of her life crying over man? Just who did they think they were, making woman suffer for *their* sins?

He started this masquerade, damn him, and he was going to put an end to it himself; it was up to him—otherwise he could go straight to hell.

But how, she wondered just as she drifted into arms of sleep, how was he going to accomplish the impossible?


Bran sat alone downstairs in the big oaken settle, ruminating as he stared into the flickering flames that cast a yellow radiance to the place before the fire. Not even once had he looked up at the sound of a creaking board or windswept shutter slamming against a window recess. It was deep into night.

Bran stroked the black fur of the pantherskin beside him. He had been staring for so long, unblinkingly, stroking, staring, stroking absently. But now his long, thick black lashes flickered.

Bran squared his broad shoulders, trying hard to

wipe out the vision of tragic beauty, the beseeching violet eyes like heather gracing the moors, which he had seen mirrored in the mesmerizing flames.

He turned abruptly from the fire; the heat and flame from it seemed embedded in his eyes like crystal torches. It felt like silver fire coursing down his cheeks, but he was feeling more alive than he had in a long time. Bran dried his eyes, and then tucked his handkerchief back into his pocket as he rose and crossed the room, leaving the penumbra about the hearth and stepping into the darker shadows.

He took the stairs two at a time, sometimes three, until he reached the top. The fire crackled softly and he paused upon entering the bedchamber, then moved about slowly so as not to awaken his sleeping wife. Her hair spilled about on the pillow like black fire . . .

With his several bags of clothes packed, Bran paused in the doorway before going out. He looked about the room, as if memorizing every corner and piece of furniture. He wore his rakish riding boots and his black cavalier hat with drooping purple plume and cloak of night black. He looked like a dandy rogue.

He was remembering as he stared at the figure in the bed . . . remembering the last time he had loved her. How she had responded to him, arching her body to meet his as she moaned softly in her throat, her eyes growing wider and wider, until he knew his fire surged through her lovely woman's body, making her whimper deep inside until—she cried out the name Fay. *Fay*. No matter what she said, the masked man of her dreamworld was still very much with her. And it was . . . an illusion.

He could smell her heady perfume, aye, like spring roses, from here. He had already made a decision, though. He had dwelled on it hour after hour, so he was not going off half-cocked. He had known as he had studied the fire what he must do. It might as well be now. Now . . . or never.

## Twenty-Six

The rain came down for a whole week, the windows in the house rattling noisily and nerve-wrackingly as the wind banged against them. Aurora had escaped the Keep, riding out during the temporary lulls in the rainstorm. No one tried, not even Hetty, to prevent her from doing whatever she wanted. After all, she was the mistress now. Also, they all seemed to realize that the mistress needed some room to roam. And the Keep, great as it was, afforded her no sense of privacy, as did the woodland, and could not continue to hold her within its gloomy, oppressive walls.

On the seventh day and during one of those such lulls, Aurora took Cupid out, the mare being the more nimble of foot than the larger-structured Elektra. The turf was slippery, but not so much as snow during the winter. And she was used to riding in almost any kind of weather. However, the muddy slots occasionally slowed down her ride, and the enjoyment of exhilarating speed was hindered.

Before she knew it, Aurora had come to a halt outside the summer house. Going even farther, and as if under hypnotism, Aurora dismounted and went to the door.

A frown started and then grew until her unlined brow was unnaturally puckered, quizzically. The aura about this her childhood home now seemed to leave suspended a sense of anticipation. There had almost always been something strange about this place; Aurora concluded now, as if it had held a secret unto itself. She shivered while pausing on the threshold.

When would the house unloose its mystery? And who, she gulped, had left it unboarded?

Aurora lifted the hem of her fustian dress of violet-blue with its dainty heliotrope cross-cloth, so that it would not snag on the broken, jutting boards. With her quilted petticoats falling over each other in a tumble of creamy-white, she paused as the neighing of a horse held her poised with one foot in front of the other.

Not one horse, but two, at the side of the house nibbling on what few remaining blades of green nourishment could be found. She saw that Cupid was also foraging while picking her way toward the two taller mounts. One especially possessed great height. Nimrod. Bran's own horse. That meant . . .

Aurora crept silently through the kitchen, seeing as she walked, almost mesmerized, that the small living room was softly illuminated by flickering flames from the hearth. Her step was cautious, so as not to make the floorboards creak. She halted then, frozen to the spot by what she heard.

"He shall be back, I am certain of it. And when he does—"

Aurora could almost feel Bran shrugging at that point in the conversation—or had he stiffened? Who was he talking to? She stepped back into the shadow, then a bit to the right to see . . . Rachel! The tavern wench!

*Oh!* Aurora let herself glide backward, preparing her limbs for flight. She had to be away, before they discovered her.

"Come in, Aurora."

Aurora felt rather than saw her husband stand up from the sofa he had been sitting upon . . . with her! And how did he know she was here? Had she gasped out loud just moments before, giving herself away?

Suddenly his tall frame was silhouetted in the doorway, his countenance dark and unreadable. It was all she could do to keep herself from turning tail and fleeing like a coward. Tall and lean and overpowering, he seemed to fill the length and breadth of the opening he stood framed in. Rachel came to stand beside him. Aurora stared first at the tavern wench and then at him, wildly, seeking mutely for the truth of what they had been doing here—just the two of them.

"Mayhap I should be going now," Rachel said all of a sudden. She looked askance to Bran, her look telling him he should take it from here.

"Aye, 'tis a long ride back to the Randolph house." He paused as if in indecision, before he went on. "Will you—ah—be staying there long—just in case—"

"Of course!" Rachel interrupted. "Jake and I will be tying the bow before long now. You'll get an invite to the wedding"—she turned to acknowledge the other woman's presence—"And you too, Mistress Ravenleigh."

Aurora looked down at the extended hand Rachel was offering her as if it were poison.

"I am sorry, but it's not like you're thinking," Rachel tried, then let her hard fall back down.

"That was not very nice of you," Bran admonished after Rachel had made her exit as graciously as possible.

Acting very unlike herself, Aurora brushed past Bran as she walked haughtily into the living room. She noticed that the sheets had been removed from all articles of furniture and that the floors had been swept free of dust, the corners erased of their cobwebs. Aurora now spun about, her back to the crackling hearth, her hands clutching the back of the sofa as if to tear it to shreds.

"Whether it was nice of me or not is of little importance. 'Twas a very cozy scene I had walked in on, in fact." She could not suppress her shrewish laughter. "And what, pray tell, are you doing *here* in the first place."

She was feeling very possessive of her childhood home. But now she should have expected to arouse his wrath by her question. His eyes were broodingly dark as they fixed themselves upon her heaving bosom.

He laughed shortly. "I have been living here. Or haven't you noticed my absence from the Keep?"

She shrugged indifferently. She would not yield that she had indeed missed him for many days. But it did not sit well with her that he had moved out of his own house. This only proved to her all the more that he had little love for her.

Bran came farther into the room. "And as to what I

am doing here—if you recall, sweeting, this humble domicile happens to belong to me."

"And Rachel, she also belongs to you?" She lifted a dark, feathery eyebrow.

"You heard her, she is soon to become wife to Jake Randolph. But I must admit one thing"—he moved closer to her—"I found Rachel's company more pleasing than yours."

While she squirmed about, he began to remove the pins that had held her midnight hair in a sleek knot at the back of her head. Next, he snatched off the heavy cloak she wore; she stood stunned while her hair came down and streamed about her shoulders, and he tossed the cloak aside.

The sight of her now so sweetly innocent and at the same time womanly seductive, stirred his blood. He said her name, softly, like a purr from a hunting cat's throat.

"You know what this means, don't you?"

She tilted her chin to look at him, laughing nervously to cover up her apprehension.

"It means that I am your captive . . . and that you shall keep me here against my will, to do with as you please?"

"How well you have read my mind, my dear!"

With rounded eyes, Aurora backed up and spun away from him. She kept her distance from him, on the other side of the sofa, while he glared at her with his nostrils flaring.

"I was merely jesting! Surely you would not—of course you could not keep me here against my will!"

"And why not? Who would say me nay—but you?"

He folded his arms across his chest in superior gesture.

"After you have bedded your wench here"—she swept a hand about the room—"you expect me to—to—No! Never!"

He too gestured about the room cast in a reddish glow from the hearth.

"So, then, do you see a bed here anywhere?" he asked in a more quiet tone now.

Her regard indicated suspicion as it fell to the sofa.

"Ha! On that bit of furniture? A pair of dwarves couldn't even *make* it there!"

The sofa she remembered was indeed short in length and lumpy to boot. She stifled a giggle at the thought of making love on such humpy cushions!

"'Twould be ungodly!" she said beneath her hand.

Bran fingered his chin in thought.

"Yet, if you should be inclined to—I could think of something."

She pointed a finger at him as if it were a weapon of accusation. "You! You have thought to fool me. I happen to know that there are beds upstairs. Where no doubt you, milord, tumbled your wench!"

Black fury raged within him, but he checked it. "Ah-ha, yes. *But* there are none to speak of now. You see, they have been burned. I felt it rather a pity to burn the bed my wife slept on as a little girl."

"Why then did you?"

"Tell me, love, do you like rats?"

Aurora shivered. "Oh, I see. Well then—"

"The pantherskin. 'Tis large enough to lend some comfort to lovers."

"I did not mean *that!*" she said. Her cheeks reddened hotly.

"Why not? We are husband and wife." He stepped to the end of the sofa. "Come here. Meet me halfway."

"I—I cannot."

"Please. I love you."

"Don't. You—you do not mean that," she said.

He reached down to dig something out from beneath a pile of sheets. Thunder rumbled in the distance, invading the peaceful quiet surrounding the summer house. But inside, as Bran fitted the silk vizard to his face and fastened it, Aurora felt as if the tumultuous storm had closed in and entered her whole being. Next the cloak appeared, as if by some incredible magic. With his already dark attire, the costume was soon complete—and he had become Fay.

Fay. The dark ranger. The night-rider. Her phantom love.

She stepped backwards in alarmed dread. He stalked her in a menacing manner.

"You are not going to—please, Bran, take the disguise off. I—I—"

"Nay, my love. I am Fay. Bran loves you, but I merely want to make love to you. I am your lover, nothing else. When we are done here, I shall disappear."

"You—" was all she said.

"Aye, your lover. 'Tis what you want. What woman wouldn't want a dark, handsome lover, a mystery man?"

He was close enough for her to smell the manly

odor permeating from the folds of the cloak. He cupped her chin, studying her reaction from slits of silver. Fingertips brushed the pale bruise high on her cheekbone.

"Do you remember the last time I rode between your sweet thighs?" he said in a near whisper.

She slapped his hand away. "Cease this game—Bran."

The rain splattered against the panes as the storm began in earnest, but all she could sense was the thunderous slamming of his heart. The night was coming down fast to cloak the summer house in a shroud of black—black as the vision that stood threateningly before her. Suddenly his swift movements brought her skirts up in back and he took her buttocks in his large hands, one lovely cheek molded in each hand. He pulled her close to his throbbing manhood.

"Aurora, do you want me?"

Before she could answer, his lips came down to capture hers, enticing in a teasing promise. His male body was hot, churning deep in his vitals. He wasn't giving her any room to breathe, and he knew this. She moaned softly as he dealt her a heavy rain of wildly savage kisses, matching the pouring rain pelting the rooftop. His hand moved slowly around to her front, gently cupping and squeezing a pointed breast.

Aurora swayed dizzily when he said nothing as he abruptly left her, going to the corner of the room to busy himself there with rummaging through an old sea chest. Just as a feeling of utter relief swept over her, as she thought he would end this frightening but somehow exciting game, he turned.

An ear-splitting explosion of a thunder-clap shook the small house and lightning struck somewhere outside close by. The war of elements raged, illuminating the windows in a flashing display of light. He held something in his arms, something she had thought to never see again. It was sleek—and black.

# Twenty-Seven

Roughly he grasped her shoulders as he pushed her back firmly onto the pantherskin. With hands tightened on her wrists he pinned her down before she could even utter the smallest protest. He didn't even bother to undress her, but tossed the cloud of skirts high, probed gently but deeply enough between her long, beautiful limbs that made a white blur of movement as he spread them, and then tried to mount her. She wriggled too much.

"I mean to have you," he said roughly, "so be still!"

He had removed his finger and now replaced it with a longer, throbbing hardness. In half a heart beat he had plunged deeply, not bothering to enter slowly as he had in the past.

Even though she became excited against her will, Aurora fought and whimpered now in protest, as he continued to thrust mercilessly, far into her, his lips clinging to hers, rushing his breath into her mouth as she tried biting his pliant mouth with little teeth.

He was driven by his long-unsatisfied need—and something else. There was a method to his madness, while even knowing there might be a big price to pay in the end.

Aurora watched this stranger—aye, that is what he had become—this man above her who ignored her useless struggles, even when she was beating wildly against his rising and falling chest. He shifted the driving shaft and Aurora knew a tormenting ache begin inside of her.

"No, now, this is not love," she was murmuring. "'Tis lust and I shall not succumb. You are not—not—" She broke off and fought the panic rising in her. She was sickened and humiliated by the rape, for that was surely what he was doing—raping her.

This time when she reached up to tear the silk vizard from his face, he let her. He even managed a tiny smile while controlling the thrusts that had hurt her. Then, suddenly, the thickness between her legs was gone. Much to her relief, he had withdrawn.

"Why?" Aurora cried softly when he left her.

She rolled away from him, ashamed to see his face. Her damp cheeks pressed into the furs he had spread on the floor before the hearth and curled herself up into a little ball. Noticing that she still clutched the mask in one hand, Aurora tossed it aside hatefully.

"Now," she sniffed, "now I know why you did it. It was a cruel trick to play, Bran, and I shall forever hate you for what you did to me. You hurt me—you always hurt me. 'Twas a terrible blow you dealt me here today." But was it really, she began to wonder? She had said to herself that he must end this masquerade. Hadn't she?

Bran pressed himself against her back, curling an arm about her tiny waist. His breathing had ceased to be labored and had become normal. He made a move toward her breast, then stopped himself.

"Can you believe this? I had begun to hate the disguise, was insanely jealous of it. I was in contention with my own self—not another man. I would have killed your lover if you had one. But, Lord, it was me! I struggled with myself!" His breath stirred her disheveled hair. "Another part of me—the rebel—but I had wanted to become someone else. A new someone for *you,* not Melanie whom I had mistakenly believed was the woman I had fallen mindlessly in love with. Ironically the disguise brought you and me together."

Aurora stirred against him. "But did you have to hurt me just now?" she asked.

"I am sorry, but yes, I did," was all he said.

After a long silence, Bran continued. "Why did you tell me to go that night I slipped into your—our room?"

"It was David who had crept in there before you, and until just now I had not known it was you the second time. David had threatened to kill you if that map was not in his hands soon. After a time I realized he was not bent on murder, only mad after that treasure, having set his mind that nothing would stand in his way." She drew in a quivering breath before going on. "He *might* have killed you, for truly I discovered he was of unsound mind, but too late. I had already fallen into his trap . . . and Melanie. Oh, Melanie, Melanie, I cannot pass judgment on her now. She . . ." Her voice trailed sadly away.

Understandingly, Bran nodded against her hair. "Rufo Savage discovered Melanie's body washed up at the mouth of the cove, not far from where the

*Enchantress* is moored. There was one thing David hadn't counted on at that time. Jonsey could very well have been sleeping on the sloop the night David brought you there. Alas, I had only just sent Jonsey to stay with some relatives of his, over the winter until the spring thaw. One more day and you, my love, might have been spared all the torture and anguish suffered at that madman's hands.'' Against her belly, he clenched two great balls of fist. "I should have slain that bastard!''

A dainty finger slipped up to his lips to hush his anger, and he kissed the tip tenderly, reaching up to take hold of her hand. He kissed the palm, the back of her hand, her wrist, and finally, turning her in his arms, captured her lips of honey in soft, clinging kisses that torched her to instant flames. Their lips clung as he breathed a question into her mouth.

"Are you hungry, love?''

"Aye.''

"I have stocked the kitchen with provisions for a week.''

"A week?'' she blinked at him curiously.

"Aye, the honeymoon we never had.''

"And just how did you mean to get me here?'' she said with a twinkle in her mischievous eyes.

"You are here, are you not?''

With that he began to rise. Long, willowy arms stretched upward to circle about his neck. Bran shivered with the intense heat that began to course through his blood.

"'Tis a hunger of the flesh that I speak of, my darling.'' She delighted in the male groan of desire

464

while he buried his dark head against her throat.

He was not patient, gentle, as he began to undress her this time. With new boldness, Aurora helped him to swiftly peel off his clothes too. He at once began a slow torment to her senses, nibbling behind her ears, followed by a moist kiss to her eyelids, making a slow descent to lap at her nipples, going beneath her breasts. Down over her quivering belly, quickly to the back of the very sensitive knees. Then up, a short path again, fingers leading his hungry mouth to the jungle of pink moisture amid the silky triangle of hair.

"Nay, Bran, I do not know what you are doing to me. You have never—"

"But I shall now. Just relax, sweet, and do not fight me," he murmured against her thigh. He at once stabbed into the pink wet entrance. Aurora groaned as she began a rotation of her hips; gripping her buttocks, he tutored her with love-artful hands into an undulating motion. Her lips remained parted and he licked them with his hot tongue, sliding deeper with tiny thrusts until she couldn't stand it any longer. He jabbed into the part of her that was as delicious as warm spring rain until she began to feel herself bloom. Gripping handfuls of thick black hair she felt herself go higher and higher while she moaned in sheer delight and near painful ecstasy, strangely mingled together.

"Oh, please!" she cried. "No more. I cannot stand it!"

Tormenting her to the last, he lifted his dark head. "There is more. A beautiful end you must know."

465

"Finish! Please!"

"Please, *Bran,*" he demanded against her dewiness.

"Please! Bran! *Bran!*" the last cry coming with the final, vicious few thrusts, bringing forth a trembling culmination.

Giving her only moments to come back down to earth, Bran then moved his tall frame up over her. Still warm and tingling from head to foot, Aurora welcomed his probing member that began to pry into her deepest secrets. Squirming anew, Aurora clutched him to her as she rose and fell, meeting him and then departing while with all his life force pouring into her, she knew this fullness of love that went on and on with love sounds repeating themselves. Pulling gently on a saucy, upturned peak of breast until it grew hard under his fingertips, at the same time his giant thrusts went deeper and deeper.

Lightning flashed at the same time they came together in a final burst. Breathing heavily, they descended from the heights of bliss together, lying content in each other's arms, their bodies wet with love.

The flame burning in Bran had long ago ignited her own tiny dark ember until it now had consumed them both in one mutual burning rapture that could nevermore be extinguished. This was reality, this ecstasy shared by two, which soared and took them away as if on the wings of the wind. He took her to heaven and back, again and again, to the enchanted forest of bliss and Aurora knew courage in the name of giving.

\*  \*  \*

The pale pink curtain of day rose, and the musky smell of autumn leaves drifted on the wind, coming from some plantation yard several miles away.

He was garbed in clean trousers and a white cambric shirt that was open to the waist. When he bent over her bed of furs, with breakfast arranged on a tray, Aurora could not resist the temptation as she woke and splayed her hand in the opening of his shirt, rubbing over the furred mat of his chest. She eyed marmalade, toast, hot tea.

"Breakfast in bed, milady."

Aurora shot up to sit on her bare bottom. "Oh! I have forgotten the horses—Cupid." She felt herself being calmed by his big hands on her shoulders.

"No need for you to fly outside, sweeting. I have already seen to them. Your Cupid stayed close to my steed, and I am thinking they might have had some fun of their own during the long night we left them to roam."

"Oh, but"—she looked all embarrassed about something before blurting—"He is much too big for—she is a dainty mare and—and—"

He nearly shocked her by taking her hand and guiding it to the spot where the bulge of his manhood was to be plainly seen, should anyone happen to glance there, that is. And if it were another woman doing this, she might very well find her eyes clawed out by slim but dangerous fingernails.

"You are but a dainty mare," he began huskily, "and I am a great big steed. Did you find my thrust overly painful in our matings, my hot little vixen?"

She lowered her eyes demurely. Her head moved in a negative shake that caused her hair to brush the

467

auburn tips of breasts. He cupped one small white dove and soon found himself forgetting all about the breakfast for two that he had fixed. She giggled behind a hand while his trousers were nearly rent in his swift stepping out of them.

"Bran! I am famished, and besides, the food will cool—"

"A willful man will have his way," he said.

He took her hand and closed it over his erection, and very soon she was like a child experimenting on a new toy, a very large one indeed as she remarked the huge, swollen length of him.

"Good Lord. Are all men like *this?*"

"How would I know? I haven't made it a habit of asking around or matching trusty blades with others of my kind." His chuckle was deeply stirring. "And I am not certain what shape *it* will be in when we've finished here this morn."

She purred deep in her throat. "I shall take a chance that you can always grow a new one?" Lifting a dark brow at him coquettishly.

"Well—if you prefer that I do—"

She pushed him down and climbed on top of him, much to his delightful surprise. Like that, she spread herself full length and began to move wantonly.

"It is quite adequate, I believe," she said. "And I like it just the way it's fashioned, thank you. Tall and powerfully made, if you had an inch more—"

"Hush up, woman of ill-repute. Now, will you kindly leave me to my sport?"

"Yours!"

"Aye. But are you sure you are up to it again?"

"You cannot do it alone, lover." She ran cool

fingers along his ribs, breathing deeply of his manly scent. She tossed her head back. "I gladly accept your challenge! All or nothing, when do you wish to begin?"

"Immediately, if not sooner." He clutched her as if he couldn't bring their bodies close enough. "Ahhh, Aurora, sweet, sweet witch in the mist. I knew I would fall in love someday . . . for all time. . . ."

The night was bone-chilling and the moon a bright silver ball when Bran rode like a swift dark spirit to reach the little house before Aurora became too alarmed at his staying away so long. He had to ride carefully, though, avoiding holes in the horse-path lest he lose the neatly packed bags that thumped heavily against Nimrod's sides.

His violet-eyed beauty, she would be thrilled at his returning with all the new froufrou gowns he had sent for from England months before. The ship had just come in at Jamestown that afternoon; the reason for his being detained lay in picking up the parcels and stopping at Raven Keep for other items of importance.

In the living room where the honeymooners had set up house with featherbed and various furnishings, Aurora was just pouring water into the washbowl from the pitcher. She was just wondering, too, how her family had ever survived the winter upstairs in the loft minus fireplaces when Bran stepped in. Loaded in his arms he bore huge parcels and bulging bags of sacking to the table.

"So, milord Ravenleigh, you have been out looting the neighbors, perchance?"

His eyes watched her fondly as she set the pitcher down and slowly approached the loaded-down table. He drew off his leather gauntlets, stripped off his velvet cloak and baldric with its weapons, tossed them all aside to the sofa, then straddled a wicker-bottomed chair. He nodded for her to open them and she began, without another word. Her eyes, dark as French velvet now, strayed to his whipcord lean body every few moments.

The corkscrew lovelocks she had fashioned at one side of her head brushed the high-collared bodice of her modest gown while she tilted her head and then selected a smaller package first.

"Has time passed so swiftly here in our abode of love that the Yuletide is already upon us?" she playfully asked.

"Nay. 'Tis not Christmastide. But Lady Nature seems bent on seeing it so, for she wrapped me in her frigid arms all the long ride and blew her icy breath of winter beneath my cloak."

"Could sit by the fire, sweet prince of mine, and warm yourself? I have brewed some hot sassafras tea, would you like some now or before I am finished— Oh! Bran, a copy of William Shakespeare's play *A Midsummer Night's Dream*. One I've never read!"

With full heart she rushed to wrap herself in his inviting arms, looking up at him with the declaration of love shining in her breathtaking eyes. Though they shone with veritable paradise in them, her lips had to speak the words again.

"I love you so, Bran. You've chained forever my heart and put it in bondage. A nice place to be." She rubbed her cheek against his doublet of dove gray.

"Yea, and you mine, for a thousand-and-one eternities." He tilted her fine chin up. "Here now, you mustn't spoil my fun for the evening with tears." He stroked the gleaming mantle of long midnight hair she had just washed and brushed and fashioned.

"'Tis just that I am so very happy, my tears are ones of boundless joy. I would be destroyed without your love."

He slid his hands beneath her armpits and lifted her high with arms one at a time lowering to encircle her saucy bottom. He nosed her skirts up until kissing the silky triangle of black hair between smooth-skinned thighs. She squealed in delight and then begged to be brought down. He was not in the mood to release her, instead commenced with teasing the sensitive pink pearl until she had fallen sway to the magic of his tongue and sucking mouth. He clutched her closer, and in a matter of minutes every inch of her body was on fire. She began to throb deep inside, with her head thrown back and her mouth forming the words that would urge him to bring on the peak of ecstasy.

"Come deeper . . . deeper . . . fill . . . *Oh God!*"

A short time later Bran brought in the metal tub and filled it with steaming water he had heated over the fire. He bathed her first, and then took his turn while she, with her rose-tipped breasts tickling his arm temptingly, bathed him. Seated on the sofa with her emerald shawl giving added warmth to the linsey-woolsey petticoat she wore, she helped him dry himself before the blazing hearth with a fluffy linen.

"You don't have to do that, sweeting, I can do

it myself."

"I know, darling, but I cannot keep my hands off you, alas. Your male form staggers the feminine imagination and boggles the—*my* mind."

"You are quite astoundingly put together yourself, milady, but I don't think"—he chuckled—"that I could better your statement, love."

"You are *beautiful*," she purred, bending to lap up the moisture from his bulging pectorals.

When she finally lifted her head he leered at her strawberry-tipped nipples until she was kindled afresh by a thousand sparks that passed from him to her.

"I've an uncontrollable lust for you." He buried his face in her hair and whispered her name. "See here, there is something rising between us again."

There was no help for it. A deep-sinking heat began to spread between her thighs as the sexual tension began to grow between them. He lifted her gently, still buried in her hair, carrying her to the feather bed. She reached down just before he placed her in the middle of the bed and stroked the passionate purple of his pleasure dome.

"Ahh, don't, love, you may—*shall* speed me to an end too swiftly. I want to be inside you before that happens . . ."

"But," she began shyly after he had put her down, I want to kiss you too, milord."

"Oh-ho!" He tumbled into the bed swiftly. *"Oh-ho!* Come here, my hot little vixen!"

Much much later, after they had ripped apart with

472

their teeth the roasted capons Cuffee had prepared for the honeymooners, and washed the honeyed meat down with rich wine as if they had both known a ravenous hunger, the time had finally come for Aurora to try on one of the gowns her husband had presented her. Standing on a bearskin rug with the pantherskin flanking it, she stared around her at all the fine gowns arranged neatly, some draped over the couch in a pale rainbow of colors, a few in satin piles at her feet.

She had just stepped into a rustling taffeta petticoat and now Bran stood to hook the russet silk bodice and loop the overskirt back and up. She smiled saucily, postured, and twirled, while he sat back reveling in her woman's abandon and joy of feeling rich and pampered and indulged and cosseted. She sauntered by him where he sat with legs spread on the corner of a heavy piece of furniture and rubbed herself against him. Then, before he could encircle her waist with his fingers, she spun away, and he hooted and ogled her with a drop of the devil rogue blood in him surfacing.

On and off the gowns went: White lawn petticoats; mauve satin gown with bodice encrusted with seed pearls; a black half-moon face patch on the high point of her cheek ; mauve velvet cloak; black satin slippers; gowns in shamrock-green, silvery-gray satin, French green, canary yellow, and black, seductive black, trimmed with threads of gold.

All the while Bran sat there and watched, swinging his wide rakish boots and singing in a rich baritone a bold song of the Stuart court. He stopped his song suddenly when Aurora stood motionless, all the joy having gone from her face. Her head was low as she stared at all the gleaming froufrous at her feet, piled high like sparkling gems in a kaleidoscope of colors.

"Oh, no." Bran went to her.

"Oh, Bran," she said softly. "I feel like a—a pagan princess with all these bejeweled gowns surrounding me so richly."

Tears shone in Bran's eyes. "I meant for all these froufrous to have the opposite effect on you, precious." He kissed the tip of her pert nose. "What is it, pray tell?"

"I—I—do not think me silly—"

He shook her gently, bending his head over hers. *Never*. Tell, love, I would know what troubles you."

"I should—like to go to the new church in the wood, Bran, and praise the Lord."

"Is that all? My precious bride . . . we *shall* attend every Sabbath from now on."

"Hetty, too."

"Hetty, too," he repeated.

"*And* Sir Eric?"

He coughed. "Uhmmm—we shall have to work on that one."

Spinning away abruptly from him, Aurora continued with her play, pretending to be the coquette with her rakish, reckless cavalier. Suddenly he opened his arms and she rushed back into them. For some strange reason, known only to those who love hard, their tears fell and mingled together bittersweet. Bran heaved a man-sized sob against her neck.

"Ro, darling, I love you so . . . it hurts."

"I know, Bran. *Hold* me."

"A hurting happiness," he mumbled.

"Aye, I know," she soothed.

Aurora sighed blissfully with the wood crackling in the fireplace behind them. What could happen to spoil their happiness now? There was nothing, really nothing, she told herself.

## Twenty-Eight

Aurora sat on her haunches, rummaging through the trunk of clothes Bran and Tom had carried in earlier in the day. All at the Keep knew by now that they were staying at the summer house on their honeymoon.

And what a glorious honeymoon it had already been, Aurora thought, smiling dreamily. She was desired, loved with wild abandon by a powerful man. Of course it helped if that man was your husband, she softly laughed, tossing over her shoulder the seductive three ringlets she had fashioned in her hair by herself.

"Ah! Here it is!" Aurora shook out a gown of pale rose jaconet looped over a fine silken bodice and petticoat. She loved it above the others for its simplicity.

Bran had even been so gallant as to bring her the mirror from their bedchamber at Raven Keep. She smiled recalling the day before, when Bran and Tom had ridden side by side with an end of the mirror on each horse. He had even begun to furnish the place, saying with a grin that this would be their lovenest when they wanted to get away from everyone.

They had lost track of all time—or rather she had.

She didn't know about Bran. Had four days passed? Five? Six? Did it matter?

Bran had gone to get a feather mattress for the bed frame he'd put together, so it left her plenty of time to primp and make herself pretty for him. Another night to look forward to, a very long night spent entwined naked in each other's arms, sharing sleep or wakefulness, together as one.

Hugging herself in her shawl of emerald green, Aurora walked to the kitchen window. The trees were already beginning to frost in silver spurs and glazed icing and the gorgeous winter was breaking in fast.

She couldn't measure the time she stood staring out at the frosted woodland scene, but it was growing dark and still no sign of Bran. A short time ago—or had it been hours?—she had napped. Now she was feeling fresh, looking forward to yet another night of love. She should add another log to the fireplace. . . .

Suddenly she knew a prickle of fear. The door—it was open a crack. She couldn't recall Bran having left it open. That wasn't like him.

A sound from behind her made her stop halfway to the door. Her hackles rose at the back of her head, causing her to freeze, her movements like ones captured on a canvas. Finally she whirled about and instantly sighed in utter relief.

"Bran, my Lord, but you gave me a fright!" She cocked her head, indicating the disguise with a waft of her hand. "Please, love, let us not play any more silly games, hmmm?"

Her eyes narrowed and then flew wide. This could not be Bran. Though the room was quite dim by now, she could tell that the man who faced her did not share her husband's height and width. The eyes, which were of late full of love, were hard marbles of blue ice. Below the silk vizard was a mouth, set in a grim line. Out to do someone harm.

"So, this is how you and your husband spend your time, huh? You don't know I saw you and him doing it, you laying on that rug of fur and him pumping on top of you with this on." The cloak swirled in the air like a bat-wing.

"You—you, whoever you are—*saw* us? But how could you? There was no one else here but the two of us." She backed up steadily as he came closer.

"I shan't go into detail, my love," he mimicked her husband's drawl. "But I did see you, and hear you panting and crying, right through that window over there—" He jabbed a finger toward the window that could afford one a bird's-eye view of the floor at the hearth. "I knew he was *acting* like he was raping you, and you were quite the little actress—"

"You *are* going into detail. And—and you can just take that thing off and get out of here—or mayhap you would like it if my husband found you here? He would kill you for sure! Now, be gone, so that your life may be spared!"

"Ah, little Ro, leave without sampling some of what you gave him?" he laughed an evil laugh.

"David Wiley!"

Suddenly Aurora knew the fear of the helpless, in the company of a madman. He had been dangerous before, but now it emanated from him like a tangible thing. She had to think of something quick. With the fire in embers, the house was steadily growing dark. Perhaps she could hold him off until her husband showed. If not that, she could always hide. She knew all the places.

"David," she began in a cajoling tone, "why don't you light that taper over there so that I might begin to prepare dinner. Bran will be here soon and—and we can all sit down to eat, let bygones be bygones. Huh?"

David snorted. "Hah! You Jezebel, you think to fool me, don't you? And don't you be dashing off somewheres to hide before I've had my sport. First off, you and me are going to hide somewhere—together. Then when your lusty husband comes—" He shrugged, his meaning quite clear.

"He will kill *you* first, David Wiley!"

"Not if I can attack him unawares." He lunged forward and caught her by the arm. "And maybe we can have some fun while we're waiting in some dark corner," he breathed in her face with a sour wine breath.

"You are drunk again!"

"Why not, Ro, it gives me some sorely needed courage. Here," he said, digging beneath his cloak, "have a sip of this wine. 'Tis good stuff." He squeezed her cheeks with his greater strength, opening her mouth while trickling the fiery red stuff into it.

Without giving her a chance to spit it out, he clamped a paw over her mouth and proceeded to drag her forcibly into the living room. Fighting him with all the strength she could muster, Aurora clawed and bit and kicked, spitting like a wildcat into his face. Using language she would normally have not.

"You bastard! Damn you, release me!" What was it Bran had used to cuss David out—? "You son of a—"

479

"Shut up!"

He slammed her hard against the wall. Grinding her back, he emulated the motions of lovemaking, slobbering kisses of wet wine breath all over her mouth and neck, sliding down to nibble painfully at the tender breasts he had exposed. His breathing attested to his readiness and became labored while his hard, bony manhood pressed into the soft place Aurora thought no other man but her husband would ever know.

"I'm going to give it to you damn good now! And better and harder than Bran Ravenleigh ever made you burst inside."

"Oh, God, no!" Aurora screamed, struggling insanely while he pushed her skirts high.

That was where David's mistake lay. Aurora was now free to lift a knee for a damaging job—and bring it up she did—with all mustered force dead center to the groin. David howled like a wolf, at the peak of racking pain, disabled for the time while involuntarily releasing the woman he had nearly ravished.

"You—you'll regret—that—bitch!"

Not hesitating a moment more, Aurora flew from the room, unthinkingly heading in the one direction she should not have. Here downstairs, she could be assured of finding a hiding place in some nook or cranny, even have made it to the kitchen door—the only way out—but in her folly of moment's panic she had found herself scurrying up the narrow flight of stairs to the loft, where the bedrooms were.

Now there would be nowhere to hide, no kitchen utensil she could have turned to better use than carving meat this day. What if, indeed, David carried a weapon on himself? Was this the horrible fate that lay waiting here in her beloved childhood home? The place, the only place where she had shared countless hours of rapture with her only love. Bran—her *only* true love.

Oh, God! To be first raped and mauled and then left dead, for Bran only to return to a bloodied corpse, no more breath to pour into his mouth, his sweet, sweet mouth as his lips clung to hers?

David only need break her neck with one snap from one hand; he was a strong man, mad indeed, and needed no weapon to end her life.

The upstairs loft was a frustration to her efforts of finding a place in which to hide. She could only hope and pray that demented Wiley downstairs was in such throes of agony as to render him helpless in pursuit any longer. That he should quit the mad game of rape-and-kill was too much to hope for.

Lengthening shadows brought fuzzy gray fog into the small room in which Aruora stood, backing up and twisting slowly around. Merely boxes and fusty old crates and—Her heel struck something then which caused her backward step to halt.

Her old rocking horse!

Tossing aside caution and fear, Aurora bent to set the hobbyhorse into motion. Why hadn't she come up here before? Had she been afraid to? With a reminiscent smile lifting her sweet mouth at the corners, Aurora became the child again. Tears smarting, she just started to hum softly a tune, when a voice from long ago and from out of her dreams brushed her mind, but the words were for the present, and she stopped.

*Aurora, my darling daughter . . . take heed . . . do not tarry for memories' sake . . . there is someone in the house. He is coming for you now. Beware, for I hear the chopping of an ax.*

Deana's voice had ended in a spine-chilling wail—or had it merely been the wind outside the window? Aurora wondered frantically.

*Ax.* Aurora stuffed a knuckle into her mouth and bit down so hard that blood began where she broke the skin.

"Mama, where shall I hide if he has an ax?" she asked the surrounding walls but received no answer.

Footsteps brushed the stairs, coming slowly up, but each one an echoing din in Aurora's head. In her haste to do something, anything fast, she almost tumbled in a heap over the hobbyhorse. Aurora half-concentrated on stilling its rocking motion while tossing frightened glimpses over her shoulder toward the uppermost step where that first bit of David Wiley would show.

Galvanized into action, she hurried to press herself flat against the farthest wall, inching along it as if seeking a crack wide enough to crawl into and cover herself with part of the wall. But nothing, she realized with alarm, would keep David from fulfilling his singleminded purpose. To have his revenge on Bran would mean killing her. He had always been a coward, using women as a means to an end.

"Ah-hah! So here you are, my pretty! I can see you," he ended in a singsong voice of sheer madness. "I have something here I'd like to bury in your naked flesh—all you have to do is spread those lovely legs."

Wiley did not mean himself, no, he indeed was swinging weapon—an ax! Her mother . . .

He was coming toward her, she could almost feel his breath. Her mouth open in a soundless scream, with heart pounding as if seeking to escape her heaving chest, Aurora made claws against the wall until the bones in her hands rose. She wanted to kill him if he touched her with those filthy lecher's hands.

Why did she feel like retching again as she had in the hollow? But this time it was her own life she feared for. At that time her emotions had been spent for his torture—this time . . . Could it be that she was with child?

"Oh, God, spare me if this is true," she said to herself and the Almighty above.

That she could never share the boundless joy of bearing a son or a daughter with Bran was too heart-breaking to think of now.

A yellow moon had already made an appearance in the bedarkened sky, with a sprinkling of stars peeping in. Aurora perked up her ears. Did she only imagine it, or did she really hear another sound downstairs—like a door closing, a catlike tread coming across the floor below her? Why could she not scream to let Bran or whoever it was know she was up here about to be murdered?

In her throat the scream died before even being born as David attacked with renewed vigor, taking up where the earlier scene had left off. But this time he had a rope, that Aurora could feel brushing against her arm. She was only mildly relieved that he had dropped the ax somewhere behind him. She could tell that he had, for the moonlight suddenly came streaming in and shed its light upon the ominous weapon lying there on the floor. If only she could . . .

"You would not tie me up, David. 'Tis bad and cowardly, even you—"

"Too bad for you, don't you mean, bitch?" he snarled into her frightened face.

Before she could utter a word, he had picked up one ankle, making her feet fly forward—and she fell flat on her back. He then bound her ankles together, the rope cutting into her flesh and burning, for he trussed her up like a turkey.

Wiley stood her up again, as though she were but a porcelain doll, stiff and unfeeling, but still she had the use of her hands. He hadn't tied them. The claws she had made earlier of her fingers now drew blood as she raked them across his throat, damning at the same time the strength that was draining all of hers. She could do no more to hurt him. Sliding her up the wall a bit, so that he could manage to enter her secret place, at the same time David undid his breeches. The tip of a skinny shaft had just touched upon that delicate little bit when he stiffened, became dead weight against her and then cried out. He spun about as if whirled by an invisible hand, and it was then that Aurora saw the ax. It was buried at an angle in his back, his dark red blood appearing on the cloak and already staining the floor. He tried uttering words as he fell over the hobbyhorse, but they merely bubbled forth through red foam. He made a horrible gurgling sound and then was still.

Aurora stared in horrible fascination at David who

was draped over the hobbyhorse like a huge, grotesque puppet that had been tossed carelessly aside by a very bored child.

Her stare lifted, widening at the shape of a woman who stood silhouetted against the moonlit window. Her face was a dark mystery, but when she finally spoke, Aurora could not help but loose a surprised gasp.

"May you now be free to love without fear in your heart the man Bran Ravenleigh who never loved me but gave me the fine gift of freedom from an evil man's clutches. The one who walked beside this also evil bastard!"

"Captain Strang," Aurora said the name like a soft curse.

Downstairs Bran had just entered by the kitchen door. Tossing off his cloak, he halted and stood very still, listening, glancing up sharply as a frail and mournful sound lifted and hung in the rafters. Like death itself. Just like the first time he had stood there listening to the sweet voice of a little girl.

As he never stopped to light a candle to show him the way upstairs, he collided into the soft shape of a woman just coming down. She hastened to the window and there ripped down the new curtains Aurora had just hung. She held something in her hand for Bran to see.

"For your Mistress Ravenleigh, milord."

Staring down, Bran dropped the linen covered basket of roasted capons. He looked back up at Rachel.

That was all that passed between them before Rachel tossed the bloodied ax aside, the weapon she had only just dislodged from Wiley's cracked rib and pierced lung. Before Bran rushed up to the bedroom loft he watched for a moment as Rachel stepped out of the room. He already knew he would never see her again; it would be for Aurora too emotional a scene. David Wiley was dead, that much he knew too for certain.

"Aurora!" Bran cried for the first time in his life as he took the stairs two at a time in his haste to be at her side.

Neither Bran nor Aurora attended Rachel's wedding ceremony. She had sailed for England but a few days after Jake Randolph had made her his bride. But they stood silently together on the *Enchantress* while David Wiley's body was being lowered into the deepest part of the river. His body had been wrapped in canvas and beneath that he was dressed as Bran found him—in cloak and black silk vizard. The masked man was no more.

## Twenty-Nine

The first of the season and the loveliest of all snowfalls. Snowflakes, curling their feathery way in front of the walking horses, halting for a moment in time, then twirling off like hundreds of ballerinas in every direction.

The young woman's windblown hair was a mass of raven-black in disarray, but she didn't mind the white flakes of snow that nestled atop her head like diamonds upon black velvet. Her cheeks were pinched a healthy, more-filled-out pink, and her heather eyes danced now with worshipful love when Bran helped her down from Cupid's back.

Bran recalled a like scene when three days back he had stood in this very hollow with her, burying his fingers in her shining hair and, with one long arm snaked about her waist, dragged her gently and lovingly against him while kissing her thoroughly. He had sensed that her eyes widened in pleasant surprise where they stood beneath the barren branches of the ancient oak tree; gnarled with age, its roots stretched out in all directions like gray-brown tentacles half-buried in the turf. . . .

"What is it, love. What could be more interesting than being kissed by your ardent husband? Shame, opening your lovely eyes like that, you are supposed to—"

"Bran!" She twirled happily from his arms. "Look, look at this tree. My lone tree! I have discovered the treasure!"

"My love, I don't see how. We have, Tom and Rufo and Harris and myself and practically the entire male staff, dug up this place from rim to ravaged rim." He swept his gloved hand wide.

Aurora had not been listening. She was like a child thrilled at her first birthday party opening up a gaily wrapped package. She was running her slimly tapered fingers over some carvings in the old tree.

"*Your* tree? Silly little lady," Bran said smilingly as he ran his large hand over her softly curvaceous buttocks.

"Stop that now! 'Tis no time for making love!" she chided, then breathed the answer to his question. "Aye, my lone tree, the signs of three trees carved into this ancient wood! See here?"

Bran himself caught her excitement. "So, the treasure is here, buried beneath this fat old sentinel, stand-guard jealously all these years, ha! While we sweat and toil the length of this spongy tract, breaking our backs, the towering oak stands here creaking its limbs in laughter at all the bloody fools!"

Aurora too fell to laughing as together they leaned to the tree, their fingers tracing the carved drawings of three fully matured trees. In the middle tree a bird had been carved upon a branch.

"Look, 'tis a raven!" Aurora announced, shuddering, then falling to fits of giggles, saying, "And I thought you could turn yourself into a bird!"

"Ah! Ravenscar could have, perhaps, but not I, sweeting. I was merely jesting the day I said that I could materialize. I simply had moved fast, and let me tell you, my wounded leg practically killed me as I flew"—he chuckled—"I mean *ran* up the stairs!"

They then exchanged looks that spoke of their having no secrets between them, for they had adapted to the understanding that not knowing what the other was about kept their love from reaching total maturity. Their great love had blossomed into the fullest, most glorious flower ever. A shining, golden twin rose. Bran held but one thing from her in the certainty that nothing mar their flawless love. That being his past, those meaningless love affairs.

"Did the killer raven belong to Ravenscar?" Aurora wanted to know, thinking of the one that had attacked Melanie and caused her death—so she thought.

"There are no killer ravens here, love," he said tenderly, wrapping his long arms about her again. "And if you are thinking of Melanie's cruel death, Tom Bone discovered a bruise on her ankle when he and Rufo buried her—she had a heel mark made by a heavy boot. No raven did that, Aurora, she was tripped. Aye, 'tis true the raven went after her, but she must have first off—in fact I know she antagonized the bird into flying at her."

She lifted an eyebrow. *"How* do you know that for a fact, Bran?"

He shrugged it off easily. "I just know, that's all."

"I shall accept that, lover. I adore you too much to ever doubt your word again. Never again shall I be so

489

blind, you *know* I shan't."

He knew exactly what she meant. She had always known inwardly of his dual identity, it was just that she too had been so afraid, so had closed her eyes to the fact that Bran was also Fay. He had wanted to shed his rogue's image, and she had always feared that which Melanie had revealed long ago, that Bran was a callous lover. . . .

Now, today, as the white swirling mists in the hollow mingled with the white white snow coasting softly down about them, Aurora thought the world incredibly lovely to be in and greeted each sparkling new day with delight and fresh enthusiasm. The days were bright-hued, the nights wine-dark with passion. With Bran's total love surrounding her, she had been given a new and clearer vision.

Aurora was prepared for anything—even for what she was about to learn of her husband.

"Please tell, Bran, tell me what they meant to you, those other women in your past?"

"Aurora, love—" Bran tilted her chin up so that he could study her heather-dark eyes.

"I am afraid no longer."

"Do not ask this of me. I would not hurt you, for, dearest, you are the very breath of my life."

"Please, Bran, no more secrets between us?"

He took a deep breath, as if it hurt him, then went on to tell her of his lonely boyhood and the restless spirit of early manhood that had driven him from mistress to mistress, and to the wenches in the streets of London.

"Even then, I hunted for Aurora, my little goddess of the dawn. Only back then I didn't know what I sought for so insanely. Even Melanie—"

"Shh," she placed a finger to his sensuous lips. "I have heard enough, my darling. Look, over there beneath my tree."

Tom and Rufo had brought up the last of the treasure. There were three chests of booty, several kegs of gold and silver coins, spilling onto the ground, gleaming dully among the scattered gems, and goblets imbedded with rubies, sapphires, emeralds. It was all too dazzling for the eyes and the soul to comprehend, as the treasures flashed enticingly there among the flakes that drifted down and melted soon thereafter.

"Fortune, in more ways than one can count, is indeed smiling upon us." He turned his back on the treasure, leading her away from the edge of the hollow, his arm curled about her waist.

"Bran, what about the treasure?"

"I shall make a trip to England in the spring, you see, the booty is most likely Spanish, and we shall have to share it with the Crown. Some of the jewels will go into your coffer, milady. Would you like that?"

She rubbed her cheek against his shoulder kittenishly. "Just a few pieces, darling. I have my treasure, the one I had searched for ever since roaming these woods, seeking that special something, someone, on the other side."

"Aha," he chuckled. "The little herb-maiden. Remember this?" He dug into his breeches' pocket and there nestled the old herb-pouch in his hand.

"Alas, where did you get that? I have not seen it for years!"

491

He related the time he went to the summer house and the magic spell of a child's lingering aura that had even back then captured his heart and soul.

"Oh, Bran!"

The snowflake stars nestled in his jet hair as he bent his head; she rose on tiptoe to receive his warm kiss. His lips clung to hers as he murmured into her sweet mouth.

"Tell me, Ro, that you love me as much as I love you. Speak the words, my precious, sweetest treasure."

She pressed eagerly against his hard male form. "I shall show you how very much I love you . . . soon."

Silent, Bran lifted her onto Nimrod's high back and leapt up behind her, taking up Cupid's reins to follow behind them. His breath tickled the nape of her neck and she leaned back, warm and secure in his encompassing love. She closed her hands over one of his as he reached around to take the reins. Nimrod tossed his huge head, blowing puffs of moist breath that wreathed about the snuggling couple.

"Home, Bran?" she murmured against his cheek.

"Aye, love."

## Epilogue

Sympathy for the Baconians faded, and several of the most important surrendered. By mid-January it was safe for Sir William to return to the mainland. Those rebels he could lay his hands on were immediately rushed to trial and execution as a ghastly warning to future rebels. A few lucky ones were never found.

Sir William reasserted his authority without assistance from the Crown. King Charles was enlightened to the governor's acts of vengeance. On January 29, 1677, an English fleet appeared in the James. It carried troops of the Crown, bearing a royal commission to investigate the causes of the rebellion and restore order to the Crown's most valuable colony. They came armed with pardon for all the rebels; for some it was too late. They also brought news that Sir William Berkeley was to be superseded as governor of Virginia. He was ordered to return to England.

A new plan would be adopted to deal with the natives, a modification of Berkeley's blockhouse system. Patrols of scouts, to be lead by the representative of Elizabeth County, Bran Ravenleigh, would rove the frontier to keep the colony posted on all untoward movements. Defensive maneuvers were out. Any hint of an uprising would be dealt with by direct and aggressive action. They desired principally to shift political power from the central government back to the counties, where it had been before Berkeley came to power.

Returning home now from visiting the Tobies, the sound of bells jingling gaily on the horses' harnesses brought Aurora out of her reverie. There was yet a worried frown between her heather-dark eyes as she studied her husband. He looked painfully handsome this afternoon, in full-sleeved leather jerkin and doeskin breeches.

"What will happen now, darling, that you have surrendered?"

Bran peeled off a gauntlet to caress the seed of their boundless love growing in her belly. His eyes were diamond-bright as he spoke softly, the rich timbre in his voice full of love for this one precious woman he would forever and ever adore.

"A few days ago a bailiff arrived here bearing a writ issued by the Crown. This writ is legal and shall be executed, bearing the king's seal. Too, the new but temporary governor is a peaceminded man and will hang no one. Darling mine, I am no longer a rebel. Are you happy now, sweeting?"

Violet eyes met silver ones as she murmured:

"Aye, love, I am a woman complete and my heart is glad."

# BLAZING CIVIL WAR SAGAS!